RONIE KENDIG

DISCARDED HEROES # 2

# DIGITALIS

"This is one pulse-pounding adventure you don't want to miss."
—Robert Liparulo, author of *Comes a Horseman, Germ,* and the *Dreamhouse Kings*

Kimberley Falk

PRAISE FOR THE DISCARDED HEROES SERIES

Nightshade kept me up all night! A tight plot, heartthrob heroes, and description so rich I could hear the jungle noise, feel the heat slide down my back. I'll be clearing out a shelf to make room for Ronie's books!

—Susan May Warren, RITA award-winning author of *Nothing But Trouble*

VALOR, ACTION, ROMANCE, HEART. . . *Nightshade* is the perfect blend of everything I like best in a story. I can't recommend it enough!

—John B. Olson, author of *Powers*

In *Digitalis*, Ronie Kendig again displays her superb ability to reach from the page and pull the reader into a world of heart thumping espionage and richly flawed characters. Her heroes are some of the best I've read, and they are so unforgettable.

—Dineen Miller, author of *Winning Him Without Words: 10 Keys to Thriving in Your Spiritually Mismatched Marriage*

Balancing a story of high action and deep emotions isn't easy, but with *Digitalis*, author Ronie Kendig pulls it off with the casual grace of a truly talented storyteller. I don't know what kept me on the edge of my seat more, the fast-paced military intrigue or the powerful tugs on my heart. Doesn't matter: This is one pulse-pounding adventure you don't want to miss.

—Robert Liparulo, author of *Comes a Horseman*, *Germ*, and the Dreamhouse Kings

Digitalis kept pace with thrilling suspense and strong characters that will live long past the last page. None of us realize the dedication of those who keep our world safe.

—DiAnn Mills, author of the Call of Duty series

An action-packed thrill ride from start to finish. . .if you liked CBS's long running hit series *The Unit* you're going to love Ronie Kendig's *Digitalis*. Enjoy the ride and the read. I only have one question. . . where do I sign up for Nightshade?

—Bob Hamer, veteran FBI undercover agent and the author of *Enemies Among Us*

Fast paced and deliciously intriguing, *Digitalis* delivers military high-octane with just the right amount of romance and suspense. Kendig knows how to keep readers flipping pages until the wee hours of the night. Don't miss this one!

—Robin Caroll, author of *Fear No Evil* and *In the Shadow of Evil*

RONIE KENDIG

DIGITALIS

DISCARDED HEROES #2

BARBOUR
PUBLISHING

OTHER BOOKS BY
RONIE KENDIG

Nightshade (Discarded Heroes #1)

© 2011 by Ronie Kendig

ISBN 978-1-60260-783-5

Scripture taken from the HOLY BIBLE, NEW INTERNATIONAL VERSION®. NIV®. Copyright © 1973, 1978, 1984 by International Bible Society. Used by permission of Zondervan. All rights reserved.

This book is a work of fiction. Names, characters, places, and incidents are either products of the author's imagination or used fictitiously. Any similarity to actual people, organizations, and/or events is purely coincidental.

For more information about Ronie Kendig, please access the author's Web site at the following Internet address: www.roniekendig.com

Cover design: Müllerhaus Publishing Arts, Inc., www.Mullerhaus.net

Published by Barbour Publishing, Inc., P.O. Box 719, Uhrichsville, OH 44683, www.barbourbooks.com

Our mission is to publish and distribute inspirational products offering exceptional value and biblical encouragement to the masses.

Member of the
Evangelical Christian
Publishers Association

Printed in the United States of America.

DEDICATION

Major Loren D. Kendig (Ret.)
Humble. Honorable. Patriot. Hero.
THANK YOU for your admirable and distinguished service
to our great country, at war and at home.
I am proud to be a part of your family!

ACKNOWLEDGMENT

Special thanks to:

My husband, Brian, and my amazing children for your patience, understanding, and excitement. I love you all so very much! I couldn't do it without you!

Steve Laube—my agent, for believing, understanding, and accepting me.

The Barbour Staff—y'all rock! Special thanks to Rebecca Germany, Mary Burns, Shalyn Sattler.

Andrew Kendall – for the amazing Nightshade insignia!

Chuck Holton – for being part of my "arsenal" for military advice/direction. (Any mistakes in the Discarded Heroes books are purely mine.)

Yitshak Kugler, Eva Marie Everson, and Dr. Heater—for extensive help on Israel.

Critique Partners, Readers, & Endorsers: Dineen Miller, Kimberley Woodhouse, Robin Miller, Jim Rubart, Rel Mollet, Sara Mills-Mills, Shannon McNear, Bob Hamer, DiAnn Mills, Lori Twichell, Lisa Harris

Candace Calvert for help with trauma and medical questions. You're a gem—thank you!!

Chaplain Carlton D. Hall—for your encouragement and help regarding our veterans and PTSD.

Wes & Jane Thornton for sharing from your hearts and lives.

# MARINE PRAYER

Almighty Father, whose command is over all and whose love never fails, make me aware of Thy presence and obedient to Thy will. Keep me true to my best self, guarding me against dishonesty in purpose and deed and helping me to live so that I can face my fellow Marines, my loved ones, and Thee without shame or fear. Protect my family.

Give me the will to do the work of a Marine and to accept my share of responsibilities with vigor and enthusiasm. Grant me the courage to be proficient in my daily performance. Keep me loyal and faithful to my superiors and to the duties my Country and the Marine Corps have entrusted to me. Help me to wear my uniform with dignity, and let it remind me daily of the traditions which I must uphold.

If I am inclined to doubt, steady my faith; if I am tempted, make me strong to resist; if I should miss the mark, give me courage to try again. Guide me with the light of truth and grant me wisdom by which I may understand the answer to my prayer.

MARSOC—*Silent Warriors. Always Faithful. Always Forward.*

THE INVITATION

Invaluable skills came with bloody faces and dead objectives that left Colton Neeley wishing he could rub his eyes raw. Those same skills were the reason Uncle Sam had denied his request for an early exit from his commitment with the Marine Special Operations Command/Team. And the same reason he couldn't muster enthusiasm for his friend who'd been granted his freedom.

"Never thought you'd get out." Colton slumped back against the wood slats of the lawn chair, watching his four-year-old daughter, McKenna. She sat on the fifty-foot dock that stretched over the private pond. She tossed a pink lure-tipped line into the water as his dad helped.

"You and me both." Beside him, his partner and MARSOC buddy Griffin Riddell sat with his elbows propped on his knees. "What about you? Thought you wanted out."

"Denied." The word felt like a weight around his gut. Colton shifted his gaze to the water rippling around Mickey's bobber. "Eleven years wasn't enough for Uncle Sam. Said my sniping and recon skills were too invaluable."

Griffin whistled. "Man, after what you went through in Fallujah, I half expected them to toss you without so much as a thank-you-very-much." His grunted. "How you doing with that?"

Colton picked up his soda and took a swig. "S'pose I'll be all right." He glanced over at the grill. Probably should get up and flip the meat in a few.

"Two months as a hostage. That don't just disappear, know what I'm saying?"

Oh he knew all right. More than knew. Though Colton didn't

8

want to remember, the mention of that city and what happened snapped faces into his mind like a flickering silent movie, bringing with it phantom pains in his spine and legs.

"What about the flashbacks?"

"Daddy, look!" McKenna's mouse-like voice squeaked as she giggled. With his father next to her, she held up the end of her fishing line. "I caught a seaweed." Another giggle.

"Save it, Mickey," he called toward the pond, where his daughter sat between his mom and dad on the short pier. "We'll grill it."

She batted white-blond hair from her face as her papa took the rod. "Daddy." The cutest scowl tugged at her fair features and blue eyes as she planted her hands on her hips and turned to him. "You can't eat it, silly. It's a *weed*."

He chuckled as she and his mother baited the line, while his father pointed out that if they'd use real worms, they'd catch something besides weeds. Naturally, Mickey and his mom ewwed out the option.

Though Colton's attention never left his family, the patient, waiting gaze of his buddy burned through Colton's resolve. He shook his head, knowing he wouldn't get out of answering that question. About the flashbacks. *Fallujah. The girl. . .* "I see that kid's face every day and every time I look at Mickey." The brown eyes. The misinterpreted trust.

Clearing his throat, he sat up straighter. "Started therapy last week." He shrugged, scrounging for hope that this would be over soon. "Like the counselor. Joined an experimental group for a new med—seems to be working."

"Going all the way, huh?"

"I want to be whole. Get out there and play with Mickey and forget that two months of captivity almost paralyzed me, that the hum of a light isn't my brain getting fried." He roughed a hand over his face. "Forget it, man. This is the Fourth. We have a barbecue."

Colton pushed out of his chair and strode to the covered patio, where plumes of heat rose from the gas grill. As he worked the steaks and burgers over the cast-iron grate, he let the tendrils of smoke carry off the depression and haunting images. As the meat finished cooking, he stood in silence, soaking up the laughter of his family and guests, Griffin and his ten-year-old nephew.

Ten minutes later, they gathered under the covered porch to

munch on the cooked-to-perfection corn on the cob and meat. Once their bellies were full, they leaned back and sighed as the fans circled lazily overhead.

"Now, that was a meal," Griffin said as he clamped a hand on Dante's shoulder. "You need to learn to cook like that."

Dante grinned. "Yes, sir. Grandpapa would love it."

Gathering plates and dishes, Colton's mother waved them off. "Y'all go on and enjoy your time. Colton, get the sparklers for McKenna and Dante while I clean up."

The blond wonder jumped up and down, squealing. "Yes, Daddy! I love them! Please—please—please?" She threaded her hands in mock prayer.

"All right, darlin'." He rustled her hair. "I'll be right back." He stepped into the dark night and headed to his truck, where he'd left the small bag of sparklers. Reaching behind the front seat, he cocked his head and groped for the fireworks. As his fingers grazed the bag, which scooted farther out of reach, he spotted his Remington 700.

Regret choked him. He paused and leaned against the seat. Hung his head. *God. . .please. I just want a clear mind.* With a final grunt, he snatched the bag and slammed the door shut on the truck and on his shaky thoughts. "All right, Mickey, here we go."

Bouncing from the back porch toward him, she squealed. "Dante, look, look! Daddy got sparklers and poppers—my favorite."

A noise screeched through the night.

His heart jack-hammered at the familiar sound.

Crack! Boom!

He dove to the side. Hearing hollowed out, he blinked. A dusty road spread before him. Shouts pervaded the Iraqi street. Men darted for cover. Colton scrambled, feeling the weight of his gear on his back.

"Take cover," he shouted to his team as he rushed up against a building. Spine pressed to the wood, he reached for his radio. Gone. He cursed. Under attack and no backup, no airstrike. He searched the street, his mind pinging.

Movement to the side flared into his awareness. Instincts blazed. He grabbed his weapon—but it wasn't there. *Oh God, no!* He patted the ground, his hearing still muffled by the first IED detonation. *Where's my rifle? Where'd it go?*

"Cowboy?"

"What?" he shouted, searching for his weapon.

"What're—"

Kaboom! Pop-pop-pop. Multi-colored flashes lit the bloody day. Colton scrambled for cover beside the Humvee. He scoured the dust and smoke for his team. Where were they? He glanced over his shoulder—then remembered the Remington.

As he rushed to the back door of the Humvee, another blast shoved him against the steel. *Oof!*

"Cowboy!"

Yanking open the door, he noted civilians on the other side of the Humvee and hoped they stayed clear of the violence erupting around them. He didn't need to find another foot—or any other body part—during cleanup. He lifted his weapon and only then realized it was empty.

Sound from behind yanked him around.

A white-haired man rushed toward him.

"Get back!" Without his weapon ready, it'd be hand-to-hand. But he wasn't letting his weapon go. No way would someone find him with his pants down. Not here. He wasn't going to die in Iraq because he didn't have his gun. They did that to the civilian contractors. But not to him, not to a MARSOC sniper.

"What are you doing? Don't do this."

When the haggard man rushed him again, Colton drove a hard right into his face. The old man flew back and slid across the hard-packed earth. Colton quickly eased a slug in and chambered the round.

Crack! Boom! Pop-pop!

He ducked, and when he came up, a girl with wide brown eyes appeared out of the dust. His heart rapid-fired. No. Couldn't be. He'd killed her already. The villagers had used her as a suicide bomber—then captured him and nearly killed him. No way, no how was he going back there so they could drive a thousand volts through his body.

He dropped to a knee and lined up the sights.

The girl drew back and yelped. "I'm scared."

Why was she speaking English? He shrugged. They'd trained the children to gain confidence and intelligence. He'd fallen prey once. *Won't happen again.*

"*Maa-i-khussni,* not my problem," he said, all too familiar with the way the radicals worked the American soldiers. Soldiers who were here trying to help.

"Cowboy, it's"—*Boom! Crack-crack-pop!*—"girl."

"Don't care, man. I'm not letting them take me again." Sweat slid down his temple into his eye. He blinked—

Wait! Her eyes. How had they changed from brown to blue? He shook his head to dislodge the disparity. The heat. Had to be the heat. Using his upper arm, he swiped away the sweat. Realigned the sights. His heart rate ratcheted when more civilians emerged around the girl.

"Ambush!" He lowered his head and peered through the scope. Focused on nailing the shot, holding his position. Considered the elements.

"Colton! No!" a familiar voice shouted.

But they didn't know. Hadn't been there.

"Marine, stand down! *Stand down!*"

His finger slid into the trigger well.

It's a girl. A little girl.

And they'd used her to get to him, to extract information and kill him. Never again.

Target acquired.

Why are her eyes blue? No, not blue. He was seeing things. They were brown, and he wasn't letting this happen again. No remorse. Gently, he let his finger ease back on the trigger.

Forgive me, Father, he prayed silently, as he did with every kill.

A tremendous weight slammed into him and knocked him sideways. *Crack!* As the weapon's recoil registered, so did the fact that he'd lost his gun. He went flying. Hit the ground—hard. *Thud!* Stars sprinkled through his eyes. The edges of his vision ghosted. His ears popped. He howled at the pain. Blinked.

Night? Why was it night?

"Colton!"

Again, he blinked. A man almost as dark as the sky behind him loomed over him. "Legend?" Aches radiated through Colton's body, leaving him disoriented. "What. . . ?"

Screams and cries suffused the night.

Something ominous clouded Legend's face. He straddled Colton, pinning his arms to the sides. "You with me, Cowboy? You here?"

"What are—get off!"

"Where are we?"

"What do you mean?"

"Where are we? Answer me, Marine!"

Qualms squelched by Legend's drill sergeant voice, Colton paused. "My ranch." A horrible, horrible feeling slithered into his gut. The events crashed in on him. The screaming. The little girl in Fallujah. *Blue* eyes. "No!" Everything in him went cold. For a split second, he locked gazes with Griffin, then jerked his head to the side. Strained to see.

A half-dozen feet away lay his Remington 700. Beyond, his mother and father huddled over—

"McKenna!" The pounding roar of his pulse deafened him.

The small huddle shifted. His parents parted, and Mickey sat up.

Colton squirmed, but Griffin held him down. "Get off me now, or so help me God—"

His buddy shoved off and cleared the path.

Scrabbling over the dirt drive, Colton pushed the weapon out of reach and dove toward his daughter. When she saw him coming, Mickey screamed—and lunged for his mother.

Her rejection punched him in the gut. He sat, stunned. "Mickey." His voice cracked. He reached for his beautiful, precious four-year-old with a trembling hand.

Liquid blue eyes came to his as his mother let out a sob again, pushed to her feet, and rushed up the steps into the house with McKenna.

Colton dropped back, numb. *I almost killed my daughter.* A half moan trapped the air in his throat.

"Son?" Blood dribbled down his father's chin.

Did I. . .punch him? Appalled at himself, Colton pushed his father away. Stumbled to his feet. Staggered to the barn. *I almost killed my daughter.* Arms and legs felt as heavy as cannons. He couldn't tell between reality and the nightmare of captivity. Couldn't tell the difference—he gasped for air—between his own daughter and an insurgent's pawn.

He swayed. The heady scent of the barn lured him inside. How. . . how could he do that? Lose grasp on reality like that? He gripped the half wall of a stall. Gripped it tight. Wood dug into his hands. *What's wrong with me?* He shook the wall. Shuffled back—and drove his heel through the wood. It splintered and swung inward.

A horse shifted aside and nickered in protest.

Colton spun around and grabbed his head. Anger burned to

rage. Seeing Mickey's stricken face. Knowing what he'd almost done. Almost put a sniper bullet through his daughter's tiny frame. The impact alone would have ruptured every major organ in her body.

Colton wobbled. Hot tears streaked down his face. His knees grew weak, and he stumbled. Fell and dragged himself to the wall. With his back against the steel of the barn, he again held his head. A demonic-like growl clawed through his chest. Tears slid over his cheeks.

"God, where are You?" He rammed his elbows into the steel. "Why? Why. . . ?" His fingernails dug into his scalp, wishing he could gouge the memories from his mind. He growled—sobbed. Banged his head. He let out a loud, stuttering moan, still shrouded in disbelief and pure agony.

A hand clamped on his shoulder. Griffin. He'd been the voice in the flashback, ordering him to stand down.

Humiliation cloaked Colton in a suffocating fabric. "I told them. . . ." He groaned. "I *told* the Brass I had to get out." He smeared the tears away, then wiped his hand down his jeans. "I need time. . . ." The memory of Mickey's terrified expression strangled his words. His chin quivered. "To heal up."

Shoes shuffled and crunched against the dirt and hay.

Colton rubbed his face and shuddered as he looked up. When he saw his partner crouched in front of him, he wanted to say something—*anything* that would explain how he'd become some monster who couldn't tell the difference between pure innocence and a girl with a bomb strapped to her chest.

Fingers threaded, Griffin took a deep breath, then pointed his fingers at Colton. "I met a man not long ago who can get you out."

Wariness wedged into Colton's ability to believe his partner. "No way. I'm locked in."

"Not only get you out but give you the time you want."

Colton shook his head. "Stop messing with me. I can't take jokes right now."

"No joke." White teeth shone against Griffin's ebony skin as he smiled. "I tell this guy I need you, he'll get you out."

"Need me? For what?"

"I'll give you all the time you need to get your mind back where it should be." Griffin straightened and towered over him. "But then you're going to be part of a very special team."

CHAPTER 1

Fifteen months later.

One shot. One kill.

The sniper's motto streaked through Colton Neeley's mind as he lay with his arm folded under the stock of his Remington 700. Dampness soaked into his sleeve, evidence of the swampy terrain. He eased his hand toward the trigger well. A bead of sweat rolled down his temple and slid past his eye pressed to the scope.

"Tangos en route and twenty yards," whispered his spotter, Marshall "the Kid" Vaughn, from his four o'clock position.

"Roger that." Synchronization between him and the Kid helped Colton focus on the mission. Peering past the crosshairs, he watched their team leader, three-quarters of a mile away, signaling a heads-up to the others.

Colton gently nudged his weapon, sighting the guerillas trekking north of the team. If all went well—which the elite team of former spec ops soldiers would ensure it did—they'd be on a C-130 back to the States and out of this mosquito-infested jungle by morning. He'd already spent thirty-six hours longer than he wanted in the vegetation. It'd rained for the first twenty, leaving him drenched and cold. But crawling in early gave them the advantage of locating their objectives and the guerrilla group holding them hostage.

Once again, he verified the position of the team. Nothing would ruin a mission like friendly fire taking out one of their own. At his two, he sighted Frogman hunkered down next to a boulder. Greased up, Max Jacobs had the perpetual scowl that marked him as the man in charge—and a grump. Nobody minded. The former Navy SEAL had come through a lot.

Behind him slunk Canyon "Midas" Metcalfe, probably the sanest of the group, even if he had once been a Green Beret. And they forgave him for that.

"Heads up, Frogman," the Kid whispered into his coms, alerting the team. "Six headed your way for a party."

Checking his nine gave Colton a close-up of Griffin "Legend" Riddell, his Marine Special Operations Team buddy, as he took up point. Even from this distance, their movements felt silent, deadly. During the thirteen months Nightshade had been operational, it had built a phenomenal record, but nobody took that for granted. Each mission could be their last.

"Target," called his spotter. "Sector B, TRP-1, right fifty, add fifty."

Colton harnessed his energy and mind on the mission. He had an excellent shot-kill ratio, and he wanted to keep it that way. Mishaps exponentially increased the chances of being spotted and sniped back. In other words, dead.

"Roger," he replied as shadows morphed into solid shapes of Cuban rebels and their exhausted captives. His objective was the leader. "Sector B, TRP-1, right fifty, add fifty." The repetitive dialogue gave him an added measure of comfort.

"Dumb and bald soldier, M16 in right hand, cigarette in left."

Leave it to the Kid to give a snarky description. But he was right. The leader had taken the hostages into a jungle easy to maneuver and hide in, but also one easy to track. "Dumb and bald soldier, M16 in right hand, cigarette in left." Colton took a minute to assess the man behind the crosshairs. "Target identified." He measured the marks on the vertical bar. "I have two mils crotch to head."

"Roger, two mils crotch to head." Leaves on their ghillie suits and the low-hanging branches rustled as the Kid made his calculations. Air crackled beneath the gentle urging of the wind. "Dial five hundred on the gun."

Colton adjusted the optics. "Roger, five hundred on the gun. Indexed."

"Wind right to left, six miles an hour, hold one-quarter mil right."

"Roger, wind right to left six miles an hour, hold one-quarter mil right."

"Take the shot."

Quiet confidence roared through Colton as he eased the trigger back. The tiny sonic boom signaled the firing and sent the bullet spiraling toward its target. "Broke one-fourth mil right." While Colton immediately followed through and chambered another round, the Kid would eye the vapor trail of the bullet to check for precision.

"Center hit," the Kid confirmed. "Stand by."

"Roger, center hit, stand by." Waiting, he kept his scope on the guerillas—minus one. Frogman and Legend disabled the remaining bad guys without a hitch.

Pop! Pop! Pop!

"Taking fire. Taking fire!" Frogman shouted, diving over the hostages to protect them.

"Find him," Colton growled to the Kid. Blurs blended into the foliage as Colton swept his scope over the jungle. Tension ratcheted with each second—each second that meant the enemy sniper could reacquire and kill.

Father, guide my eyes.

A subtle difference in color, shade, and texture caught his eye. The left side of his mouth tweaked upward. *Amateur.* A tank would've been more stealthy. "Shooter spotted, blue 2."

Within seconds, the Kid provided the range to target. Colton set up the shot and lured the trigger back. Three hundred yards away, the branches swayed. A solid mass slumped into view. "Tango down," Colton voiced into the mic.

"Moving out. Rendezvous in sixty," Frogman ordered.

As he hiked down the steep hill, Colton kept his rifle slung over his shoulder. Leaves and mud squished underfoot as the Kid brought up the rear. There'd be no talk between now and the rendezvous. They were alone and in a hostile environment. No need to wave to the bad guys on their way out.

That gave him an hour to pray the images from his mind. While lying behind the Remington and firing off a round, he compartmentalized. Strategically boxed up what he had to do. Yet even now, guilt harangued him. He reminded himself the guys he took out were wicked men. Many around the globe had problems with Colton's area of expertise, but he knew God had given him this talent for a reason. And thanks to that talent, Nightshade had been able to intervene in hot spots no nation or government would touch.

Like today's objectives. A politician on a secret mission flies over the Cuban jungles and gets shot down. Taken hostage. Held for political maneuvering. Getting him back, along with the wealth of knowledge in his thick skull, was a priority for the U.S. government. Yet if they were caught, Nightshade would be disavowed. Their lives would be forfeit—all of them.

That wasn't going to happen if he had any say in it. He lifted the miniature dog tag embossed with Mickey's picture and kissed it. *I'll be home soon, darlin'.* Although he hated being away from his daughter for any amount of time, his parents filled the gap. Eventually Mickey would be in school and his absences wouldn't be felt as severely. At least, he hoped so.

His mother's rant filtered through his head, and he leapt over a large, fallen trunk. *"If you'd get married and settle down, you wouldn't have to worry about leaving McKenna."*

If only that were true. He'd have more to worry about if he let that happen. A woman he loved *and* a daughter? No, it wasn't worth the risk. He'd already failed one woman—his sister. The memory assailed him—the detonation, the fire, the screams. . .finding her broken body under a table and part of the counter from the Israeli café.

No, he'd hurt too many people over the years. He wasn't about to leave the door open to failure and more bad dreams by taking a wife. Besides, what woman in her right mind would take a guy like him?

A rustle somewhere north elicited his training. He dropped to a knee behind a tree, his rifle at the ready. He peered down the scope, searching for the source of the noise. All at once, he registered the Kid taking up position behind him and the shifting of branches thirty yards northeast. To maintain a calm heart rate, Colton drew in a slow, deep breath—

A dull bird call trembled through the humid air.

He eased his face away from the butt. Relaxed—the Nightshade signal. Colton responded with a similar bird call and stood.

A half-dozen forms emerged from the trees. He grinned at the cocky, dark-haired man moving toward him with an M4 cradled in the crook of his arm. With the green and brown paint, Frogman's smirk seemed more pronounced.

"Nice job up there, Cowboy."

"These guys are amateurs—I think they pegged this gig on luck." Colton patted Frogman on the shoulder, then reached for the hand of his MARSOC buddy, Legend Riddell. The burly man grinned, his pearly whites brilliant against his dark skin.

Legend said, "Once again, perfect shot. Remind me not to flinch when you're taking aim."

"You could stand to lose an inch or two," Colton teased, then looked to their leader. "Sitrep?"

Frogman handed him the GPS. "About a klick northeast of rendezvous. Objectives are intact."

"Twenty minutes," Colton said as he returned the device and looked at the rescuees.

The politician slumped on a fallen tree, sweat ringing a shirt once starched to perfection. A grimacing woman struggled to sit on the log next to him, make-up smeared and white-blond hair askew.

Colton secured his rifle, then shifted to Frogman. "With the extra shooter I took down, I suggest we keep moving."

"Roger that. On your feet, people," Max ordered with a tight, controlled whisper.

As they hiked over the uneven terrain, the clouds let loose again. The grassy areas became slicker than the ground after Dolly calved last year. Colton pulled up the rear of the marching column, having to stop each time the woman slipped and tripped. He eased into position to help her. No sooner had he stepped behind her than her foot caught between two rocks, wrenching her ankle.

She cried out, but Colton clamped a hand over her mouth. Her wide eyes snapped to his.

"Quiet," he hissed, his eyes darting out over the hillside.

Midas let down his medic's pack and knelt in front of her. With her ankle between his hands, he probed and prodded, making her wince and whimper. "No break. Torn ligament, most likely. She can still get around."

"Good. Everyone move," Max snapped in a low, but effective tone.

The politician grunted. "You're not seriously going to make her walk—"

Max drew himself up straight. "We're only five minutes out, and a delay could mean death."

Colton watched as the woman absorbed Frogman's point with a slow nod, then worked herself upright. Propped on her toe, she faked a smile. Metcalfe supported her arm as she hobbled behind Frogman, weaving around trees and boulders. Her injury made the slow journey slower, more arduous. More dangerous. His senses were pinging. As if the rebels breathed down his neck this very second. Finally, crouched at the hem of the hill, they waited for the chopper.

Sitting ducks. He couldn't help the thought and tried to wipe it away with the thick sheen of sweat on his face and neck. The familiar *thwump* of distant rotors stirred his heart. Another few minutes and he'd be on his way back home to his daughter. To his ranch. As he smiled and kept watch on the swaying limbs and leaves, he felt a pressure on his arm.

Eyes lined by hardness and wrinkles glared back at him. Salt-and-pepper hair clung to the politician's face. "If you tell anyone about us... about this..."

The good ol' boy thought he had a secret Colton would be interested in. He grinned and winked. "Don't worry, partner. We don't exist either."

"How do you deal with it?" the woman asked, her voice shaky and hoarse. "Killing people, slaving through a jungle, hiding like criminals..."

"Criminals? Nah, never thought of it like that." Besides, who dealt with war? "You shove it down and pray hard."

"Chopper!" The Kid grabbed his pack.

Aboard the Black Hawk, Colton let the steady, deafening drone of the rotors lull him to sleep. Three days without a decent amount of rack time left his muscles aching and eyes burning. Images took on ghostly forms in his dreams, snapping him out of the slumber. He sat up straighter, rubbed his eyes, and swallowed against the metallic taste in his mouth. Colton bent, his arms propped on his knees, and prayed. Prayed for God to protect his heart and mind. He'd never pray to forget. Forgetting meant repeating mistakes.

After safely delivering the politician and crew to the U.S. Embassy in Mexico, the team boarded the private plane back to Virginia. At the converted warehouse base, Colton stood at his locker, holding two shirts. Stripes or just blue...?

"Time for another trip to Hastings?" Max laughed as he clapped him on the back. "What're you going to buy from her this time? Lingerie?"

"Go home to that wife and kid of yours, and leave me alone." He shoved his friend out of the way.

"Hey!"

Peeling out of his grimy duds, he let his mind drift to the woman at Hastings as he headed to the showers. Though he gave Max a hard time, the guy was right. Colton intended to stop by on his way home, just as he had every time for the past eight months.

So what if he couldn't bring himself to ask her out? That wasn't a bad thing, considering his past.

"My daddy is lost."

The squeaky little voice drew Piper Blum away from arranging the line of cosmetics. She shifted to the opening between the two counters. Beneath a coral-colored floppy hat peered the brightest blue eyes.

Piper smiled and leaned toward the girl. "Your daddy is lost?" She tried to hide a laugh when the girl propped her hands on her hips.

"Mm-hm. I told him I was going to look at the toys." Her lower lip pouted as she pointed to a display of Gund stuffed animals. Fear trembled through her chin. "But then he just left." Her voice cracked as she tossed up her hands. Puddles formed in the cobalt eyes.

Crouching, Piper rubbed the girl's arms. "Don't worry. We'll find him, sweetie." She led her around to the white leather barstool and helped her up. "What's your name?" Folding the hat rim back, she brushed the white-blond bangs from the girl's face.

"Mickey."

"Okay, Mickey, why don't you sit here, and I'll call your daddy."

"You can't." She huffed with another quiver of her lip. "He forgot his phone at the house, and we live out in the country, so it's too far to drive." She wrinkled her nose. "He's not having a very good day."

The laugh bubbled up over Piper's resistance. "Well, what about your mother?"

"I don't have one."

The matter-of-fact statement stunned Piper into silence—and drew out her own pain at that comment. She smoothed her hands over the pale pink Maxximum Girl jacket. "Why don't I try to call your daddy through the speakers here in the store?" She lifted the phone from the cradle. "What's his name?"

"Cowboy."

Phone in hand, Piper paused and looked at the little cherub. The coral cowgirl boots matched the hat. Jeans. A cute white eyelet top. The name for her father shouldn't have surprised Piper. But she couldn't exactly use that over the intercom. "Does he have another name?"

"Poppa calls him Colton."

Okay, that was better. Not much, but she could work with it. She pressed the number code for the intercom and shifted, facing the long aisle that reached for the escalator. A man darted toward the sliding staircase, his movements rushed and frantic.

"McKenna?" he called as he spun and scanned several directions.

It didn't take a genius to know this was Mickey's father. The black Stetson gave it away. Cowboy. Yeah, he had the jeans and boots, too.

Piper replaced the phone and moved into the open. "Sir?"

He spun, his eyes practically hidden by the tip of his hat. "Have you seen—" His gaze lit on the girl on the stool. "McKenna!" He rushed down the aisle, his strides determined and powerful. "Thank God!"

Piper inched away, propping against the counter as the man swept his daughter into his arms. His hat flew off. Disbelief sent her composure spinning in a dozen different directions. This was the same man she'd seen in the store over the past several months. She couldn't help but notice him because her typical customers were elderly ladies and young mothers with strollers. Not strong, muscular cowboys who bought towels.

But watching him embrace his daughter. . . She choked down the lump rising in her throat. The moment felt painfully familiar. And yet so distant.

He set his daughter on the floor and knelt. "Where'd you go?"

"I told you," his daughter said. "I went to look at the animals. But you left." Her face then brightened as she pointed to Piper with a big smile. "I did like you told me, Daddy. I told this lady you were lost. And she found you!"

How this man ever disciplined his adorable daughter, she'd never know. All Piper wanted to do was laugh.

"Well," he said, glancing at Piper, then back to Mickey as he replaced his black hat. "I guess we should tell the pretty lady thank you."

Pretty lady?

Mickey nodded. "Yep, or Nana will make us come back to do it."

22

Piper choked back a laugh and quickly covered her mouth.

The man rose, towering over her. His presence swallowed the entire aisle between the counters. A deep tan accented eyes born of the sky. Shadows from the rim of his hat skimmed his face and made him appear more mysterious. More handsome.

"I'm sorry about all this. But thank you for keeping her safe." He offered his hand.

Piper's heart skipped a beat as she placed her palm against his, surprised at the size and warmth. "It is no problem." Anxious to hide the jitters swarming her belly, she straightened the girl's hat. "Mickey and I were just talking. Here," she said, stepping behind the counter and retrieving a pink- and white-striped bag that held a mirror, a sample lipstick, and perfume from the Maxximum Girl line, extras from a spring promotion. "This is for you, sweetie."

Mickey's eyes widened—then darted to her father. "Can I, Daddy?"

He drew up his chest and held a breath, slowly letting it out as he tucked a hand in his pocket, which seemed to emphasize his broad shoulders. "Alright. I s'pose that'll work." A small grin tweaked the corners of his lips, drawing a dimple-like line down his cheek. He had a nice smile, one that could put anyone at ease.

"Thanks again." With that he led his daughter away.

The sight made her heart clench. Father. Daughter. Hand-in-hand. She chewed the inner part of her lip, willing the tears back.

"Bye-bye." Mickey's sweet voice snatched Piper from her grief.

She waved. "Bye, sweetie." And once again, her gaze collided with the girl's father.

The memory of shaking his hand swept through her. She smiled.

"Who's the hunk?"

She spun at the voice, startled to find Charmagne, her coworker, donning her pale pink lab coat. "Oh, well, his daughter came to me and said her daddy was lost. Isn't that the most precious thing you've heard?"

"Uh-huh." Charmagne just looked at her. "I guess they found each other."

"It was really cute."

"So is he."

Piper ignored the comment and returned to organizing the products in the new display box. In so many ways, the little girl reminded her of herself. Her father had always made her recite Bible verses to help tame her tongue and curiosity, but it hadn't worked. Not really. And Mickey seemed to have a wild streak that rivaled her own. *"Again, Lily, what does scripture say?"* Even now, his gentle rebuke carried through time and distance, reminding her that physical attraction to a man wasn't as important as a heart attraction.

But somehow. . .she sensed Colton Neeley—she'd memorized his name since the first time he'd purchased towels at her counter—had a good heart. Of course, he probably wasn't steeped in his religion like her father. Few were these days. But the way he treated his daughter, doted over her. . .how easily he'd called her *pretty lady*. . .

"Wow, what else did he say to make you grin like that?"

Heat infused Piper's cheeks. "He said nothing." That was a lie. "He was just concerned about his daughter." With a smile, she carried the items to the display. Once done, she found herself staring at the bar stool, remembering the precious little blue-eyed girl. Heart heavy, she logged out on the register. "I'll be back in an hour."

"Smart. Hit the food court before the crowds—and maybe that hunk is still out there."

More heat crawled into Piper's cheeks. She snapped the tray into place and washed her hands at the small sink.

Charmagne laughed. "You know, Virginia is laden with soldiers, agents, and other government-types. You're far too pretty to remain here long without a boyfriend."

"I have my college classes, and that's enough for now." She slipped out of the pale pink coat and hung it in the narrow closet. "Bye."

With her purse slung over her shoulder, she smoothed out her long hair and took a calming breath as she headed to the food court. Charmagne wanted her hooked up. Why, Piper didn't understand because the woman was miserable in her own marriage. Besides, like Char had said, there were tons of trainees hanging around. They were exactly the types Piper couldn't afford to get involved with. Which was maybe why the cowboy made her heart skip a beat. His calm demeanor spoke of rock-solid maturity. Something 99 percent of the men she'd encountered didn't have.

All the same, she had enough stress in her life. Studying. Staying hidden.

The smell of eggrolls and sweet-and-sour chicken wafted thick and heady through a small, fast-food restaurant in the mall. As a matter of fact, too thick. Piper detoured to the pizzeria, enticed by the tomato sauce aroma. She stepped to the counter and ordered a slice of veggie pizza and water.

"Four eighty-three," the cashier said.

Piper dug into her purse—just as a hand slid past her with a five-dollar bill. She snapped her gaze to its owner.

CHAPTER 2

A quart of oil would've pumped faster through his heart. Colton managed a smile. "It's the least I can do."

Her caramel eyes peered at him, digging deep into his soul. Piper straightened, brushing her long, silky hair from her tawny face. Her features had wrestled his mind over the last eight months as he tried to pin down her heritage. Almost a Middle-Eastern touch, but with a slightly American aspect. Intriguing.

"That is not necessary," she said in a quiet, embarrassed voice as she watched the greasy cashier snatch the bill from his hand.

"Yeah, actually it is." He tucked his fingers in his pockets and leaned against the counter. "See, when I get home, Mickey there will tell her nana what happened back at Hastings. My mother's interrogation about how I lost my daughter will pale in comparison to her questioning on how I showed you my gratitude."

Her laughter was natural and light. Nice. Real nice. "Thank you." She gave a slight nod as a rosy tinge crept into her cheeks.

Dawg. She twisted up his heart and mind in ways that made him wish he'd kept his dealings with her professional—only behind the counter at Hastings. Not here in everyday life where normal things like pimple-faced teens and greasy food amplified her beauty.

"Hey!" Mickey rushed toward them, caught Piper's hand, and tugged her toward the table. "Come eat with us!"

"McKenna—" Colton moved to intercept his daughter. "Now hold on there. We can't be intruding on her day any more than we already have."

"Daddy." Swiping her bangs from her face, his daughter rolled her eyes. "She has to eat *somewhere*."

"You aren't intruding," Piper said with another stop-him-cold smile.

"See?" Mickey led the graceful woman to their table in the corner. It looked right and good the way Mickey took to the woman, natural like the fields welcoming the sun into a new day.

Shaking himself from the thought, he cringed. She'd taken his seat, the one facing the door. The one that kept him alert, able to anticipate sudden noises that could render him a fool.

"Sir?"

He jerked toward the employee, who slid a red tray with a slice of vegetarian pizza and a drink across the counter. *Vegetarian?* What's the point of a pizza with no meat?

Tray in hand, Colton glanced toward the entrance once more, then pushed himself to the table and placed it in front of Piper.

"Thanks, again," she said as he eased himself onto the seat across from her.

"My pleasure." As soon as the words escaped his big mouth, Colton wondered how common courtesies like that took on new, full meanings in her presence. And then that meaning received appreciation with another melt-his-heart smile.

He ran a hand down the back of his neck, wishing he could push off the thoughts as easily so he could eat in peace.

"What's your name?" Mickey munched a fry, assembly-line style.

"Piper."

Mickey scrunched her nose, which made Colton wince at what would come out of his daughter's mouth. "That's a funny name."

"It's different." Piper agreed as she sipped her drink. "What about yours? Mickey seems more like a name for a mouse."

"That's my nickname."

"Oh, I see. So, what's your real name?" Smiling, Piper cut through the pizza and used a fork to slide the first piece into her mouth.

"McKenna Margaret Neeley." She took a bite of her burger, tucking the wad of meat and bread to the side of her mouth like a chipmunk. "My nana's name before she married Poppa was Margaret McKenna."

"Don't talk with your mouth full, Mickey," Colton said.

"I see. It's a very pretty name."

Colton ate quietly, listening to their conversation, surprised Piper endured his daughter's endless chatter. She had a lilt to her words, almost like an accent. Not only that, but she seemed to talk differently. And she had a way with children, which was good because—well, it just was.

In the store when he'd looked down after buying Mickey a new pair of jeans and discovered her missing, he'd panicked. How fast she could've been another missing child case. Where were all his stealthy reconnaissance skills when he needed them most? It reminded him of another time he hadn't been paying attention—and it had cost a life. *Emelie.*

Wanting to push the memory back into his past, he glanced over his shoulder and swept the fast-food restaurant with his gaze. Satisfied, he finished off his second slice of pizza, watching the enigmatic woman. He hadn't intended for her to join them. He felt bad for her, actually, with Mickey's incessant chatter—a sound he thrived on. Nothing like coming home and hearing the sweet, squeaky voice rattle on. He never tired of it. But. . .a stranger, someone not used to precocious children, probably felt their ears talked off.

"Darlin'," he said to Mickey. "It's time to eat and let Miss—" He popped his gaze to Piper in question. An easy tactic to gain information.

"Blum."

And she fell for it. "Let Miss Blum eat her lunch, too."

McKenna pushed up onto her knees and pointed toward the play area the food court straddled. "I'm full, Daddy. Can I play?"

Ditching Piper now would be rude, since they'd all but invited her to eat with them and she still had more than half her food to finish. But this was as good a time as any to bail. "I. . ." When he glanced at Piper and their gazes locked, he lost the power to think. Despite eight months of watching her, he still found her riveting. Gorgeous caramel eyes. Glowing tawny skin that accented her hair.

Piper tossed down her napkin on her food. "I should return to work anyway."

His left eye twitched. Something about the way she said that told him she wasn't being straight with him.

"Yay!" Mickey jumped down and started for the playground.

Afraid to lose her again, Colton started after her. Then

remembered Piper. He shifted back around. "Thanks for your help earlier. I 'preciate it."

"You're welcome." As she pushed from the table, she smiled again. "Thank you again for my lunch."

He'd pay for anything she wanted him to.

Accursed thoughts. Five years ago, he would've invited her out the first time they met. Asked for her number. Gone on a date. Let the night lead where it willed.

Leave before you do something stupid. "Well, I reckon I'll see you around."

"I'd like that." She tucked her head a mite and smiled.

His heart hitched and stuck in his throat. Dawg, his skills hadn't failed him. He'd been right—she *was* attracted to him. But he'd have to unearth too many dark secrets to let a woman into his life again.

Ask her out.

He stretched his neck, trying to dislodge the thought. That was the old Colton, the one who didn't give a rip what happened. He couldn't go there again.

Turning away had never been so hard. His boots felt like cement had filled them, weighting him with each step. He circled the play area, found a spot, and planted himself on the stone bench with strict orders to keep his eyes to himself.

Disobeying orders, his gaze drifted to her long, graceful form as she cleared the restaurant. When she turned toward him, he averted his gaze, feeling as silly as a schoolboy with his first crush. He removed his hat and brushed the rim. Straightened the band. Anything to keep his disloyal thoughts and eyes out of trouble.

"Mr. Neeley?"

When he glanced up, a thrill rushed through him at the sight of Piper standing beside him. He shoved to his feet, his heart tripping over itself. "Colton. Call me Colton."

Rosiness filled her face. "Colton." The silky softness of the way she said his name tied his mind in knots. She held out the little striped bag she'd given Mickey at Hastings. "I found this on McKenna's chair."

"Thank you. There'd be crocodile tears once she figured out it was missing."

"Well. . ." She tucked a strand of hair behind her ear. "I should get back to work." As she walked away, he was riveted to the bounce of her sandy blond hair. Why hadn't he asked her out? What if God had given him that opportunity right there to open the doors to. . .

The idea was all he needed. "Hey, what if. . ." he called after her. When she spun toward him, expectation in her beautiful eyes, he realized he'd lost his mind. But how did he recover from the hope he saw in her expression? "Maybe we could catch dinner or a movie sometime."

What are you doing, Cowboy?

Did she have to smile like that? His legs went weak.

"I would like that. Here—" She drew a card out of her purse and scribbled on the back, before handing it to him. "If you can't reach me at home, well. . .you know where to find me. Or if you need more towels."

Surprise jabbed him at the obvious taunt. He paused as a slow grin plowed into his face. Had she figured him out, that he'd been shopping in that fancy store just to see her? "I think we're stocked good on towels now."

She chuckled. "You should be." She *was* teasing him.

"We got a lot of bathrooms back at the ranch."

"Probably goes well with the luggage set."

His chest puffed up. "We travel."

This time, she laughed full out. And so did he. His cover had been blown.

"Daddy, watch!" McKenna shouted from the playground.

"I'd better go." She turned but kept her gaze over her shoulder. "Bye, Colton."

Mouth dry and brain dead, he gave a curt nod. *What have I done?* What was he thinking, stepping over his self-imposed line?

Too many things. What woman wanted a damaged Marine like him? And then there was the niggling feeling he had, things that snagged his instincts—instincts that had been dulled as his attraction took over.

He narrowed his eyes.

She was intelligent and spoke with proper English. Almost *too* proper—look at the way she ate pizza for pity's sake!

"Daddy!"

He pulled himself around and caught sight of McKenna as she slid down the tall slide, then leapt to her feet as if she'd dismounted the thing.

"Ta-da!"

He applauded her, then motioned her over. "Mickey, let's go, darlin'."

In his dualie, he buckled her into the booster seat and climbed behind the wheel. With one last glance at Hastings, he began the forty-minute trip home. Mickey quickly dropped off to sleep, affording him time to organize his thoughts and responses to his mother. Between her and Mickey, he had enough estrogen streaming through his life to know she'd demand an explanation. No matter how much he tried to convince himself he shouldn't call Piper for a date, that he should dismiss her from his life, his mind lingered on the beautiful woman.

Piper Blum.

Why was she sad? He'd seen the look when he and Mickey left the store before lunch. He'd almost swear there were tears in her eyes. She carried herself with poise that spoke of prominence and privilege. Then again, the clothes she wore didn't bear witness to a wealthy upbringing.

Hiding something. Keeping secrets buried tightly beneath the lid of composure.

Just like me.

Blum. A German-Jewish name. Of course, her conservative nature that he admired could be because she was Jewish—that might explain the veggie pizza because she couldn't eat pork sausage. Was his mind reaching too far with that one?

He blinked. Ten minutes out from the house, and he'd done nothing but think about Piper Blum. He slammed his hand against the steering wheel. "Rein it in, Cowboy!"

"What's wrong, Daddy?"

He glanced in the rearview mirror and found his sleepy daughter looking out the window, rubbing her eyes. "Nothing." He steered onto the dirt road to the house. Almost as soon as the crunching under the tires pervaded the interior, Mickey squealed, spotting his parents on the front porch.

His father met him as Colton stepped from the truck and shut the door. "Did you get the table for your mother?"

"Yessir." Colton let down the tailgate and dragged the large box from the bed while his mother retrieved Mickey from the backseat of his dualie. "Ya know, I have no idea why she wants an assembly-required table when you can make one twice as nice for her."

"Because I can't wait until I'm dead and buried to get it!" His mother laughed as she held her granddaughter close.

"Look, Nana. I got this at the mall from Piper."

Dawg, she starts fast. He hoisted the box up and corrected his daughter. "Miss Blum."

His mother's eyebrow arched. "Miss Blum?"

"She was a really pretty lady, even Daddy said so. She helped me when Daddy was lost. Then she had lunch with us. But she gave me this bag." Mickey took a breath, then rushed on.

Seizing the chance during his daughter's ramblings, Colton escaped into the house with the box. His mother and Mickey had more in common than any granddaughter and grandmother should. Inquisitive nature, incessant chatter, and relentless nagging.

He left the box by the living-room entrance, where his father would spend the next day or two assembling it, and strode into the kitchen. Not that Colton minded helping, but his dad enjoyed doing things like this. Made him feel useful, he said. After pouring a glass of iced tea, Colton grabbed a roll from a bread basket and stuffed several pieces of ham into it.

"Who is this Piper Blum, and why is she giving McKenna gifts?" His mother's folded arms and deep-brow scowl reeked of jealousy.

Colton almost laughed. "Your granddaughter was lost at Hastings. Miss Blum found her, and Mickey was upset, so she gave her a gift."

Her expression didn't change. She moved to the counter and began wiping down the mess he'd made with his sandwich. Towel tossed down, she planted a hand on her hip and shifted to him. "Why'd you have lunch with her?"

Colton nearly choked. Pounding a fist against his chest, he coughed to clear his throat. "It wasn't what you think. Mickey insisted that—"

Brr. Brr. Brrr.

He yanked his phone from the holster. When he saw the coded message, he planted a kiss on his mom's head. "Don't get any ideas. Lunch was merely a thank-you gesture. She's not a love interest or any other type of interest." He stomped down the side hall to his bedroom at the back of the house.

His mother called after him, "It wouldn't hurt you to take *some* kind of interest in a woman."

With a smile, he swung his door shut, then dragged his rucksack from the top shelf in the closet, his mind already on the new mission. Adrenaline surged through his veins. Where would they head this time? What adversary had popped his head up and proved too volatile for traditional military tactics? He lived for the missions, for Nightshade.

God, protect me and mine.

Getting caught meant death.

But she had no choice. Piper hit SEND and sat back against the hard chair in the law library. Hand on a textbook, she stared at the words in the pretense of reading and turned a page. Her gaze skittered between the text in the book and the glare of the monitor, waiting.

Minutes passed. Nothing.

Piper glanced at her watch. Checked the aisle to the right where mammoth oak bookcases stretched until they seemed to bleed into one another. To the left. She barely saw the edge of the main door. She shouldn't have sat this close. Too exposed. Someone could see her.

The Web site sat, staring back at her, lifeless, as if expecting her to do what a normal person would do—click on a link. Maybe she'd misread the note. She dug it out of her jeans pocket and smoothed the crumpled paper. Scanning the message, she read through the obvious to the code. Nonsensical code that demanded another level of deciphering to reach the intended message.

Today was the twenty-sixth of January, wasn't it? She flipped open her phone and checked the calendar. Yes. The twenty-sixth.

Another minute vanished. The Web page remained unchanged. Her heart worked a little faster. What if something had happened? Her mind galloped through scenarios. Had he been caught or arrested—or worse?

No. She had to keep hope alive.

She stared at the screen. An online pizza shop in SoHo. The site the griefer had given her. She double-checked the URL. Yes, it was correct. So, what was wrong? Why wasn't it—

A large spaceship suddenly slid across the lead banner. Lights around the top dome flickered, sending out distressing strobes of light. She blinked quickly. Letting out a breath she didn't realize she'd held, Piper smiled. She clicked on the pepperoni slice and logged in, using the provided code. If it all worked right. . .

> Shepherd: *Hello?*

Her heart jolted at the simple greeting waiting as soon as the black page loaded. She typed back:

> Ewe: *Vegetarian pizza, please.*
> Shepherd: **smile* So glad to hear your voice.*

Relief flooded her at the response. Quickly, she pecked on the keys.

> Ewe: *The joy is mine. How are you?*
> Shepherd: *Yeshua is with me. You?*
> Ewe: *Sad. Lonely. Praising Him for griefers. *smile**
> Shepherd: *As am I. It will not be long.*

Her pulse raced. How could he promise that?

> Ewe: *Have you found a way?*
> Shepherd: *In time, my precious. In time. Be strong. Keep your eyes*
>   *open, watchful. Do not trust easily.*
> Ewe: *What is wrong?*
> Shepherd: *They close in, but I. . .I will be fine. Must go. Keep*
>   *the Faith!*
> Ewe: *Love you!*
> Shepherd: *And I you.*

Piper sat staring at the dialogue as it faded from the screen along with dozens of green Martians, handiwork of a griefer named Shu Tup. In the world of griefers, little truth existed except the fact that their kind thrilled on causing angst to Web site owners and gamers. Getting paid to set up the rendezvous sites with her father was just an added bonus to her cyber friend.

But the conversation had been entirely too short. As she X-ed out of the browser, the ache to be with her father, to hug him, to hear his gruff but kind voice overtook her. Tears streamed down her face. She despised having to speak to him in code. Anger chipped at her courage. She wanted his warm arms around her. To feel his beard against her cheek.

"Excuse me?" The masculine voice stabbed her alert.

Spine rigid, Piper pushed herself up in the chair and swiped at her tears, keeping her face down. "Yes?" She slapped her books closed and grabbed pens and pencils, using her hair to shield her wet face from the man standing beside her.

"Are you using the terminal? I need to do research."

"Sure. Okay." Books gathered, she nudged back the chair and rushed from the hall. She had to be more careful. Sitting there pining over things she couldn't change left her vulnerable and brainless.

Out in the warm night, she hugged the books to her chest, still riding the high of knowing that, at this very moment, her father was still alive! Giddiness wove a sickening concoction in her belly. The last few weeks had taken their toll as reports of unrest in their homeland consumed the news. Unable to talk to him on a regular basis, she had to settle for nights like this. Nights when thirty seconds of conversation would have to hold her for months.

A block from her apartment, she stopped at a convenience store and grabbed an energy drink and a fruit bar. Anything to help her stay up studying. With finals in a month, she didn't have time to lose. The adrenaline from the online rendezvous was bottoming out, and exhaustion gripped her in a tight vise. If she went home and tried to study without a sugar rush, she'd be face down in her books within minutes.

As she waited in line, she noticed a keychain with a small pink poodle on it. A little girl's round blue eyes filtered into her mind. Piper tugged it from the rack, smiling as she remembered McKenna. . .and her father. Handsome Colton Neeley. She'd had to feign ignorance on his name, but she'd watched intently each time he'd scribbled his name over the credit card slip. Strong hands. Callused. Hard working. He fit the tall, dark, and handsome bill to a T. What would it be like to be in *his* arms? Fire raced through her cheeks. Her father would surely send her to the scriptures again for that thought.

As if Bapa forgot about the Song of Solomon, the ultimate love letters.

Piper paid for her items and hurried from the store, her mind still on the charming stranger. She'd hoped that he'd come into the store to see her, but he'd always had a ready explanation for each purchase. Yet he'd given himself away at the mall. She sighed, her breath swirling in the chilly night air.

The last few feet to her apartment sent fear racing up her spine. She swallowed as the hairs on the back of her neck stood on end. Hesitation pushed her gaze around the street, stabbing the corners where the shadows hid from the light. She spotted her elderly neighbor sitting in her rocking chair. Somehow, the three steps up to her door and the yellow hue of the porch light gave the woman a creepy appearance, almost as if she were glowing.

Piper waved as she passed the woman's section of the building. "Evening, Mrs. Calhoun."

"Out late, aren't you, dear?"

"A little." Unable to shake the unease, Piper quickened her pace and rushed to her door. "Have a good evening." She scanned the jamb, spotted the twine stretched over the lower corner, and jabbed the key into the lock. Inside, she spun the locks and whipped the chain into place before she blew out a breath.

Once she dumped her books and bag on the small, cedar table, she withdrew her small flashlight-mace combo and walked the tiny apartment—but her gaze quickly pounced on the answering machine. Disappointment sagged within her. Would Colton ever call to ask her out?

She refocused on her apartment. The sliding glass door. The kitchen window. Her bedroom door. No need to worry about the bed since there was no "underneath" to conceal a predator. She eased into the room and spotted the blinking sensor sitting on the windowsill. Checked the closet.

Satisfied, she flipped on the light and grabbed a pair of shorts and a shirt from the dresser. She sat at the kitchen table minutes later and opened the energy drink. Over the next four hours, she studied case law and procedures pertinent to economics. Despite the sugar overload, seconds took on the weight of hours, and by midnight, the sharp claws of sleep scratched at her resolve for an all-nighter. With a long day of work ahead, she headed to the bathroom.

Bent over the sink, she washed her face and groped for the hand towel on the counter. . .but it wasn't there. She blinked through the water. *Where did it go?* Finally, she saw it on the vinyl floor.

Piper froze, her mind whipping through her walk-through protocol. Nothing had been out of place. Had it? No. It hadn't. With a huff, she snatched a clean towel and dried off.

She grabbed her flashlight-mace from the table—and the poodle keychain caught her eye. She picked it up and placed it on her nightstand. Alarm set, she slid under the sheets and reached for the light and turned it off. Would she have the chance to give the poodle to McKenna? Why hadn't he called yet? Maybe he'd changed his mind.

She groaned and rolled over. Good things didn't come to her. They never had. Only pain and the opportunity, as her father said, to be longsuffering. She shouldn't expect anything different. Besides, relationships were only entanglements that endangered lives. No way would she do that to the beautiful blond girl and her handsome father. She wanted a happy ending. Not a nightmare. And the people hunting her father would stop at nothing to kill him.

"Showers're out," Max growled as he pushed through the front doors of the base.

Colton glanced down at his muddied duds, considered the stench that seemed to lift like steam from the caked-on earth, and huffed. He got to be Swamp Thing for the next hour—and pray hard his truck didn't soak up too much of the odor.

The trip home carried him down the highway—the one that passed the mall, the mall with Hastings, where Piper worked. For two seconds, he entertained rushing in and just buying. . .towels. His mom needed some new towels. Hastings had new towels.

"No!" He wrapped his fingers tightly around the steering wheel and kept driving. Even with the vents open, the unique swamp odor wafted around him. He twitched his nose and rolled down the window. Good thing he'd opted to head home. If he hadn't already scared Piper off a month ago during the impromptu lunch with Mickey, he would with his Eau de Jungle.

When he pulled into the drive, he slowed at the sight of a blue sedan. Whose car was that? Was his mother having company? Finally resuming her ladies' afternoon tea?

RONIE KENDIG

He eased his truck around the vehicle and parked in his usual spot at the back. Although his parents loved entertaining, they'd done little since moving to Virginia two years ago. Hard to do when living forty-minutes outside city limits. From his truck bed, he grabbed his gear, then stomped up the side porch, thanking the good Lord he'd built the addition at the *back* of the house. If Mama did have company, she'd light into him for coming home like this.

He stepped onto the hardwood floor and paused to ease the screen door shut. Spicy smells embraced him as he dropped his gear. The taunting aroma of lasagna and bread drifted down the hall from the kitchen, making his stomach grumble and his mouth water.

He frowned. Must be really special guests. Had the pastor come to call?

"Daddy! Daddy!" Mickey sprinted around the corner, her face beaming.

Yeah. This is what kept him going, made him feel like life was worth living. "Hey, darlin'." He knelt and swept the sweet-smelling bundle into his arm. "I sure missed you."

She threw her arms around him—and jerked back. *"Ew!"* She pinched her nose. "You stink."

Colton snorted. "What's wrong? You don't like my new cologne?" He tickled her, eliciting peals of laughter that did his soul good. That helped him remember that no matter how bad it got out there, he had *this* to come home to.

"What are you doing here looking and smelling like a sewer rat?" His mother's words assailed him with their intensity and pitch.

"Didn't have a choice. Showers were broke." He stood and moved toward his mother. "Come here. I'll give you a hug you'll never forget."

She flapped a towel at him. "Get lost, Colton Benjamin!"

He grinned—then froze, a full view of the kitchen. And another person. A woman. A tall, beautiful woman. Chest tight, he cleared his throat and nodded at her. "Piper."

CHAPTER 3

He looked wonderful. He looked terrible.

Piper let a tremulous smile into her lips. "Hello, Colton." She thought of the moment he'd asked her to use his first name, and how comforting it felt as she'd said it.

Slowly, he backed up, his gaze still riveted to hers. "If you'll excuse me." He looked at his mom. "Can I speak to you for a minute?"

Hesitation crept over Mrs. Neeley's face for a second, then twitched away beneath her always-present smile. "McKenna, why don't you show Piper your princess dishes in the kitchen?"

Piper felt the little girl's fingers wrap around her own, but the expression in Colton's face pinched her stomach together, making it impossible to look away. He wasn't happy about her presence. Disappointment clogged the thrill of seeing him.

"What's wrong with you?" His mom's terse voice darted out, just above a whisper.

"I've told you before, don't bring anyone here unless you clear it with me first. There are. . ."

His words faded, but not the rebuke. He'd aimed it at his mother, but the words had stabbed Piper right through the heart. So. His not calling her had been intentional. He didn't want a date with her.

"C'mon, Piper!" McKenna tugged on her.

When she took one last glance down the hall, her gaze collided with Colton's. His crystal blues held hers as if sending a silent message. What that message was, she couldn't decipher. But his words had left no doubt. He didn't want her here. With a shake of his head, he turned and clomped down the hall, his broad shoulders drooped.

McKenna jerked hard, pulling Piper into the kitchen, where she opened a cabinet. "Look, we got them at the princess palace!"

Piper tried to redirect her focus onto the pink, sparkly dishes. "They're so pretty." But her attention was still hung up on the horrible mistake she'd made in letting Mrs. Neeley talk her into coming for dinner. It'd seemed like an answer to prayer. A hope so deep and desperate she'd ignored good, common sense.

His eyes had pervaded her thoughts last night, and the resounding bass of his laugh rumbled through her dreams. Anticipating a phone call or answering machine message had gotten her through the first week or ten days following their mall encounter. After that, she started losing hope, wondering if she'd misread the twinkle that had made her stomach queasy—and found herself stranded on Desperation Island.

She ran her fingers through her hair, frustrated with herself. What was wrong with her? Mooning over a man who didn't reciprocate admiration and respect. *Oh just be honest—the attraction, too.* She had to hand it to him. Hands down, he was the most gorgeous man she'd met, with his barrel-thick chest and long legs, the trimmed-close hair.

And the dimples. *Yeshua* should never have done that to a woman. Adam probably had dimples—and that's what made Eve lose her mind over a stupid piece of fruit. Probably concentrating so hard on the dimples she didn't realize her folly.

If only the Fall could be explained so easily. Or her own stupidity. *Just leave. Make it easy on everyone.* Yes. Yes, she could grab food from Mr. Tang's on the way home and wallow in her own pity. Just like every Saturday night.

"Honestly," Mrs. Neeley said as she entered, her words weaker than before. "I don't know what's gotten into him. He's never come home like that."

Piper stole a glance at his mother as she went to the sink and washed her hands. In jeans and a short-sleeve sweater with appliqués, Mrs. Neeley stood several inches shorter than Piper's own five-nine, but there wasn't an ounce of average in the woman. Even though the cinnamon-colored hair was perfectly coiffed, Piper knew it was colored. But tastefully. Like everything the matriarch did. She had it together. A husband, a home, family, and everything else Piper didn't have that she so earnestly wanted.

Ack! She had to get out of here before she became completely depressed. "I really appreciate your inviting me out. I've had a wonderful time." She pushed to her feet. "But. . .uh. . .I have an assignment due soon." And she did. In two weeks. "So, I'm just going to head back to town."

"Oh, please—"

"No, really. I'm not sure I can find my way back without daylight, anyway." It sounded good, but the more she convinced Mrs. Neeley she should leave, the more Piper wanted to cry. Why on earth were tears threatening?

Because she'd wanted this—all of this—so very badly. The family, the laughter, the handsome hero to save the day. But of course, she should've learned years ago that good things weren't meant for her.

Mrs. Neeley's eyes rounded. "But dinner—"

Piper lowered her head, mustering her courage and resolve. . .but found none.

Colton's mom came to her and gently braced Piper's arms. "Please, stay for dinner."

Gazing down into the pretty brown eyes, Piper felt herself crumbling. "I don't want to make him mad," she whispered. Not when she'd been hoping for a first date. It was her turn to fake a smile as she patted the woman's hand. "It'll be okay. Thanks for a wonderful afternoon." She grabbed her purse, heart racing as she forced herself to carry through with this. "Again, thank you."

Out the side door, down the steps, and onto the gravel drive she rushed. Only as she rounded the big split oak did Piper realize she'd been holding her breath. She let it out and plunged her hand into her purse, digging for the keys and reminding herself that this was best—for both of them. Colton clearly didn't want her here. And getting close to anyone risked exposure. Risked her big mouth getting the better of her and revealing all her secrets.

Where were her keys? She stomped to her car and dropped the bag on the hood, then rummaged through all the paraphernalia: Maxximum Girl cosmetics, pens, an address book, her phone, a hair elastic. . .

"No keys." She huffed. Dug again. They had to be in there somewhere.

"Looking for these?"

Gravel crunched and popped as she whirled toward the husky voice. She gulped the burst of anxiety, that sinking feeling of being trapped in an awkward situation. Colton stood on the porch in jeans, a T-shirt, and wet hair. He started toward her, dangling her keys.

Those dimples pinched his cheeks as he grinned. "You turnin' tail and runnin'?"

He closed the gap between them. Soon he stood before her, gaze on the ground, then slowly he brought those blue eyes to hers—and pocketed her keys.

He tilted his head to the side slightly. "Don't you know it's rude to refuse Southern hospitality?"

"We're not in the south."

His smile widened, then a seriousness overtook his expression. "I reckon I owe you an apology for the way I acted when I came in."

"It was certainly within your right—"

"Nah." He shook his head. "It's just that. . .the last thing I wanted right then was for you to see me looking like that."

"I. . .I'm sorry."

"Don't be." After a shy grin, he scratched the side of his face. "Truth be told, seeing you made the day seem a bit brighter." Chin tucked, he peered up at her. "Stay for dinner?"

Piper couldn't think with him looking at her like that. She peeked at the house and saw his mother watching through the window. "Your mom's been working on that meal all afternoon." Pulling her gaze back to his made her stomach knot up. Did he have to be so gorgeous?

"Besides the food, if I can't convince you to come back inside, she'll tan my hide, and I won't hear the end of it for at least a year."

She didn't want to laugh, but the teasing light in his eyes plucked it out of her. Confusion slipped in under the lightheartedness. Was he asking just because his mom made him?

Colton reached out and touched her elbow. "Please?" All the joking disappeared. "I'd like for you to stay."

Well. . .if he wanted her to stay, wanted her company, why hadn't he called her? What stopped him from coming into Hastings over the last four weeks?

"Okay," she whispered.

Together, they made their way back into the house. No sooner had they entered the kitchen than McKenna plunged headlong into Piper, wrapping her arms around her legs. "Yay, you came back!" She squeezed tight, then looked up at her. "You won't leave me like my mommy did, will you?"

Shrapnel hitting him didn't hurt the way Mickey's words had. It stole his breath as the wound went deep. Especially with the wild look in Piper's eyes. He had to rescue this situation, deep-six the mortifying morsel his daughter had tossed out there.

"Mickey," he said, lifting her into his arms. "Why—"

"Hey, what's holding dinner up?" His dad stepped into the kitchen, hands on his hips as he glanced around. "Son, glad you're home."

He gave his father a one-armed hug, and that fluid move shattered the awkwardness created by Mickey's question. For a second, Colton marveled at the weight his father had lost during the two weeks while he'd been gone on a mission with Nightshade. How had he lost so much that quick?

"Benjamin, be nice." His mother hurried to the counter and handed his dad a bread bowl and pitcher of tea. "Take that to the table. Colton, here, come grab this casserole bowl."

The deafening silence of that moment still rang in his ears an hour later. His parents had buried their embarrassment in the meal, chattering like chipmunks over a mother lode of acorns. Piper seemed to recover over the course of the meal, but he spotted her eyeing Mickey with a look in her eyes he couldn't quite decipher. Pity? Maybe Mickey's comments had scared her off. What woman wouldn't bolt?

Truth be told, Mickey's words haunted him. How had she found out about Meredith? He'd vowed not to tell her until she was old enough to understand things. She didn't need that burden, and definitely not this early in her young life. He'd have to question his mom about it later, find out how Mickey could've learned about her mother.

Much as he tried to shift his attention to the beautiful woman who'd almost slipped out of reach tonight, he couldn't help but wonder if the earlier fiasco was divine intervention. Losing his head over a woman would only add to the complications already in his life. But even he had to admit he was losing that fight. He liked having her here, liked her smile and the smooth sound of her voice.

Maybe they could take a walk after cobbler and ice cream. He could explain a few things—of course, nothing that would put his life in danger. Or his heart. What if she found out about his breakdowns?

He stretched his neck and rubbed the knot forming in his shoulder. Stress was piling up again. Good thing his appointment with Pastor Roy was next week. He could unload the weight he'd carried around.

"Cast all your anxiety on him because he cares for you."

How many times had Roy quoted the words of 1 Peter 5:7 to him? But prayer and faithfulness hadn't healed the fracture in his psyche, the one that leaked ghoulish memories into the middle of perfectly good moments.

What would Piper say when she saw the first flashback? Because sure as heck if she stuck around, he'd have one eventually. God hadn't seen fit to heal him miraculously. A point of contention that had compounded the frustration of the flashbacks. What if she saw him, his mind anchored in some past event, and it freaked her out good? Made her run. His chest squeezed.

"Colton?"

He blinked at the sound of his mother's voice. "Ma'am?"

"Your ice cream's melting."

Shock riddled him as he stared down at the bowl of cobbler and cream. When had she put that there? Numb, he lifted the spoon and ate the first bite. It tasted sour. Mingled with bad memories and humiliation. He had to clear out, get away, get some fresh air.

"I'm full." He shoved away from the table. "Going to get my boots and check on Firefox. If you'll excuse me..." He couldn't look at Piper, couldn't face it if she was disappointed.

"Oh," his mom said. "Piper, why don't you go with him? Firefox's our mare. She's ready to foal any day."

His gaze slammed into Piper's. Question and uncertainty swam through her delicate features. Forcing himself to swallow past the lump in his throat, he gave her a slow nod.

"I want to go," Mickey said as she climbed to her knees in the chair.

"No, young lady. You need a bath; then it's bedtime," Colton said.

"I'll take care of it." His mom bobbed her head to Colton and Piper. "You two go on."

Colton headed to the back door, then paused when Piper came around the corner. "I'll get my boots and be right back." In his bedroom, he sat on the edge of his bed and stuffed on a pair of socks and his old work boots. When he returned to the side door, the hall sat empty. He glanced back into the kitchen, but crunching noises drew him outside. Hunched down, Piper rubbed a hand down the spine of a gray-striped cat.

"Can't seem to get the thing to move on," he said as he stepped onto the porch.

She straightened. "He's not yours?"

"It's a she, and nah. She had a litter in the barn back in the spring, and they've all scattered, but she seems to like it here."

"I can understand that."

Good to know. He pointed out toward the east pasture. "Foxy's in the barn." A warm breeze followed him across the backyard.

"Has she had a baby before?"

"This is her first." The soft rustle of tall grass soothed him as he glanced up at the sparkling blanket of black. "She's a champion I bought for breedin'."

"So, you want to breed horses?"

"Nah," he said, grinning. "I leave that up to the mares and stallions."

A loud whinny burst into the warm September night.

"Foxy." Colton sprinted the last few feet and jerked open the door. As soon as he came around the first stall, he saw her shifting and bobbing her head in the birthing stall he'd finished just last month. Then she went down.

Colton motioned to Piper to slow down. "Keep it quiet and still. She looks spooked."

"She's not the only one."

"Then stay here. She'll sense your fear and feed off it."

Piper rolled her eyes. "I meant you."

"Hey," he chuckled at her spunk. "This ain't my first rodeo."

The rueful look Piper shot him did strange things to his breathing, but he tucked that aside and stopped at Foxy's stall.

"Looks like the water sac has broken," she said, nodding toward Foxy's straw bed.

"How do you know so much about horses?"

Piper eased her hand toward the mare's hindquarters. "My grandfather raised goats."

"Goats! What's that—"

"A girl in labor is a girl in labor." Caramel eyes held fast to his. She smiled. "Whether a horse, a goat. . .or a woman."

His mind hung up on the day McKenna was born. He'd missed it thanks to a tour of duty. Not that Meredith cared. She'd never wanted him or the baby in the first place, but—thank God—she didn't want an abortion either. He couldn't help but think that he'd never been a real good judge of character when it came to women. His mind had been on other things. . .curves. . .smiles. . .long hair.

He roughed a hand over his face, and then he noticed Firefox seemed to be growing restless. She lifted her head up and whinnied at him again. He'd seen many a mare give birth, but this was Firefox, the foal he'd nursed from the brink of death, the one that made him feel like he had a new lease on life. And she was in distress.

"Something's wrong." He eased himself into the stall with her. "S'okay, girl," he spoke to the mare. As he worked his way around to her flanks, he felt his heart stutter. "Lost leg."

"What?"

"The foal only has one leg out." He smoothed a hand over her hind flank. "It's okay, girl. Just relax." His own hands would be too big to help Foxy. "I'm going to need your help."

"O–okay."

With a quick glance back toward the stall gate, he knelt behind Foxy, amid the wet hay and lone leg. "Wash up at the trough by the door."

She hurried away without a complaint or hesitation. Admiration ran anew at Piper's undaunted spirit. But the distraction was momentary as another contraction hit Firefox. She neighed and almost seemed to moan as her body worked to push the foal out.

Whispering more encouragement to Foxy, he mentally noted the water shutting off. Feet padding back toward them.

"What do I do?"

"Come in, but talk to her. As you come up on her, keep talking, tell her you're going to help." He could only hope Piper's presence didn't add to the mare's stress. He placed a hand on Foxy's flank again and reassured her in firm but soft tones as Piper did the same.

He watched. Admired. Knew he was falling hard in love with the woman who showed no fear in coming to the aid of his mare in distress. Might seem fast to most, but he'd spent eight months getting to know her. On his own, but he knew her all the same. Most likely, he had collected more information about her than most men learned about their girls in six months of dating.

Soon, Piper knelt at his side.

"I'm going to push the foal back in. When I do, I need you to reach in and find the other leg, draw it out." He shifted a bit more to the right to give her more room. "The leg's probably folded up."

She swallowed. "We did this once."

He considered her.

Nervous eyes came to his, clearly looking for encouragement. "On a goat."

"Just a bigger animal, but you'll do fine." He watched as Foxy reacted to another wave of birth pains. "Okay, after this contraction, we need to work fast."

A nod as she positioned herself.

He waited, his heart thrumming. As Foxy's body relaxed as much as it could, he strained to see her head over her body and made sure she was still focused on birthing, not on them. Once he confirmed her almost trance-like state, he gently grasped the leg above the fetlock and guided the foal back up the birth canal, careful not to stress Foxy or injure the foal.

"Okay, Piper." Warm goo coated his arm. "Go ahead."

Her delicate hand slid into the birth canal. She shifted as her arm vanished to the elbow. "I think. . ." Her eyes darted back and forth as her cheek twitched. "I can't find it." Frantic, she looked at him, her arm rubbing his as they both worked to aid the labor.

"Nice and easy. You can—"

"There!" Face alight, she slowly brought her arm back out. "It's coming!" Gooey and warm, her arm retraced its pattern until out came the other hoof.

Colton drew back and allowed Firefox's body to take over and finish the delivery. No sooner had he and Piper stood and cleared the area than Foxy went through another contraction.

The head emerged with a white blaze.

Piper gasped, covering her mouth with her clean hand as she inched back to give mother and foal more room.

"Come on, girl." Colton prodded Foxy on, his gut seized up. Quietly, he led Piper to the side as they awaited the finale. "She's almost got it."

Another contraction. Foxy moaned through it.

"That's it, that's it. You can do it," Piper quietly cheered next to him.

After a short relaxation period, Firefox endured another contraction. Within minutes, a *whoosh* delivered the gunk-covered foal onto the bed of hay.

"Oh!" Piper spun and threw her arms around his neck. "She did it!"

Surprise lit through Colton, and he lost his good mind, wrapping his arms around her and pulling her against his chest tightly. In the seconds before sheer satisfaction closed his eyes, he saw Foxy rolling to her feet so she could tend her baby.

Piper slowly eased out of his embrace, her head down and cheeks filled with a rosy tinge. "I'm. . .I. . ." She held her left arm awkwardly to the side. "I got your T-shirt dirty."

"I don't care." *Marry me.* His mind had gone rogue. "It'll wash." But his feelings wouldn't. He was in deep. The thing that irked him the most: He didn't want out. He wanted Piper. Wanted a life with her.

But that meant telling her.

Everything.

He couldn't do that.

DAY ONE

Saudi Arabia, 20:43:18 hours

Crimson curtains hung like sentinels on either side of the massive marble columns lining the entrance to the ballroom. Women dressed in expensive fabrics and jewels adorned the gilded hall, their heels clicking over the highly glossed floors. Men sporting their military regalia puffed their chests as much in salute to the women on their arms as to the gold glittering on their lapels.

Rich fools, all of them. They had a traitor in their midst. One besides him.

And that made his instincts blaze. Who'd beaten him to the general? Fingering the buttons on his suit to make sure he'd fastened them, he let his gaze roll lazily over the sea of people, tucking aside his fury.

Armed with the keys to the Hummer he'd lifted from an overstuffed diplomat, Azzan hustled down the expansive steps leading to the circular drive. At the water fountain, he banked right. Toward the parking area where hundreds of vehicles waited.

A guard stepped toward him.

Clapping a hand on the man's shoulder, Azzan Yasir smiled. *"Assalaam Alaikum."* He gave the familiar peace-be-upon-you, which demanded the other person reciprocate.

Wary and uncertain, the guard finally gave a slow, furtive nod. *"Wa Alaikum assalaam."*

Relief sifted through Azzan, no doubt undetected by this ill-trained guard who held his weapon as a prize, not a part of him. "It is a quiet night, yes?"

The guard nodded. *"Al hamdu lillah."*

Praise be to Allah? Afraid not. Azzan could only hope this guard did not delay him much longer and tangle him in the ensuing chaos when the body was discovered.

"You are leaving early." The man's words were quiet, probing.

"Too much ego." Azzan wanted to laugh at the man's feeble attempts to extract information, but the uncertainty lingering in the guard's words made him turn the conversation from himself. "You are the lucky one, stuck out here guarding"—Azzan waved his hand over the sea of fiberglass and metal—"the cars." He tsked and nodded at the man. "A waste of such a fine soldier."

The guard's shoulders squared.

"Maasalaamah," Azzan said, hoping the good-bye would give him a clear exit.

"Fi aman allah."

The conciliatory farewell blended with the gravel crunching beneath Azzan's Versace shoes as he strode toward the Hummer. Lousy shoes were as uncomfortable as they were ugly, but the mission demanded the price tag. He climbed into the vehicle and stuffed the key in the ignition. As the engine turned over, several thoughts assailed him. The throaty rumble as the vehicle roared to life. The guards and soldiers rushing from the front entrance, shouting. The odd reflection of blue glinting off the front windshield. And the soft rustle of fabric in the seat behind him.

Azzan whipped his weapon to the back. What registered in his mind almost made him hesitate. A white hijab draped her head and framed her oval face. Thick dark hair curled at the temples. Terror-stricken eyes.

"Out!" He stared hard at her, the tip of her nose almost touching the steel barrel. The darkness pulled at him again, plunging him into the despair that had wrapped its tendrils around his soul. No, he must do this. With the weapon, he motioned her out. "Get out, or I will kill you."

The girl cowered and drew back as tears pooled in her eyes. She glanced at the palace, then met his gaze and gave a small but frantic shake of her head.

He jabbed the muzzle against her cheek and nudged so that her head tipped back. "You think because you are young and beautiful, I care? Your brains look the same as anyone else's splattered over the seats." Words like that usually had their effect on weak-minded females.

She whimpered as her attention darted toward the royal palace again. "They're coming," she whispered, her Arabic quick and nervous.

A flurry of movement reflecting against the heavily tinted windows affirmed her words. The men rushing toward them were too close. He didn't have time to drag her out of the car. He'd have to kill her.

Dod would tell him to reach for the light in his soul, avoid the darkness.

No time. Azzan grasped the threads of reason his sage uncle's voice offered. He reared his arm back and slammed the butt of the weapon against her temple.

CHAPTER 4

Heat swirled through his gut, matching the temperature in the first level of the brownstone. Colton sat on the edge of the flowery couch, arms propped on his knees, turning the Resistol Cattle Baron in his hands. Smoothed a hand over the black felt. Ground his teeth and felt the tension radiate across his jaw, down his neck, and into his knotted shoulder muscles.

Why? Why did Lambert have to require a monthly meeting with a shrink?

He wiped the sweat from his brow. Max had just about erupted when the general informed the team they each would be required to meet with this Dr. Avery or resign their positions on the team. Although Colton had calmed down his friend, he sure understood the reticence. He'd rather—

"Well, he was certainly accurate." The woman's voice snapped Colton to his feet.

"Pardon me, ma'am?" Who was accurate? What was she talking about?

A smile filled her smallish face as brown eyes sparkled back at him. "Why are you here?"

He handed her a slip of paper. "I have an appointment with Dr. Avery." He glanced toward the stairs, wondering how the woman had approached without him hearing. Had he been that wound up in his own thoughts that he'd not heard her coming down the steps?

"Dr. Avery is ready to see you. Follow me."

Colton had to temper his large strides as she led him around the stairs and through a small door at the back of the hall. There, she opened a larger door to the right, stepped in, and waited for him to enter.

Feeling closed in and cramped in the small office, he focused on the window. He shifted and turned around.

The woman shut the door and moved to a small cabinet. "Would you like a bottled water or a soft drink?"

"Um," he glanced at the door again, wondering where the doctor was. "No, I'm good. Thank you."

"Well, have a seat, please." She motioned to two large, overstuffed chairs opposite the desk. One with its back to the door.

Colton tugged the hard, wooden chair next to the bookcase closer and sat. If the doctor was late, did the time spent waiting count toward his sixty-minute requirement?

Armed with a bottled water, the woman reclined against the credenza stretching the length of the suffocating office. She took a sip, her gaze never leaving his.

With the Resistol balanced on his knee, he peeked at the door again. "Did he get lost?"

"No, Dr. Avery is right here."

He felt the color drain from his face. "Oh. You're. . . ?"

"Dr. Katherine Avery, at your service." She tilted her head to the side. "I can see why you've been given the nickname Cowboy—which, as you know, is the only name provided to me by General Lambert." She drew in a slow breath, then leveled a steady gaze at him. "You're nervous. Can you explain why?" She kept her distance, but eased into one of the two chairs. "Do you find me threatening?"

"No, ma'am." Had it gotten hotter in here? What was Lambert thinking, putting the team in the hands of a woman who seemed fragile enough to break if you looked at her wrong? It was hard enough to talk to Max and the guys—but an attractive woman who was disarming and intelligent? Not that she had anything on Piper. She didn't. But still. . . "I meant no disrespect. I was. . .well, fact is, I assumed I'd be seeing a male doctor."

She smiled. "Most men do."

He nodded, more unnerved and agitated than ever.

"Tell you what. Why don't we take a walk? I'm hungry, what little air is seeping through the windows isn't enough to keep me breathing, and there's a fabulous hot-dog vendor down the street." She stood and grabbed her keys and small wallet. "Come on, Cowboy."

When they strode down the hall, she explained to her receptionist that they'd be back in thirty minutes, then stepped out into the bright afternoon. But Colton couldn't shake the humiliation of getting mixed up.

Donning his Resistol, Colton fell into step with her. A breeze wafted over the cement, and he took a deep breath, ready to savor being out of that confining office. But instead of clean air, he inhaled her floral perfume.

Okay, see? There. That there was a problem. It was distracting. A guy doctor wouldn't be wearing something to make Jell-O out of a man's mind.

"So," she said as she peeked up at him. "Tell me your thoughts on the military."

"It's necessary."

She arched her eyebrow at him as they rounded the corner. Shade draped over them instantly, bathing them in coolness. "That's a convenient answer. Going to the bathroom is necessary, too."

"Do you want to know my feelings on that, too?"

She laughed. "Fair enough. I asked for that one."

Colton felt the first smile tug at his wound-up mood.

Thud!

He flinched and whipped toward the noise, his senses buzzing. A guy in a blue uniform pushed an upright dolly away from the back of a large, white delivery truck. Heart chugging, Colton tried to refocus on the doctor. He could see her lips moving, but the sound didn't reach his ears.

She pointed to the side. He followed her finger and saw the hot-dog vendor. As she gave her order, he eased back and stretched his jaw.

"You want anything?"

Besides leaving? Colton eyed her, then shook his head.

His gaze roamed the busy street until it hooked on the small park that sat adjacent to a school.

"Mmm," she said as she brandished a dog laden with sauerkraut and mustard. "Nothing like it."

"Ma'am, no disrespect, but that's just wrong. A hot dog should have ketchup and relish, maybe a bit of mustard, but sauerkraut?"

She shrugged. "Raised in New York. You should be thankful it's not onions; we still have thirty minutes."

"Now, see, that's why I stay south of the Mason-Dixon."

Dr. Avery laughed but then took a bite. They quietly walked, and Colton found a bit of comfort in the fact she was leading him to the small park. At least there, they'd be far enough from sudden noises and sounds. He wouldn't make an idiot of himself.

They sat on a bench that straddled the space under a shade tree while she finished off her lunch. He stifled a yawn as he monitored the foot traffic. The office building across the street with its two-story parking garage.

A chill scampered over his shoulders. It seemed familiar—but he knew it wasn't. He'd never been here before. But the tall building, the quiet section of street. . .watching his kid sister get blown to bits.

Colton lowered his gaze and shut out the memory. Couldn't think about that.

In his mental memory banks, the sound of dribbling concrete raining down on him pulled his mind into another scenario—when he'd been ambushed and taken captive.

He pinched the bridge of his nose.

"How bad are the flashbacks?"

Despite the gentle, caring tone, Colton snapped his gaze to hers.

Steady brown eyes held his. She sat attentive, positioned toward him. Nothing threatening in her posture.

His attention drifted back to the ground. To his booted feet. "Bad." He drew in a ragged breath. "I can go months without one, but then—"

"A simple slamming door triggers one."

Surprise lit through him, but he offered only a slow nod.

"You aren't sleeping."

He felt his brow tense and forced it to relax. "How. . . ?"

"I can see the circles under your eyes, and you've yawned four times since we stepped into the sunlight." She leaned forward, matching his posture. "Cowboy, we have a lot of restrictions on our meetings, compliments of the good general. I will do my best to not ask *too* much, but I do believe I can help you."

"I can't say much. Can't talk about what happened." Well, maybe he could talk about Emelie. "But I want this to go away. I just want things to be the way they were."

"That's not going to happen." Something akin to grief washed over her face. "I'm sorry, but it won't. You're a changed man. Now, my job is to help you reintegrate, to work through the nightmares and flashbacks."

Maybe...maybe if this worked, he'd have a chance with Piper.

"Don't do this for a girlfriend or a loved one, Cowboy. Do it for yourself. You've sacrificed everything for your country. Now, it's time to sacrifice for yourself."

Plausible deniability. They'd demanded it of him, his Joint Chiefs brethren and the president.

So Olin Lambert delivered.

Right down to the last bullet.

Warm lamplight spilled over the litter of pages. Angling the light for a better position, he let his dry eyes rake the information. The death of Oscar Reyes put Nightshade one member short. Desperately short in a six-man team. But measuring up candidates against the perfection of this black ops machine made it nigh impossible to find the right match. Especially with those photographs they'd discovered in the Philippines. Who'd taken them? That alone made Olin leery of recruiting. But the team couldn't go forward without another team member.

Even now, a year after constructing the team, he'd kept their identities a secret. Each of the six-man—*five*-man, he corrected himself—unit was a virtual ghost. An analyst might detect personality traits or flaws, but that'd be it. Someone desperate enough might be able to guess the team's movements, but they could never pin down the individual identities of Nightshade. He'd made sure.

Fingering one profile sheet filled with mind-numbing data— sans biographical information—drew a smile out of his unwilling face. The composite of the team leader with the designation of Nightshade Alpha. Max Jacobs. The man's wife had tracked down the team six months ago, which warned Olin to take this process slow, be meticulous. He couldn't afford any mistakes. Nightshade couldn't afford any mistakes. He would endure painstaking precautions in recruiting a replacement.

Sifting through the pile, he dragged another profile closer. A chuckle drifted up his throat. Digitalis. The Cowboy. Never met a man he liked more. Calm, easy personality, and the former Marine dug into the trenches for the long haul, stuck it out, no complaints.

Now Wolfsbane had a killer instinct and efficiency, which is why

Canyon Metcalfe had received the code name of the man hidden within the wolf-like persona. The man was as loyal to the team as he was to the beach. He also had an ocean full of dark secrets.

Much like Griffin Riddell—Firethorn. The only member of the team Olin had consulted on the initial selection process. A man wanting to do his job and be respected, only to end up unjustly accused and pushed to the point of breaking—or killing, as the case was.

The Kid. Olin clenched his hands as he thought of the young man. The Kid had so much potential bunched up inside him but had no idea of the greatness within himself. One day, he'd see it, and exploit it for the benefit of everyone. That's why Olin had codenamed him Bloodroot. . .some day, maybe he'd find out what blood coursed through his veins.

Glorious. Ingenious. No recorded Christian names. A giddiness soaked Olin's old muscles. He slumped into the leather office chair that creaked and tilted to the right—his wife had always said he leaned to the right, toward conservatism. To Olin, the leadership placed on him by the United States government could only have happened because God gifted him with the fortitude to speak sensibly and plainly in the face of certain opposition. Because of his reputation, his dream had come to fruition: a deadly, stealthy team moving in the shadows of night with the skill that left the uninitiated blinking and their tongues hanging out.

Yet with the brilliance of the team, the delicate nature of the missions, and the absolute demand for anonymity, adding one member, bringing on a newb, put every one of them in jeopardy.

Every. Bloody. One.

Until the team had its sixth body, Olin would have to pray they weren't called upon. Being one man down—

"Lambert?"

Olin looked up from the chaos spread before him.

The Chairman of the Joint Chiefs stood in the doorway, worry gouged into his weathered face. "Been to the carnival lately?"

At hearing the code phrase and with his spine vertical, Olin tugged his jacket straight. So much for laying low. "Love the cotton candy." Hot and cold swirled in Olin's gut as he gathered the documents into the file and stored them in the safe. He couldn't tell the chairman they'd lost a man. The information would be a blinking, neon-lit trail straight to the team.

The chairman pivoted and left—and with him went Olin's hope. He'd wanted time to let the team heal and fill in the missing man. But tonight's venture to the carnival would launch one more mission.

They'll never make it out alive.

No. He'd assembled that team. Men with brutal dedication and loyalty. A group that functioned with the perfection and beauty of a stealth bomber. And they'd better.

Or he'd be looking for more than one replacement.

CHAPTER 5

Dark brown eyes. Curly hair. Blood dripping down the face.

Colton shifted, ran a hand over his stubbled jaw, and readjusted on the chair that felt like a rock. Pressing his head back, he fought for another measure of sleep.

Almost instantly, more eyes. This time, caramel. Haunting.

They swam through his mind amid screams. Amid rapid-fire. As a sniper, he came eye to eye with every one of his victims. Faces of those he'd killed. *Neutralized* was the sanitary term that made politicians feel better. To him, that was only a Band-Aid on a gaping wound. He'd killed. Yes, each had been mission-integral, but the faces still haunted him.

He sat up and leaned forward, elbows propped on his knees. Covering a fisted hand, he pressed his knuckles to his lips and looked out the window of the private plane. And closed his eyes. Prayed once again that God would forgive him and allow a good night's sleep. Save him from the dark cloud that invariably descended and devoured his soul, tempting him to end it all, give up on the emptiness that left him thinking life would be better off without him.

It was foolish to focus on those thoughts. A slap to the face of a God who'd created him and loved him. He knew that. He did. But. . . the thoughts were still there, battling him. Weighting him.

Something hit his shoulder and snapped him out of the private moment. He yanked toward the aisle seat.

Max dropped into the chair. "Take a look," he said, handing him a phone. "Syd sent photos of Dillon's first tooth."

The chubby face drew a smile into Colton's face. "Good thing he looks like his mother."

"Amen." Max laughed but grew serious as he eyed his son's image. "So what's eating you?"

Colton glanced down. "Nothin'."

"Come on, man." Max shifted to face him better. "We've done enough time in the bush for me to know something's off." He nudged him with an elbow. "Besides, we're friends. You saw me through a lot. I'm going to do the same for you. Now, cough it up."

With a ragged breath, Colton supposed the guy was right. He studied the industrial-grade blue carpet below his feet. Talking about this could get him yanked from the team. But what could he do? He'd tried everything else. "Each hit is getting harder. . .after."

"You're getting old."

"True." He'd be thirty-seven in a few months. But it was more than that. "I see them. In my dreams. In the day." The only other image that even remotely countered the oppression of the dead was a beautiful, caramel-eyed woman. He hadn't talked to Piper since she'd jumped into his arms after Firefox foaled. She'd been so excited about the foal, and he loved that she seemed at ease with animals the way he was.

"Uh-oh."

Colton flinched.

"I know that look."

"What look?"

A low laugh slowly worked its way through Max's chest. He covered his mouth with his fist. "What's her name, Cowboy?"

"I don't know what you're talking about."

Max pushed to the edge of his seat, his face alive. "Oh wait! It's that girl, isn't it?" He hooted, drawing the attention of the guys on the plane. "This girl you keep going into that store for—what's it called?"

"Hastings," Griffin said from across the aisle, his bald head resting against the seat and eyes closed.

"That's it! You go in to Hastings." Max's eyes widened. "Wait, wait. I'm getting the picture now. You go in there not to buy stuff, but to see her." His coal black eyes glistened with his bright idea. "Am I right?"

"What's this about Cowboy and a girl?" Midas glanced back from his seat one row up.

The Kid rushed from the rear of the plane. "He's got a girlfriend?"

"No, I ain't got a girlfriend." Colton felt the heat creeping up past his collar and hated himself for the way his drawl thickened and he reverted to his cowboyisms.

Max chortled. "You still haven't asked her out?"

The heat blazed a trail up his neck, mingled with his frustration, and simmered into anger. Hatred. "I'll do it when it's the right time." Why did he suddenly feel the need to run home and talk to his dad?

He pushed his gaze to the window, furious with Max's jeering that drew the attention of the rest of the team.

"No way, man. You gotta ask her out," the Kid prodded.

Colton glared at him.

With a staying hand to the Kid, Max looked at Colton. "What's holding you back?" Max moved a seat closer, gaze on the floor. "The Cowboy I know is confident and assured."

Besides the breakdowns and flashbacks? Besides wondering if he'd kill her in his sleep one night? Besides the niggling in his gut that something was...*off* about Piper? All the same, he hated talking about this. "I want to be sure."

"Of what?" On his feet, Canyon folded his arms. "You're MARSOC, recon—don't you think you'd have the pieces put together by now?"

"It's not that simple, and I don't want to rush things."

Max nodded. "But if you wait too long, it might never happen."

"Could be better."

When a chorus of mocking laughter and *aww man*s rang out, Max stilled the team again, this time telling them to back off and give him some room. Watching in the dingy reflection of the plane's window, Colton waited till the others left before he looked at Max again.

"I could kill you for that."

Max's dark eyes held Colton's with an intensity he'd seen many times in combat. "Colton," he said—which was plain weird because Max had never called him anything but Cowboy. "If you really believe she's not worth it, why are you still sitting here, tormenting yourself? Why did the guys' reactions tick you off?"

Right as Max was, Colton didn't have to admit anything. He stared at his hands, calloused hands stained with the blood of far too many people. If he took this road, he'd have to tell her about his past, what he did, what he was doing right now. And that brought up the bigger issue. "She could put everything at risk." The team, their missions. . . his heart.

"Only if you're serious about her."

Colton cast him a firm glare. Would he be talking about this if he weren't?

One side of Max's mouth curved upward. "Thought so." He lowered his head. "Yeah, we put the team at risk with anything new. Lambert's looking to replace Reyes, so the dynamics will change, but I think each man on this team has your back if she's important to you."

It wasn't easy to accept that his teammates would put themselves at risk for this. Granted, they did that every day in the field, but for a woman?

"Is she worth the risk to you—and the team?"

The question pricked Colton's conscience. "I've been in that store once a week for eight months—except while we're out on missions, of course—and I still can't answer that question."

"Dude," Max said with a laugh. "I know you're uptight-methodical in lining up a target, but this is obscene—*take* the shot."

Take the shot. What did Max know? He had a wife and a kid, had things good and right. Of course, they were good and right because Max had taken the time to fix things.

Well, Colton's life wasn't messed up from his lack of trying. But the flashbacks had a way of dropping in on him the way a B-2 dropped its payload on unsuspecting terrorists. Coupled with his skills and big bird flying high over enemy territory, the method was effective. Unlike every prayer, counseling session, and attempt to straighten out his mind.

It was time to stop hiding.

He adjusted his Stetson, stretched his neck, and strode into Hastings. How pathetic that he had every aisle memorized. Knew the sales ladies for every department. It was wrong. Just plain wrong. A man ought not to know that stuff. If it hadn't been for his mother asking for that perfume last Christmas, he wouldn't be here. And he wouldn't have met Piper. That bottle had sealed his fate.

A woman he'd seen before at the counter with Piper walked

toward him—and recognition lit her ebony face. "Afternoon. Are you finding everything okay?" she asked with a little more curiosity than usual.

He tipped his hat, mumbled a "just fine, thank you," and kept moving, afraid that if he'd let anyone stop him full on, he'd never get his nerves—or his feet—working again.

As he rounded the corner, he darted a glance to the Maxximum Girl counter. There! Bending toward the illuminated displays, Piper reached under the glass top. She angled her body to reach farther into the cabinet—and her gaze slid right into his.

He'd swear he felt the impact. It had slowed him.

Lips slightly parted, she straightened as he approached. "Colton." She locked the display and placed her hands on the glass. With a coy smile she asked, "Have you lost McKenna again?"

He wasn't sure if her humor made it easier or harder to get on with this. "No, actually, she's with my parents visiting family in Texas right now." Heart thrumming, he glanced around—and spotted a couple of sales ladies watching. Dawg. "You busy tonight?"

Wow, that had a certain. . .idiocy to it. And a heaping dose of desperation. Not exactly the way to woo a woman. Where was all his southern charm? He yanked off his hat. "Sorry. What I meant to say—"

"Then you're not here for more towels?" The playful tone in her words and the way she cocked her head to the side told him she wasn't going to make this easy.

It was time to own up, come clean. Stop hiding behind towels and perfumes. "No," he said, firm and certain. At least something in him was. The other parts screamed this could be his biggest mistake ever. *Get on with it!*

"You get off at six, right?"

Amusement danced across her face. "You know my schedule?"

Could this go any worse? But no more hiding, so. . . "Darlin', I don't think there's a thing about you I don't know."

Piper blinked and squared her shoulders. "Yes, I get off at six."

Here goes nothing. . .or everything. "I'd like to take you out."

"Where?"

"To dinner."

"Why?"

What on earth. . . ? "What do you mean?"

"I—" She lowered her head and tucked a strand of hair behind her ear. "I'm sorry. I was just wondering why, after all this time, you finally decide to ask me out."

All this time. . . She'd been waiting. For him. To ask her out. His heart stumbled over the grenade-like revelation. He traced the band of his Stetson, hating that he didn't have an answer. At least not one that wouldn't make him sound like a big fat chicken. "Does it matter?"

A small smile teased the edges of her lips. "No."

Her soft reply did his heart good, picking it up off scraped knees of his own bumbling attempt to be dignified in asking her out. "Good." He gave her a slow nod as a customer walked up to the counter. "I'll wait."

"Good afternoon, ma'am. How are you?" Piper greeted the customer, but her gaze kept bouncing back to Colton.

Thirty minutes till she got off. Any other time, he might get himself a drink, check out the boot shop. But he knew better than to leave. Staying was crucial for two reasons. One, he got to watch Piper, and he'd pay to do that any day of the year. Two, if he left, he'd either end up in some wreck, get summoned on a mission, or he'd just plumb turn yellow and never come back.

But the more time he spent with Piper and realized her feelings most likely mirrored his own, the less he felt inclined to avoid her. Actually, it made him want to be with her at every opportunity. Max's suggestion that Piper could be *the one* had lodged in his chest, digging deeper with each thought that passed by it.

As the customer bent over the counter, Piper's gaze drifted to his. A smile filled with pleasure and expectation assailed his senses. Yes, he wanted to please her, wanted to meet that expectation. . . .

But he knew better. He'd fail her. Sure as night turned to day, he would. Just the way things worked with him and dating.

CHAPTER 6

The grim reality that she could never be completely honest with Colton tempered Piper's enthusiasm over the romantic dinner date. Even now as she sat across from him, a white tablecloth dusting her legs and the flickering candlelight casting shadows over his rugged face, she ached to tell him. Everything. But necessity—and her father's life—demanded her silence.

Though clean shaven, he had a slightly shadowed line running along his angled jaw that made him appear rougher around the edges. And that dimple winked at her each time he chewed. Instead of being hidden by the big black cowboy hat, his eyes were shielded by the low lighting—which was probably a good thing since he always melted her resolve when he probed her with those blue irises.

"You don't talk much about your family." He slid a chunk of steak into his mouth and shifted his gaze to hers.

She sucked in a quick breath at the statement and darted a glance at him, then down to her salad. Family. . .she had all this rehearsed; why couldn't she think what to say now? "My. . .um. . .my mother died when I was young." That wasn't one of the rehearsed stories. While it wasn't a disastrous tidbit, she had to rule her tongue before it destroyed her.

Colton stilled. "Piper, I'm sorry."

She brushed the loose hair from her face. "It's okay. I was ten when it happened. She died giving birth to my brother—he died, too." *Kelila Liora Rosenblum!* She could hear her father's remonstration. In the days before sending her to America, he'd had spies test her. She'd been heartbroken that he'd tested her, but even more so that she'd failed. But those trials had hammered into her the importance of *not* failing on nights like this.

"Wow, that's. . .I'm sorry. I had no idea." Colton touched her hand.

Drawing up her wits, she forced a smile, determined to deflect the questioning from her family. "Like I said, I was young. I don't remember much." Not entirely true, but she had to push the conversation away from herself. "What of your family?"

He winked. "You met them, remember?"

Think, Piper, think. "What about McKenna's mother? I've never heard her mentioned." When Colton's face fell, she immediately regretted the maneuvering of topics. "Colton, I shouldn't have—"

He held up a hand as he placed his napkin on the plate. "No, you're right. We don't talk about her with good reason, but you deserve to know if. . .if this thing between us is working."

The insinuation tickled her hopes and brought a smile to her face.

"All right, then." He cleared his throat. "I reckon I messed up real bad with Meredith. Had no business gettin' involved with her. I was a cocky Marine, thought I owned life." He huffed and shook his head. "When I came home after my first deployment, I met her at a frat party with my college buddies."

Regret chugged through her veins, making her wish she'd never brought this up. She could tell it was hard for him, and she hated hearing about him with any other woman.

"Anyway," he said and ran a hand through his hair. "When she told me she was pregnant, I. . .well, I ran. My unit got orders, and I'd never been so glad for deployment."

Was she understanding this right? "You ran from your wife?"

"Meredith and I were never married."

"Oh."

"When I came back, I tried to do the right thing, tried to marry her, but she wouldn't have anything to do with it."

Why on earth wouldn't a woman want to be married to Colton?

"After McKenna was born, Meredith took off with some guy. I'm on a ship somewhere in the Arabian Sea when I get a call that she's been found dead, OD'd on crack or something. The guy, too." He let out a long sigh as he wiped the beads of sweat from his tea glass. Slowly his gaze came to hers. "I'm not proud of my past. Matter of fact, I'm pretty ashamed of it."

Not everyone had been raised by a father who'd insisted on the absolutely pinnacle of upright and moral living, but somehow, she was disappointed. The handsome hero before her had fallen from his steed. But it was years ago. Piper wrestled, uncertain how to feel.

"I made my peace with God about it, and I've worked double-time ever since to make up the days I've lost with Mickey." He nudged his glass aside. "I've avoided dating, afraid of the way I used to be. I did a lot of stupid things where Meredith was concerned. She wasn't exactly a saint, but she didn't deserve how I treated her either."

Piper swallowed, feeling as if the earth had shifted from beneath her feet. "I can't. . .I can't imagine you being like that."

Colton nodded. "Reckon that's a good thing—maybe it's proof I've changed my ways, which I have." His earnest expression carried with it a heavy silence that fell over the dinner.

What could she say? That it was okay? But that'd be a lie. She knew American culture sanctioned just about anything that made a person feel good, but she hadn't been raised that way.

"I can see I've disappointed you."

Wanting to allay his fears, she scrambled for something to say, something to soothe that wrought expression darkening his blue eyes. But she couldn't.

Who was she fooling anyway? When Colton found out who she really was, how would he react? Probably with the same shock and loss she felt right now. And her father would never approve of Colton, not with his past, no matter how much he'd changed. His recklessness in his youth would disqualify him immediately.

That he'd never married the mother of his daughter frightened her. In essence, he'd abandoned McKenna's mom.

Bazak and her father abandoned her. True, there were legitimate reasons, but. . .she was alone all the same. On her own. Her heart hung heavy and aching.

The waiter removed Colton's half-eaten steak and her potato, asked about dessert, but Colton handed him a credit card and waved him off.

Arms folded, he leaned forward. "Since we're putting all the cards on the table. . ."

Her aching heart trounced in her chest. What did he know? No, there was no way he knew the truth about her. She wasn't sure how much truthfulness she could handle in one night.

"When I mentioned being in the military the other night, you reacted."

"Did I?"

"Is that a problem for you, the military?"

"A problem?" It'd killed her brother, alienated her sister, and stolen her father. Why was he asking about something like that? He wasn't in the military now. She tried to remember what he'd said about being a Marine. He was out, wasn't he?

"Does it bug ya?"

"No." It seemed to be the answer he wanted. "I'm fine."

He smirked with a half chuckle, then scratched his chin as he pushed back against his chair. "See, that's part of the problem."

"What?"

"My military training involves reconnaissance." Colton's eyes bore into her, piercing her deeply held secrets. "I can tell right now you don't believe what you just said. You're holding something back, and I have a feeling it's right important to you."

Something about his challenging tone pushed her. "You're right. My brother was in the army." He didn't need to know which one. "He vanished two years ago, and they found his charred, beheaded body not long after."

Blinking, Piper sat stunned. She'd never told anyone that. Such a brutal crime could be easily—*very* easily tracked. In one evening, she was undoing thirteen long months of preparation and secrecy. What had she done? Her father—they'd find him. Kill him. She tried to pull back the tears that stung her eyes, but one slipped past her hold. "My father. . ." *Stop! Don't say it.* "He never got over it." Okay, good save.

"Apparently, neither have you."

Another tear slid down her cheek as she shook her head. "Ba—" She bit off her brother's name. "My brother was my twin," she said, trying to smile. She wouldn't tell him about Dodie. All the same, she felt herself crumbling. To pieces. In front of the man she wanted to impress, a man whose approval she wanted to win.

"I'm real sorry. I can relate to losing a sibling. My sister died a few years back."

She touched his arm. "I'm so sorry, Colton."

He gave a grim smile as he paid for the food. Then Colton pushed to his feet and took her hand. "Come on." He led her through the congested restaurant. As they neared the front door, a man stepped into her path and knocked her sideways.

She recovered and muttered, "I'm sorry."

Dark eyes rammed into hers.

Colton pulled her through the knot of customers as the man's gaze triggered something in her mind. Something dark. . .familiar. Hateful. With a quick glance back, his shadowed face disappeared into the crowd.

Did he know her? Why would he glare at her like that? Just as the dread trickled into her veins, Colton drew her closer. "I'm sorry, Piper. I didn't mean to stir up bad memories." At his truck he stopped next to the passenger door and stood in front of her. "Seems we both have some things we don't really like talking about."

She dipped her head and wiped at the remaining tears.

Gently, Colton nudged her chin up. "Hey," he said, his voice soft.

She met the blaze in his blue eyes.

"I'm not like that anymore."

Like what—oh, right. Her mind snapped back to the present, away from the haunting feeling that skittered up her spine as they stood in the cool night.

Colton leaned toward her, his gaze intense. "It's important to me that you believe that. Okay?"

"How. . . ?" Yeshua forgive her, but she had to ask. "How can I know that?"

"Might sound a bit silly, or perhaps a bit cliché, but I gave my life to God after Meredith's death." He slid both hands around hers. "I've made every change I could think of—moved out here, gave up dating and drinking, went back to church, dedicated myself to being the best father I could be to Mickey, and the best son who would honor my parents—to separate myself from the shameful man I was back then."

"God changes the heart, not man." Her father had said that so often she'd wanted to scream at him.

Colton hesitated, his gaze assessing. "You're absolutely right." He inched closer. "I still make my share of mistakes, but. . .I just. . .I won't let it. . ." He fisted a hand. "Agh! Woman, why is it so hard to talk to you?"

"Because you like me?" Sometimes, her tongue really should be cut out of her big mouth!

"Oh, I think it's gone beyond that." His unrelenting gaze seemed to absorb her every reaction. "Piper, don't pass judgment on me, okay? Give me a chance to prove myself."

"Your actions toward Meredith frighten me." With more boldness than she'd experienced since leaving her homeland, she placed a hand on his chest. Beneath her fingers came the steady thump of his heart. She kept her gaze down, knowing she would lose her focus if she looked into those eyes. "But I feel that I know you—the man you are, the man who is unafraid to do the right thing, no matter how much it hurts. Your heart speaks to me. Somehow, I know. . .I know you're not like that anymore."

His hand rested over hers. "I hope I can prove it to you for a long time to come."

The promise that lingered in his words yanked her gaze to his. What was he saying? His hand slid under her hair at the base of her neck. With an almost unnoticeable tug, he pulled her closer, his gaze dropping to her mouth.

Her heart sped.

Colton pulled off. "Now, see?" With a silly grin and hooded eyes, he tried to recover. "I said let me prove myself, and I almost failed."

"I—I—" Her voice cracked, and she cleared her throat. "I wouldn't have called that a failure. Maybe. . .a promise."

His smile went lopsided. "Sealed with a kiss."

Her father would beat her, but she nodded.

He laughed in a way that made her feel silly. "As much as I want to kiss you, and as much as I know I'd thoroughly enjoy it, I'm going to do this right. I promise you—I'm going to prove I'm not like that anymore." He stepped back and opened the truck door. "Let's get you home before I get myself in trouble."

High on anticipation and the thought of Piper, Colton strode into the Tank, the nickname the team had given the warehouse where they met, trained, and debriefed. His boots thudded through the cavernous space as he approached the black Chrysler 300 perched in the loading bay.

A door opened. General Lambert emerged. "This is very unusual, Digitalis."

"I reckon so, sir." He shook the man's hand, admiration and respect thick. "Thank you for taking the time to meet with me."

"My time is short, as I'm sure you can understand."

"Of course. Let me get right to it: I'd like you to clear someone for me."

"A recruit?"

"No, sir."

"A woman, then?"

"Yes, sir." Why did he feel like a thirteen-year-old kid talking to his dad? "I'd like to introduce her to the team—once you've cleared her, of course."

The lines in Lambert's face crinkled. "Already being done, son."

Colton's amusement fled. "Sir?"

"She's been under observation and investigation since she went to your home a month ago."

Blood slowed through his veins, and he felt the pressure build in his chest. "Mind explaining how you knew she's been to my house?"

Lambert laughed and turned toward his car. "There are no secrets here, Digitalis." Hand on the door, he glanced back. "And if there are, you can be sure that we will expose and exploit them."

Colton's hands fisted.

The general's gaze bounced between Colton's fisted hands and his eyes. "Good, that's a good anger. Remember, you're protecting your team, as well as your family." With a curt nod, he said, "You'll hear from me."

Sirens wailed. People screamed as they ran for cover, shouting for loved ones. The camera panned toward a woman, on her knees as she clutched a lifeless body to her chest. With her head thrown back, she clearly wailed, yet the sound was lost amid the warbling sirens.

Blinking back tears, Piper held a hand over her mouth as she listened to the reporter continue:

> "This in the latest violence in the region. The rocket, fired from Palestine, decimated several buildings in Ashdod. Another rocket struck the outskirts of Beersheba, killing dozens."

Piper's knees buckled. She scrambled to sit on her small sofa.

Huddled against the wave of shock roiling through her, she stared at the screen. And in a split second, it transported her back to her homeland. To the rancid smell of human flesh burning. Air thickened by ash and smoke. Heart-piercing screams.

"*Baba*," she whispered, calling for her father. She threaded her fingers together and squeezed them, drawing upon courage she'd not had to use in many months. But the words staggered. "Yeshua, please. . ." Tears streamed down her face.

She didn't know where her father had taken shelter over the past year, but she knew that street, knew what buildings had once stood there proud and white. What if. . .what if he'd never left Beersheba? What if he'd been killed in that attack?

Hope vanished as the camera angled in on a robed body near a demolished mud-and-brick home. "No," she mumbled. "It can't be." But that sweater! She'd given it to him for his birthday last year.

No. No, she would not believe he was dead. That all these months had been for naught. She smeared the tears from her face. Punched to her feet. There was only one way to find out. Piper grabbed her purse and keys before she darted out the door.

The images of her beloved Beersheba in ruins chased her into the night-darkened street. She jumped in her car, sped through town to the university, and parked at the law library. Hurrying up the steps, she shoved aside the thought of her father lying dead in a burnt street and focused on getting through the front doors.

Rushing between the towering sentry shelves, she indiscriminately grabbed a volume as she made her way to a terminal at the back. Quiet and dim lighting packed heebies on top of her jeebies, but she didn't care about being frightened. She had to know if her father was alive.

Piper slid into the hardwood chair and glanced around before she let the book fall open on the desk. With trembling fingers, she typed the fake login.

A yellow caution sign with a red exclamation point blinked at her. In her frenetic pace, she'd mistyped the ID. She worked to steady her nerves as she pecked out the ID once more. This time the terminal granted access.

Another few clicks brought her to a business site. She worked through the layered pages until she finally came to the maintenance department and selected the janitor. With a press of the mouse button, the browser opened an e-mail program. Piper entered the coded message she'd conjured up en route to the library and hit SEND.

Letting out a slow but long exhale, she pulled her eyes from the monitor and glanced at the textbook, forcing herself to look as casual as possible. Look like she was studying. But she'd never be able to study until she knew her father was still inhaling the cool, dry air of Israel.

And then. . .the only glimmer of sunshine in her life—Colton—trickled into her thoughts. If she could reach her baba, she'd tell him about Colton. It would help her father concentrate on his mission, on getting back to her. Undoubtedly, he'd question her choice if he found out about Colton's past, but he didn't need to know. Only that she'd found a good man, that he'd take care of her. . .assuming it went that far.

She scanned the words in the reference book, but nothing seeped past her anxiety. She'd broken protocol by contacting him. He'd have to deal with it. She had to know. A message dropped into the in-box. Her heart hitched.

Then plummeted.

The message read:

I'm sorry. You must have the wrong dept.

Breath backed into her throat, she stared at the screen. No. . .no, no, no. What did he mean *wrong department*? She'd used the same link as always. Only as her mouth dried out did she realize her jaw hung agape. She clamped it shut and straightened.

He must understand. What if her father needed to warn her? What if—? She gasped. What if the attack was intentional, and someone found him? He'd try to warn her, right?

She hacked out another message, knowing this one must be more urgent, more direct:

Imperative contact is made. Potential endgame may have been effected. Must establish veracity of recent reports regarding Raven.

She hit SEND again and hoped she hadn't made a mistake to be so open about her purpose for the protocol breach. But it was a risk she had to take.

Her lower lip trembled as she thought of her father...worried over him. Elbows on the table, she buried her face in her hands. What if he needed her? The walls holding her together were crumbling like Jericho. *Is he dead?* Was she all that was left of her family? Her back slumped, dragging her shoulders down as a sob wracked her.

Bang!

The loud noise jolted Piper from her misery. She snapped her gaze to the right, then left. Was a book dropped on a table? A door slamming? Listening, she silently chided herself for losing control and focus. If anyone saw her, they'd grow suspicious. She was supposed to be studying. Piper dragged the reference book close again and rested her arm over it, her gaze stabbing the dark corners in the library. It'd been too dangerous to do these cyber-rendezvous attempts on her personal laptop—too easily traced. But she hated coming here, sitting in the dank, depressing building.

As she dragged her gaze back to the monitor, she sucked in a breath. Another reply:

Get out. You've been found.

CHAPTER 7

He finally found the girl he wanted to spend the rest of his life with. Eight months of recon told him what he'd felt in two seconds—she was the one. But if—no, *when* she found out about the flashbacks, she'd be gone. Colton stabbed the bale of hay with a particularly hard thrust and flung it toward Maverick's stall.

Don't even get him started on that feeling at the back of his brain warning him something wasn't right. Nothing worse than that with zip to substantiate it. He rammed the tongs of the pitchfork into another bale. He tossed it toward Foxy's enlarged stall, and it hit the iron rail. Her new foal, Hershey, started at the noise and darted around the pen.

"This wouldn't be about Piper would it?" His father ambled to the tack rack and drew down another pitchfork.

Colton eyed his father. Eyed the way his shirt seemed to hang off his tall, once-muscular frame. Eyed the way he thought he'd help. "Pop, I can handle this."

"I know," came the familiar drawl. "But there aren't many times we can do this together anymore."

Who was his old man fooling? He wasn't here to work. Cradling the fork's handle in the crook of his elbow, Colton removed his hat and wiped the sweat. "Not in a talkin' mood today, Pop."

"Then quit your jabberin', son." His father worked the bound hay near Maverick's stall and spread it over the ground.

Nope, that wasn't going to work. Not this time.

Colton delivered the last two bales to the other stalls. Then he grabbed the shovel and went to mucking Foxy and Hershey's stall. Satisfied with the job, he grabbed the brush and smoothed it over the honeyed coat of Maverick. The horse swished his tail at Colton. "I know, boy."

As he wiped down the flank, he couldn't help but think how much the stallion's coat looked like Piper's golden-blond hair. Well, not quite golden, more of a straw color. Nah, that wasn't right either. Maybe coffeelike, with a little creamer. But soft the way Mickey's baby skin had been.

"Son!"

He jerked around—and Maverick whisked his tail right into Colton's face. Flinching, he soothed the horse as he met his father's eyes. "What?"

"Where's your mind? I asked you a question."

Colton waited. Wouldn't admit he'd been distracted.

"You bringing her to the barbecue?"

Knew it. "Haven't decided."

"Why not?"

"Told you," he said as he went back to grooming Maverick, "I'm not in a talkin' mood."

"She's not Meredith."

That yanked Colton around and earned him another smack from the stallion. Aggravated with both his father and the horse, he left the stall and moved farther down the barn. He eased into Foxy's stall and grinned as Hershey hesitantly came over to inspect him.

His mind flicked back to the night Hershey was born, to the way Piper had thrown herself into his arms. She said her grandfather had raised goats. He'd never known anyone to do that intentionally—raise goats? Was she serious? She was the quirkiest woman he'd ever met. Beautiful, too. But there was something. . .

"Might wanna move," his father's voice—which was all too close—broke into his thoughts.

He glanced back to his father, who now stood leaning on the gate to Firefox's stall. "Come again?"

"Imagine your leg's about to get a bit warm."

Colton looked down just in time to see Hershey take aim to relieve himself.

"Boy, your mind's doing a lot of talkin' for ya. Eventually, that's going to leak out—either through more flashbacks or through your mouth." His father tilted his brown Cattle Baron from his brow, revealing the clear blue eyes Colton had inherited. "Now, I'd prefer mouth to flashback, but it's your call."

Armed with a soft lead, he returned to Hershey. With quiet talk to the foal, he eased the harness over his head. When Colton stalked toward the gate, his father didn't move. He grinned at the man he was becoming more like every day. "You gonna let me out, or you planning to hog-tie me so I'll listen to your lecture?"

"Champion rodeo cowboy in my day." His pop lifted the lead from the tack and entered the stall, where he harnessed Firefox.

Colton ran a hand along Hershey, whose eyes seemed to widen and flit from Colton to his father. "Yes, sir. You don't let me forget."

"But you've been the most pig-headed and the hardest to wrestle." Colton chuckled as his father brought Firefox alongside.

"What's eating your brain cells?"

"Like you don't know."

His father nodded. "Thought so."

"I–I'm crazy about her. . . ."

"That's news to only one person—you." His father laughed, but then grew serious again. "I feel a mighty big *but* coming on. Let's have it."

Colton removed his hat and used his shoulder to swipe away the sweat. "I dread the day she sees me go through a flashback. Or finds out about Emelie. I know it'll happen, and. . ." He swallowed hard. "I can't stand the thought of her thinking less of me." He fisted a hand. "Who wants a messed-up cowboy?"

"Can't believe you're still trying to lay claim to what happened to Em. Being hard on yourself, aren't you?"

"Not hard enough." Maybe if he had kept his head together, a lot of heartache could've been avoided.

"I might not be the brightest bulb in the pack when it comes to women, but I'm fairly certain Piper likes the man she's getting to know."

"I'm a brand of trouble nobody wants." Colton stretched an arm around Hershey's chest and the other arm around his bum. "She deserves better. You and Mom didn't deserve even this." He glanced at his father over Firefox. "You ready?"

"Yeah—and what *this* are you talking about?"

"Babysitting me! Sticking around because nobody knows when I'll try to kill someone again because I'm plumb out of my mind."

"Son—"

"No, don't, Pop. Not now. Please." He sloughed a hand over his face. "I'm not going to pretend anymore. Don't nobody need or want that trouble. I hate this about me—"

"Colton—"

"*Hate* it." Long-suppressed feelings surged to the surface of his carefully held frustration. "Why? Why won't God heal me? How could He let me take Em over there just to kill her?"

"Well—"

"I pray all the time, *beg* Him to heal those memories, to help me forget—"

"Colton!" His father's near shout siphoned the strength from his tirade. "Son, quit stewing over what you can't change."

The comment knocked him silent. Mad, but silent.

Finally, he said, "Let's just. . .get this done." Using Firefox's lead, Colton held Hershey in a firm hug hold and led him to the open paddock. His father led Foxy a few paces ahead as incentive to get Hershey to follow. Some people didn't start them this young, but Colton felt it was wise to get him used to being handled by humans. At the paddock, his dad released Foxy, who trotted around. Colton eased the foal free and closed the gate.

Together, he watched with his father as the foal and dam reconnected, then trotted around.

"Looks to be a strong one," he said, hoping his dad would abandon the heart-to-heart.

"Firefox is good stock." His father hooked his arms over the wood fence. "Colton, I want you to stop dragging your sister's memory into your depression. She did what she wanted to do. Let Emelie go in peace."

Colton closed his eyes. *I can't. . . .*

"And if I know you—and I do—you're taking two and two and getting five."

"Always was bad at math," Colton mumbled.

"Lumping Piper in with what happened to Emelie, and what Meredith did to you, well, it's just going to leave you crazy. 'Sides, you're not giving Piper a fair shot."

Guilty as charged. "In case you haven't noticed, Pop, I don't do real good with women. Only God knows why He gave me a daughter." He shook his head again as he opened the iron gate to the outer pen and allowed Hershey to dart into the open.

"If you'd just show a girl the same care you give that there foal, I think you'd be off to a good start."

"Somehow, I doubt Piper would take kindly to being harnessed."

"What do you mean you can't give me money?"

"I'm sorry, ma'am, but your name is on the list."

"What list?"

The teller darted a nervous glance around the small bank. "The one from OFAC." He shifted behind the counter.

"Look, I don't care what list you put my account on, I want my money, *na*—right?" She gulped hard at nearly using the foreign phrase. Tried to keep her voice steady. This couldn't happen. She needed that money. "I'm talking about my money I placed in this bank—"

"I'm sorry." He straightened in his chair and took on the appearance of a brick wall. "Your account has been flagged by OFAC."

Her pulse picked up speed. "What. . .what is that?"

"The Office of Foreign Assets and Control." Fingers threaded he looked straight at her. "It's a government branch that flags accounts with suspicious activity related to terrorism—"

"I'm not a terrorist!" She heard the shriek in her own voice and tried to catch her breath. Foreign Assets? How. . .how could they know?

"I'm sorry." Face as stone, he remained unfazed as he handed her a piece of paper. "You can contact this number to rectify the situation."

Piper tried to swallow against the adrenaline pouring through her veins as she pushed to her feet. That ten thousand dollars was her lifeline, her only means of survival now that she'd turned in her resignation at Hastings. She ran a hand through her hair, panicked. Flashed him a conciliatory smile. "Thank you. I'll call them."

Only, she wouldn't—couldn't. This was her last stop before she headed out of town. She'd spent the day closing accounts, paying debts, and turning off her cell phone. Now she had no money.

Piper stepped out into the early evening with a heavy heart but alert to her surroundings. Her gaze rose to the dull gray sky. . .so much like her life. What would she do?

Once she swept the parking lot and convinced herself the white minivan wasn't filled with Palestinian terrorists, she climbed into her car and locked the doors. The twenty dollars in her purse wouldn't fund another night at the hotel. She'd stayed at the Grand Inn last night, too afraid to return to her apartment and find men waiting to drag her back. . .to pry answers from her unwilling lips.

She shuddered at the same time her stomach gurgled. Too bad. Until she had more money in hand, she wasn't going to squander her last bill when she could easily go a while longer without food. For now, the priority was finding a place to stay.

Her mind drifted to a handsome cowboy and a pair of blue eyes that made her warm and happy inside.

Absolutely not. Completely out of the question for two reasons. One, she'd have to tell him the truth or lie through her teeth. She wasn't going to do either. She'd gotten this far on half truths and knew exactly what her father would say about that: *A half-truth is a whole lie.* And two, if she was followed back to the Neeley ranch, those intent on getting to the truth would use Colton and his family as a means to extract the information from her.

Trapped. Stranded. Alone.

Piper dug her fingers into her hair and screamed behind squeezed lips. Why? Why must it be this way? She just wanted some hope that the insanity that had stolen her life would end, that her father would be saved, and that she would have a chance at a happy life.

A familiar melody dropped into her mind—the *Hatikva*. Hope infused her to the very bones. The national anthem of Israel spoke of hope. Was that a sign, a message that things would turn out okay?

Yeah. Right.

The ache burned raw and hot. Every good thing in her life had been crushed or stolen. She banged the back of her head against the head rest. How could she be so idiotic as to think she could fall in love with Colton and have a happy life? Things didn't work that way for her. Her mother and baby brother died. Then Bazak. When Dodie left her, the only family member she had left was their father. . .who also stepped out of her life. Yes, for her own safety, for his safety, for the safety of a nation, but that still left her alone. Utterly alone.

Tears streaked down her face. "Oh Yeshua, help me."

Again, the Hatikva played through her mind. Sitting at a red light with the crimson blur splashed over her windshield, she let out a shuddering sigh. Then gasped.

The music box. She had to get the music box. Which meant she *had* to go back.

When the light changed, Piper drove on, peering in the rearview mirror at the ever-shrinking bank that had put a huge roadblock in her escape plans.

She slapped the steering wheel. How could the bank keep her ten thousand dollars like that? It was all she had left of the trust fund that had kept her afloat. It was her entire life—how would she survive on her own?

And how on earth did the griefer know?

Her heart skipped a beat. Then two. The only way he could've known was if her father had sent a message. Right? The griefer didn't know who she was, so how could he tell her she was found?

Desperation chased her through the streetlamp-lit city, clogged with heavy traffic and a mountain of fear. She had to do something. Maybe. . .maybe if she parked at the strip mall and walked back, she could spy out her apartment, see if anyone was coming or going.

Parking in front of the pizzeria gave her little comfort despite the throng of cars. Still, she had to do what she had to do. Piper left the car and hurried down the street. Near the park, where she had a bird's-eye, though distant, view of her apartment, she sat on a swing and waited. And waited. Once dark nestled in for the night, Piper made her way closer.

She tugged her lightweight jacket around her shoulders. Every shadow seemed to come alive as she passed it. The alley next to her building twisted the wind into howling ghouls.

Crossing the corner to her street, as the trees seemed to move aside and grant her unfettered access to what lay before her, she spied Mrs. Calhoun rocking on her porch.

Piper's hopes soared. Of course! She quickened her steps until she came to the side of the neighbor's fenced-in front yard. Gripping the iron bars, Piper waved at the lady, hoping to get her attention without yelling.

Mrs. Calhoun finally must've seen her. She looked over her shoulder. "Oh. Well. What are you doing over there?"

"Just out for a walk," Piper said, trying to make her voice sound casual and light. "How's the neighborhood tonight?"

Mrs. Calhoun wrinkled her nose. "Oh, you know that Jenkins kid is always causing trouble. But I did see Reverend Mason earlier. Nice man of the cloth."

"Sounds like a quiet night."

"Mm-hmm," Mrs. Calhoun said, rocking once again.

Then maybe nobody had been to her apartment. Chewing her lower lip, Piper once again allowed her gaze to probe and stab every corner and crevice of the building, of her front door, the windows. Was it safe? She no longer had a cell phone, so if she got in trouble, she was out of luck getting help.

"Girl, what are you doing standing there?"

Piper blinked out of her thoughts. "Just thinking."

With leaden legs, she pushed herself down the sidewalk, her gaze glued to her apartment. *Yeshua, guard my steps.* Up the path to the stoop.

She drew the mace-flashlight out of her purse and held it down, low and out of sight.

"Night, Piper!"

Without looking away, Piper took the first step. Better not call out and alert whoever was inside. . .if someone was inside. She waved night to Mrs. Calhoun. Took the second step. Her two-year stint in the Israeli military made her wish for an assault rifle. The Tavor would do nicely against anyone in her apartment.

Her brown door loomed before her. Gulping the burst of warmth that squirted down her throat, she scraped her gaze along the jamb. Everything looked to be intact. Quietly, she slid the key into the lock and turned. With practiced agility, she flung the door open and stepped in, aiming the flashlight into the darkened apartment.

A flutter by the window made her breathing catch. The curtains. She dragged the flashlight over the couch and end table. Nothing. She must have rustled the curtains when she shoved open the door. Quickly, she flicked on the lights and checked behind the door— clear—and closed it. Flipped the locks. Now she had either locked herself in with an assassin, or she'd locked the assassin out.

Beyond her own ragged heart rate, she heard nothing save a car passing on the street as she searched the apartment. Instinct drove her to the music box. . .but she veered off. If someone was here, watching, she didn't want to tip off her only passage to freedom. If they'd somehow bugged her apartment or installed a camera. . .

The thought drew her gaze around the room. To the air vents. To the lamps. The ficus tree in the corner. She cleared the kitchen and closet, the laundry room, the bedroom and its closet, then the bathroom—where her heart stalled.

Again, the washcloth she always set on the corner lay on the floor.

Heat splashed down her neck and back. She backed up. Glanced around. Behind her. Someone *had* been here. But they didn't want her to know. Which meant they hadn't found what they were after.

All the more reason to believe they'd planted a device to uncover her secret.

Back in the living room, Piper sat on the couch. Chewed her thumbnail. She didn't have any money, so she couldn't stay at a hotel. What if she went to the law library for the night until the bank opened?

The idea took hold. Better than staying here and waiting to be captured.

Piper darted into her room, packed a bag of clothes and necessities—just enough to get her through until she could buy more without notice. She grabbed her backpack and filled it with snacks, legal documents, and her MP3 player. As she passed through the living room, she went for the music box when the phone rang.

She hesitated. *I put in a disconnect request.* Why was it still ringing? She went to the kitchen counter and stared at the phone. The ID showed UNKNOWN NAME. If she didn't answer it, would the bad guys assume she was gone and come in?

She snatched the phone from the cradle. "Hello?" Her voice cracked.

"Piper?"

The bass of Colton's voice vibrated against her ear, soothing her instantly. "Colton."

"You all right?"

She licked her lips. "Yeah, sure. I'm fine."

"You're not convincing me." The concern that laced his words bespoke the manners that had told her he was the type of man who'd fight to the death to protect someone. Just like a soldier.

"No, really. I just. . .it's late." She set the heavy backpack on the counter, eyeing the music box.

"Oh." He cleared his throat. "Right, sorry. I'll be quick. I'm having a barbecue here at the house next Sunday with some good friends. I'd like you to be here, if you're interested."

He wanted her to meet his friends. "That sounds nice." If only she'd be here. But she wouldn't. And she couldn't tell him. She closed her eyes and fought the tears. Oh, she didn't want to do this to him, not to Colton. Or McKenna. The two had wormed into her heart. It'd be like losing Dodie and Bazak all over again.

"Great." But he didn't sound happy. "I'll pick you up Sunday—is one o'clock too early?"

A tear squeezed past her resolve. "Um. . ." She pressed the heel of her hand to her forehead. Crying thickened her voice. "Yeah, that's fine." He'd hate her.

"Piper?"

She sniffled. "Yes?" The word squeaked.

"Are you crying? What's wrong?"

Tilting her head back, she ordered herself to dry up the tears and not give herself away. "I'm. . .cutting onions." She bit her tongue on the lie. And that made her want to cry all the more.

"All right." He didn't sound convinced. "I'll see you Sunday."

Crack!

With a gasp, Piper spun toward the front door.

CHAPTER 8

At least this time nobody could say he failed for lack of trying.

Colton rapped hard on the door three times. When he'd talked with Piper, she had hung up too quick. Or maybe too quick for his liking. With a step back, he planted his hands on his hips. He took a cursory glance around the darkened street, still not liking the way that black sedan sat hovering at the corner.

Piper had been off her game when he'd talked to her a half hour ago, and he'd be hanged if he just let it go. Something was wrong, and he had to know for himself that she wasn't in some sort of trouble.

Truth be told, he'd have used any excuse to see her. He'd dropped by Hastings to invite her to dinner, but she wasn't there. Called in sick. That just didn't sit right with him. Had she found out about the general's investigation? His gaze bounced to the car again. Was that bona fide U.S. government issue? Or was it trouble?

He shifted and pounded on the door again. Where was her car? Why hadn't he seen it in its usual spot? And why wasn't she answering? He raised his hand again to knock.

"Who is it?" Her soft voice carried through the door.

There it was again—that something off in her tone. He cocked his head, and his gaze hit the mucky spot on the stoop. Were it not for the street lamp and the way it struck the indention, Colton wouldn't have seen the muck, which wasn't a surprise. It'd been raining earlier. What bothered him was the footprint outline. Too big for Piper. Not his.

"It's me, Colton." Who had visited her? He should relax. Piper had friends—any of them could've come over. But in the rain? At least, the way the heel smeared right made him think the print had been made just as the rain let up. "Thought we could talk."

"Uh. . ." Shuffling noises carried through the door.

The sound of her voice made his heart skip a beat. It sounded strained, nervous-like.

"Just a min—"

He couldn't be sure, but it sounded like the word had cut off. No, not cut off, *choked* off.

His gaze scanned the doorframe. He spotted her tape and string in various spots. Oddest woman he'd known to be so uptight about security, but it'd kept her safe, he reckoned, so he hadn't said anything. Then he hit the scrapes along the lock plate. He ran a thumb over the gouge. That wasn't there before. With another step back, he let his gaze retrace the door. Was it off alignment, or was that just his overreacting mind?

Tension rolled into Colton's muscles. Mentally, he checked the MEU .45 concealed at the small of his back. Hands to the side, he scowled as he honed his attention on the noise behind the door. Shuffling. He squinted when he thought he heard a whimper—

The door opened.

Colton let his recon-sniper skills loose, assessing and reconnoitering. Half a muddy footprint on the tile matched the muck on the stoop. Piper's bare feet. The way Piper practically hugged the door, using her body to shield the entry.

Warmth spiraled through his veins. "Evenin', Piper," he said, trying to keep things natural. If she was in trouble, he needed to figure out the best way to help her.

"Colton."

Stiff, almost unfriendly. She sure hadn't been the night before when she'd all but begged him to kiss her. In his periphery he saw a shadow shift in the one-inch sliver of space between the door and the jamb. "Thought I'd drop by, maybe talk awhile."

Her eyes cut to the side—to the door. "I. . .uh. . ." She winced and froze.

That was all he needed.

Colton kicked the heel of his right boot into the door. A loud *crack* rang out. He let his momentum carry him forward and shoved Piper to the side. In one fluid move, he swung around the corner. A gun wobbled inches from his face. The man behind it had been stunned but was recovering. Colton snapped his right hand against the guy's wrist and simultaneously grabbed the handgun with his left, effectively confiscating the weapon. He flipped it around and aimed it at the man before he could blink and realize what had happened.

The shock didn't last long. Tango One lurched at him. Colton angled his shoulder down, spun around and rammed his elbow into the guy's gut—doubling him over. Then he drove his elbow into the back of the man's neck—raising his leg so the man's face collided with Colton's knee.

Crack!

The gunman stumbled and dropped like a rock.

Behind him, Piper gasped.

Colton shut the door, then cleared the weapon of chambered bullets, dropped the magazine, and removed the slide. "You okay?" he asked as he checked the assailant. When she didn't answer, he glanced up.

Trembling hands covered her mouth. Eyes glossed behind tears.

"Piper!" He hated yelling, but he needed her with him. "You okay?"

She blinked. Several times. "Y–yes." Then she sucked in a hard breath. "There's another. I don't know where he went." Suddenly, her face paled.

He took her cue and whipped around, ripping his weapon from the holster. A blur of black came at him. Adrenaline boomed through his veins as the attacker tackled him.

Colton went down hard but alert. Aware of the haphazard way the guy fought. The kid—and the young and almost beardless face bespoke his youthfulness—had to be running on pure fear and adrenaline. Which gave Colton's second nature instincts the advantage. Twisting his legs around the guy's, he flipped him. Straddled his body. Got a hard look at his face. Middle—no, not quite Middle Eastern. Something different.

With one hand against the kid's throat, Colton aimed his weapon at him. "Hands! Show me your hands!" he roared. His mind registered the beads of sweat. The tunic-style shirt that tugged to the side, revealing Arabic script tattooed along the man's collarbone.

Over his shoulder, he ordered Piper to call the cops. As she rushed into the kitchen, he turned back to his prisoner.

Behind him, the floor creaked.

He glanced—and something flew into his face. Knocked him

backward. Stars sprinkled through his vision. The back of his head hit something solid. Fire licked through his head, feeling like a thousand tiny needles darting down his spine.

Head cleared a bit, he came up—straight into the barrel of a weapon. Tango One towered over him, kicked at Colton's hand and dislodged the MEU pistol from his grip. But as he did, Colton sideswiped the guy's legs. Knocked him flat on his back.

With a hard right, he knocked him out cold. Maybe he'd stay down this time. As Colton struggled to his knees, squinting through the pain, he sighted Tango Two scrambling toward the kitchen—toward Piper.

Colton rolled once, twice, snatched up his weapon and rolled onto his belly. He lined up Tango Two behind the sights. He eased the trigger back. The guy crumpled, his body straddling the threshold to the kitchen.

Piper screamed and jerked around.

The first tango bolted out the door. Dawg, the guy must have a steel skull.

No. Couldn't let him get away. He pulled around and fired, but the man made it through the door. Colton shoved to his feet and stumbled after him. Out into the dimly lit night. The dull yellow glow of the streetlamp made specter and ghoul out of every shadow. By the time his vision adjusted, the street lay empty. Quiet.

He attempted the three steps and nearly landed on his face. His knee grazed the cement. He dragged himself upright. Propped against the wrought-iron fence, he holstered his weapon and tugged his phone from his pocket. Dialed.

"Go ahead."

"I got a mess you're going to want to clean up." He gave the address, then scanned the street one more time before pocketing the phone.

"Colton!" Piper's voice stabbed his conscience and drew him back to the steps. He started to climb, but the effort made his head swim. He slumped onto the concrete and pressed a palm to his temple.

"Oh Yeshua, thank you!" She hustled down to him. "Are you okay? Colton, are you okay?"

"I'm. . .fine." He pressed his palm harder against her loud words and the throbbing pain in his head.

She lifted his hand and winced. "Ouch."

"Yeah," he said with a wince. "That's one way of putting it."

"The cops are on the way."

"Good. I made a call myself." He traced the bloodied spot on his knuckles where he'd made contact with the first attacker, then considered her. "You okay?"

"Yes, for the most part."

"Who were those guys? Did they tell you what they wanted?"

Her eyes took on a distant hue. "I. . .I. . ." She narrowed her eyes, gaze aimed at the street. Then, as if remembering he was there, she blinked and looked at him. "I don't know."

While it comforted him that he'd intervened and stopped her from getting hurt, something bugged the tar out of him. Piper wasn't rattling on about what happened, she wasn't hysterical—not that a person had to be—but she didn't seem scared. At all. Matter of fact, she seemed distracted.

He'd done enough time working to extract information from the unwilling that he felt his gears change. "Do you know something? About those men or the reason they came at you?"

Her gaze came to his quickly, riddled with surprise—or was it fear?—and just as quickly she looked down. "No." Piper glanced at him with a smile that definitely didn't reach her eyes. Barely made it past her upper lip. "I wasn't sure what they wanted or were doing, but then you came."

He wasn't going to break eye contact. "Just in time." She was hiding something, and if he had to back her into a corner, he would. "You don't seem scared."

A siren wailed as a squad car burst around the corner.

Without answering, Piper stood and motioned to the police.

Yep, she was hiding something.

He knew she was hiding something. His crystal blues told her. What good would she do in the political arena, defending her homeland, when she could not even convince one man that the men in her home were strangers?

The arriving ambulance and police cruiser saved Piper from having to lie yet again. She hated herself for being stupid enough to think she could get involved with a man and that it'd work out. She had too many secrets for that to be plausible. She'd studied public relations, and yet she'd been unable to negotiate a path to peace in this situation. Did it matter?

Piper crossed her arms and hugged herself against the cool wind that stirred up and took over the night. Time seemed to vanish with each blink of her eye. Questions, interviews, photographs...It felt like too much. Too much to hide. Too many secrets.

She watched Colton, who sat with an EMT working on the bloody spot on his temple. She'd never forget the sound of her wood sculpture when it thudded against Colton's head. Or watching him fly backward and hit the pine table. How had he known how to fight like that? The skills, the maneuvers, spoke of advanced training. Like Mossad. Was Colton some type of elite soldier? Hadn't he said he got out of the military?

It was time to move on, move away from Colton or anyone else before they got hurt. She'd vanished once before. She could do it again. She simply had too many secrets to hide, her father to protect until he could prove what he'd unearthed.

A sleek black sedan and an SUV pulled to the curb. No sooner had the doors opened than Colton was on his feet, excusing himself from the care of the EMT and the questions of the officer. He strode toward an older, white-haired gentleman and a broad-shouldered African American man. He clapped the latter on the back and shook his hand.

Piper frowned. Who were they? A suit cut into her view, and she strained around it to see.

"Miss Blum?"

She jerked straight and met the steely gaze of a man in khaki pants and a sweatshirt with three gold letters over the left breast. FBI. A metallic taste filled her mouth.

"Miss Blum." An officer appeared beside her. "This is Agent Morris with the FBI. He'd like to ask you some questions, pretty much the same ones I asked."

"My answers haven't changed," Piper said as she stood, hoping the move made her appear stronger and more confident.

Agent Morris smiled. "Actually, don't mind Lansing. He thinks I'm encroaching."

Piper glanced between the two men and saw the rivalry, even in the dim light provided by her front porch and the streetlamp. And once again, she recounted the entire ordeal. She would've finished the tale faster, but her gaze kept wandering to Colton, who huddled with the other two men in deep concentration and discussion.

"Ma'am?"

"Yes?"

Agent Morris looked toward Colton and the others. "The assailants—have you ever seen them before? Did you know them?"

She shook her head. "No, I've never seen them before." Just as the words slipped past her lips this time, she recalled the date with Colton. The man who'd bumped her shoulder. Was he. . . ? No, he had eyes she'd never forget. Eyes that said he didn't do anything lightly.

The high-pitched whine of a sport bike screamed into the night, severing her ability to even hear her own words. She looked toward the street where a black motorcycle screeched to a halt near Colton and the others. The rider removed a helmet and toed the kickstand. Colton gave the man the same welcome he'd afforded the others.

"Do you know who those men are?" Agent Morris asked, nodding to Colton and the other three.

Should it bother her that the local authorities did not know Colton or the men he stood with? "I know Colton but not the others."

"And Colton is. . . ?"

"The cowboy, the tall dark-haired one in the middle."

"No," he said with a soft chuckle, pulling her attention back to himself. "I meant, who is Colton Neeley to you?"

She peeked at the cowboy who had captured her heart, who'd shown more strength of character than perhaps her own father. How would tonight's events change the budding relationship? Was he going to leave her, too, because things were too tense? "A friend."

Agent Morris eyed her, then the officer, then her again.

"What?"

"A friend, who comes out at nearly ten o'clock at night—on a hunch?"

"He has strong instincts." Piper shrugged. She really didn't feel up to any of this. She wanted it to go away, wanted to disappear.

"Agent Morris, I believe?" A strong, firm voice intruded on the questioning.

Morris and Lansing turned away from her.

The older gentleman stood directly behind him, with Colton and his two friends. "I believe this call is for you." The white-haired man handed Agent Morris a cell phone. As the agent took the phone, the older man smiled at Piper. "Good evening, Miss Blum. Quite a little circus we have here, wouldn't you say?"

Piper darted Colton a nervous glance. And winced at what she saw lingering just below the small white bandage on his temple. Accusation. Questions. Anger. Her defenses snapped into place. So she was going to be alone in this. Again. So be it.

"Certainly doesn't make for a quiet night." She furrowed her brow. "I'm sorry, who are you?"

Agent Morris returned, stuffed the phone at the older man. "I don't know how you pulled that off—"

Shorter, but larger by the size of his powerful presence, the older man glared down the FBI agent. "I believe your work is done here, Agent Morris. Thank you for your time."

The African American man wrapped an arm around the FBI agent and led him away. Something inside Piper coiled up, ready to strike—to protect herself, no matter the cost. The way this man operated felt entirely too familiar. Though her body tensed and drew back, she steeled herself. She'd faced Mossad agents and survived. She could face this man.

But Colton. . .

The thought jarred her, but she recovered.

"Officer Lansing, might I have a word with you?" The older man talked as he walked, the two of them meandering toward the police cruiser.

He hadn't answered her question. The situation made her feel as if a hundred roaches darted over her torso. Instinctively, she rubbed her arms and neck as she turned to Colton. "What's going on?"

He glanced toward the house. "Cops found a gas leak, think the line was cut—intentionally."

She widened her eyes. "They were going to blow up my house?"

"Fire department is on the way." Colton rested his hands on his belt. "You're going to need to stay elsewhere tonight. We've got clearance for you to leave the scene, as long as you're available for questions later."

"Okay. . ." Irritation skidded into her crawling skin and made her irritable. Colton wasn't answering her questions either. Something was going on here, and clearly they didn't intend to tell her what. Her stomach churned.

"Do you have parents or siblings we can call for you?" the man next to Colton asked. His dark eyes probed her.

That question was far too specific. He was fishing for answers. "They don't live close."

"What about friends?" he asked.

"No."

"You don't have friends?" his tone went incredulous.

"They're married. I'm not intruding on their lives!" It was true. Mostly.

"Piper," Colton said softly as he leaned back against the half wall she'd propped herself against. "You seem defensive."

"Honestly, I'm a bit frightened by the display of power. I've seen things like this before, and they didn't end well."

"No need to worry." Colton motioned to the man who stood before them. "This is my friend Max Jacobs." He nodded to the street where the African American now stood conversing with the older man. "The big guy is Griffin Riddell, and that's General Lambert with him. I work with these men. You can trust them as much, if not more, than me."

Max's eyes bored into her.

A general and Colton worked with him? But Colton had said he got out.

Piper swallowed. "I'm sorry. I just. . .I don't know; maybe it's all getting to me."

"Shock."

At the softening she heard in his voice, she looked up at Colton. Oh how she longed to have him take her into his arms, tell her things would be okay. To tell him everything. To break this barrier she'd lived behind for the last couple of years. She wanted that freedom, yearned for it.

"Pardon us, coming through," someone said amid a clanking noise.

Max stepped to her left as the coroner and his aid carried a gurney with a bagged body down the steps, then rolled it down to the vehicle.

Piper rubbed her temple. *Oh Yeshua. . .*

Warmth wrapped around her shoulders—Colton. He pulled her into his arms. She curled her fingers around his shirt and held on tight. How had they found her? Would she ever be safe? One step closer, and they'd have gotten her father, too! What if they succeeded next time?

"Hey," Colton said softly. "Don't cry. It'll be okay."

Only at his encouragement did she realize she was soaking his T-shirt with her tears. Embarrassed, she clung tighter. She felt so out of touch with her life, her plan, *herself*. All this time she had studied to be an ambassador, to speak on behalf of her country regarding peace. To stop the senseless violence like what killed her brother. To stop the pain.

"You're sure?"

Griffin Riddell gave a curt nod, his lips thinned. "Intel just came in."

Olin let out a long sigh. "We need to let him know."

With a large, but gentle hand, Riddell stopped him. "Be careful. I think his heart's involved. More stress could push him into having flashbacks again. It's been nearly six months since the last one."

"I know, but we can't keep this from him. He must be made aware."

"I agree." Riddell grunted. "Just. . .pad the news."

Olin smoothed his jacket. "I'm not sure news like this can be padded." He strolled back toward the apartment and called Colton over, then waited for Colton to join him. The team depended on the cowboy, relied heavily on his mature guidance and looked up to him. Riddell was right—this had to be handled carefully. Olin prayed silently for wisdom as Colton left the girl and walked toward him. He knew what it'd taken for Colton to come to him and launch the investigation on Piper Blum.

Protective mechanisms triggered in Olin—Colton was like a son to him. All of them were. He wasn't going to let anything happen to them.

"She doesn't have any family around here." Colton leaned against the car. "Far as we can get out of her, no friends either. She's right defensive, too." He shook his head and frowned. "Odd."

"I'm afraid that I have some disconcerting news." So much for padding.

Colton stilled, his expression shifting from surprise to guarded-ness, to downright depression. "All right." He folded his arms over his chest as if bracing for the news. "Go ahead."

"She has terminated her lease, effective Sunday."

Colton's gaze shifted to the woman standing in her fenced front yard. "People move."

"There's more. All utilities—gas, electric, landline and cell phones are turned off."

"That'd explain why she didn't answer when I called back."

Despite the raw ache clearly scrawled over Colton's face, Olin knew he had to tell him everything. The news wasn't good, not in a situation like this. "About three hours ago, we intercepted traffic from her bank that indicates she is closing the account and withdrawing the funds."

The cowboy watched her. His brow furrowed. Left eye twitched. "She's running."

"My thoughts, too."

"Like she knew these guys were coming after her. . ." Colton rubbed his jaw.

"In situations like this, it's normal to give a directive to avoid contact with the subject at all costs." Lambert glanced toward the house where the other two Nightshade team members kept the girl distracted.

Colton snapped a glare at him. "She's not a threat."

"Can you guarantee that? What if she *does* know these men?"

"She said she didn't." He worked the muscle in his jaw hard.

"You've developed feelings for her—"

"That doesn't matter."

"Quite the contrary, Digitalis." When the cowboy started to object, Olin held up a hand. "It does matter, and it may work to our advantage, at least until we have some solid answers."

"How so?"

"I suggest you put that guest room at your sprawling ranch house to use."

Colton frowned. Then his eyes widened. "It ain't proper to have her stay with me at the house. 'Sides, what if trouble follows us out to the ranch?"

"I've had your name removed from all records related to this incident. That should not be a problem. Think of it, Digitalis. You take her out there; you can keep a watchful eye on her. Buy us time to get the investigation done and find the answers we're looking for."

"Like what?"

"Like why Piper Blum doesn't exist."

DAY TWO

Saudi Arabia, 21:44:01 hours

Objective Terminated.

Through his secure phone, he sent the coded message. Terminated. Yes, he'd fired two bullets into al-Jafari's brain—the same brain that held the information Azzan wanted—*needed*. Had defied orders to extract. Though he would like to take credit for the assassination, the man's sluggish response warned him that the man had been poisoned.

Someone else wanted General al-Jafari dead. But who? The man had as many enemies as mistresses. Azzan could spend from now until eternity considering the prospects. He would not waste his time.

Right now, he needed to make it to the Dead Sea, which felt a lifetime away. Especially with the woman knocked out in the backseat. If he was caught with her, he'd be executed without question, and al-Jafari's guards would make sure it was a slow, painful death. At the first village, he'd drop her off and be done with it. Her blood would not be on his hands.

An hour into his drive, the veil of clouds lifted, and moonlight skimmed flat rooftops of a cluster of homes wedged into a mountain. He glanced back at the girl. Still unconscious. That served him well.

Pulling off the road, he killed the lights and slowed as he came alongside a dilapidated structure. He rammed the gear into PARK, climbed out, and opened the rear door. Grabbing her ankles, he heard crunching behind him. Quiet, light-footed, but not sneaking. A villager. Not to worry.

As he dragged the girl across the seats, a soft moan emanated from her. She turned her head back and forth.

He tugged.

Her hands flew, grasping, groping for traction as she came awake. Azzan hauled her out of the Hummer. She writhed and yelped—screamed.

Pinning her against the sleek hull, he clamped a hand over her mouth. She gripped his hand with both of hers. Wide eyes sparkled in the moonlight. An angry welt puffed and bled against her pretty face, eliciting a strange feeling in his gut.

He shrugged it off. This had to be done. It was this or kill her. All his training demanded her death—if he didn't, she could finger him, point him out to authorities.

Azzan held the muzzle of his gun to her temple. "Quiet!" His hand shook, one voice in his head telling him to pull it, and a second voice begging for another way. Pressing her against the side of the vehicle, he searched the dark, crumbling corners of the village. Shadows morphed into scrawny, vacant-eyed bodies. Odd noises pulled at his decision. This wasn't right.

Panic streaked her beautiful eyes. She wriggled against him. The hijab slid off her head. Dark hair spilled over her shoulder, framing her flawless features. In that instant, Azzan's stomach cinched tight and froze him. She had the same eyes, the same piercing gaze.

No, it wasn't possible. His target didn't have daughters. She was just some rich girl wanting to sneak away.

She used his hesitation to yank his hand from her mouth. "Please—please don't leave me here." Desperation clung to her words with a healthy dose of panic. "Take me with you!"

She deserved to be left behind. To let these people—his gaze skimmed the six. . .no, sev—*eight* men lingering on the fringe of the road and death—strip her of the expensive silk hijab and dress. Rip the gold rings and necklaces from her fair skin. Sell her off. Maybe she could buy some humility with a few years' service.

As he pivoted to climb back into the truck, she grabbed at him. "I beg you—"

Behind the wheel, he tried to shut the door.

She wedged herself in the way. "You're an assassin."

He glared at her. "Which is exactly why you should get out of the way before I do what I do best."

"Please. . .I don't know why you were at the palace, and I don't care. But don't leave me here, please. The Bedouins will sell me. Allah wills it!"

He flashed his eyes at her. "I have no use for you or your god."

"I can offer you money."

He sneered.

"I—I. . ." Her eyes darted, as if searching for something to bargain with. Suddenly, those gorgeous eyes brightened. She flashed them at him. "You're Palestinian."

How could she possibly know that?

"I know who you're looking for. I can help."

He tried to push her aside, but with her standing and him sitting, she had the advantage in leverage. "Why would I trust you or anything you say?"

"I know. I know where they have him and why you came to the palace." Confidence overtook the frantic desperation that had tightened her features. "Help me, and I'll help you."

With a firm shove, Azzan tried to pull the door close again. "I don't know what you're talking about."

"General al-Jafari said everyone was searching for a *particular man*."

She couldn't know why he'd gone to the palace. Al-Jafari told a woman of his plans? Impossible!

But. . .what if she did know?

When he lunged out of the car, she stumbled back. He caught her and noticed the crowd gathered nearby. "Stupid woman! This is the last time," he yelled at her and grabbed her arm and shoved her into the car, hoping the theatrics convinced the villagers. After kicking the door for good show, he glanced at the men and tossed up his arms. "Avoid women. They will drain your money and mind!"

The men roared in laughter as Azzan got behind the wheel and pulled out of the village. Back on the highway. Fingers coiled around the wheel, he peered in the mirror again, ignoring the reaction he felt when he saw the whelp on her forehead where he'd hit her.

"Al-Jafari wouldn't share strategies or information with a woman. Unless you were one of his mistresses."

She gasped. Then lifted her chin, exposing a long, graceful neck amid that river of dark hair. "My name is Raiyah al-Jafari. My father is Bashar al-Jafari."

"He didn't have daughters."

"That's what he told me a thousand times, even as he tried this very night to sell me to a fat, balding prince so he could take their oil." She let out a disgusted sigh. "I will help you get the old man if you will promise to take me to Israel."

The daughter of the man he just killed. He shouldn't trust her. The name alone meant she had blood as disloyal and wicked as the devil himself. But something in her gaze, in the hurt coating the words she'd just spoken, told him those disloyal tendencies could work to his advantage. That is, if they were talking about the same old man.

CHAPTER 9

If I am inclined to doubt, steady my faith. . . ."

The line from the Marine Prayer sifted into Colton's mind as he aimed the truck onto the gravel drive that led to his house. He tried to ignore the way Piper sat next to him—staring straight ahead and hands clutched in her lap as if she were holding onto something, tight. Real tight. The ride home had been that way the entire forty minutes. Complete silence.

And he'd rather leave it that way than dig into the silence and open the can of worms hiding behind her tight composure. The questions plagued his mind all right. Like what the general told him. And more.

Beside the house, he rammed the gear into PARK and climbed out. Hand on top of the tailgate, Colton hesitated. His southern upbringing insisted he open the door for her, but he didn't want to be close, didn't want to see the betrayal in her eyes.

Only when the passenger-side door opened did he grab her bags from the back and start for the house. Behind him came the quiet crunching of her steps. Colton ground his teeth, wondering how he'd managed to convince her this was the right choice when all he'd wanted was to walk away and forget they'd ever met.

You're buying into this too quick.

Yeah, and it'd taken his girlfriend ODing in the arms of another man for him to believe the lies about her. Tightening his grip on her bags, he reached for the side door—but it swung out toward him.

"I've been worried si—what on earth happened to your head?" His mother stood in her robe and house shoes.

"Nothin'."

Her attention drifted past him. "Piper, is that you?" Brown eyes came to his filled with questions she'd just have to keep to herself because he didn't have any answers.

"Is the guest room ready?" Guilt prodded Colton to inch back and let Piper enter first. He might be irked, but he wasn't going to be rude. All the same, he kept his gaze on the tiled floor as she swept past and looked at him.

"Of course it is." His mother wrapped an arm around Piper as she led her toward the kitchen. "What happened? We can talk about it over a cup of herbal tea."

Colton kicked the door shut and followed them down the hall to the kitchen.

Piper glanced over her shoulder at him, then pulled her attention back to his mom. "Actually, I'm pretty tired. But thank you."

His mom drew back, a bit surprised, but then patted Piper on the shoulder. "That's just fine. I understand."

Did his mother notice Piper didn't answer the question about what happened? Surely she did. That woman never missed a thing.

"Guest room's this way." He stomped through the kitchen and living area, then down the small hallway to the guestroom, where he nudged the door open. He dropped her bag by the foot of the bed and slid the suitcase up against the closet.

"I cleaned the sheets last week after my sister and her brother visited," his mom said as she moved across the room to the nightstand, where she flicked the lamp switch—*Pop!* "Oh. My. Well, I'll get another bulb."

Colton angled around Piper—ignoring the way she smelled—like spices. He had to get his head together. "You've got a bathroom all to yourself, which should be nice." Nice? Having her own shower? What was wrong with him?

"Colton, are you angry with me?"

There it was again. That particular note in her voice that plucked his heart strings. The words sounded small, weak. Everything in him wanted to take her into his arms the way he'd done back at her place—the only thing that felt right in years—but he forced himself to remember the things Lambert had told him. The phones, utilities, lease. . .

Why was she running?

It gnawed at the little confidence he had left, at the inkling of a notion that she might actually be the one for him. Who was he kidding? He'd already set his heart on her. And that hurt bad, real bad, knowing she had planned to leave him. And McKenna.

Which was all the more reason this idea of Lambert's was stupid. Piper would be around Mickey more, and it'd only make things worse when Piper left. He could abide her leaving him—

Dawg, he wasn't fooling anyone. He couldn't abide her leaving. Period.

"Colton, please talk to me," Piper whispered as she stepped closer and placed a hand on his arm. "I..."

He fastened his gaze to the doorjamb. Didn't know what everything meant, but it sure bugged him that his instincts had been tingling since she came into his life, then all the stuff Lambert mentioned, and then... "Your bags were already packed."

A quiet intake of breath drew his unwilling gaze to hers. Piper's chin trembled as wide eyes darted over his face. Her lips parted as if she was going to say something. Instead, her eyes glossed. Vulnerability colored her tawny features.

Everything in him went rigid as her eyes filled with tears, but he couldn't—wouldn't—give in. Not this time. He'd been hoodwinked once by pretty eyes. How idiotic could one man be?

He'd learned a few things since then. "Were you going to leave me, Piper?"

Again, she sucked in a breath and gulped it down. Her nostrils flared.

He gave a curt nod. "Thought so." Colton stepped away—

"Wait." She clamped a hand on him again and wedged herself between him and the doorjamb. "Please let me explain."

He snorted. Couldn't help it. Did she really think any excuse she had would repair what she'd damaged—like his trust? "It's late. I need to get some rest." Colton pushed himself away from her, stomped down the hall, around the corner, and stopped short.

His mom jerked off the wall and swiped her face. She gave the fake smile he'd seen many times before. "Well, I finally found the bulb," she said and held one up. "Good night, God bless." She tiptoed up and planted a kiss on his cheek.

Colton fisted his hands, thinking of the way Piper was hurting his family. The way she'd hurt Mickey, pretending to be nice and all sweet, when she so clearly wasn't who or what they thought.

He tromped back to his room, yanked off his boots, and dropped them against the hardwood floor. Unbuttoning his shirt, he fell back against the mattress. Groaned. He tried to batten down the swell of anger and frustration. Colton roughed a hand over his face and groaned again. How did this always happen to him?

A gentle knock pulled him straight. "Come in."

The door opened, and his dad slipped into the room looking weary and drawn.

Colton frowned. "What're you doing up? Are you okay?"

"Couldn't sleep."

"You mean Mom woke you."

"Something like that. Wanna talk?"

Flopped back against the bed, Colton studied the beam directly over his bed that stretched across the room. "Not really."

"I'll wait."

Colton couldn't help the smile. He'd gotten his tenacity from his father. It's what made his dad a great chopper pilot in Nam. "I *can't* talk, Pop."

Quiet fell between them as Colton once again found himself staring at the beam. Even if he could bring himself to talk about it, he had no idea where to start. Had no idea what he believed. The sincerity in her voice, in those tears, told him she had a legit reason behind the packed bags.

"Son, the heart finds a way to talk."

Prying himself off the bed, Colton sighed. "I did what you've been telling me for the last two years—I took a chance." He removed his shirt and tossed it in the hamper. "And I got burnt." Threading his arms through a T-shirt, he suffocated the voice that said he was jumping to conclusions. But what other conclusion was there when she had her bags packed and utilities shut off? "Whatever I thought might happen with her is gone."

"You brought her back to the house."

"Not by my choice. And since you brought that up, nobody takes her anywhere or lets her drive. No phone calls either."

"Crust of bread, cup of water?" Mischievous eyes peered up at him. The comment punched. "Just trust me on this, okay?"

"On one condition."

Colton paused, reticence choking the breath from him. He hated it when his father did this because the condition always coiled and struck like a viper.

"You know I stay out of your affairs for the most part."

With a hesitant nod, he conceded the point.

"But I want you to keep your mind and heart open where Piper is concerned."

Colton shook his head. "I know too many things."

"Well, son, that might be your problem."

She had to leave. Staying here jeopardized this family—the people who'd welcomed her so wholly and willingly. Fully clothed and propped on the edge of the tub, Piper cupped her hands over her face. Tears streamed down as fast and hot as the water in the shower behind her.

Confusion and chaos choked her mind. She couldn't remain here—it put the Neeleys in danger. Yet she couldn't leave either—she'd never find her way in the dark and on foot.

But she had to try. She wouldn't hurt this family, not any more than she already had. Thank goodness McKenna was already asleep. The little one wouldn't ask her father where she was in the morning because she'd never know Piper had been here. The men had found her apartment and tried to force her to show them where the chip was, but she'd denied knowing its location. About the time they figured out she did know where it was, Colton had showed up.

Piper shoved the thoughts of Colton and his magnificent handling of the men from her mind. She had to be focused—on getting away from them. From Colton.

Her chest constricted—she didn't want to leave him. Especially not with him thinking horrible things about her, which she saw as clear as the sun reflecting off the Sea of Galilee. And the stiff way he had pushed her aside. His actions had said one thing, but the tone when he'd asked that question, the one that stabbed her straight through the heart—*Were you going to leave me, Piper?*—told a different story.

She was wasting her breath and precious minutes. People still wanted her to get to her father. And they'd stop at nothing to make sure that happened. Her father held powerful secrets he was never intended to access, and those most affected by that knowledge wanted him dead. Baba was a master at hiding, and once he'd sent her here, he'd vanished into the Israeli air.

The only way to contact him was a chip with encoded IEP addresses, chosen in a particular pattern. When she accessed one, it activated his and opened that site. Afterward, the code dissolved and the program waited for her next access.

That was what the men wanted. That was what would help them find her father. It was the only weak part of Baba's plan. Yet he'd insisted they maintain a way to stay in contact.

If she left here, left Colton, he and his family would be safe.

She would not.

Here, she had a modicum of assurance that her life was not in danger. That Colton would save her, no matter the cost. But what right did she have to put his life or McKenna's at risk to save hers?

None.

She had to leave.

Piper hung her head and stared at the brown tiles. *Yeshua. . .*

She didn't know what to pray. Leaving felt like an egregious betrayal toward Colton. So did staying.

Yeshua, guide me. I don't know what to do.

A series of rapid thuds snapped her out of the prayer. Piper pushed to her feet, unsteady and shuddering as she stumbled from the bathroom.

More banging. "Piper, it's me." Colton's voice drew her to the bedroom door. "Open up."

She hurried toward the door. A *whoosh* draped the air with the scent of him.

"Just wan—" He snapped his mouth closed and frowned.

Only then did she wonder what her face must look like. Were there black streaks down her face from the tears? "Sorry. I. . ." Absently, she wiped at her face, surprised at the discoloration on her palms.

"I'm setting the alarm."

Should that mean something to her?

"Opening doors or windows will set off the alarm." Hands on his hips, he scowled. "The cops will come."

Slowly, realization dawned. "You think I'm going to leave?"

He held her gaze evenly. "I don't know what I think right now."

"Well, you're obviously not setting the alarm for all the hoodlums wandering the pothole-eaten country roads." Indignation swelled in her chest. "This isn't exactly the crime capital of the world, is it? I mean, probably the biggest crime is having a cow stolen."

His face reddened.

"If you want to accuse me—"

"Night." He spun on his bare feet and disappeared around the corner.

Numb, Piper stood there, staring into the darkened hall. Her heart dropped into her chest. She padded after him, unwilling to let him think. . .whatever he was thinking! In the living area, she caught sight of his broad form as it entered the kitchen.

"What are you afraid of?" she hissed across the room. "What have I done to you?"

Like a phantom, he suddenly rushed toward her and loomed over her. Expression darkened, eyes filled with fury, he ground his teeth—the muscle popping in his jaw.

This isn't what she wanted—his anger. The anger and frustration whooshed out of her. She wanted. . . Her shoulders sagged. "Why won't you talk to me?" she whispered. His visage blurred as the stupid tears came again.

"If you want to talk," he said with a tight tone, "we can talk in the morning."

"What's wrong with right now?"

Brow furrowed and lips taut, he took a step back. "You don't want to hear what I have to say tonight." Without a word, he went to the front door. Soon, a beeping sound poked into the thrumming quiet of the house.

Colton returned a moment later. Nodded. And vanished into the darkened hall that led to his room.

Piper stared at the front door, at the red light glaring at her from an instrument panel. No way out. Nowhere to go. Physically and emotionally trapped.

But I don't want out.

She wanted to stay. Wanted to be a part of this family. Startled at the thought, she blinked and looked back toward the darkness of the hall. Would he ever forgive her for this disaster? Would he understand all the secrecy, the. . .deception?

Why should he? Piper hung her head. But then a renewed resolve settled into her heart. She wouldn't give up without trying.

Was it—was he worth fighting for? She raised her chin and glanced around the house, filled with every nuance of all that was Colton Neeley.

Yes. Definitely.

She went into the kitchen, pulled the kettle from the gas stove, filled it with water—which reminded her she'd left the shower on—then placed it on the stove. Back in her room, she turned off the shower, grabbed her journal, and returned to the kitchen.

Armed with a steaming mug of tea, she sat at the kitchen table, determined to make sure she saw Colton first thing before he left the house to work, or do things around the property, or whatever. She wouldn't miss the opportunity. She'd tell him as much as she could without jeopardizing her father.

Over the next several hours, she wrote her heart out on the pages of her leather-bound journal, what she'd tell him, what she wanted him to know. It wasn't until she stared down at three little words that she felt her breath back into her throat.

I love him.

Did she really love him? What was love? Was it the way his smile made her heart skip a couple of beats? And why on earth would she think she loved him? Was it his gentlemanly charm? Good looks? The way his drawl thickened when he was flustered? Or maybe the ache deep in her that made her want to convince Colton she wasn't lying to him, that she wasn't a bad person? She wanted that so much. . .almost more than she wanted to protect her father's whereabouts.

Almost. The fate of a nation depended on his safety, and nothing was more important.

After three mugs of herbal tea, nature called. Piper set her mug in the sink and went to the bathroom. Stifling a yawn, she returned to the kitchen—and froze. Colton stood at the table, her journal in hand. His dark look drained her courage. A chill scampered over her shoulders.

He tossed down the book, spun around, grabbed a duffel bag from the doorway, and stormed down the hall.

"Colton?" A series of beeps pervaded the hall, then the side door opened, pulling Piper from her shock. "Where are you going?"

He punched open the door and stepped onto the covered porch.

Piper raced down the steps after him, cringing as cold gravel poked into her bare feet. "You said we could talk this morning." Come to think of it, what time was it? She pushed the long strands from her face as he followed him to the garage.

"No time."

"But you said—"

"Plans change. I got a call."

Piper stepped on the cement slab that bore his massive truck and folded her arms against the early morning chill. "You don't have fifteen minutes?"

"Not this time." He swung his bag into the passenger side of his truck. Grabbed another pack from a corner and stowed it in the back.

Taking tentative steps, she worked up her courage. "I stayed up to make sure we could talk."

"I could tell. You look drawn."

She blinked, surprised at the curt comment.

Colton glanced at her and huffed. "Now, don't go lookin' at me like that. You had a bad night. You need the rest, that's all I'm saying." There went that thick drawl. "It's part of the healing process."

"Did you sleep?"

His blue eyes darted to her again. Then away. He adjusted a strap on one of the bags and rethreaded. "I didn't wake my folks to tell them I got called up." He looked at her.

"I can tell them."

He paused, then met her gaze. Colton sighed.

Piper joined him and placed a hand on his forearm "Colton, please give me ten minutes. I have some things I want to tell you."

With a step back, he seemed ready to run.

"Did you read my journal?"

To her surprise, his face reddened.

Her heart tripped over the realization of what he'd no doubt seen. "It's true. I love you." The words, so sweet and tender, felt like a balm as they crossed her lips.

His brow took a nosedive toward his nose. "Do you know how old I am? What about my favorite dinner? Do you know what I do for a living, Piper?"

Her declaration, weighed against his confrontational tone, seemed silly and irrational. She let her hand slip from his arm.

Colton jerked the big duffel toward himself. Ripped open the zippered pouch.

A bunch of gear gaped at her. Gear that looked like. . .*military gear.* Her throat closed up. She braved a look at him.

Hands on his belt, he glowered. "I seem to remember you having a problem with the military. Isn't that right?" Colton patted his chest. "That's what I do for a living. That's what I am. A Marine."

"B–but you said you got out."

"I did." He raked a hand through his hair. "I get called up. I go. That's my job. I can't talk about it or tell you anything." Leveling a shoulder at her, he narrowed his gaze. "You know nothing about me, yet you dare insult me, expecting me to believe it when you tell me that you love me. I might be a simple cowboy with a lot of land and money, but I'm not a simpleton—"

"I never said that."

"And clear as the stars above, I know you aren't being straight with me. If for one second you got it in your pretty head that I'm going to bend when you're keeping secrets and ready to bail on me and mine, you've got another thing coming."

"I'll tell you." Was she out of her mind?

He eyed her.

"Everything."

CHAPTER 10

Somewhere in the Middle East...

Y ou are lame."

"Hey," Colton said as he pointed to the scope. "Eyes on the target."

The Kid shook his head as he leaned toward the bi-pod-mounted device. "Tell me you've kissed her already."

For the first time, he understood Max pummeling the Kid on the island last year.

"Quiet," Colton said low and slow. "We didn't have time to scope this gig, so pay attention." Irritation skidded up his spine as he stared out over the dilapidated structures. This had once been a small but thriving city. Now a few of the buildings served as shelter for homeless people. For the most part, this location held the desolation of the desert surrounding it.

"Come on, man, you—"

"We don't have someone on the ground to watch our back, and the team just went in. Now, shut it, and do your job."

This thing with Piper was bringing out the worst in him. She'd offered to tell him everything, and his response? *I'm outta time.* Hollow words from a coward—he'd run from her. Peeling paint and dirt crunched beneath Colton as he shifted his weight on the top floor of the small warehouse. Lying prone, he used the scope to aim through the ten-centimeter hole in the wall. Sure, the call had escalated the urgency, but he could've sacrificed five minutes.

All the same, Colton didn't want to sit through more lies. The very thought nipped at his conscience. He really didn't think Piper was like that, but how could he explain the trail of proof?

"With me?"

He ignored the Kid and forced his attention to the small town. "Where d'you think I am?"

"Your big oaf body's here," the Kid said, his voice strained as he peered through the Leupold spotter scope, "but your mind is elsewhere. I've been taunting you and haven't gotten punched once."

Colton grinned. "I'm not Frogman."

"True, very true—and thank God!"

"I'm monitoring, remember?" Minus a man on the team, he didn't have his six covered the way he'd like, especially here where unfriendlies didn't have any compunction about shooting a man in the back, and that put a burr the size of Texas beneath his saddle. With Frogman, Legend, and Midas bounding cover up the stairwell, their one-man-down status rankled him.

"Need another man."

Hearing the Kid echo his thoughts unsettled him. Was it that obvious they were weakened? His mind flittered to the sensor he'd placed by the main door downstairs. The only "man" covering him and the Kid.

"Piper." The Kid chuckled. "Pretty name for a pretty—"

When the sentence went unfinished, Colton looked at him, noted the hunched shoulders and rapt attention. "What's wrong?"

The Kid shook his head. "Nothing, brain's fried."

So was Colton. "All the same…" He scooted behind his Remington. Staring through the window a dozen feet from his boot, he saw Midas step inside and close the door. "They're in."

"Roger," the Kid mumbled.

He scanned the town. Nothing seemed irregular.

Unlike Piper. So many things made his instincts ignite.

"I love you."

He'd heard those thousand-pound words from Meredith. It'd netted him a daughter and a truckload of heartache. So why did hearing those words from Piper make his heart ricochet through his chest?

When she'd said she would tell him everything, curiosity made him want to stay. Fear—and the call escalation—pushed him into his truck. He wanted to bury his heart, bury this whole segment of his life. . .but he couldn't. Something was off. It was like not being able to see the forest for the trees. The facts pointed to good cause to be suspicious of her. Yet life had taught him things aren't always what they seem.

Had he been so ready to cling to her guilt to save himself some pain?

"Hey!" The Kid hissed and swatted his leg.

Colton blinked. Movement in his scope registered. Mind synched, he focused every muscle and firing neuron on the scene before them. Even in his initial assessment twenty minutes ago, he didn't like that building. Narrow and three-story, it screamed ambush. With the team snaking up the back firewall about now, he should be paying better attention, not worrying about Piper.

If they didn't get or kill their objective, Bashar al-Jafari, a radical bent on disrupting peace negotiations by forming deadly alliances against many Middle Eastern countries, there could be a lot of heartache.

Colton eased back and grabbed his thermals. He propped his arm and studied what the scope revealed. Quickly, he located the team huddled on the upper portion of the firewall between the second and third levels. Colton moved the reticle to the left. Al-Jafari should be in that room.

"Where'd they go?" Knots formed at the base of his neck. "The room's empty. Where's the team?" He dragged the multicolored lens farther left. . .alley. . .building. . .nothing. He keyed his mic. "Alpha One, hold."

"Roger, holding."

He shifted, teeth clamped as he studied the small village. How had the mood changed so rapidly? Had he been *that* distracted? "This isn't. . ." Where were all the villagers? Not even a dog or cat trotting the road. "I don't like it." He swept right. Left.

"What's the word, Cowboy?" Max whispered through his coms.

Colton's skin was crawling as he scoured the streets. "Hold your—" His thermal bled red—and lots of it. *Oh God, help us!* In a split-second he counted a half-dozen hostiles, high-powered weapons and RPGs in a building behind and two down from where the team sat. And they weren't there for coffee and donuts.

"Abort!" Colton said with a growl. "Abort, unfriendlies in red four. Objective missing."

Through the thermals, he watched the team move without

reservation. "Copy that. Aborting," Max confirmed.

Beside him, the Kid cursed. A second time. A third. "They're coming—right for the team!"

Beep–beep–beep–beep!

Colton wanted to curse this time—that was the motion sensor he'd set up. "They're in our building, too."

"On it." The Kid punched to his feet.

Listening to him move into the hall behind their position, Colton swung his scope from the team toward the hostiles. A line of rainbow-lit figures streamed out of the building. They traveled across the street and down the alley, right next to the targeted building. As if they knew he'd given the abort.

"Nightshade, ten well-armed tangos headed your way."

"Copy."

Thermal stuffed away, and eye trained on the movement through the rifle scope, Colton targeted the tango with the most armament and fired. The guy dropped. Chambering the next round, he then hit the point man.

Pop–pop–pop! Pop!

"Taking fire, taking fire," the Kid's voice pierced the coms.

Steeling himself against the Kid's near scream, Colton focused on protecting the team. Downing two more unfriendlies bought the team the necessary time to clear the building.

"Kid, en route!"

"Negative, negative. It's hot, too hot. I've taken cover."

"Cowboy, clear out," Max's authoritative voice cut through the panicked moment. "Rendezvous at evac point."

"Copy that." Colton whipped into action, slinging the rifle over his shoulder and drawing his handgun. Hunching at the door well, he slipped down his NVGs. "Kid," he whispered. "What's your twenty?"

"Avoid the stairs."

"That doesn't tell me where you are."

"You always were a geniu—"

Crack!

A grunt punched through the coms. "I'm hit."

Urgency pushed Colton into the hall. He cleared the right, then swung around and hustled down the dusty corridor. Streams of light, compliments of bullet-holes, poked the dark space. Sweat dribbled down his temple. He didn't care. The Kid was down. Had to get to him.

Ears attuned and eyes focused, he sought out his spotter. Where was he?

Colton eased toward a juncture and pressed his back to the wall, listening for movement, voices. He should be at the juncture that led to the main stairs. Which was the perfect place to get ambushed, just like Nightshade had been. With great stealth and care, he lured the thermal scope from his pouch and peered through the wall.

His pulse spiked. Three men stood strategically placed on the steps, aiming their weapons up. At him.

"How ya doin', Kid?"

No response.

"Kid?" Colton bit through his frustration, knowing his spotter was either down or captured. He pulled back and reconfigured his position. More than half of the back stairs were missing. The drop would break his legs.

Noise from the stairs nudged him backward. He hustled back down to the room where they'd set up and flanked right. Bullet holes had eaten the floorboards. Colton eyed one, mentally plotted what he knew of the building. If he could find one that peeked out onto the main foyer, maybe he could figure out where the Kid was. Finally, he located a hole that went all the way through. He stared through the hole—and ground his teeth.

Four men stood with their weapons aimed at a fifth man, curled up on the ground. There were too many to take them out and not get himself killed, so Colton leaned back on his haunches.

Colton keyed his mic. "Alpha, they've got the Kid," he whispered as he moved toward the hole where the shaft gaped.

"En route."

But even if they had humped it the way they should've toward the extraction point, the team wouldn't make it back this far. Not in time anyway. On his feet, he stalked the hall, praying for an out. Praying to find a way to get the Kid out alive.

As he passed a massive hole in the wall, he tried to think—Wait! He backed up three paces. An elevator shaft, the dangling cables awash in green, gaped at him. He cocked his head. Peered down the well. A shaft of light at the bottom gave him hope. Maybe he could. . .

He reached into the black void and grabbed the cables dangling ominously. With the rope he carried, he fashioned a harness and secured himself with the cables. He rappelled quietly, both hands cinching him down. As the bottom rose to meet him, he quietly pressed both feet flat against the wall and braced himself.

Again, he nudged his NVGs up and used the thermal to peer through the wall. Dawg. His scope wouldn't penetrate the steel shaft. *God, sure could use a break here. . .*

He'd have to lower himself head-first if he planned to get a shot before they clipped his legs or knees. Colton replaced the thermal. Winding one leg around the cable and the other crossed over that leg, he slowly and carefully lowered himself another five feet. The edge of the shaft crawled into view.

"Where is he?" a man shouted in English thickened by a foreign accent.

Gripping the cable tight, he held his position.

"I told you, man," the Kid said through fits of coughing, "he's dead. Got nailed."

Boots thudded overhead, most likely grunts searching for Colton.

Sweat slid down his back, across his neck and tickled as it streaked past his ear. Colton eased the silenced MK23 SOCOM out of his chest holster. With his NVGs on, he appreciated one of the few good things about the oversized pistol—the LAM. The Laser Aiming Module provided an invisible/visible laser, only apparent with the use of NVGs. He could pinpoint his target in the dark without the target knowing.

Colton let himself down another two inches. He peeked under the top of the elevator wall. A wash of green highlighted three men monitoring the still-kneeling Kid. Three? Where'd the other two go?

He winced. Had they sent two more men to find him? If they did, they'd figure out real soon that he wasn't as dead as the Kid claimed. A full engagement hunkered just minutes out.

"Twenty yards and closing," came Max's sitrep.

Answering his team leader would give away his position. And they were too far out to help. He had to take care of this now, or the Kid would be dead.

Just as Colton extricated himself from the cables, booted feet toeing the ledge of the shaft, he saw a gun raise toward the Kid's head. With a thrust, he landed on the first floor. He leveled out and fired at the gunman.

Shots flashed in his green field of vision.

Colton dove for cover behind a half-blown counter. He fired. As the dust cleared and he was able to take a solid assessment, Colton spotted the Kid on the ground, crawling across the open area toward him. With the two tangos on the ground, there should be at least one, if not two more, somewhere.

A dark shape moved.

On a knee, Colton provided suppressive fire as the Kid dragged himself around the corner, clutching his chest.

"There's five of them." The Kid breathed heavily and coughed. "Three on the stairs, covering the door."

Colton glanced at the Kid's wound, the blood oozing past the gloved fingers. "Nightshade, pinned down and under fire."

"Ten feet and closing," came the panting voice of Frogman.

"How. . .how we doing?" the Kid asked.

Colton peeked up—just in time to see the butt of a weapon flying at him.

Bam! Crack!

His head snapped back. Blackness swallowed his vision, taking his hearing with it. With the threat of imminent death and a bad guy looming over him, he flipped himself onto his back, leveling his weapon in the direction he'd been hit.

"Flash out," Midas warned.

Tink-tink-tink!

Colton flopped onto his belly and covered his head.

Boom!

White light exploded through the warehouse.

He pulled himself off the ground, pain vibrating through his head. . . his neck. . .shoulders. *Splat. Splat!* Blood pooled under him, dripping from his nose.

"All clear," Frogman called.

"Move out!" Legend shouted.

Colton pushed to his feet, blinking and dreading the giant migraine he'd have by the time they hoofed it out of here. He wiped the blood dribbling down his chin, noting that his nasal passage was closing up.

"Not bad, huh?" Frogman grinned at him.

"Wha's that?" Colton sniffed and wiped more blood.

"They broke your nose. We broke their back."

"Hey, what about me? They shot me!"

"Aw," Legend said in a baby voice to the Kid. "Your first combat boo-boo, and you're whining like a baby."

"Hey. I'm *shot*. Does anyone not see this?"

Nightshade Base, Virginia

"We were ambushed." Team leader Max Jacobs folded his arms over his chest, a storm brewing in his dark eyes.

Sitting in a folding metal chair, Colton lowered his gaze, glad to relieve the strain against his eyeballs. Wasn't his first broken nose, but it hurt as bad as the first. Throbbing pain muddled his ability to focus. He nudged the Cattle Baron off his forehead, relaxing a smidge when some of the pulsing pain eased—not a lot, but at least it wasn't annoying to have the hat brim pressing against his temples.

The team had neutralized his attacker, thankfully. No doubt the guy would've finished him off. He'd never seen him coming. Maybe that was part of the problem—he hadn't been paying attention from the beginning. "I was distracted," he mumbled to himself.

"Come again?" Legend growled.

Sitting straight, Colton winced against the ache in the back of his neck. "Just sayin', if I'd had my head in the game, I could've—"

"We were a man short." Max glared at him. "That's it."

General Lambert's shoes squeaked as he turned toward Colton. "What do you mean, you were distracted?"

Gut it up, and tell him. "I was thinking about Piper, what happened at her house."

Lambert nodded.

"Cowboy's the best. I don't believe for one second he's responsible for what happened."

Hand up, Lambert laughed. "Easy there, Alpha. I'm not looking to blame *anyone* in this room. Fact is, I think you're right. We were fed faulty Intel, and I'm going to find out why."

Max straightened. "And we're short a man."

After a hearty sigh, General Lambert nodded. "I am all too aware. I'm working on it. As you all know, adding to your team is not as easy as walking into a recruiting station or picking them off the field."

"Why not?" The Kid babied his shoulder, nursing all the sympathy he could get. "I mean, that's what you did with us, isn't it?"

"Trust me enough to fill the slot with someone you can all trust and rely on. I won't rush that decision."

"We need another player, and fast. Someone could've been killed—me!" The Kid's voice squeaked on his last word.

"The general is right," Legend said. "We rush that; it could screw us up royally."

"Thank you for the confidence, Legend."

"I'm outta here," Max said, his ire apparent.

Colton pushed to his feet and joined Max as he grabbed his helmet by the door. "Feel like some pool?"

Max hesitated. "Sorry, Sydney's birthday."

Colton nodded, heart heavy. He needed to talk through what happened, what he was feeling. The last thing he wanted was to go home. . .to Piper. He clapped Max's shoulder. "You enjoy that family of yours."

With a grin, Max straddled his bike. "Don't worry about that one." He revved the engine and left Colton standing there, alone. . .depressed.

"Cowboy, let's talk."

He turned to find the general standing a few paces away. Tempted to tell Lambert he didn't have time or to pull the wounded card, he knew he needed to face whatever was coming. If he was to blame for what happened, he was to blame.

Lightning cracked, splintering the night sky just over the slimy warehouse windows. Lambert strode toward his Chrysler 300 and climbed in.

Colton folded himself into the vehicle and removed his hat. With the Cattle Baron resting on his knee, he glanced at the man in the driver's seat.

Olin's gaze darted over the storm clouds.

Thunder rumbled, followed within seconds by another crack of lightning.

"Ever notice storms don't just come out of the blue?"

Colton shot a glance to the sky, then back to the guardian of Nightshade. He'd missed a point here somewhere. "Yessir."

"I mean, we see them once they're there. But in the hours and sometimes days leading up to their presence, we feel it coming."

"Sir?"

A half-smile pushed against Olin's lips as he lowered his gaze. Lifted a folder from between the small space between his seat and the console. "The thing with storms is they have two potentials—to be a cleansing, bring about a freshness." With a sigh, he handed it to Colton. "Or they can wreak devastating destruction."

Colton eyed the folder. No markings. He hesitated and double-checked Olin for more direction. None came. He balanced his hat and drew open the file. His heart caught as a familiar pair of caramel eyes stared back at him. Apparently taken at her work, if the pale pink lab coat and name pin were any indication. He turned a page. Scant details. Her address, phone number, license. "I don't understand. . . ."

Olin cleared his throat. "Neither do I." He shifted against the cream leather. "That's all we can find on her."

"There's nothing about her parents, her background."

"That's because there isn't any. At least not on Piper Blum."

Colton slapped the two-page file closed. "What're you sayin'?" A sorrowful expression tugged at his aged face.

Teeth clamped, Colton stared at the general.

"The team was ambushed. How did our targets know you guys would be there? Only the pilot, the chairman, and myself knew you were heading in there. So, who set us up?"

"That's something I'd like to know." Realization hit him. Anger flashed through Colton. "You're suggesting she sabotaged us?" He shook his head. "No way."

"I agree. It's an outlandish possibility," Lambert said as he looked out the window again. "But a possibility all the same. Keep your eyes open and your heart closed on this one, Digitalis."

Colton gave a soft snort, dragging his gaze back to the storm raging outside. "Look, she might not be who she claims, but there's no way Piper tried to get us killed. The logistics—it doesn't add up. She knew I left but didn't know where we were headed. I'm telling you, it's not her."

Aged eyes studied him. Then a slow smile. "I'm too late. You're already in deep with this girl, aren't you?"

Dawg. Colton swiped a hand over his mouth. "Yeah." He hated admitting it. "I know it goes against reason, but I just believe. . .she's not a threat, not in the way it might appear." That sounded as stupid as stupid could get. "A threat but not a bad threat." That sounded worse. He groaned. "I can't put it to words. . . ."

Lambert nodded. "Give me the time to prove you're right."

"Ya always did have a way of putting a nice spin on things."

"No spin. Just years of experience."

The confidence in the general's words made Colton pause. "You know something."

Tucking his chin, Lambert couldn't hide his smile. "I think I know something. That's a huge difference."

Irritation skidded down Colton's spine. He set the folder down and lifted his hat. "Keep me in the loop."

Lambert caught his arm. "Digitalis, whatever her vacant record means, don't tip her off."

With the Cattle Baron in hand, Colton trudged back to his truck, allowing the rain to needle his face and shoulders. Piper wasn't Piper. At least, she wasn't the innocent, wholesome, demure woman he'd fallen for. How had his months of recon missed it? What. . .what had he missed?

She's too perfect.

Had to give her that. In his truck, he tossed the hat on the seat and stared down the street, where the beads of rain blurred the taillights of Lambert's car in bloody streaks. . . .

His mind snapped to Borneo. Shouts and screams. Rain driving in such fury it almost blinded him. He'd tried to peer through the scope, but even under the makeshift tarp, sighting the target was difficult. His spotter had been taken out, leaving Colton to finish the job on his own. Then a distant *crack* echoed through the deadly night. Seconds later, a limb dropped on him. A branch sliced his face. Unmoving, he waited for the enemy shooter to show himself.

Rain rushed the path of his own blood down his face. Across his eye.

There! He eased back the trigger, the smear of blood adding to the eerie night.

Lightning cracked.

Colton flinched, his attention brought back to the present. His spotter had died in a storm in Borneo eight years ago. Now, his dreams had died in a storm in Virginia.

DAY THREE

Saudi Arabia, 01:50:48 hours

If you are wrong, I will kill you," Azzan hissed into her ear as he tightened the stranglehold he had on her throat.

Grunting, she held his arm. "If I am wrong, I *beg* you to kill me. But if you don't release me, nobody will believe I brought you here."

Trust. A virtue an assassin didn't have. It was a risk like everything else. "Just remember, I have the weapon." He let her slip from his grasp.

As they rounded yet another marble column and glided across slick floors, Azzan considered the royal beauty beside him. She had all the earmarks of a spoiled, pampered Arabian princess. Jewels, self-confidence. . .beauty. An inner strength that he wished he'd found in more women rather than sultry body language.

He chided himself, his memory jogged by the fact someone had poisoned her father. This mission had grown convoluted and complicated. He'd need to swing this back to his favor soon.

Swiftly, she made her way through the maze of halls and doors. "When we get down there, let me do the talking. You're just a hired gun." Her confidence reared its head again.

Uncertainly flickered through him. Who was in control here? "Just remember who has the gun." He gave her a curt nod, but knew the only important thing was this coup d'état.

If he could get the old man, it'd turn his superiors on their ear. His pulse quickened while silently alarms rang through his head. What if he was walking into a trap?

After she accessed a secure, vaultlike door, he couldn't help but glance at her. How did she come by the codes to this facility?

She shrugged and smiled, the sequins of her lightweight dress sparkling under the lone light. "My brothers were careless around me."

He arched an eyebrow. "I won't make that mistake." Did she understand he'd do whatever it took to get back across the border? Tamarisk wouldn't be pleased with this diversion, especially since Azzan hadn't called it in and this would mean a delay.

Raiyah paused at the top of eight cement steps. "Perhaps you already have?"

His heart jammed.

All amusement faded from her face. "Israel," she whispered, eyes purposeful.

The meaning speared him: She'd betray him if he didn't get her to Israel. Why was the daughter of a very powerful general, one who stood to command the Republican Guard in the area, so anxious to flee her homeland?

"The old man," he countered.

With that, she lifted her hem and descended the steps. Azzan hovered at her elbow, mentally checking his weapon holstered at his back. Again, her diminutive fingers danced over a keypad. The door hissed open.

After another glance at him, she entered. "Assalaam Alaikum, Taufic," she greeted a guard sitting behind a arc-shaped desk.

"Wa Alaikum assalaam, Raiyah." Hesitation and concern flowed from the voice. "Why are you here?"

Azzan slipped into the room behind her, ensuring the door stayed ajar just enough that it looked closed.

"What is the meaning of this?" The man staggered to his feet, his uniform buttons struggling to hold his wide girth.

Tempted to go for his weapon when he saw the man's hand slide toward a gun on the desk, Azzan paused as the girl stepped between them.

"Relax, Taufic. You are far too paranoid." She glided across the stone, her hips swaying.

Azzan flicked his gaze to the man, noting the leer on his face. Something in Azzan twisted and nudged him to kill the man anyway.

"Believe it or not, my family has finally decided to trust me." She sashayed toward the man, popped out a hip, and folded her arms. "I'm to bring a prisoner back to the palace. My father is having a closed meeting and wants to parade his trophy before the others."

"That. . . Are you certain?"

"Well, Faisal wasn't." She chuckled. "You should have seen him. He ranted and yelled that they could not trust the product of a village harlot. It was Hamzah who finally cajoled Faisal into relenting."

Taufic shook his head as he moved closer to her. "Hamzah always was soft on you."

"So, you'll help?" Raiyah glanced toward the far wall, and Azzan followed her gaze. A clock. She gasped. "I'm late." She whipped back toward the fat man. "Please help me, Taufic. You've always been so kind."

The rotund man glanced toward Azzan. "Who is he?"

With a long glance over her bare shoulder at him, Raiyah sighed again. "General Sadik's personal guard. They did not believe I could handle the job." She sighed, those full lips set in a resolute pout.

"My purpose," Azzan interjected, "is to ensure your safety and that no one intervenes." He pushed as much accent into his words as possible. "As you said, we are late."

Raiyah leaned closer, her eyes on Azzan as she whispered to the guard, "I heard he's a skilled assassin. No doubt he can ensure the safety of the prisoner, no?"

A smile pulled at Azzan, and he let it show, especially when the guard shifted uneasily under the news. The guard turned back to Raiyah and retrieved a ring of keys. "Who are you here for then?"

She glanced back at Azzan. "What was his name, assassin? I forget."

He realized her ploy. Realized how truly incredible and intelligent the woman was. He'd never confirmed the name of the man he wanted. And this would show his hand. "Perhaps you are not equipped for this mission."

Fire flashed in her eyes.

Taufic laughed. "Come. Rosenblum is our only prisoner left." He lumbered toward a steel door. A grating noise echoed through the steel-reinforced room as the door swung open. With it, a gust of wind. Rancid and thick, a foul odor assaulted him.

The telltale stench of torture.

Fury coursed through Azzan as he stumbled back and shielded his face.

Raiyah cried out and spun back to face him, horror gouged into her features. Tears welled up and glossed her eyes. "I can't do this. He's dead."

"No." Azzan knelt beside the frail body. This is why he had chosen his profession. It was humane, at least more so than plucking out a man's fingernails and gouging out eyes. Cutting off ears.

His stomach roiled as he nudged the shoulder. Bad as his torture had been, at least so far, this man had been spared the worst of such atrocities.

"No!" the old man shouted, waving his arms. "No more."

They didn't have time for belligerency. Azzan caught the old man's shoulders and tugged him upright. "Listen to me. This is your chance to escape. But you must get up and walk."

Wizened but wearied eyes fixed on Azzan. A crooked smile. "Escape?"

"Only if you can walk."

Then a frown. "No, they will kill me, shoot me in the back."

Azzan hauled the old man to his feet. "Not if I can help it." Tucking an arm under the old man gave him support, but he could tell there wasn't much strength left in the aged legs.

"How. . .how will we get him out of here?" Raiyah's soft voice pulled at Azzan.

"Put him in a trash bin, for all I care." Taufic narrowed his eyes at him. "Is there a problem?"

"You expect me to put this man in a garbage can," he said with a growl. "And present him to my general like that?"

Taufic's arrogance faltered.

"My father would be humiliated! He'd have you shot, Taufic."

"Use the wheelchair. I don't care. It wasn't me who did this to him."

No, but you didn't stop it, did you?

How he wanted to snap the neck of the fat, overbearing man. Then string him up the flagpole and let his disgrace be displayed for women and children to see.

Raiyah shifted toward Azzan. "I'll get the chair."

When she returned, Azzan carefully lifted the old man from the floor, noting the bandaged hands, the innumerable cuts, pocks, and the horrendous way his—

The old man felt light. . .too light. Fear rushed into him. Would he make it? He had to. They needed the information he had. The information al-Jafari had tried to pluck from his body.

"You'll need to bring the SUV," Raiyah said as they headed toward a back entrance. "I'll wait with him here."

Hesitation trapped him. Could he trust her? If he retrieved the SUV, would he come back to find an ambush, or both of them gone?

She stepped closer and placed a hand on his arm. "My father killed my mother, sliced her unborn child—another daughter—from her womb. Right in front of me." She looked directly into his eyes, but he felt her probing go deeper, much deeper. "I see my pain in your eyes. I'll be here, waiting."

Feeling as he had been sliced open, Azzan sprinted into the open. Anything to get away from her reading his soul. He darted to the Hummer, started it up, and raced back to the entrance. The door swung open.

And he stopped cold.

Taufic held Raiyah in a choke-hold, a gun pressed to her temple. The man sneered at Azzan. "Thought you could fool me, huh?"

He held his hands out in surrender. "I'm not sure—"

"Bashar al-Jafari is dead. Killed by an assassin."

Raiyah released the hold on the man's arm and jabbed her elbow into her captor's manhood. Taufic grunted and jerked forward, his hand outstretched.

Azzan seized the weapon and simultaneously swung a hard right into the man's face. "Get Rosenblum out of here." He angled his body in and threw another punch, finding the courage to keep fighting as he heard Raiyah grunting and pushing the wheelchair out the door and into the sun.

Finally, with one last blow, he dropped the guy. Azzan whirled toward the door.

Ping! Tsing!

He dropped to a crouch and tucked himself to the side, away from the line of sight of whoever was shooting at him. When he tried to peer around the corner toward the desk, a searing trail of cordite whizzed past. He jerked back, eyed the SUV, then launched himself out the door.

Fire lit through his arm. He winced, knowing he'd been hit, and dove into the SUV.

Raiyah huddled in the backseat with Rosenblum.

Azzan punched the gas and roared out of the compound. Bullets pinged the hull.

Crack! Glass shattered.

Raiyah screamed.

CHAPTER 11

Ominous thoughts scampered into Piper's mind as a loud *boom* thundered through the stormy sky. With Mr. and Mrs. Neeley—or Margaret and Ben, as they'd insisted—staying in town because of the storm, Piper grew restless. She couldn't leave McKenna alone. They'd done this on purpose, to keep her here. Colton had probably suggested it. Nerves had her checking the doors, the windows, and Colton's precious daughter, over and over. She'd never forgive herself if, because of her, they got hurt.

She peered through the rain-splattered window in her bedroom. Large trees swayed under the control of strong winds. Pulling a light jacket around her shoulders, she plodded through the house in her bare feet to McKenna's room.

Gently, she eased the pink and brown quilt up over the small shoulders. Piper lingered there, softly brushing aside the little one's blond strands.

McKenna's eyes snapped open. "Is Daddy here?"

"No, it's just the storm—the thunder rumbling overhead."

"I heard his truck." With a yawn, McKenna let her eyes drift closed. Then was wide awake once again. "Will you wake me if he comes? Nana always does."

"Sure." Piper waited with the little girl until she rested in the warm comfort of a good sleep and ached for the reassurance McKenna had that her daddy was coming home.

Piper glanced toward the door. Would he? Would Colton return? Over the last four days since he'd left, she'd begged God to see him safely home. Yet she remembered her promise to tell him everything, and that made her dread him walking through the door. She'd kept everything secure in the vault of her heart.

Locks keep out only the honest.

Remembering the way her father had repeatedly said that through the years brought an unwilling smile to her face. What would he say about her love for Colton? Although he wasn't Orthodox anymore, he did adhere to strict moral rules. He wouldn't like that Colton had fathered a child out of wedlock. Surely he'd see that Colton had changed. That she was in love with the rugged cowboy.

Though Piper scrambled to rationalize revealing her darkest secret, one thought plagued her: What if she told Colton everything, and her father died because of it?

A noise drew her into the living area. On the threshold, she let her gaze rake over the room. Light smeared over the large, open den, fading more with each inch as it reached toward her. What had she heard? The windows creaked under the force of the wind. She skated a glance around but saw nothing out of the ordinary.

After another perusal, she shrugged. Must've been the wind.

Needing to busy herself against the storms outside and within her own life, she went into the kitchen. And grunted. She'd already done the dishes. Swept and mopped the floor. Couldn't vacuum without waking McKenna.

Laundry! Mrs.—Margaret—had been doing laundry before they left. In the mudroom, she pulled the load from the dryer and deposited them on the counter behind her. Once she switched the wet clothes from one machine to the other, she started folding.

Piper slowed when she came to one of Colton's olive T-shirts. Stretching the sleeves out side to side, she marveled at the enormous size. The shoulder stitching started almost at her elbows. She giggled.

Creak!

Cold darted through her stomach. She snapped her gaze toward the darkened hall.

Groan. Creak.

Someone was coming up the side steps!

Pressing herself against the wall, she chided herself for leaving McKenna—and coming in here. She was trapped. One way in and out. The alarm was set, so whoever came in had roughly ten minutes before the authorities came. At least, that's what Mr. Neeley had promised just before he activated the alarm and left.

A peal of thunder rattled the hardwoods beneath her feet, sending the tremor up through Piper's legs and straight into her chest. She gulped back the adrenaline. Stuck in here, she had no way to protect McKenna. She needed something—and quick—to defend herself.

Turning a slow circle, she looked for a makeshift weapon. Hanging behind the door, a broom called to her. She lunged toward it and flipped off the light. As her hand closed around the wood handle, the front door opened.

Beeping pervaded the night, drowned for a second by the angry storm outside.

Just as fast, the door closed.

Piper held her breath and gripped the broomstick like a bat. She wasn't going to let anyone hurt this family—or her! She inched closer, trying to peer around the corner.

A strange sound like swishing reached her ears as a series of beeps interrupted the constant stream of the screeching alarm.

They were deactivating it!

She took another step—a big one—into the hall.

Colton shook the rain off his coat and froze.

A figure stood in the door to the laundry room wielding. . .a broomstick? He flipped on the light. And almost laughed. "Piper? You planning to use that on me?"

"Colton." Her breath and his name rushed from her lips. Just as quick, she dropped the stick and flew into his arms.

His own shock couldn't suppress the incredible way it felt to have her rush to him. As if it'd been instinctive to seek his protection, to hold him.

"I was so scared," she spoke into his chest.

Slowly, he let his arms close around her waist, reveling in her warm sweetness. He'd wanted this for months. Wanted her in his arms. Even though his internal sensors buzzed, he drowned them out and buried his face in her neck. She smelled wonderful. Sweet. Like honey. The way she trembled in his arms, her fingers gripping his shirt tightly beneath the jacket as she curled into him, made everything primal in him rise up.

"I was so scared. So scared when I heard someone coming."

"Shh."

"With the storm, I couldn't tell who or what—and everything, I..."

His mind whirled with her emotion and the feel of her softness.

"I was scared you wouldn't come back to me."

His heart hitched. *To me. . . Come back to me.* Was she serious? Colton drew back and studied her face. "I'm here. It's okay." He smoothed the strands and tears from her face.

She blinked, surprise dancing over her sultry face. "You're hurt."

She'd said something more—he saw her lips moving. But that was just it. Those lips, calling to him. He tilted his head. Dusted her lips with his.

He felt her draw in a silent breath, but then she wrapped her arms around him.

Colton eased into the kiss, savoring the silkiness of her hair and skin. As he tugged her closer and she melted into his arms, he deepened the kiss. Though he told himself to step off, he couldn't. He'd wanted this—*her*—for so long. She belonged with him. They belonged together.

A sob racked through Piper, breaking the kiss. She burrowed into him, shuddering through her tears. "I'm sorry. I'm so sorry." She latched onto him and kissed the side of his neck. "Please. . .please, don't hate me."

Holding her, Colton swallowed hard. Dread dumped on him the way the sky had let loose its load and quickly cooled his passion. He shouldn't have kissed her. Shouldn't have gotten weak and stupid. Then again. . .

He loved her. He knew he did. There wasn't any other way to explain the torment and affliction of the last five weeks. "Piper. . ."

She stepped back but held onto his waist. "Colton, please let me explain. Listen to me."

Reticence grabbed him by the throat. He ground his teeth. "All right." It was the least he could do. If she wanted to offer information, he was all ears. "Let me say hello to Mickey and my parents. Then we can talk."

"Your parents aren't here."

Every muscle in him knotted. They'd left her here, alone? "Where are they?"

"Your dad had an appointment in town, they went to supper,

and then the storm came. They said the road had wiped out, so they wanted to stay in town until morning."

Colton gripped his duffel and slid it down the hall, aggravated with his dad. "Road's fine." He turned and headed to the kitchen. "Pop just doesn't like to drive in rain or snow. He had a bad accident a few years back."

"Oh." Piper seemed to weigh what he'd said. "Do you want some coffee or tea for our talk?"

Dawg. She sounded like his mom. "Reckon that'd be fine."

She quirked her lip. "Well, which do you want? Coffee or tea?"

"I don't drink tea."

Piper laughed. "I know."

Amusement swirled through his chest. She was teasing him. Reminded him of when she'd taunted him about the towels. His traitorous mind slunk back to the kiss he'd just stolen. Her willingness... her sweetness. . .

Aw man, maybe he should go get his parents.

"McKenna wanted to see you when you came home."

Colton nodded and strode to the back of the house. What was he going to do about that talk she wanted to have? This wasn't exactly what he wanted to come home to—the kiss, yes. The talk, no. Then again, he wanted absolute honestly. But he was head over heels for the beauty. What if in his weakened mental state, he bought completely whatever it was she wanted to share?

Truth be told, he was scared. Scared to find out what she had to say. What could explain her running, two attackers at her apartment... her missing identity. More dread churned in his gut as he entered Mickey's room.

She lay sprawled on her back. Blond hair akimbo, she clutched the pink poodle Piper had given her. Colton knelt and pressed a kiss to her forehead.

Her blue eyes shot open. Tiny arms locked around his neck. "Daddy! I missed you!"

With the little monkey wrapped around him, he pushed up and sat on the edge of the mattress. "I missed you, too. But I wasn't gone so long this time."

Mickey shook her head and yawned. "I told Piper I heard your truck."

"You're so smart." He brushed the blond bangs from her face. "Now, go on back to sleep and get some shut-eye. Maybe we can go to the mall and ride the carousel tomorrow."

She worked her way under the quilt, then looked up at him with those big blue eyes. "Can Piper come?"

"We'll see." He planted a kiss on her cheek. "Night, darlin'."

"Night, Daddy."

After a slight detour to double-check windows, doors, and rooms, Colton took his time returning to the kitchen. *Lord God, I feel like I'm facing the executioner on this relationship.* When he finally made it, he stopped, taking in the kitchen—more accurately, Piper standing at the sink, washing something. Her hair stretched down her back. Couldn't help but remember the feel of those soft strands. How they smelled of honey and spices. He pushed his gaze to the table.

A mug of coffee and a bowl with apple pie à la mode waited for him. "Trying to sweeten me up?"

Piper spun from the sink. Flipped off the water and dried her hands. "I. . .your mom had it made, ready for whenever you came home."

As he slid into the chair, he smiled. "Always does." When he lifted the fork, only then did he realize she didn't have anything to eat. "You eating?"

"Honestly, I'm too nervous to eat."

Fork halfway to his mouth with that delectable first bite, Colton paused. "Honesty might be painful, but it's always the right thing to do." He took the bite.

She sat across from him, wariness edging out the light and sparkle he'd seen right after they kissed. "I'm not convinced it's right, but I can't stand the thought of what you think of me."

"And what is that?"

"I see it in your eyes, in the way you treat me—well, before. . . before you came home tonight."

He stifled the grin that tried to leak into his face as hers went crimson. "Well, I'm about done with this pie, and you haven't even started."

She cradled the mug of tea between both hands. "I. . .what I'm about to tell you could put someone I love in horrible danger."

Colton set down his fork and shoved the plate aside. "Go on."

"I. . ." Caramel eyes came to his, uncertain and afraid.

He held his peace.

She shrugged. "I'm not really sure where to start."

"How about with those two men."

"I. . ." Images of her father flashed through her mind. Images of what the men who'd come after her were notorious for doing to their captives.

Panic thrust its greedy fist up her stomach and clutched her throat. She couldn't do this. Telling him *anything* meant telling him *everything*.

But she loved Colton. Promised she'd tell him the whole sordid story.

As if her heart were experiencing a great earthquake, she felt it rent in two by the seismic pressures of her conflicting loyalties.

Colton folded his arms on the table and leaned in. Didn't he realize how commanding his presence was? How much she wanted to tell him whatever he wanted to hear, just so they could move past this? But lying and deceiving would only destroy what little trust he placed in her by agreeing to talk.

She darted him a nervous glance. "I'm trying to figure out what to say."

"Those men at your apartment, did you know them?"

"No, not directly."

A half-grunt pushed him back. "What do you know, indirectly?"

Each word could be her undoing, could kill her father, so she took her time formulating the correct response. "They may be connected to an organization that prides itself on being forceful and deadly, on wielding their power over. . .others."

"Why were they after you?"

Slowly, she shook her head. "Perhaps they thought I had something they wanted."

A slow nod. "What was that?"

"I'm not sure, really." Had he rigged her to a polygraph, he'd know her heart rate was through the roof. Didn't he know this was killing her? "They didn't steal anything, and they didn't hurt me."

Colton grinned, but she saw the first tinge of disgust color his face. "Darlin', I could've told you that."

He wasn't buying it. She wouldn't be able to keep this up.

On his feet, he carried his plate to the sink and set it to the side. Piper watched from her periphery, unable to face him. He wanted and deserved the truth. She wanted and yearned to give him that truth. But her father would die.

"Why were your bags packed?"

"I was going to leave." Numb, she drew in all the tendrils of her heart that she'd wrapped around him, fearful once he knew the truth, he'd shove her away.

"So, you *were* leaving me."

"Town. I was leaving town, moving."

"You were leaving *me*!"

She swallowed—hard. "I had no choice."

The storm had drifted through the window and into his face. "You always have a choice."

She jerked toward him, her heart speeding through her chest. "When they call, you go. Do you have a choice?"

He frowned. "That's different."

"How?"

"When I go out there, when I leave my family, I'm protecting lives."

Piper narrowed her eyes. "So am I."

"No, you don't understand—"

"It's you who doesn't understand." She found herself on her feet, hands fisted. "You aren't the only one in this world with secrets that protect other people."

"Who are you protecting, Piper?"

Her courage failed. "I cannot tell you."

Then, without warning, he grinned. Leaned back against the counter. "Nicely done."

"What?"

"When I walked out the door the other night, you said you'd tell me *everything*." He cocked his head and pursed his lips. "I'm thinking you haven't made good on that promise and don't plan on it."

"I can't."

He straightened, towering over her. "Can't? Or won't?"

"It's the same thing in this case."

A myriad of things flashed over his face, each one registering with the impact of a brick wall to Piper. Hurt. Anger. Rejection. Grief. " 'Nough said." He stomped toward the door.

"Why won't you trust me. . . ?" Her words trailed off, lost in her realization that the question had answered itself. He couldn't trust her. Who would, when she wouldn't give him answers? When she hid everything about herself? He wanted more than she could give.

"Why won't I trust you?" His laugh proved hollow and grating. "I won't trust you because you've all but admitted you're lying to me, hiding things, and then stand there and say you won't tell me the truth!"

Piper's vision blurred beneath the tears. "I can't tell you!" she shouted. "He'll di—" She clamped her mouth shut as a burst of dread and panic shot through her belly.

"Die?" Eyes narrowed, he pressed into her space. "*Who* will die?"

She shook her head. "I can't. Please, please don't ask me. . . ."

Colton raised a hand, then lowered it. "Never mind." With that, he stalked down the hall to his room.

What a stupid, idiotic dolt she was. To think she could find a way to skirt the truth yet provide morsels of it at the same time. She'd nearly endangered her father. And lost Colton while doing it.

This story didn't have a happy ending. It never would.

Piper peered after him once more. When she heard the shower turn on, she dragged her gaze back down the hall. . .and settled on the boots lined up by the door, directly under the alarm.

Her heart caught.

Green. The alarm wasn't on.

Piper spun and, on her tiptoes, she sailed across the living room, down the rear passage to the guest room. She changed into her jeans and a shirt, then grabbed her pack and a jacket. Back at the side door, she stuffed her feet into the big wading-style boots and snatched the rain slicker from the rack.

Rain hammered her as she stepped into the dark night. The darkest night of her life.

No, she had to be positive. Had to be. . .

She screamed into the deafening elements. There was no more positive. Only surviving. Getting through. She was fed up with trying to be the good little girl. The one who did what was expected of her. The one who didn't complain or argue. Prim and proper had gotten her nothing but pain. When Baba told her his plan, she'd tried to object, but he'd used his fatherly authority and forced her to comply. She should've used the good brain she'd been given.

Then again, considering the situation she was in, who would say she had a good brain? Wouldn't someone intelligent have found a better solution or path? A way to get their father to safety with his proof?

Puddles sloshed mud up at her, but she didn't care. She stomped onward, the adrenaline pumping her legs hard and fast. She wouldn't be stopped. Not again. She had to get far away from. . .everyone.

Plodding on became more like trudging. Then dragging. The water grew higher under the flash-flooding along the side of the road, and the sludge thicker and more difficult. Though she looked for higher ground, she couldn't see more than a few inches with the sheets of rain. Piper drifted to the side, where the pothole-laden country road provided little difference. At least she was trying to wade through a river of mud.

She pitched forward. Mud splashed into her face. She braced herself. . .but slowly sunk in the muck. Panic thrummed against her chest as she struggled to get back on her feet. Finally, she stood, slopped the hair out of her face, and pushed. . .dragged on. Compliments of the mud and muck, just moving forward, what normally required no effort, now demanded a full athletic workout.

Piper had managed no more than six slogging steps before she did another face-plant. She yelped as pain stabbed through her ankle. She shoved up out of the filthy water, sputtering and gagging. Spitting the mud from her mouth, she wiped her face.

Unable to move, she ignored the pain and worked to free herself. Submerged, her foot wouldn't budge. Her fingers ached as she reached through the cold needling water and traced the spot. Somehow, she'd gotten wedged between some rocks.

Headlights broke through the black void of the storm.

Coming straight at her.

She gasped. If they didn't see her, they'd run her over. She waved her arms. Pushed against the rocks with her free foot—only to get it caught too. Rain pelted her face. She heard it hammering the steel barreling toward her.

"Stop," she screamed and waved again as she battled the elements. "Stop!"

But the car came unheeding.

Piper hauled in a breath as the vehicle approached. Fire jolted up her leg. "Please." She kicked, wiggled, and thrashed, crying.

A dozen feet away. Tires sluiced through the downpour, forming a small squall that rushed onto the sides of the swelling road.

Blinding, she jerked away. "Yeshua, help me!" She threw herself to the side, hoping to protect most of her body. The car would run over her legs, but. . .

Brakes squawked almost in her ear. Tiny rocks peppered her face as the car swished to a stop, sliding right up until the bumper nudged her shoulder.

"What on earth. . . ?" a voice called.

Piper bent around and stared up. In the split second that a bolt of lightning streaked through the sky, she spotted a large star decal on the driver's side door. Sheriff. She blinked and strained to see past the water rushing down her face.

An old man scowled down at her. "Waddya doin' out in weather like this?"

"I'm. . .my leg. I'm stuck."

"What a fool thing," he mumbled as he climbed out of the cruiser. "Nearly gave me a heart attack. Don't you know ain't nobody gonna see you in the weather?"

That was the point.

He bent and flashed a light on her foot. "Here, just hang on a sec." With a slight turn of her foot, he managed to free her. "Now, that wasn't so bad. Can ya stand?"

Piper batted the hair from her face and tried to push herself up.

"All your panickin' probably made ya not think straight." He helped her to her feet and wrapped an arm around her. "Come on. Let's get you out of the rain."

Never so glad to be rescued, Piper hobbled to the back of the sheriff's car.

"Don't think ya broke it. But you got a mighty nice sprain." He eased the door closed and climbed into the front. A wire rack formed a barrier between them as he put the car in gear, then lifted a phone to his ear. "Yep, I found her." The sheriff nodded. "Sure thing, Colton. I'll bring her back."

CHAPTER 12

Beams of light shattered the darkness and streaked over the pocked kitchen window. Colton pressed the phone to his ear as the police cruiser lumbered onto the flooded stretch of road that led to his driveway.

"Jacobs."

"I could use some backup." When Max didn't respond, Colton wondered if he was expecting too much. But he really wanted the support. "If it's a probl—"

"I'll be there." The line went dead.

He holstered his phone and watched through the kitchen window as Bart eased the car up to the side of the house. From the rack near the door, he grabbed a hat and slid it on as he stepped into the pelting weather. He peered through the downpour toward the car.

Colton flicked his gaze from Bart in the front seat, talking on his radio, to the backseat. Piper sat, her head down and shoulders sagging.

Good.

In the half hour since she'd fled the safety of his home, his parents had returned and the sheriff had set out, lured into the storm by the silent alarm Piper's sudden departure triggered. Hands on his hips, he worked to temper his anger, the hurt, the complete failure he'd felt like knowing she preferred an early winter storm to his company and protection.

The screen door squeaked behind him. "She looks upset," his father said.

"She ain't got nothing on me." He stepped into the rain and hurried to the cruiser.

Bart climbed out. "Hate to dump her and run, but I got another call—old Nessie's squawking about someone being in her barn." As he opened the rear door he said, "Her ankle's wrenched. Don't think it's broke."

Colton let the piercing drops and whipping wind needle his mood. What was so dawg awful about him that she fled? He bent in.

Hands in her lap, she was a sight. Mud smeared over her face— several streaks almost washed clean. Tears? He frowned as his gaze tracked her hair hanging in muddy strings. She kept her gaze down and made no response as he knelt on the seat.

All the anger, all the frustration, leeched out of him at the brokenness he saw in her posture, her normally vibrant face. He held out a hand. "Let's get you inside."

Willingly, she scooted out of the car and stood—yelped and crumpled against the car.

Colton scooped her into his arms and rushed her into the dry warmth of his home. He carried her to the couch.

She tensed as he lowered her toward the leather material. "No! I'm filthy. I'll ruin your furniture."

With a grunt, Colton set her down. Did she really think a couch was more important? "I need to get a look at your ankle."

"Please. . ." Piper slumped and sagged again, shivering. Beneath the shudders and utter defeat written over her dirty features, she had a blue tinge easing into her lips.

"Stay put." Colton hurried to the hall closet and snatched a fleece blanket. He returned and wrapped it around her. Caramel eyes flitted to his and away quick as a hummingbird. The swell of emotion crying out from those beautiful irises tugged at his heart.

No heart-tugging. She fled. Into a storm. Abandoned him.

"Let me see what you did when you thought a raging storm would be safer than being with me." He knelt and removed her shoe, eliciting a quick intake of breath from Piper, who gripped the back of the sofa as if bracing herself.

He probed the sides and compared her two ankles. "It's swollen. Not broken though." He lifted her arm and looped it over his shoulder. "Let's get you showered—make it a hot one—and changed, so you don't end up with pneumonia." He hoisted her off the sofa, carried her through the house, and deposited her inside the bathroom.

Colton moved away, glancing around the room. "Where's your bag?"

She shrugged. "I. . .I lost it." Then her eyes widened. "No! My bag. We have to find it."

Had the woman lost her fool mind?—well, yes, she had. "Nobody's going out in the storm."

She hobbled toward him and nearly slipped onto her backside because of the puddle her dripping clothes created. "You don't understand—"

"I'm pretty sure we've established that a thousand times over." He stepped back. "Now, shower up. I'm calling someone to look at your foot."

"You just said nobody's going out in the storm."

"Nobody meaning you or me." He pointed to the glassed-in area. "Shower."

"I—"

He shot her a piercing glare. Was she still going to challenge him? He hesitated when she withered under his fierce look. Colton drew back the reins on his anger. "What?"

"My bag. . .I don't have dry clothes."

She was taller and slimmer than his mom, but surely he could find something for the night. "They'll be waiting outside the door when you're done washing off the filth. And while you're at it, why don't you rinse with some good sense." Colton started to leave, then moved back into her view. "Oh." He drew out his MEU .45 and did a press check. "I'm ready if you want to run again."

The wide eyes and her half-open mouth told him the demonstration had the desired effect. Lord knew he wouldn't ever be able to fire on her, but the message came through clear enough. She needed the point made.

He made another call. "I need your medical expertise."

Throbbing music pounded the line. "Now? In case you missed it, there's a possible hurricane off the coast."

"When was the last time I called you, Midas?"

A thick pause pulsed through the phone line. "Twenty minutes."

With a breath, Colton felt one more tension knot release. "Thanks."

"Hey, it's what we do."

Phone tucked away, he found his mom. "Hey, I need something for Piper to put on for now. She lost her bag in the storm."

"Of course, of course. I know just the thing."

Colton followed her into the master bedroom as she mumbled

something about a sparkly sweater. "No, no sparkles." He cringed to think of Piper wearing one of his mom's sequined sweaters. Just didn't work for him.

"Oh, okay. Well, what about these pants? Jeri left them hanging in the laundry room when they were here last."

Colton accepted the velour pants. His Aunt Jeri was taller than his mom, but not quite as tall as Piper. "That dog'll hunt."

"You sure you don't want this sweater?"

One glance at the frou-frou sweater pushed Colton from the room. "No. Thanks, Mom." He trudged back to his room and tugged a Marine Corps sweatshirt from the top of his closet.

"Is everything all right?" His mom hovered in the living room as he passed her, heading back to the guest room.

"Not yet."

"Want me to talk to her?"

"No, please. Let me handle this."

His dad appeared behind her. "I feel responsible for all this."

Colton held his tongue. A good portion of his frustration had been aimed at his parents for leaving Piper here alone. "Even I know if a person wants something bad enough, nobody can stop them."

"Look," his dad said as he shifted around his wife and met Colton's gaze. "You gotta know I wouldn't have gone if it wasn't important. We weren't just out joyriding or shopping."

Colton nodded.

"The doctor had an opening, and we had to take it."

"Doctor?" Colton hated the sickening feeling sliding into his stomach. "What doctor?"

Indecision seemed to strangle his father, especially when Mom wrapped her arm around Dad and gave Colton a silent look that warned him off. Finally, his dad looked at him. "We can talk about it later, after things settle."

His mom came to him. "Please. . .just try to see things from Piper's perspective."

His will hardened. "There are things you don't know—things *I* don't know." He touched her shoulder. "Just. . .trust me on this."

She gave him a wan smile. "I do, son. It's just so odd. I see so much of myself in Piper, and I know in my heart of hearts she doesn't mean any harm."

"Maybe." He glanced over at his dad, who knelt before the fireplace, trying to get a fire going. "But she's doing an A-plus job of it so far."

"Colton—"

"Mom," he said, tugging again on the reins of his frustration but knowing he wouldn't tolerate any interference this time. "I know you want to help, and you like Piper 'nd all, but I mean it. Let me handle this."

She lowered her hands, and her countenance went with it. "Of course." Like a little puppy with her tail between her legs, she crossed the room to his father. Again—there was the look that made him feel like he was about to unload his lunch.

Colton's guilt tripled. His mother had nothing but good intentions and hated to see anyone hurting. But that was just the problem. Times of soft answers and gentle words were gone.

As he rounded the corner that led to the guest room, a thought hit Colton and stopped him dead in his tracks. What if. . .what if Piper was just like his mom? Could her racing into the angry storm be an attempt to protect him and his family rather than self-protection?

Like a jigsaw puzzle, the pieces floated before his mind. Her leaving town. . .another attempt to protect him?

Colton shook his head. Nah, he was reaching too far with that one. With a gentle rap on the open door, he entered and crossed to the bathroom door. "Piper?" The water shut off. "Piper, I'm leaving the clothes here."

"Okay," came her very dull reply.

For some reason, the broken timbre of her voice rooted his feet to the floor. He placed a hand on the door. *Lord. . .* Why couldn't things be different, simple, between them? Colton hung his head and closed his eyes.

He shut down the emotions, his longing for simple things, his longing for Piper. He was a Marine. Nothing was simple or easy. If it was, someone was cheating.

Loud knocking snapped him out of the depression clouding his heart and mind. Sounded like the side entrance. Colton cast one more glance at the door, at the shadows moving on the other side of the barrier, then left.

When he rounded the corner, voices skidded through the house. Max. Colton met his friend halfway across the living room and pulled him into a half-hug, half-back slap.

"Thanks for coming."

"No problem. Midas is about five minutes behind me."

Colton frowned. Why would he know that?

"Dude got lost, called for directions." Max hoisted up a dripping, muddy pack. "Found this in the road not far from your drive."

"Piper's." Colton took it and tossed it to the side.

In the dark eyes of his friend, Colton read the myriad of questions. Rather than open that nightmare in front of his parents, he motioned to the kitchen. "Coffee?"

"Caffeine this late?" Max shrugged out of his leather jacket. "Must be serious."

Colton retrieved two mugs from the upper cabinet and filled them with the black brew, then passed one to Max, who sipped it straight. "No creamer?"

Max grunted. "What's the point?"

Colton grinned and added creamer to his.

"So, what's eating you?"

"She tried to escape—ran into the storm. Injured herself."

"Wow, never thought I'd see the day where the cowboy would need help keeping a woman in his sights."

The taunting cut sideways through Colton. "Ya know," he said, staring into his mug and tempering his frustration. He looked up. "I'm not really in the mood for jokes tonight."

Max's dark eyes held his. Then a nod.

Unbelievable how irritable this whole thing had made him. Normally, he'd roll with the punches, turn the other cheek, but this mounted one insult and burden on the other.

"So you called Midas?"

Colton bobbed his head. "She hurt her leg. I'd like to make sure it's not broken."

Left eye twitching, Max set aside his drink. "What aren't you telling me?"

Relief rushed through Colton. This is why he'd wanted Max here, why he was willing to tell him almost everything. "While she was out there in the rain, I started thinking about the attack at her place." With a heaving sigh, Colton ran a hand through his hair. "They didn't steal anything. They didn't kill her. They didn't rape her—and they had time to do all of those things."

"So, what were they after?"

"Exactly. I asked her if she knew who they were, and she said she didn't know their names. But she was hiding something." He shook his head, hating the fact he had to hash this out at all—he wanted to bury it. Why did all the threads feel as slippery as a snake out of water? "Then, when the sheriff brings her back tonight, he says a neighbor lady a couple of miles away reported someone in her barn." Colton checked on his parents.

On the sofa with firelight flickering over their faces and his father's arm draped around his mother's shoulders, they sat quietly, no doubt listening to his conversation.

"What does it all mean?"

"I don't know." He didn't want to voice his thoughts. Didn't want to breathe life into them and unleash what he feared hovered on the horizon.

"That's not the Cowboy I know." With a gentle, back-handed slap, Max thumped his chest. "You've got killer instincts—literally. What're you thinking?"

"My theory—she knows the trouble chasing her, but not directly. Know what I mean? I think she wanted to protect me and my family—that's why she tried to leave tonight."

"That or stupidity," Max mumbled, then grinned. "Sorry. Exploring options. So. . .in that brilliant Marine recon mind of yours, how does it all add up?"

Colton ground his teeth together and tasted the bitterness of his next words. "They're coming for her."

"Then it's time to lock and load."

"You're sure?"

"Yes, sir. One hundred percent. I verified it before I came to you."

"Thank you, Robert." Olin stuffed his arms through his suit jacket as he stormed out of his office and past his secretary's desk armed with the file his attaché had delivered. "Bonnie, call Charles Falde and tell him I'm on my way to see him."

"Yes, sir."

The closing elevator swallowed her words.

Unbelievable. No wonder Piper Blum didn't exist. But. . .but what did this mean? How deep, how entrenched—why?

The questions were endless, and trying to hash them out en route would only frustrate him more. Yet a hope ignited in him. Perhaps Digitalis wasn't in the boat of trouble he'd begun to suspect. What if he had a national treasure at his house?

The thought buckled Olin's knees. "Oh merciful God!" Pushed him forward. The doors opened, and it took every ounce of strength for him to walk down the hall...to the car.... By the time he reached Falde's Virginia farm, he had a dozen theories, each more unlikely than the previous.

Charles met him on the porch with a broad smile and a steaming mug. The scent of coffee drifted through the piney setting. "Must be a mighty big problem to bring you to my doorstep. I've been inviting you out here for years."

Olin peered up at the man. On the top step, he paused. "What do you know about Yitshak Rosenblum?"

His face suddenly pale and gaunt, Charles dumped the coffee and the smile. "How do you know that name?"

DAY FOUR

Saudi Arabia, 02:01:03 hours

Be sure to send a lazy man for the angel of death." A throaty chuckle emanated through the thundering chaos as Rosenblum pushed himself upright, dusting the litter of glass from his lap. "I believe higher powers are sending the fat, lazy men our way." Another chuckle.

The old saying grated on Azzan's nerves. He'd heard it too many times. He glanced in the mirror to the road behind them. Far in the distance, a black spot appeared on the horizon. Two. Three. Plumes of dust rose from the ground. Al-Jafari's men.

"Those cars aren't fat and lazy. I might have gotten you out of there just to be killed on the road like a dung beetle." He glanced at Raiyah—and froze. Jerked back and took in her appearance. "Where are you injured?"

Blood poured down the side of her face. She looked at him. Blinked. "I'm...okay. Just...the glass." She nodded to the window that had cracked.

Azzan tightened his grip on the steering wheel. Bit back the curse on the tip of his tongue as one more peek in the mirror told him he didn't have the hour it'd take to make it to the border. Had to get off the road. Take cover. He exited the highway and navigated a small but thriving city, tangled with many vehicles and people.

He pulled up along a building and eyed the foot traffic.

"What are you looking for?" Raiyah whispered.

"Trouble." He unbuckled and removed his jacket, wincing at the sting on his arm. When he saw the blood stain, he pinched his lips together. He'd have to grab another shirt, something dark to hide the blood. "Stay down and stay here. I'm going to find something else to drive."

On foot, he stalked through a market and walked the perimeter. He bought a black T-shirt and moved on. As he did, a feeling skated down his back. One of being watched. Trailed. Trusting his instincts, he ducked into a shop, cringing at the ox bell that announced his presence. Head tucked, he raised a hand in greeting to the man behind the counter and quickly strode to the back. He'd no sooner put his hand on the doorknob than he heard the bells.

"Stop!"

Azzan sprinted into the alley. He rounded a corner. Kept running, staying in the shadows as he ripped off his shirt and changed into the T-shirt. By staying on the move, he managed to come full circle. . . almost back to the Hummer. He slipped into the market. Snagged a ball cap. Tucked it on.

His foot hit the street.

Boom!

The concussion of an explosion knocked him backward. Onto his backside. As he pulled himself off the ground, he glanced around, searching for the source of the detonation.

His heart sunk into his stomach.

The Hummer—what was left of it—lay in flames.

CHAPTER 13

Dad?" Colton swung around the door to the stables, scanned the stalls, and double-checked the tack room. "Dad?" he called again, stepping farther into the heady, stuffy building. Max had reported seeing his father come out to the barn, which made no sense at this hour.

Leaning against the last stall, his dad made no move or response.

Colton glanced around, confused. Finally, he closed the distance between then. "Pop? What's going on? What're you doing out here in this weather? Let's go sit on the porch."

"They might overhear."

"Who?"

"The womenfolk. Those friends of yours."

"I. . .I don't understand. What don't you want them to hear?"

After several minutes of the deathly silence, Colton tried to wait it out, but there were way too many things pulling on his energy and focus. "I need to get back in. . . . Things are crazy right now."

"Uh huh." His father stared at the bed of hay where Firefox had given birth a month or so back.

Colton jerked his gaze to the side. He balled his fist and clamped his other hand over it, rubbing his knuckles. Something was seriously wrong. He'd never seen his father like this. "Pop? What's this about?"

"Piper's a good woman."

Grinding his teeth, Colton tried to respond respectfully. "She fled—from me. She says she loves me one minute and then darts out as soon as my back is turned."

"Always a reason a woman does things. Have you asked her?"

He'd asked. And she'd promised to tell, then broke that promise.

Refused. And it ate at him. "This isn't the time, Pop. Can we go back inside?"

His father drew up his chin. "I'd hoped to see you married. . . ."

What the. . . ? Was his father off his rocker? "Pop, we've got time—"

"No, son." His father's voice cracked. "I don't."

He snickered. "Pop, come on—"

"Found cancer."

A cannon ball through the chest wouldn't have had the impact those words did. Colton stared at his father, waiting for a laugh, a sideways punch with an "I'm kidding."

Silence.

"Pop, you're serious?" his voice pitched.

"Doc gave me weeks to live, Colton." Pursing his lips, his father slowly turned to him. "*Weeks.*" The eyes he'd inherited slowly became a plane of liquid blue. "Don' wanna die slow and ugly like. Ya know?" He bit back the sob and looked around. "Don' want your mama seeing me like that, nursing me while I lose my faculties."

Slumped against the fence, Colton held his head, tried to breathe, tried to process the fatal diagnosis. It helped him understand Dad leaving Piper alone at the house, his weight loss. . . .

Colton's world was collapsing from the inside out. First Piper, now his father.

Merciful God, Almighty. . .

His throat swelled with the roaring emotion and burned. He sucked back the tidal wave of sorrow. "Dad. . ."

"Wished I could die in my sleep, ya know? Get it over with. No bittersweet times. No lingering, no depression." He shook his head. With fierce determination, he turned to Colton. "Promise me you won't let her go or push her away."

Confusion raked across Colton's raw heart. "Sir?"

"Piper. She belongs with you. I can see it in your eyes, in hers. Love don't need weeks and slow processes to know it's there. You either do or you don't, Colton." He pointed a shaking finger, tears rushing down his weathered face. "You love that girl, and I don't give a donkey's behind what you think you're protecting. She's the one."

"Pop—"

"No. I *know* it, son. I do."

Shoulders heavy with the realization of what his father was saying,

Colton had to tell him. It didn't matter anymore, not if his father was dying. "My boss found out some stuff about her."

"Like what?" Defiance leeched into his father's words.

"We aren't sure."

"So!" His father grinned, chin raised in triumph. "You don't know." His eyes all but glittered. "But I *do*. I'm telling you she's the one."

"How?" Colton rubbed a hand along his jeans, aching to believe what his father was saying. "How do you know?"

"McKenna."

Colton drew his spine straight. "What's Mickey got to do with this?"

His father grinned. "She said Piper was going to give her a baby brother and sister."

With a snort-laugh, Colton relaxed. "She's always wanted a brother and sister. But that doesn't mean—"

His father dragged a crumpled picture from his pocket and shoved it at Colton. "She drew this picture three months ago."

A weird feeling slithered through Colton's stomach as he stared at the paper. Five stick figures, crudely representing a man and woman and three children—and a dog. "Three? She drew this three months ago?" He gaped. "She hadn't even met Piper yet."

"Exactly." Exultant, his dad grinned as he pointed to the characters. "But she has you, her, and a woman with long, golden hair. Just like Piper."

"That could be anybody." Except for the fact he'd never brought *anybody* home. Colton roughed a hand over his face. "Pop, look, I don't like the turn this has taken, but—"

"For once in your life, stop expecting something to sabotage your happiness. She's not Meredith, and she's completely in love with you. Everyone can see it but you."

"No," he said with a half chuckle. "I can see it."

His father jerked toward him, his eyes wide. "Then, what're you waiting—"

"Let me handle this. My way. Carefully." Dawg, he didn't like this one bit. "My career demands I exercise caution. Lives could depend on it."

Jaw jutted, his father stared out of the barn. "I can understand that." He nodded. Once. Twice. His throat processed a hard swallow.

"I stopped by Thomas's on the way home this afternoon. Named you as executor." A small chortle. "Did you know, the last time I updated my will, you were five?"

The burning at the back of Colton's throat returned. Too reminiscent of the night he'd held Emelie's broken body in his arms as she bled out. Colton dropped his gaze, shouldering the thought out of the way.

"You'll take care of your mama when I'm gone. Make sure she's happy."

Rubbing his knuckles, Colton nodded. His eyes burned now, too.

"Don't put her in one of them homes."

"No, sir." He straightened and let out a thick breath. "She'd never let me."

"She'll need something to keep her busy, which is why. . ." His pop cleared his throat. "Why I wanted you to look after Piper and the thing between y'all. Don't let details get in the way of what your heart's telling ya, son."

"Details could mean the difference between life and death."

"Without a heart, what does it matter?"

A damp chill swirled around her throat and head as Piper limped from the bathroom. With a hand against the jamb, she listened to the tangle of masculine voices coming from somewhere near the family room. She hobbled down the hall and peeked around the corner.

Colton leaned against the back of the sofa, talking in quiet, terse tones to two men. With a start, Piper recognized the shorter of the two men—the one with black hair and midnight eyes. He'd been at her apartment. What was his name? Mark. Mack. *Max!* Arms folded over his chest, everything about the guy screamed he was ready for a fight. And by the looks of those biceps, he took care of whoever he went up against.

The third man wore a pair of black slacks and a royal blue silk shirt that hung loose just past his waist. He oozed calmness, but a quiet focus radiated from his eyes. "I'll get changed and walk the perimeter, check things out, then report back." Flickering shadows from a fire danced over his sandy blond crop.

Hands on the spine of the sofa, Colton nodded. "Thanks, guys. I appreciate your help."

She gulped when her gaze collided with Max's. She felt like a moving target, knowing full well she'd been caught and couldn't evade his sights.

Colton pushed to his feet as he looked at her. "You shouldn't be walking."

Limping, she stepped into the open. "It's not as bad as before."

He pointed to the oversized chair and ottoman. "Have a seat," he said as he nodded toward the blond man. "Check it out, Midas."

Tensing as thick cushions enveloped her, Piper carefully set her foot on the ottoman and regarded the slick guy as he crouched by her leg.

"Don't worry. I know what I'm doing." With that, he cradled her heel in the palm of his left hand. With his right, he slowly rotated her foot.

When he went to the left, Piper flinched at the stab of pain that darted up her leg.

"Is it broke?" Colton loomed over them both.

Midas looked up at her through sandy eyebrows as his hand probed her muscles and tendons. "Never seen him this grouchy." He pinned her with pale blue orbs. "What'd you do to him?"

The accusation poured heat into her stomach, drenched with dread—that is, until she saw the smile peeking through Midas's query. She darted a glance to Colton, who brooded and scowled.

What had she done except run away from him? Colton's curt words spoke of his hurt and anger. She didn't expect to have to face him after she left the house. It would've been better. . .easier. . .if he'd just let her go. Why wouldn't Yeshua help her?

"Well?" Standing over her, Colton planted his hands on his hips. The roaring fire inflamed his rugged face, making it seem to glow. "Is she going to be okay?"

He was worried? About her? Piper studied the man more. The way his black hair curled around the nape of his neck, the dimple in his cheek pinching and winking. His muscles pulling against the untucked, button-down shirt.

Midas pushed to his feet and gave Colton a cockeyed grin. "She's fine."

"Fine?" Colton frowned. "It's swollen."

With a shrug, Midas grinned even wider. "She wrenched it.

Stretched it too far. Might've bruised the bone itself, but no real injury to the tendons, ligaments, or bones. Of course, without an X-ray, I can't be one hundred percent."

"Why are you smiling?"

"Because I've never seen you so wound up." He glanced back down at Piper but still spoke to Colton. "I wondered what it'd take to make the cowboy human like the rest of us."

Max laughed.

Which reddened Colton's face.

"Come on, Cowboy," Max said, still chuckling. "You walked right into that one. Even I saw that coming."

"Back off." Colton's face darkened.

"I. . .I don't understand," Piper mumbled, feeling self-conscious and concerned. The last thing she wanted was someone teasing Colton and making him angrier with her. "What's funny—what's. . . ?"

"Nothing. Never mind." Colton motioned to Midas. "You have a shift to work."

"Yessir." Snickering, Midas saluted Colton, then headed to the back of the house.

Piper's stomach knotted at the expression on Colton's face—consternation knitted his brows, his color went red, and his body language warned he'd take on a champion bull if given the opportunity.

"Come on," he said to Max a minute later. "Let me show you something." He took two steps, then stopped and looked at her again. "Stay there. My parents are in bed already, but my guys have orders to shoot."

A swarm of emotions tightened her stomach as the guys vanished down the hall, their voices seeming to indicate they'd gone to Colton's room. Indignation and humiliation at the way he said that, the way he embarrassed her in front of his friend. Then again, she deserved it, so the guilt harangued her and kept her mouth shut. But the hurt. . .the hurt she saw on his face, the hurt she felt knowing she'd destroyed a chance of anything with Colton.

Though she attempted to save him from the heartache she was heading straight for, she'd failed. Were she to be honest with herself, she'd know she didn't want to leave Colton. She wanted him to protect her. To love her.

Hot tears streaked down her face at the revelation. Yes, she'd wanted to be protected. It seemed every time danger arose, she was pushed away from those she loved. She burrowed into the chair and drew her legs to her chest. Piper buried her face against her knees and cried. . .prayed. . .begged Yeshua to show her what to do. How to protect Colton and his family.

Amid the popping and crackling from the fire and the roar of the elements outside, she heard a quiet voice. *"In his heart a man plans his course, but the Lord determines his steps."*

Piper stilled as the words from Proverbs drifted into her mind and settled into her heart. Her father had often repeated that to her when she'd rushed ahead with her plans, failing to inquire of the Lord and seek His will. Piper seized the solitude to remedy her mistake. Head lowered, she closed her eyes and stilled her mind.

Yeshua wanted her to understand something.

And in the next heartbeat it came to her—Yeshua had her right where He wanted her. With Colton. Here. With him, not running from him.

"No," she said, straightening and lowering her feet. Frantic at the thought of what could happen if she stayed with him, she shook her head. "He'll get hurt. They'll kill him." But even as she said it, peace settled within her like a hot cup of herbal tea. Soothing. . .warm. . .relaxing. She was supposed to be here. Belonged here. There was a purpose.

Shouts jolted her attention.

Thud! Crack!

On her feet, Piper limped through the kitchen. More shouts— angry and heated. It sounded like Colton and Max. Were they fighting? She hobbled quicker. What if something was wrong—what if. . . ?

Oh please, no. Please no. She used the wall to support her as she hurried.

Thud! Crash!

By the time she reached the laundry room, Max stumbled into the hall. Holding a fist to his mouth, he came toward her. Grinned.

"What—" When she saw the blood on his lip, she gasped. "Did he hit you?"

"I warmed him up." He winked. "I think he's ready for you now."

Automatically, a hand went to her stomach.

"Don't worry. He won't hit you. It took a lot to get him this mad," Max said as he pointed to his mouth. Then chuckled. "It was worth it."

"Worth it?" She gaped. How could he intentionally provoke his friend and say it was worth it?

"Yeah—Cowboy doesn't let go much. And he's built up too much steam. Trust me," Max said as he zipped his jacket and paused with the back door ajar. "It's a good thing. I think he knows—" He looked down the hall then nodded. "Yeah, now he knows what he's fighting for."

"And it took a fight?"

Max grinned. "Don't worry. He doesn't get worked up like that most times. I just knew the words to say to hit the right nerve."

"I'm not worried about him hitting me. I'm wondering why his friend felt it necessary to provoke him into a fight."

The humor vanished from Max's face as he stepped in and let the door close behind him. "You gotta understand. I'm a squid; he's a Marine. We're trained to do what we have to do and stow it all in a steel vault that we deep-six." He raked a hand through his dark hair. "Sometimes, we're so boxed up. . .we don't even know it." Then, that easy smile returned. "Colton knows now." He nodded down the hall. "Go on. I think you two need to talk."

Max disappeared into the rain and wind, the door clattering behind him.

Swallowing her swirling potion of fear and panic, Piper glanced down the hall. Dare she? Dare she go down there when Colton was so angry he'd punched his friend? What exactly did Colton do that he could summon men to his home? Men who clearly had military training? Everything in her told her to go back to the living room, sit by the fire like a good girl. He'd told her to stay there.

But her love for him pulled her down the hall.

Light spilled from his room, and she stopped at the line between darkness and light. So symbolic of her life. If she crossed this line. . . would things change?

I need a change. I want a change.

Piper rounded the corner and halted.

Seated on the bed, Colton sat hunched with his hands cradling his head. In a white tank, his muscles flexed and retracted as if. . . It was then she noticed his hands clenched into fists. Flexing. Unflexing. He rocked.

Even as she took the first step over the threshold, Piper felt her chin quivering.

A board creaked.

Colton jerked to his feet. Braved a glance to the side—but not at her. His gaze hit her feet. "I told you to wait in the living room." His breathing was heavy and deep.

She crossed the room to stand in front of him. With an uneven breath, she brushed the wet strands from her face—and saw the red stain on his knuckles from hitting Max.

Piper caught his hand and ran her fingers over the injury. When she looked at him, it broke her heart to see such a wounded, tormented expression marring the strength of the man. Couple that with the way he avoided looking at her, and Piper struggled not to cry.

"He told me what happened, that he provoked you."

Slowly. . .unwillingly, his gaze rose to hers. Red streaked his eyes. "Doesn't matter. I lost control." His voice cracked.

"Maybe that was a good thing." She couldn't believe she said that, but maybe that was Max's point. Colton kept everything tight and tidy.

He pulled his hand free. "Hurting those I love and care about is never acceptable," he said through tight lips.

He was right. That was part of what she loved so much about him—his absolute dedication to those he loved. Even now as the truth of his words bounded through her chest, they reminded her of the promise she'd made. She had to tell him. No more dodging the truth. She inched closer, nervous—would he let her close? More than anything, she wanted to be in his arms again.

Warily, he watched her.

"I broke my promise to you." Tight and raw, her throat constricted. *Yeshua, protect Baba.* "The person I'm protecting is my fa—"

A scream severed her confession.

CHAPTER 14

A nightmare unfolded like a slow motion movie sequence. Colton's heart stuttered when his mother's scream reverberated through his being. Was it real? Was this really happening? Or was it another of his flashbacks, another moment to humiliate him?

Caramel eyes widened, soaked in fright.

Adrenaline surged. Colton grabbed Piper's hand. "C'mon!" Sprinting down the hall, he harnessed his mind against the million different directions it'd plunged. *It's real. . .it's real.* A large knot kinked his stomach as he dodged the kitchen chairs and bolted into the living room.

"Colton," came another half-shriek from his mother.

"Where are you?" he shouted as he pushed himself harder, faster. Past McKenna's room. She didn't have to answer because his trained mind latched onto her broken sobs—in their master bedroom.

With one foot in the door—he stopped cold. Two frozen seconds, suspended in the ghoulish nightmare, gave him just enough time to see the vital points. His father, down. In a pool of blood. His mother, cradling his father, gawked at the window.

Colton jerked backward. "Mom, get down!" he shouted as he swung a hand back and secured Piper against the wall. "Get McKenna, but stay down." Once she acknowledged the order, he scrabbled into the master bedroom.

His mother, flattened on the blood-drenched Persian rug, peered through black-marred eyes. Mascara smeared down her face. "Ben! Ben, please stay with me."

Colton hooked his arms under his father's shoulders, pushed

up on his haunches, but stayed as low as he could. With a grunt, he dragged his father into the hall.

Crack!

Thud!

Colton cringed at the familiar sound and the plume of gypsum board that puffed out. "Stay down," he shouted when he saw his mother pushing up. "They're still shooting!"

In the hall, he laid his father down gently and moved to assess the injury. What felt like a punch in the gut was the blue tinge sucking the life-color from his father's skin. "Pop?"

"He was about to climb in bed, then just—" A sob choked off the words. "He's not breathing." She lifted her hand to her face and stopped short of touching her mouth when they both noticed the blood that covered her hand.

As he clamped a hand over the chest wound, Colton heard a noise to his left. Piper scurried around the door with a sleepy McKenna wrapped around her. She cupped Mickey's head to her chest, apparently pinning his daughter so she couldn't see his father.

The thought snapped his attention back to saving his life. "Pop." He nodded to the hall closet behind her. "Stay low," he said to his mother, "but get me a towel, anything, to staunch the flow."

She'd always liked to be doing something, and he saw the focus return to her glazed-over eyes. A second later, she thrust a towel at him. He pressed it against the wound. Footsteps pounded against the hardwoods.

Without thinking, Colton shoved to his feet, assumed the stance, and drew his MEU .45 as he took aim at the shadows creeping through the den. Whoever had come through the back door better have a really good reason. Because he had a heckuva reason to end their progress.

The steps raced toward them.

"Cowboy." Max's terse voice served as an announcement.

Colton shoved his weapon back in the holster and knelt beside his father. Midas literally slid across the floor on his knees and skidded to a stop next to the still form.

"What happened?" he asked, breathless.

"Someone hit him."

"We were coming to report—movement sighted in the south-western quadrant."

"A little late."

Midas looked at Max. "We need a rig—he has to get to a trauma center. Call it in. Now!" He tilted his father's chin up, checking the airway. "His breathing's agonal. Get the shirt off! I need to see the wound."

"Got it," Max said, whipping out a phone.

On his knees, Colton ripped the shirt off, his brain cells plummeting into a combat scenario even though the carpet beneath them was fibers not grass. *Don't give up, Dad. I need you. . . .* But even Colton knew by the blue-gray hue eating away the lively shades in his father's face that this wasn't good.

Shaking his head, Midas's expression grew grim. "Pulse is thready." He probed the wound. Colton knew it had to hurt, yet his father did not respond. Blood smeared over the chest as Midas began compressions.

Time seemed to come to an agonizing halt. Minutes felt like years.

"C'mon, c'mon, c'mon!" Midas grunted.

His friend's frantic pleas scraped Colton's nerves raw. He'd been here—dozens of times in combat. Far too many times he'd inflicted the wounds that severed life cords. But here? In his own home? With his own father slipping past the edge of life?

Crawling over to her husband's side again, his mother reached for him with a trembling hand. Smoothed small hands over his father's cheek. "Benjamin, please. . .please don't leave me." Tears slipped down her face and landed on his father's cheek. "Ben, please. . . Oh God, please don't take him."

Colton drew his mother into his arms and let her unleash her grief in his chest. He closed his eyes, battling to erect a fortress around his heart. Desperate to wall off this pain and. . . What? What exactly could he do?

Find whoever did this.

He'd already put together the pieces of this tragedy. Whoever had come to his land, his home, and taken that crack shot at his father. . . Piper hadn't fired the weapon, but she was the cause.

His heart skipped a beat at the thought. He didn't want to go there, didn't want to place the blame at her feet, but if his father died, there was no other choice.

"Mom," he said as he nudged his shoulder, pushing her back. "Take McKenna to the shelter."

Fiery darts shot out of his mother's normally peaceful blue eyes. "I am not leaving him," she growled as she motioned to his father.

"Mom—"

"No. I'm not." She tugged free and hovered beside her husband—his father—the dying patriarch of the Neeley family. So much lost.

"Emergency services are on the way," Max said as he stood over them. "And the team."

The words drifted past Colton's mind like a mist, barely noticeable and chilling. Midas paused and checked for a pulse. He stared at the ragged rise and fall of his father's chest. Again. . .again. . .

Then. . .nothing.

He swallowed. Hard. *No.*

Colton lowered himself to the floor and leaned toward his dad. "Pop?" He touched his bare shoulder as Midas quickly resumed compressions. "Pop." He'd seen death firsthand many, many times. Close-up and personal through his scope. But not. . .not like this. Not his own father.

Midas's compressions slowed.

A sob wracked his mom's body.

"I'm sorry. . . . I tried. . . ." Midas eased back.

In the fringe of his awareness, Colton heard the ghastly silence that should have, at the least, carried his father's breathing. He pulled his gaze to the floor. To the blood. So much blood. His father's frozen-in-death expression bore the same shock riddling Colton. And just like that frozen expression, his heart went cold and hard.

Colton bent toward his father and wrapped an arm around his head and pressed his forehead to his father's. He couldn't help but think that his father's skin wouldn't stay warm long. Eyes closed, he struggled to hold back the stinging tears that rose. "I'll find them, Pop. I'll find them and make sure they pay."

He didn't know what to feel or think or do. Where did he start first? *God. . . ?*

"Don' wanna die slow and ugly like. Ya know?"

The ominous words his father had spoken all too recently pinged into Colton's conscience. While he might in some sick way be grateful his father's death wasn't slow, he would never forgive whoever did this.

And the blame started with Piper.

A solid pat to this shoulder snapped his gaze up.

Max studied him for a second. "We have a shooter to neutralize."

Empowered by the thought of hunting, Colton took one last look at his father. Tucked away the grief and anger into a package of die-hard determination. Climbed to his feet.

Max nodded to the room. "Single shot through the window?"

"Another when we tried to move him."

"So they can see into the room."

"Blind's down." Colton folded his arms. "Means they have thermals."

Max again nodded.

"I was watching from the loft in the barn. Nobody came close to the house," Midas said, then excused himself and darted into the bathroom.

Soon, the sound of running water filled the hall. Washing away the lifeblood that had been his father's. Lifeblood that had steered Colton through bad choices, saved him from heartache, and guided him with wisdom and love. Lifeblood now being washed down the drain.

If no one had come close to the house, and his father was dead— the thought wrangled more ferocity out of Colton than he thought possible. That meant one thing. "Sniper."

Max merely waited.

Colton ground his teeth and looked at his mother, devoured by her grief. "Mom."

Gaze glued to his father, she hook her head.

"Mom, take Mickey to the shelter." When she didn't respond, Colton moved to her side and squatted, cutting off her view of his father's bloody form. Dazed eyes came to his. "Mom," he said, softly and gently as he touched her shoulder. "Take Mickey to the shelter till we get this sorted."

She blinked, as if her thoughts had just come into focus. "Shelter?"

He squeezed gently. "I need your help to keep her safe. Can you do that?"

"Yes. . . ," she said, her affirmation weak at first, then stronger. "Yes." She climbed to her feet with Colton's help.

He walked her into the hall. When she shifted and tried to glance back, he shouldered into her way again. "Let's remember him strong, okay?"

Tears welled up in her eyes. Her smile wobbled against a trembling chin. She patted his chest. "He was so proud of you." Her blue irises glossed as tears spilled over.

Colton choked back his own tears. He gave her a curt nod. "He'd want you safe."

"You'll take care of your mama when I'm gone."

His knees almost buckled as his father's voice echoed loudly through his head. "Let's get you to the shelter."

Crack!

Midas lunged toward them and slid along the slick wood floors. "Shooter at the side! Shooter at the side!"

The attack that killed her mother wasn't half as terrifying as this.

Because this time, she was to blame.

Piper stuffed her guilt, stuffed her panic, and forced herself to stay calm. Getting panicked, getting stupid meant getting killed.

"Where's the shelter?" Max sidled up next to them, his back against the wall as he pulled out his weapon and checked it.

"My room. Gun closet. Behind there," Colton said. He turned toward her and yanked McKenna out of her hands.

"I've got her."

Max grunted. "We'll cover you and the women. Get them to safety. Regroup. . ." He eyed the living room.

"Laundry room." Colton mumbled something else to his friends as he drew his mother closer. Finally, he glanced back—not at Piper, but at his mom. "Okay, run as fast and low as you can to the shelter."

"Where?" Piper let her question die on her lips. She didn't deserve shelter. In fact, shouldn't she walk out and offer herself to the shooters? They wouldn't shoot her. They'd snatch her. . .and then they'd hunt down her father and kill him.

But what did anything matter anymore? Because of her, they'd just killed Colton's father. Her gaze drifted toward the window. How would she let them know it was her coming out? Would they just take her and leave this family alone?

She had to try.

Colton would never let her do this. She could see the thirst for vengeance in his brilliant blue eyes. He'd want to kill those men. And while she wanted those men dead, too, she couldn't bear to risk McKenna's life, or his mom's, or Colton's.

As it was, she'd already lost everything.

"I'll cover you," Max said as he darted to the kitchen entry and crouched.

"Go!"

With a crying McKenna in his arms, Colton pushed his mother ahead of him and grabbed Piper's hand, drawing her to her feet. He nudged them onward, his mom in front. Quickly, he released her as they hunch-ran toward the small hall leading to the laundry room.

Piper slowed. Glanced toward the dining room, past the table and bay window to the front door. She could end this all. Right now. Save everyone.

She straightened. Turned.

Gunfire erupted around them.

Behind her, she heard Colton hustling his mother and daughter to safety. As it should be. He should protect those he loved.

As if the door held the answer to all the problems, to all her heartache, Piper took that first step.

As she crossed the threshold into the dining room wood splintered and peppered her face. She blinked, feeling disoriented as she glanced at the doorjamb. A hole gaped through it. Warmth slid down her face. Gingerly, she touched the spot. . .surprised to find the slick dark red of blood on her fingertips.

"Piper!" Mickey's scream shattered the slow motion shock that engulfed her.

Realizing she'd been seen, Piper rushed forward.

Pressure clamped onto her from behind. Dragged her back.

She screamed. Grabbed the doorjamb.

"What're you doing?" Colton roared in her ear.

"Let me go. Just let me go," she cried as she clawed to be free of him. "I can stop this. I can stop it."

Without warning, she was lifted off her feet and flung around. Tossed over Colton's shoulders, she watched the front door recede in the darkness. Only then did she realize she couldn't let him take her back.

She wiggled. "Put me down. Please. I can end this."

But the bounding way he jogged through the house cut off the words and objections. He made a sudden right from the hall, and darkness devoured them.

"I can't get the combination to work," came his mother's voice, stressed and slightly pitched.

Colton planted Piper on her feet, but wedged her between the wall and his body with one hand on her shoulder. "Once in, secure the locks. Do *not* open up until I'm here and give you the password."

His mother nodded, her face gaunt and tear-stained as she huddled in the corner, smoothing McKenna's blond hair against her shuddering form.

Piper dropped her gaze, hating herself for this. For causing this. For tearing his family apart.

A door groaned, then hissed. Colton pushed against the heavy steel barrier. "Go on."

Mrs. Neeley rushed into the small room, and instantly a light sprang to life, activated by motion. She set McKenna on a small bed and turned back to the opening. "Come on, Piper."

Piper jerked to Colton. "Please, let me go out there."

His muscle popped and danced along his jaw. He pushed her into the safe room.

"No," she said, trying to hold her own.

"Get in the room." The terse tone knifed her resolve.

Then hardened it. She'd lost him. He'd never forgive her. She had absolutely nothing to lose. "I'm not going in there." She lunged toward him.

He grabbed her shoulders. "You don't have a choice."

"I don't deserve to be in there." Hot tears streaked down her face.

"You got that right!" His eyes blazed.

"Please—it's me. They want me. My father. They want to get me to find my father. I can stop this. I can. I'm sorry. I'm so, so sorry, Colton." A cry wracked her, but she gulped it and rushed on. "I never meant for this to happen. I love you, and I love your family."

Wrestling him was like wrestling a tank. But she had to try. Tried to wiggle past his oversized chest. Holding her upper arms, he pinned her against the wall.

The sob escaped this time. She dropped her head forward, sobbing. His grip lessened.

Piper seized the lessening and tried to shove past him.

Colton slammed her between the wall and his body. "I don't have time for this or you. Now get in there!"

She went limp and fell into his chest, gripping his T-shirt. "I'm so sorry. I'm so, so sorry." She cried harder. "Let me"—*shudder*—"do this. Let me go"—*shudder*—"out there. They'll leave you alone." She hiccupped. "Please." She looked up into his eyes. "This wasn't supposed to happen. I never wanted you or your family to get hurt. It's why I tried to leave. I love them. I love you."

The raging storm outside had nothing on the volatile darkness that brewed in his face. Lips taut, nostrils flared, he pierced her with a lethal glare. "Get. In. The. Shelter."

"Piper, come on," his mother's gentle voice drew her out of the stinging rejection so clear in Colton's expression.

Stumbling into the small chamber with his mom, Piper couldn't look at Mrs. Neeley or McKenna. Instead, she dropped into a heap on the floor and buried her head in her arms.

"Seal the vault. Don't let her go anywhere. Don't tell her the combination. If she tries anything, shoot her."

"Oh, Colton."

"I mean it. Don't defy me, Mom."

"Now, that's enough. Just—"

"If I see her outside, I will nail her."

Even above Piper's stuttering breath, she heard his mother gasp. "Colton, don't—"

"She brought them here. It's her fault Pop is dead. *Don't* let her out."

With a morose groaning, the steel door swung shut. *Thud.* And with it went any hope for. . .hope.

Yeshua. . .forgive me. There was no way out of this. Her selfishness had killed a very good man. Her goal of keeping her father alive had cost Colton's father his life. Colton would never understand. Or forgive her. She didn't deserve forgiveness.

A warm pressure against her side drew Piper's head up. She looked to the right.

McKenna pressed against her, and when Piper lifted her arm, the little girl laid her head in her lap. "I don't like when Daddy gets mad. It scares me." Blue eyes peered up at her. "Does it scare you?"

More tears streamed down her face as she nodded mutely. If only this precious four-year-old could understand how scared—no, terrified—Piper was at this moment.

"Nana says Daddy'll be better once he calms down. We shouldn't take it personally."

Piper took in a shuddering breath. Personally was the only way to take it because she'd earned his hatred. She braved a glance at Colton's mother, who sat on the edge of the cot, staring at her feet.

I robbed her of her husband.

Again, Piper dropped her head into her hands and sobbed.

Tiny, cool arms wrapped around her shoulders—but not quite all the way. "I love you, Piper." McKenna's sweet voice was a balm to her soul. "God will make it all better. Right, Nana?"

Piper couldn't look. Didn't want to be here. Didn't want to hear or see the woman's scathing hatred for what she'd caused.

"Let's just pray, McKenna dear." His mother's voice sounded unsure and strained. "That's the best we can do."

The woman's quiet words battered Piper's desperation and plucked the last thread of control from her fingers. "It's all my fault. I'm so sorry. I didn't mean for this to happen."

"I. . .I don't imagine you did." Mrs. Neeley looked down again.

Piper stared at Mrs. Neeley through blurry eyes. She used her sleeves to dry her tears. "How. . .how can you be so? . . . I killed your husband!"

CHAPTER 15

W hat do we know?"

Colton passed Max a carbine. "At least one shooter, probably not working alone."

"Why do you say that?" Midas glanced over his shoulder from where he kept point.

"Sniper's shooting. . . What's he planning to do, kill us all?"

With a shrug, Midas turned back to the hall he monitored. "He's got the lead. Why not?"

Threading his arms through a flak vest, Colton shook his head. "No. They came for Piper."

Max seemed unfazed as he went over the M4 with a practiced eye.

The news brought Midas around. "Piper?" He hadn't been there the night Colton, Max, and Griffin cleaned up after the mess at Piper's home.

"Don't ask because I don't know." He knew people were after her. The why was another thing. And the truth of that grated on Colton.

"That's going to change," Max said as he donned his own vest. "What's the plan?"

He appreciated his friend's like-mindedness. "I'm going to the roof. I can get there through the loft. I'm going to find them and take them out."

"Whoa," Midas said. "Don't we want information from these guys?"

Colton couldn't hide the glare. "They aren't here to talk. If they were, they'd have rung the doorbell."

With a curt nod, Midas accepted it.

Max pulled a hat brim down low. "I'm going to head out the back, see if I can track down the movement we caught out by the corral."

"Be careful," Colton said. "Tucker ain't had the hay loaded, so there's lots of places for them to ambush us from. If you can get to the gazebo, there are enough shadows to conceal you—but not if they have thermals."

"Which you thought they did."

"Which I plan to remedy first thing."

Max waited.

"The only place they could've gotten such a clean line of sight on my father was at the old Johnson house across the way. It's been empty for the last two years. Nobody'd know if they were there."

"Except you."

Grim at his plan, Colton nodded as he passed out the ear mics. "And I don't take kindly to trespassers."

"I'm going to the barn." Midas slung an M16 around his shoulder and then stuffed a Glock in his leg holster. "Man, you sure know how to stock up." He grinned as he assessed his weaponry. "What an arsenal!"

"It wasn't meant to be an arsenal. Just. . ." His heart squeezed. He gripped his Remington tight, his pulse thundering. "It's what we used to do, my pop and me. Collect guns." His graze raked over the treasure. The early nickel Remington Model 1875, single action Army revolver. Or the Winchester 1873 Saddle Ring Carbine with the special butt stamp.

The ache burned hard and deep. He'd never see his father's eyes glow as he worked to restore any of the antiquated weapons or as they stalked gun shows and dealers to unearth the next treasure.

Max patted his shoulder. "We'll get 'em."

Colton wished he could say he was okay, that he'd compartmentalized again. But he wasn't, he hadn't. Everything churned like a tornado through his gut. "Let's do this."

Again, Midas gave that cockeyed grin. "I almost feel sorry for these unfriendlies. They don't know who they're messing with."

Colton hiked up the stairs, flanked right, and headed into the loft. As he moved, he heard Midas and Max leave the house. With each step, he reminded himself that if he didn't calm the rage, he'd never nail the target. Even as his foot hit the top step, the sound of gunfire cracked the stormy night.

"Shooter west of property." Midas grunted through the coms. "In position, negative contact."

"Tucker's hay. That's gotta be where he's hiding." Practiced. All too practiced at shutting down his emotional pool, Colton reached for the string dangling from the ceiling. He slung the Remington over his shoulder and tugged on the knob.

"Negative line of sight," Midas whispered.

The panel pulled downward, and a ladder unfolded. He hustled up the steps, flattening himself as he dragged himself over the wood-plank floor. Then, he turned back and drew the ladder back up. Once he secured the latch, Colton belly-crawled to the side.

He didn't need to get close to the slats in the vent. Not with his scope. Still, he prayed the sniper hadn't located him. Coming up the backside of the house, he hoped there'd been enough walls and concrete blocking his thermal pattern. Because if the sniper did have thermal imaging, as Colton suspected, things were about to get mighty interesting.

"In position," Frogman announced. "Negative contact."

Things were a mite too negative for Colton. Time to fix that.

He lay with his arm folded under the stock of his Remington 700 and peered through the scope. Black flashed against the reticle. Colton adjusted, and the scope peeked through the slats. Across the front yard. Through the pouring elements and dirt road. Straight through the sycamore trees to the abandoned house. He lifted his head and used his own thermals.

"Cowboy in position." He wouldn't say it. Wouldn't admit he hadn't found the sniper. That opened too many possibilities. Besides, he'd just set up shop. He scanned the roofline, taking extra time with the dormers and the ridiculous turret.

Jaw clenched, he lowered the thermal to the top floor. Swept from side to side. Nothing. Colton frowned. That didn't make sense. A sniper went to high ground for the best possible advantage. Why couldn't he find him?

Come on, you piece of dirt. Where are you?

Though common sense defied it, he probed the lower level. Everything bled a cold, heartless shade of blue. But no red or yellow, nothing indicating heat signatures.

"Do not take revenge, my friends, but leave room for God's wrath, for it is written: 'It is mine to avenge; I will repay,' says the Lord."

Colton blinked away the scripture and settled his finger in the trigger well. Refocused on finding the coward who'd gunned down his father in cold blood. His father. . .who had on his pajamas and merely wanted to climb under the covers and get a good night's rest. His father.

Through ragged breathing, Colton stared through the thermal scope. If he had to walk over there and stuff the bullet between the guy's eyes, he would.

The colors shifted. *Red!* His pulse sped. He started to ease back the trigger—but then stopped as the blur of red registered. Cat. He bit back a curse. Blood pumping, anger churning, he let out a shaky breath. Chided himself for being so out of control.

On the right side of the house, Colton heard weapons' fire.

"Tango down," Midas said with a grunt.

Which fueled Colton's desire to find this puke who'd sniped his father. Calming his breathing, he trailed the thermals along the house again. First floor. Second floor. Roofline. Second—wait!

A blue form. . .with a little green and yellow. . .shifted. A smudge of red showed, but just barely. The genius must be lying with a cooling pack or something.

Just means you'll die cold. Immediately, Colton sighted the target. Took note of the elements. "Target acquired."

"We've got inbound chopper," Max hissed through the coms. "And it ain't ours."

"How do you know?"

"Too low and too slow. Commercial grade."

Colton tuned out the chatter and dialed the gun. He wasn't going to lose this guy. And it seems he'd been waiting for his ride home. Which was just fine with Colton. He'd send him home all right. He eased the trigger back.

The tiny sonic boom signaled the firing. Colton chambered another round and stared through the thermals again. The figure lay slumped to the side. "Tango down."

Yet he found no satisfaction. None. Just a thirst for more.

"Oh sh—"

Booom!

White shattered the night. The heady roar of an explosion rumbled, bringing a shockwave that rattled the house and boards beneath Colton's belly.

He rolled onto his side, as if he could see through the rafters to the barn. The garage. "What happened?"

"They took out the gazebo—RPG." Max said. "I'm in the pond but okay."

Of course he was. Max the Navy SEAL.

"Midas, get out of the barn," Max ordered. "They're going to bring it down."

The barn. Firefox. Hershey. The others. Colton scrambled from the attic and headed for the stairs. If they took out the barn with the horses stabled, then—

BOOOOM!

The impact sent Colton sprawling. He caught himself two steps down and waited, steadying his breath. Then pushed himself to the hall. He squinted through the sheer curtains. A hole gaped in the side of the barn.

Horses darted out in wild panic. But. . .he didn't see Hershey. Or Firefox. He keyed his mic. "Midas, report."

Static.

"Midas, report!"

Static.

Colton sprinted for the back door.

Bloodied hands.

Piper couldn't drag her gaze from Mrs. Neeley's bloodied hands. Stained trying to save her husband. The husband that Piper's presence had killed.

She darted a glance around the small, dimly lit room. A roll of paper towels sat on a tall, thin refrigerator in the corner. A shelf supported the weight of several dozen bottles of water. Piper moved from her spot, lifted the paper towels and a jug of water.

Bereft, she knelt before Mrs. Neeley. Terrified she'd shove her away, fully expecting the woman's full wrath, Piper slowly unwound a sheet and tore it off. Then she dumped some water over it. . .and with a steadying breath, she reached for Mrs. Neeley's hands.

The woman pulled her arm away.

Rejection stabbed Piper.

Then, slowly, a hand returned, extended toward her.

The gesture lured Piper's gaze to Mrs. Neeley's. But the woman's gaze was fixed on some indeterminate spot by the door. Eyes glossed.

With all the care and gentleness she could muster, Piper wiped the wet towel across the woman's veiny, bony hands. So small, so delicate—yet so strong. Now, Mrs. Neeley would have to be stronger. She didn't have a husband. Though Piper had tried to keep her own tears at bay over the last half hour, she couldn't anymore. Not holding the woman's hand. Not cleaning the blood from her hands.

Soon, McKenna came and sat on the cot next to her grandmother, watching the ministrations.

What bugged Piper was the dark spots crusted beneath Mrs. Neeley's fingernails. She couldn't get it cleaned. Maybe. . .maybe if she balled up some towels. Piper did that and then poured the water straight from the jug over Mrs. Neeley's fingers.

Still didn't work.

She searched for a solution.

"Some stains you can't remove."

Her gaze shot to the woman's. And then she slumped and pressed her cheek against the semi-cleaned hand. She cried. And cried. Sobbed.

And Colton's mother sat in the silence.

At some point—Piper had no idea how long it'd been that she cried—a rumble snaked around the shelter. Her gaze shot to the ceiling, the four corners. The door. Though the steel and concrete room vibrated, she detected no structural damage.

"Was that thunder, Nana?"

When she looked back, Piper found McKenna curled up against Mrs. Neeley.

"Of course it is, sweetie. Remember, it was storming when you went to bed."

Nodding as if in agreement, McKenna's shell-shocked eyes told a different story. She was scared. She didn't believe the noise was thunder. Of course, being down in this shelter probably didn't help the story.

Piper herself didn't believe the noise was thunder. She'd heard bombings from shelters before. And that's exactly what this sounded like.

"Why don't you lie down, McKenna, and rest?"

"But I'm not tired."

"Well, I am." Mrs. Neeley stretched along the cot and pulled the little one against her. She tugged a wool blanket over them and let out a ragged sigh.

Somehow, seeing the two of them cuddling made Piper feel more left out and alone than she'd been in many months. The move told her what Mrs. Neeley thought of her. *Some stains you can't remove.* Was she saying she'd never forgive her?

And what about Colton? Oh, she had no grand delusion that he'd forgive her. But was he safe out there? Was he still alive? How she despised and hated herself, to the very core of her being. Like a rank, poisoned well. That's what she was.

She wanted to tell Mrs. Neeley everything, but the thought of sharing such a violent story in front of McKenna kept Piper quiet.

Slumping into one of the two chairs at the folding table, Piper—

A sudden, intense terror seized her. She shoved to her feet. Stared at the door.

"What is it?"

She glanced back, surprised to find Mrs. Neeley standing beside the cot.

This was it. She had to tell her. "I have something in my pack that those men want. If they get it, they'll have no reason to keep me alive—or any of us."

The woman stared at her, eyes blank, without comprehension.

"I have to go up there."

A pained expression rippled through the older woman's face. "No, we stay here until Colton returns."

"But—"

"*Don't* do this." Her eyes flamed, and her thin, wrinkled lips pulled taut. "I might be small, but I'm not weak. You're not going out there."

Piper rushed to her. "Listen to me, please." She clasped Mrs. Neeley's hands.

Wary eyes waited.

"I'll tell you what's happening, but you have to promise me one thing."

"No," Mrs. Neeley said vehemently. "No, I don't have to make any promises. Not on a night like this."

She deserved that. Piper knew she did. But it tore at her. Deep and painful. "You're right. You don't." Letting go of the woman's hands felt like letting go of hope and belief that somehow this wretched night might end without more damage or loss of life. She shuffled back to the table and slumped in the chair again. "I'm sorry. I didn't mean. . ." She snorted at the words that seemed to be the fare for the night. *I'd be better off dead.*

Metal dug into her back as she pinched the bridge of her nose.

A scraping noise drew her eyes open. Mrs. Neeley sat across from her, hands folded on the table. A steely resolve sparkled in her blue-gray irises. "Tell me."

"I'm here. I'm here," came Midas's coughed reply just as Colton stepped into the night. "Barn's blown."

"What about the horses?" Colton asked, a metallic taste squirting over his tongue.

"I don't know, man. I can't see nothing 'cept smoke and fire."

That's exactly what greeted Colton. His barn cracking and splintering, collapsing like a wounded elephant. The front went down first.

A spark to the right jerked his gaze to the sky.

His heart rapid-fired as he spotted the chopper hovering at the back of the manicured property and just over the wild tree line. A whistle screamed through the night.

Boom!

The concussion shoved Colton off his feet. He flipped and landed with a thud. Scrambling back to his feet, he stared at the house. His loft. His loft was burning. Fury coursed through him. At least his mother and McKenna were safe in the shelter. They could survive even under a nuke attack. He'd made sure.

"Tango in the south border trees." Max didn't sound happy. "How many are there?"

Another screaming shot through the dark. Colton plunged into the dirt. The boom ricocheted through the night, a latent echo of the thunder of the storm.

But just as fast, he saw another burst of light. *Again?*

The sky lit up like a July Fourth fireworks show. The chopper that had attacked spun. Flames shot out from the belly. It careened toward the corral in a blaze.

"What the heck did that?" Midas shouted as the helo tumbled and came to rest just feet from the huddled mass of a barn.

The sky seemed to shift. And only then did Colton see and hear the Black Hawk charging toward them.

'Bout time. But a little late. His panic subsided a morsel knowing Legend and the Kid would join the fight. Still, it was too late. His father was dead. His home, barn—everything obliterated.

He gripped his Remington and headed toward the front of the house. He saw a blur of movement in the house.

His blood ran cold. How'd they get in the house? He slung his Remington over his shoulder.

Who covered the front?

Colton leaped up the stairs, MEU .45 in hand. He gripped the door handle and tried to negotiate the shapes and shadows amid the hungry flames engulfing his home. Although he could make out two shapes, far apart, he couldn't decipher who was friend or foe.

Foe. Definitely foe. The girls were in the shelter.

Adrenaline spiked, he stepped into the house. Working to reduce the amount of smoke-filled air he breathed, Colton side-stepped toward the living room, where he'd seen someone.

The main beam that had stretched from one end of the living room and across the dining room, lay on the floor, in three pieces. The furniture decimated.

Crunch. Crack.

Colton whipped to the right.

A figure whirled toward him. Wide eyes.

"Mom, what're you—" His question choked off as he noticed she darted her gaze to the hall. Where his father had died. Where they'd left him.

And that's where he saw Piper.

Fury had no ally so strong as Colton at this moment. He raised his weapon. Sighted between her shoulders, the weapon blurred but her form clear and distinct. "Piper!"

She yanked toward him, panic etched into her tawny features.

He pulled his focus to the sights, her form now blurred. "I warned you."

"No, please. I—"

His mother lunged. "Colton, no!"

CHAPTER 16

If he killed her, could he live with himself?

Frozen amid that question and the downpour that forced him to blink, Colton stared at Piper. Her wide eyes. The way she kept glancing into the hall, her body partially angled that way.

"Colton, no!"

Like a distant echo, he heard his mother's shout. Heard the thunder, the steady *thwump* of the Black Hawk's rotors. The south wall had been all but blown out. Home destroyed. Father killed. . .

"Cowboy." Max's voice hissed through the coms. "What're you doing?"

What did he think he was doing? Ending this. Stopping Piper from hurting his family anymore.

This isn't about your family.

Sure it was. His father lay dead just a few feet from Piper.

It's about you and her.

There was no him and her. Not now. Not ever. He walled off his heart.

"Colton," his mother's voice, soothing and calmer—calmer than it should be—came at him. "Are you with us, son? You here?"

He blinked. Stretched his jaw. She thought he was having another flashback. But he wasn't. That was the point. He was here, in his home, decimated by grenades, gunfire, and murder.

"Stay back, Mom." He pierced Piper with a glare. "If you move, so help me God, I'll shoot." And he wouldn't miss. He'd been ingrained with the concept that if he fired, it was to exert deadly force. And with the maelstrom of fury surging within him, it'd be very deadly.

Piper propped her head against the wall, crying, as she looked at

177

him. Palms flat on the plaster, she remained still.

But. . .then he noticed. . .she was reaching for something with her left hand.

Colton tensed. Jerked his weapon firmer. "I mean it!" He moved forward several quick paces.

She clenched her eyes shut.

Hurried footsteps came from behind. "Cowboy!" Max shouted. In seconds, he sidled up next to him. A hand on the shoulder. "Cowboy," he said, this time much softer. He reached toward the MEU .45 and rested a hand on it.

Colton refused to lower it.

"The team's here. Let them take her in to Lambert."

"She killed my father."

Max squeezed his shoulder. "Let it go, man." Then, with a slow, fluid move, Max stepped in front of the weapon, barrel to his chest. "Not like this."

He met his friend's dark eyes. A knot tightened in his chest.

"You'd never forgive yourself."

It'd only been a fraction of a move, but Colton's tension relaxed.

And in that instant, Max flipped the MEU out of his hands.

Stunned, Colton glanced at his weapon. Then at his friend. Then to the scene unfolding behind them. A half-dozen men swarmed into the house, slithering across the open area with tactical precision.

Piper leaned down and lifted something. . .McKenna, from the floor.

Colton's heart crashed into his stomach. Mickey. She was trying to get Mickey? His mother rushed over the broken beam and gathered her granddaughter into her arms as the team secured Piper.

Crying, his mother buried her face in Mickey's shoulder as his daughter cried, too.

Flanked by two Marines, Piper picked her way over the debris of his home as they led her toward the gaping hole, no doubt heading to the helo.

Hands cuffed, head down, Piper looked broken and shattered.

Just like me.

Two-hundred forty-three days of reconnaissance told him she was worth getting to know. One date and one kiss told him he wanted to marry her. One disaster, and he realized he never knew her.

"Let's load up, man."

"I'm not leaving my father—"

"Don't have to. The authorities arrived." Max nodded toward the front where a gurney now bore a sheet-covered body. His father's body. In numb silence, he watched as the gurney jockeyed around the furniture, out the door, and out of sight.

Emptiness devoured Colton.

Boarding the chopper, the vibration of the helo that left his legs numb, the unloading at the warehouse...blurred in his memory. He'd brought her to his home to watch over her. It'd been an order, one he probably could've refused. But if he dug deep, if he considered his motivations in the light of honest-to-God truth, he had to admit he wanted to protect her.

He never thought he was the one who needed protection.

It didn't matter anymore. It was over.

Bang!

The sharp noise snapped his gaze to the right. He stared, adjusting his eyes to the dim lighting in the warehouse. Oh yeah. Warehouse.

A warm presence settled near him. He glanced to the side....

"Hi, Cowboy."

His heart started to find Dr. Avery next to him. Where had she come from? He glanced back down the hall. The door. Is that what he'd heard seconds earlier? If she'd come through there, then she must've walked down the hall. But her movement had never registered.

Aw, man. He wasn't up to this. He shook his head. "Look, Doc, I'm not in the mood."

"Is there ever a mood that makes a man want to talk to a shrink?"

Glancing at her out of the corner of his eye, Colton determined to brick up this chasm in his heart. "Don't reckon."

She placed a cup in his hands, and as the warmth bled through the Styrofoam, only then did he feel the chill that wrapped around him. "You've had a brutal night."

He stared at the goose bumps pimpling his flesh. "You could say that."

"They're worried about you."

"Who?"

Dr. Avery nodded toward the conference room.

The forms that had been but mere shadows in his awareness took solid form. The team—Griffin stood like a drill sergeant, arms folded and feet apart as he stared back at him. Midas and Max sat at the table, sipping something from Styrofoam cups. The Kid paced.

"Thought you weren't supposed to see us together or know who we were."

"All I know is that the man I'm sitting in front of now is a very different man than the one who sat with me in the park last month."

Colton ground his teeth. She wanted him to talk. Tell him what he was thinking. Feeling. He wouldn't. This nightmare didn't need a voice. It needed to be buried, burned, deep-sixed. Whatever it took.

"I keep losing you."

He held his peace.

"Does reality seem tenuous?"

He eyed her.

"You've been in combat many, many times. What's different?" She shrugged. "I mean, shots were fired, you did your sniper duty. What was so different?"

A demon rose within him. "My father died!" He pulled himself straight. "And the woman I thought I loved is responsible!" Colton shoved to his feet. Gathered his anger, his voice, his screaming desire to pelt this whole stupid building with a million bullets. Rigid, he gave a curt nod. "Good-bye, Dr. Avery."

He spun on his boots and stalked down the hall, flinging the cup in the trash.

"Your men want to know if they can count on you."

Just as he opened his mouth to answer, Colton saw into one of the many offices. Through one, and in a darkened corner, Piper sat in a chair. Four heavily armed soldiers guarded her. She looked up as he passed—and dropped her gaze twice as fast. The brokenness he saw in her was only a hollow echo of what had cratered his heart.

With a punch, he flipped open the door to the locker room, her words blazing a trail down his spine. *Count on me?* No. . .no, never again.

It was over—him and Piper.

It was over—him, sniping, combat.

It was all over.

DAY FIVE

A village near the Jordanian Border, 02:21:45 hours

Hidden on the roof of a nearby abandoned shop, Azzan watched. Anger coiled around his heart, the poison speeding through his veins as he watched the scene before him. Authorities encircled the vehicle. Ambulance. Fire trucks. Police. Head cradled in his hands, he stared at the scene, disbelieving how utterly he'd failed. Laid out on the thin roof, he pressed his nose against the plaster. Breathed in the dust, the smoke, the ash, the foul stench of burning rubber and metal.

He'd almost completed his mission. And now—they were gone.

Shouts drew his attention back to the scene. Police shouted to one another as firefighters removed their gear. One raised his hands and shrugged. Curious. They weren't pulling bodies from the flames. What was going on?

Two officers inched closer and tried to peek around the flames. Finally, one shook his head. Waved the others away. "Empty," the man said in Arabic.

Empty? The Hummer was empty? How was that possible? Azzan perked up.

A shadow shifted several buildings down, snagging his attention. He scampered off the roof and dropped into an alley. He slunk through the tight confines, working his way toward the place he'd seen the movement.

Jogging down the narrow space between the buildings, he maintained a watchful eye. A police car cruised past, and Azzan pushed himself into a corner. Waited till the coast was clear, then hurried on. He searched the alley. The shops. Jiggled door handles. Flung back curtains that served as doors. Nothing. He surveyed the area.

Foolish to hope. . .

Slumped against a door, he gripped his knees. Closed his eyes. It couldn't be over. Not this quickly. He couldn't have lost them, failed the mission that he'd sacrificed his career for. His head ached, and his arm throbbed from the bullet graze. Eyes closed, he tried to gather himself, tried to get his head back in gear.

He straightened, cast one more long glance toward the road, where just past a tangle of pedestrians, he could see the smoke pouring like a specter through the air. Azzan shook his head and pushed off the wall. When he turned, he found himself staring into beguiling eyes.

Heart kick-started.

Raiyah stood in a shop, behind a grimy and cracked window.

After double-checking the alley, Azzan hustled into the shop.

Surprise and tears lit through her eyes. She nodded.

"Where is he?"

She motioned toward a corner, where a weakened frame sat propped against the wall. A crooked smile came into the gaunt, bearded face. "Azzan."

"We need to hurry."

The old man sighed and rubbed a bandaged hand over his bearded face. With a frustrated huff, he glanced at the dingy wrappings and shook his head. "We are out of time."

"I know."

"No. They've begun. . .f–final phase." A mottled lower lip, fattened by abuse and reddened with dehydration quivered. "I did not find the last piece." A long, ragged breath issued from him. "Bombs. . .on. . .way."

CHAPTER 17

Air rushed in under the door, dank and damp. A piece of paper carried on the small current, swirled and fluttered over the dull gray cement floor. For a second, it settled over a crevice, then another draft caught the scrap and flung it against the desk. Yet again, it moved. . .slid, flipped away under the forceful fingers of the stormy wind punctuating the foul night.

Clomp!

Piper jumped as one of the soldiers stamped his booted foot on the paper. Heart racing at the sudden move, she realized how much she and the scrap had in common. Swirling, caught in a current and driven without control. Then stomped—her heart. Smashed. Smothered.

She lowered her head.

Light spilled across the floor as a door opened and drew her gaze up. A woman in a gray wool skirt and black heels stood on the threshold. "Miss Blum?" She motioned Piper into the small office.

Hesitantly and with quick glances to the heavy guns guarding her, she rose, clutching her backpack to her chest, and crossed the dark space. Her steps slowed at the threshold. Carpet glue stared up from a stripped floor, looking forlorn and aged. Dingy white walls did little to lighten the semi-darkened room. Even the bulb hanging from the ceiling couldn't chase the shadows from the corner office. No doubt hiding its secrets as well.

The old man she'd seen at her apartment—was that really just a week ago?—rose to his feet behind a large oak desk. Flanking him from behind, two more men dressed in black from head to toe and cradling M4s in their arms leaned back against the window ledges.

One man she recognized from the night her apartment was hit—the one on the right who looked more like a tower of muscle than a guard. She wondered at how that flak vest fit over his large chest and shoulders. Younger, the other guard wore his youthfulness well, but his edge was no less than his counterpart. Both seemed ready to kill her.

Piper skated a look around the room. A divider blocked her view of the far left corner. A door sat ajar, but not enough to reveal what it contained.

"Please," the older man said and extended a hand toward the chairs that faced his desk. "Let's talk. My name is Olin Lambert. My position, well, isn't something you need to know at this point."

As she tucked herself into the nearest seat, Piper groped for the faith that had carried her through the last year. It felt out of reach. . . out of date. This man clearly had power—both of presence and firepower, which told her this wasn't a typical interrogation. This wasn't the police department. FBI? He hadn't shown her a badge—wasn't that required?

Beside her, the woman eased into the remaining chair and crossed her legs.

"I daresay there's a lot to cover," he said as he lowered himself back to his chair. "So, let's establish one thing, right now." His aged but penetrating eyes pinned her to the seat. "Absolute honesty. Are we agreed?"

Honesty? Was he going to reciprocate? What did it matter? "I'm tired. I can't. . .can't do this anymore. No more secrets." She smoothed her hand down her jeans. "No more running."

He leaned forward, folded his hands over the clean desk. "I'm listening."

Piper's fingers coiled around her backpack again. She tightened her grip, sighed, then began rummaging through it.

Quick movements jerked her gaze up.

The soldiers, in a snap, had their weapons trained on her. Their precision and quick reflexes bespoke military training. She should know. She'd done her stint in the Israeli Army. And for that reason, she paused.

Mr. Lambert raised a hand. "Stand down, gentlemen."

Gaze skipping between the men, who lowered their weapons but not the heightened alert she saw in their eyes, she dug into the pack.

Traced the contours of the box. Prayed beyond her most desperate hopes this wasn't a mistake. She lifted out the key to her father's location, and set the music box on the desk.

The old man didn't budge, flinch, or blink. He wasn't going to make this easy.

Slowly, she let her fingers trail away from the box, from its familiarity, the reassurance she'd found just having it in her possession. Piper let out a long breath. Steadied herself and gave herself one last admonishment that this had to be done. There'd been too much bloodshed.

She gulped the acid pooling at the back of her throat. In essence, she was about to hand her father over to people she did not truly know. She pinned her gaze on the man studying her. "My name is Kelila Liora Rosenblum." Though she'd wanted to appear confident and assured, the way her name came out, almost whispered, betrayed her.

Something in the weathered face shifted—the soft lines gone. "Piper Blum is the name I was given," General Lambert said. "One of my best men came to me, said maybe he'd found the girl he wanted to spend the rest of his life with."

Heat and cold washed down her shoulders at the same time. Colton.

"Guess you had him fooled."

"I—I . . ." Piper let the words die on her tongue. She'd lost Colton. No matter what she said, it didn't change all the things she'd done wrong and the deceit she'd had to employ to stay alive and keep her father safe. She captured her lower lip between her teeth to stop the trembling.

He considered her, his aged eyes betraying nothing of what he thought or felt. "You see, he was required to have you vetted. But you aren't quite what you told him, are you? Tell me, Miss *Rosen*blum, why did you drag him into all this?"

"Me? I didn't. . . . He invited me. . . . I . . ." She gulped back the tears. "I'm here because of what I've done to him. I'm willing to give you all my secrets, all I have . . . anything to . . ."

"Please—go ahead." His brows knitted. "Enlighten us."

She flashed her eyes at his taunting. If she didn't keep going, she'd lose the nerve. Maybe it was too late, but her father never would've wanted someone to die. "My father is Yitshak Rosenblum, a member of the board of directors of the National Strategic Studies Institute." She tried to wet her lips, but her mouth was as parched as her lips. "Approximately eighteen months ago, he discovered a massive plot against Israel."

"That's nothing new." He sat back, almost disinterested. "Nations and leaders for thousands of years have tried to wipe out the Jewish nation."

"This plot, he'd said, would make Israel hemorrhage from within." She shook her head. "I know no details beyond that. I cannot answer what he found." A point of contention between them because Baba did not trust her enough to even provide her with that information. "Whatever it is, he feared for his life, yes. But his greater concern was for our homeland."

"Why go into hiding? Why not turn over what he found to the authorities at once? Was he a coward—protecting only himself?"

A dart of fury speared her. "My father is no coward." She gulped and tried to slow her hammering heart. "He did not have all the puzzle pieces but enough to know the threat was beyond imagination. He said the betrayal was too deep and far spread to know whom to trust."

Silence dropped over the room. Only the rustle of the soldier's material and the rain tapping against the windows could be heard. Piper waited, staring at the box. Hoping she hadn't just murdered her father.

Finally, a squeak from his chair snapped her gaze up. "What's the music box?"

"It is the only way to contact him. Within it is an encoded chip that contains passwords, so to speak, that will transmit messages to him. He has a duplicate. It's the only way I have been able to speak to him."

Mr. Lambert sat forward. Flipped open a folder. "You entered the U.S. five years ago as an exchange student."

Her heart skipped a beat.

"Two years later, you returned to Beersheba with a bachelor's degree."

He knew? Her identity?

"How did you reenter the U.S.? You did not use your passport."

She swallowed. They could ship her back, accuse her of espionage. Throw her in prison. She'd thought of these things many, many dark nights as she lay in her apartment, alone and scared. "My father handed me the passport with my new identity as he put me on the train for the Tel Aviv airport." She shrugged. "I don't know how or where he got it."

"But you have a suspicion."

"He had many friends—*loyal* friends, more like family than friends, in addition to hundreds of admirers for his extensive work with NSSI."

"Intriguing—you don't know who?"

"No."

"What of family?"

She let out a soft snort. "My father's brothers adhered to the old ways. Baba—my father's acceptance of Yeshua as the Messiah severed their relationship. They would no more help him or me than they would a terrorist."

"No aunt or...uncle?"

A figure emerged from the adjacent room. "Ah, Lily. It has been a long time, has it not?"

Piper lunged to her feet. "Uncle!"

"It's just temporary." Colton draped his hand over the steering wheel, staring through the rain-splotched window.

His mother harrumphed. "Don't even suggest—"

"Mom, it's not a suggestion, and it's not a favor." It took every ounce of effort and control he had left to keep the ugly out of his voice. He was tired. It'd been a long twenty-eight hours. He aimed the truck toward Reagan International. "It's just what is. Stay with your brother until I have something set up, until I know the danger has passed." He glanced across the cab of the truck at her. "Just do this—for me. Okay?"

She huffed. And he almost smiled as the quiet trip dragged on with the steady drone of the engine, the thwump-thwumping over the bridge, the quiet *swish* of the rain washing away the filth of the city streets, and the occasional squeak of the windshield wiper blades. They all weakened his resolve—that and her soft sniffles.

Colton glanced in the rearview mirror and eyed his daughter, sitting in her car seat, sucking her two middle fingers. His heart clenched. She hadn't done that since she was two, when Meredith died.

"We haven't even buried him," his mother whispered through her tears.

"I know." And they couldn't. Not for another three weeks since burials at Arlington were backed up. "I want Pop to have his full honors." Didn't want to settle for something quick just so they could get on with things. "It'll be done right."

She patted his leg. "Thank you." Tears glittered against her red-stained eyes. "You're just like him, keeping your calm in the face of trials."

"Don't know about that." He'd certainly lost control regarding Piper and wanted nothing more than to put her down, so quick to believe she was trying to escape again.

As he took the exit for the airport, Colton steadied the truck as it hit a rut of water—hydroplaned. He tightened his grip and worked to control the truck—and his thoughts, which were just as contrary, slipping and sliding straight into the eyes of a beautiful woman. He'd wanted so much with her. . .a life. A family. His heart seized as he realized all the dreams he'd secretly imagined with Piper at the center. Why. . .why did it have to turn out this way?

"Where's Piper?"

His mother's question speared his heart. "In custody."

"Oh, Colton—"

"Mom, don't." He followed the road around to the departure terminal, bright lights glaring and agitating his thundering headache. After a quick check of the departure schedule, he nodded. "Looks like things are on time."

She shifted to him. "Please let me stay. I'll find a place, set up home while you're gone."

He put the gear in PARK and unbuckled. "Mom, I want you and Mickey somewhere safe while I'm taking care of things. Okay?"

"I want to stay. . .with you." She licked her lips, eyes glossing over. "I need family. You, McKenna. You're all. . ." Her lips trembled. Then a sob. Buried her face in her hands. "He's gone! Oh, God help me. He's gone."

Colton drew his mother into his arms and held her close. Kissed the top of her head as he battled his own tears. They sat for several minutes in the twinkling darkness, a busy world whizzing around them and ignorant of the heartache tugging at their very souls.

"I feel so numb," she murmured against his shoulder. "But I know God is with me. He's going to take care of me."

Although he listened, Colton—for the first time in a very long time—noticed her words bounced off his hardened will. The realization stung. Thought he'd grown more than that, dug in deeper into his faith. Thought when push came to shove, he'd find his trust in God rock solid. More like putty-flimsy.

The back of his throat burned. The only thing he could think to say was, "It's not going to be the same without him."

Wow. Understatement of the year, genius.

"No, of course not. But I have you and God." His mother drew away and took a shuddering breath. She tried to smile, but he saw it for what it was: her pulling herself together, determined to be strong. With a pat on his chest, she nodded. "I'll be okay."

"I know you will. Pop always said you were cut from steel." He climbed out and walked around to the passenger side and opened the door for her.

She swung her legs around, and red eyes narrowed. "Promise me one thing, Colton."

"Sure thing, Mom."

"Don't blame Piper."

The impact of a .308 had nothing on those words. "Can't promise that."

She hopped out and planted her hands on his chest. "Colton Benjamin, if I know one thing, I know you love that girl." Cold fingers traced his cheek. "Give her a chance—"

He caught her hands, tightening his lips and heart. "Leave it alone." Though everything in him wanted to shove her back, shove away her thoughts and imploring, he ground his teeth and let go. "Please." He hated the way that word cracked and twisted.

He opened the rear passenger door and worked the buckle and harness to free Mickey. "For pity's sake, Colton. I thought I raised you better than that."

He blinked. Had she forgotten? "Pop is *dead*."

She winced at the intensity of his words. "Yes, and he was dying—and I can't help but think he's glad it was over quick instead of wasting away. But that's beside the point. Piper was protecting something very special to her."

"And it cost Pop his life." He lowered Mickey to the ground and lifted her small black duffel from the back.

" 'Greater love has no one than this, that he lay down his life for his friends.'" She smiled as the verse sailed across her lips.

He jerked back to his mom. "Yeah, a *friend*—not a woman hiding things."

"Oh," she said with a vehemence yet a gentleness that snapped something awake in him. "I beg to differ, young man. Your father believed, unequivocally, that Piper was his friend—and your soul mate. He saw it, Colton. Told me he couldn't be prouder."

"That was because he didn't know her, the *real* her."

"And who is the real her, Colton? Who is the real us?" She tapped his chest. "You have so many secrets hidden in there Who are you really? Colton, my son? Colton, the Marine? Colton, the cowboy? Tell me—what of *your* secrets? Your secrets so deadly and horrible that they have you whipped out of your mind at times."

"That's not fair, Mom. It's not the same thing." Shoulders slumped, he tried to. . . What use was it? She was right. He was whipped.

"It's a nightmare, Charles."

"Yes, but one that's been brewing for years."

Olin rounded the desk and leaned against it as they stared out over the bay of the warehouse. "Do you trust her?"

Falde chuckled. "The question is—do you?"

Running his knuckles along the edge of his jaw, Olin watched as Griffin entered the building with Max, both chatting quietly. "What I know is that she brought one of my most impervious, unassailable men to his knees." Hands on his belt, he let out a long exhale.

"Come now," Charles said as he pushed out of his chair and joined him at the window. "You cannot blame Lily for one of your men—"

"I can." Olin snapped his gaze to his old friend. "And I will. These men are the best. The best! If he hesitates. . . You don't realize what that man means to this group."

"You must realize what Lily has been through. She's a wonderful girl." His gaze skidded to the floor below.

A brand-new Camaro rolled into the parking bay, and by the time Canyon emerged from his car, the Kid arrived in his luxury SUV.

"They're all here. Except him." Would Colton show up?

"You should know, Lily is like a daughter to me. I know her. And this. . .tragedy has had a horrible toll on her." Charles turned to him with a sad smile. "For what it's worth, I know she loves this man."

"It may be too late for that." But curiosity gripped Lambert. "How can you be sure?"

"For the last eighteen months, a young girl with no resources save a pittance of an account—"

"Ten thousand dollars is not a pittance."

"Olin, she opened that account with fifteen thousand. Eighteen months ago." Brown eyes bore into his. "She has a car, a home—"

"Had. She cashed it all in, remember?"

"Exactly what Yitshak instructed her to do. She must've figured out someone was close to finding her."

"She figured it out a bit late."

With a conciliatory nod, Charles smiled. "Put aside your protective urges for this man you think she's harmed so gravely—"

"His father is dead. Killed by a sniper!"

Charles hopped out of the chair, much faster than his rounding belly should've allowed. He hurried to Olin and hovered over him. "Look at this with the skilled eyes of a general who commanded thousands, instead of a father pouting over his son." His eyes narrowed. "Do you see what I see? A twenty-six-year-old woman who thrives on family and friendship, living alone, isolated in a paltry apartment wondering if her father—the reason she's in exile—is still alive. Or if something she'd said or done has killed him. If her confessing to you has, after all this time, sent her father to his grave and wiped Israel from the map.

"She's worked hard, kept to herself—survived. Alone for a year and a half. Spent every night and weekend in a lonely apartment, afraid to make a friend or acquaintance who might be an enemy. Never dating or letting someone into her home for fear they might figure out her secret." His chest rose and fell raggedly.

Olin tried to allow the thoughts, tried to understand the sacrifice. It just seemed so small. . .but maybe because his first duty was to America. Hers was to Israel. *Pray for the peace of Jerusalem.* He stilled as the scripture sailed through his mind.

"Isolated," Charles said, his voice a pained whisper. "The concept goes against Lily's very nature." He smoothed a hand over his balding dome and returned to his chair. Let out a heavy breath. Then nodded. "What I want is to meet the man who drew my beautiful goddaughter out of that darkness, pushed her to sacrifice *everything*. Even her father."

A throaty rumble rattled the rafters of the warehouse, drawing Falde to the window once again.

"You're about to get your wish." Relief coursed through Olin as he slid his hands into his pockets, finally feeling a semblance of hope tinge his outlook. "But you may not like it—he does not look happy."

CHAPTER 18

Dawg if the team wasn't all here. Colton climbed out of the truck and adjusted the Cattle Baron, bringing the brim lower. Could he conceal what he felt if the hat shielded his eyes? When he shut the door, he spotted the silver Lexus SUV the Kid drove. Then Midas's shiny new sports car. The black Escalade. The motorcycle.

He paused, hand on the door of his truck. Considered getting back in and leaving town. Never looking back. All he wanted right now was to beeline it to Lambert's hovel on the second floor and do what he came to do. Weren't no good way, so he'd just do it and be done with it.

Instead. . .he was going to have to face the team.

As soon as he stepped into the main bay, a small crowd formed. Griffin. Max. Midas. They greeted him, their welcomes somber. But they didn't bring up the attack. For that he was glad.

He glanced up at the dingy window. "What's with the AHOD?"

A strange, knowing look drifted over Griffin's face, but then he shrugged. "He's been up there since I got here."

A cackling laugh rattled Colton's nerves as the Kid entered. "Man, it is good to be back in action." He clapped his hands twice and rushed toward them looking every bit the eager, uniformed beaver.

Colton stepped back, eyeing the stairs. . .the window. . .the stairs. "Hey, I—"

Thunk!

The echo of a slamming door snatched Colton's words and attention. He spun—froze.

His gaze rammed into Piper. She stood at an office door with Dr.

Avery and two guards. A smile that moments ago had lightened Piper's face vanished like a phantom, leaving a pale hue to her normally tawny face. Her lips hung apart as they stared at each other, until finally her gaze fell.

Aches tore through Colton. Anger over his father's death. Anger over her lies and deception.

"Whoa!" The Kid whistled. "Who's the babe?"

Colton whipped toward the runt and glowered.

Max shifted toward Marshall. "You really gotta learn when to stow it."

"What?" Ignorant as always, the Kid raised his hand toward Piper. "Look at her. She's got supermodel written all over her. She's hot!"

With a fist, Max backhanded the Kid's chest.

The look of pain exploded over Marshall's face. "Hey! I was shot there."

"Yeah," Max said as he grabbed the Kid's leather jacket and shoved him toward a huddle of tables and chairs that served as the conference table. "Well, I'm gonna shoot you somewhere else if you don't clamp that mouth."

Griffin grinned. "I think I'll help." He and Midas sauntered over to the table, each popping the Kid on the back of the head and eliciting more objections and curses.

Colton would've laughed. But considering what he'd come here to do. . .he realized how much he'd miss the guys. Their friendship. The camaraderie.

Clicking heels warned of the ladies' approach from behind.

Shoulders burning with tension, Colton held his ground, afraid if he moved he'd lose control. Lose himself.

Closer still. . .

God. . .why? Why are You doing this to me?

"Cowboy?" Dr. Avery's soft voice flitted into his mind. A warm touch to his arm. "Are you okay?"

Though he hadn't looked, he knew Piper was there. He could smell her—that unique light, floral scent that was everything Piper. Muscles trembling, he worked to open his eyes. "Doctor." The stiff, barely formed word ground from between his lips, but his gaze wasn't on the team psychiatrist. It was riveted to the woman who'd shaken the foundation of his life.

In his periphery, he saw Dr. Avery draw back, her eyes revealing surprise at his greeting as she turned toward Piper with a protective touch.

"Why are you here?" Colton asked Piper. She should've been arrested. Removed from here, from his life. Whatever the story, it couldn't be good or legal. She should be behind bars.

Two men emerged from the stairwell, snapping Colton's attention away from Piper. He watched as the general approached with another man.

"Please have a seat, gentlemen. We have little time and much to discuss." The general's voice boomed through the large warehouse. Specifically, he turned to Colton. "Please, join us."

He should finish this now. Like he intended. "General, I need to talk to you."

"I know." Kind, aged eyes met his. "But first—you'll have to hear me out." The smile kneaded Colton's frustration, but also forced him to acquiesce.

With a nod, he moved to the conference area. Instead of sitting, he leaned against a small, apartment-style fridge.

What bothered him, though, was the way Lambert guided Piper to the grouping as though she was a prize, an asset.

"Gentlemen, a lot has transpired in the last thirty hours."

And expired.

Like my dad.

"Our deepest regret is that our own Cowboy has lost his father."

Silence gaped loud and screaming, with each inch of space between Colton and heaven feeling like a lifetime of pain and heartache.

"Unfortunately, we do not have time to grieve." Olin's expression quickly grew grim. "I need you to hear from this young lady."

Tension coiled around his gut like a rattler ready to strike. Listen to Piper? He was supposed to shove aside his own grief to listen to her? What happened to team loyalty?

Olin nodded to her. "Please." He stepped aside as he motioned for her to stand before the group.

"You've got my attention," the Kid mused.

Colton experienced a puny amount of justice when Max popped the Kid's head again and Griffin growled for their youngest team member to shut up.

Arms folded over his chest, Colton lowered his chin. He didn't want to hear what she had to say. His heart careened through his chest and into his stomach like the chopper that had been taken down by the Black Hawk.

"My name is Kelila Liora Rosenblum."

Colton closed his eyes. *Kel-what?* Did he really not even know her real name?

"My father is Yitshak Rosenblum of the National Security Studies Institute."

"Come again?" Max's question drew Colton's gaze.

She wet her lips—and Colton nearly cursed as the moment of their kiss blasted his memory banks. "It's based out of Tel Aviv, an independent academic institute that studies key issues relating to Israel's national security and Middle East affairs."

Israel? Middle East. That had the makings of some serious trouble. Colton let his gaze skip along the cracks in the cement as he pondered that news.

"Israel," Max echoed Colton's thoughts. "As in Jews, Temple of the Mount, Jesus, and all that?"

"Please," Lambert cut in. "I know you will all have many questions, but let Miss Rosenblum finish. Our time is very short."

Time short meant a mission. A mission related to what Piper was saying?

Heart disengaged, he allowed his decision to take root—become as hard and firm as the building's foundation beneath his feet.

"Go ahead, Miss Rosenblum," Lambert said.

Her soft voice drifted into the stale warehouse air. "In March of last year, my father stumbled upon a plot against our homeland—"

"Israel." Griffin's voice boomed.

"Yes." She cleared her throat. "I—I don't know the details, but what he found terrified him. He spent every minute at the university for months, trying to unravel whatever it was. Then, one night, he flew into the house, shouting, yelling at me to pack my things at once."

The swelling emotion in her words drew Colton's unwilling gaze up—and found hers pinned on him. She continued as she looked into his eyes, "My father rushed me out of the house, into a waiting cab. En route to the train station, he hurriedly explained that there were forces so powerful behind what he'd found that he was certain they would kill us before he could unravel it all and stop them."

Was this supposed to make him feel sympathy or something? Sadly, he reckoned it did, but he stomped the butterfly flitting across his conscience and killed it.

She tucked her chin and skirted a look at the general. "In fact, he believed that is how my brother died—somehow he was connected." She shrugged, and though he wasn't sure, he thought he saw tears. "He said he was going into hiding, and that I must go to America and never tell anyone who I was."

"Why is he hiding?" Griffin asked.

Piper's shoulders slowly lifted, then dropped. "I don't know."

"No, I'm asking—why hide? Why not report whatever this was or tell someone?"

"Wait, wait, wait." Max was on his feet, knuckling the table as he stared down at it.

Surprised, Colton's attention shifted to Max and the deep, familiar scowl on the man's face. Not happy. Didn't seem to be buying Piper's tale.

"You're standing there, one day after skilled killers descend on my friend's home, kill his father, blow up his home, nearly kill me and the others. . ." Max looked around the room. Then his left eye narrowed. "And you won't tell us what your father found? Do we *look* stupid?"

Colton considered Piper, watched her flick a nervous glance to the general, then Colton, then back to Max.

Max looked to Lambert. "We're already down one man. And if I'm right, there's a mission around this woman's story. A half-cocked story. I won't let the team go into something like this without full disclosure. If she won't talk, then we walk."

Hands at her side, Piper took a step forward. "I can postulate. That's all."

Midas slumped back against his chair. "Then let's postulate!"

"My father was working on a project that would aide Israel in protecting itself against nuclear weapons and threats. NSSI's purpose is to find ways, through negotiations and other such means, to secure the hope, peace, and safety of Israel. For that reason, I have no indication of what he found or who was implicated."

"What reason?" The incredulous pitch of Griffin's voice echoed Colton's disbelief.

"The safety of Israel. He was very cautious about what he shared or revealed. Most of his work revolved around intelligence only the highest officials in Israel had access to."

"So he had a full security clearance?" Midas asked.

"Yes. Understand that NSSI employees—they're all peace-loving men." Something flickered in her expression, and her gaze surfed over the team. "Or so we thought."

"Gentlemen," Olin Lambert stepped from the side. "I understand your misgivings, but we are dealing with a very lethal threat."

"You believe her?" Max asked, his tone incredulous.

"I do. In fact, I have data that supports everything Miss Rosenblum has mentioned and much more. While I can't go into detail at this time, I ask you to trust me on this one." Olin motioned to the man next to him. "This is Representative Charles Falde, the chair of the Congressional Foreign Affairs Committee. Together, we have assembled a plan to enter Israeli territory and retrieve her father."

That was his cue.

Colton hopped off the fridge, retrieved the key from his pocket, and crossed the room. He bent over the table directly in front of Lambert, met the old man's gaze unwaveringly, and placed the key on the cold surface. "I'm out."

Shock pinned Piper to the floor. That and a healthy dose of rejection. Even though she knew he'd never speak to her again, she'd never expected him to walk out on a mission. Wasn't he the consummate solider, one everyone depended on?

Her gaze skated over the rest of the men gathered around the table. A sinking and sickening feeling washed through her as she took in their expressions. Reddened and severe, Max's face screamed his anger—and she swallowed as she rushed to the next, the large man they called Legend. Unreadable, he sat staring straight ahead, his fist to his mouth. Midas had his lips pulled to the side, as if he'd chewed his lip in deep thought.

The youngest team member just winked at her.

And one by one, they stood up and left the room. Heart in her throat, she fought against the urge to whimper. She shifted to Dr. Avery, whose compassionate smile also carried a tinge of disappointment and sorrow. "W–what's going on?" Piper hurried to the general. "Are they. . . ?" She couldn't even say it. Couldn't ask if they were quitting, too.

Hand on Piper's upper arm, the general offered a smile. "Let's take a short break."

"Please tell me they're going to help my father."

With a quick nod to the two guards and without answering her plea, he delivered her into their care.

Inside the room, she twisted toward the door to talk to Dr. Avery. But instead of the warm, caring doctor, she got the cold, hard door. It slammed. Locks clicked.

Piper spun and looked around the room. She slumped into a chair, buried her hands in her face, and sobbed. All her courage, all her hope, all that she had mustered to face Colton and the team bottomed out. Rushed out of her like a waterfall, dragging out her tears and despair. Hours slipped into the desolation of loneliness. What would she do now? The team had abandoned her, which meant whatever had happened to her father—she had no way of finding him or attempting to make him safe. If the terrorists had found her, they could find her father. Right?

Locks slammed back, and the door eased open. What, had they come to deport her now? Without the mission, without Colton, she had nothing left here.

"How are you holding up?"

Piper spun toward the old, rattling voice. Her godfather, Charles Falde, let himself into the warehouse office, armed with two diet colas. He held one out to her. "It might be awhile."

On her feet, she mechanically accepted the drink. "They're not going to help my father! What do I do?"

Sadness lingered in his brown eyes. "One thing at a time, my dear." Easing himself into a seat at the head of the table, he motioned for her to join him. "Perhaps you could talk to this Colton. The team seems to hold his opinion in high regard."

One arm wrapped around herself, Piper set the drink on the hard surface and perched on the edge of the chair. Hunched, she let her gaze trickle over her slacks. "His father died because of me. He would not listen to anything I have to say." But the thought. . .the thought that she'd lived this long and endured so much only to have her father die. . . She leaned toward him and caught his hand. "Whatever Baba found is important. He wouldn't have sent me here and done all this if it weren't." She squeezed his arm. "I—*we* can't give up. If I have to do it on my own, I won't let him die. I won't."

His gaze dropped.

Was it disappointment she saw in his eyes? "You don't think I can." The thought rammed into her chest. Knocked the breath out of her. Forced her to realize the truth. If she could not convince Colton. . . "I've already failed Baba."

He held up both pudgy hands. "My dear Lily, you did your absolute best."

Her thoughts collided against each other. "I should have left the city earlier. Should've kept running or trying to get away. Perhaps I could've hidden my identity better, not been so desperate to talk to him and contact the griefer." She put her fingers to her lips with a gasp. "Is it my fault? Is that how they found him?"

"Now, don't you start blaming yourself. There are massive forces behind all this that are way out of your control. Just because this Colton is overreacting gives you no reason to doubt yourself."

"Overreact? His father was killed because they welcomed me into their home!" Hot tears streaked down her face. She pushed out of her chair and walked to the window.

"Now, Lily. . ." He struggled to his feet.

"Please, don't try to comfort me. I don't deserve it. And I don't want it." Her father's plight felt a lifetime away compared to the heartache of losing Colton. It took a concerted effort to remind herself that she was fighting a real battle to save her father—not some ambiguous man with. . .whatever secret he'd unearthed.

After one last rub against her back, he settled against the window in front of her, but she didn't want the forthcoming heart-to-heart she saw in his aged face, so she pushed her gaze out the window. "And what *does* my goddaughter want then?"

Colton. She darted a look to Charlie, then down. "I want my father safe." Even to her, the words felt empty and rang against her conscience.

"And?" He arched an eyebrow at her. "It seems to me more was said in that conference with the men than what was actually spoken."

"I don't understand."

"You love him, yes?"

"Of course I love my father."

Kind eyes indulged her. He leaned his back against the window and smiled at the ceiling. "Connie and I did not have children, so when your father asked me to be your godfather, it was a dream come true."

And the point?

"So when I sat watching the team as you explained the story, more than once I wished for my Winchester."

"You mean the kid who kept making comments?" She laughed trying to shake off the intensity in his expression and words.

"No, I mean the cowboy who looked so conflicted and tormented but could not keep his eyes off my goddaughter."

She shifted and looked out the window. "Well," she said, barely above a whisper. "He made his decision, I think."

"This man, this Colton. . .he stole your heart. Tell me about that."

Piper's shoulders sagged again. "Baba told me never to get close to anyone. Now, I understand why. Baba's secret killed Colton's father. I love him, and when Colton sees me, all he can see is. . ." She swallowed against tears. Childish tears.

"Lily, love covers a multitude of sins."

"That's just it," she said, sniffling as she dried her face. "I don't think my feelings were reciprocated. When I told him that I loved him, he yelled that I didn't even know him."

"Do you?"

"Yes. And I don't deserve him." Hot tears won, spilling over her lids and racing down her cheeks.

An arm wrapped her in a hug. "If that man knew you as well as I, he would be proud to call you his own." He squeezed her hand. "If you'll excuse me. . ."

Piper worked to stem the flow of tears as he rapped on the door behind her. A second later, chains rattled and the door squeaked open behind her. *Thud!* The closing door knocked the tears free. The more she tried to stop them, the more they flowed. She rested her head against the rail, remembering the way Colton had aimed his gun at her, fierce resolution carved into his rugged face. How had it all gotten so terribly out of control? So terribly insane and messed up?

She searched the sky for a ray of sunshine and hope, but the gray storm clouds only served to echo the desperation brewing within her. The locks behind her and Colton's hatred locked her in a prison of her own doing. No way out. No hope. No chance her father would survive.

If he was still alive.

CHAPTER 19

Stupid pink poodle. Colton rubbed the annoying little keychain between his fingers, remembering when Mickey had asked him to hold it as he hurried her and his mom into the terminal. He'd slipped it into his pocket and forgotten about it.

Now, the thing seemed to claw at him, a reminder of when things were simple. Yeah. Like when he actually thought Piper was Piper. Now she had some Jewish name he couldn't even pronounce.

Leaning on the locker, he rested his forehead against his arm and closed his eyes. He tightened his fist around the stuffed toy and willed that he could squeeze the guts out of it. Out of this whole mess.

Voices in the hall jerked him back into action. He grabbed a pair of socks and stuffed them into the duffel, leaving the keychain with it. A plot to really hurt Israel, huh? Protecting her father. . .

He could understand that. He could. But you draw the line when it puts someone else in danger—like his father.

The door flung open. Though he wouldn't look, it sounded like the entire team was coming. Probably to talk him out of quitting. Let 'em try. He'd had enough. Just wanted to put his life back together. Save what was left of his ranch. Rebuild. Forget he ever tried to love again.

A locker hinge squawked behind him.

Then beside.

And the other side.

Colton glanced around, confused as the others drew out packs and garbage bags and began filling them. He shifted, eyeing Griffin as he grabbed a trash can, set it in front of his open locker, reached in, and scraped everything into the gray bin.

What on earth. . . ?

Max rammed clothes and shoes into a bag.

"What's going on?" Colton angled to his left.

"Cleaning out," Midas mumbled as he meticulously folded his clothes and tucked them into a pack.

"What do you mean?"

"We quit," the Kid said. "If you're out, I am, too. I'm not going into any firefight without you. No way. No how."

Stunned, Colton glanced at the others. "Come on, guys."

Then Max stood. "I gotta say, this time—I'm with the Kid. If you're out, then that's enough for me to step down."

"Wait," Colton said as he turned. "This is my choice. A decision I made for me. This has nothing to do with y'all. You don't—"

"You don't get it, do you?" Max stood up to Colton without an inch of fear, his dark eyes boring through Colton's skull. "You're the backbone, Cowboy. You pull out; we crumple."

"No," Colton argued. "You're a team. You work good—"

"The team?" Griffin clamped a hand on Colton's shoulder. "The team consists of me, Midas"—who stepped closer and nodded— "Frogman"—Max swatted his chest—"and the Kid, sadly."

"Hey!"

"And you." He shook Colton. "We ain't a team without you. Without you, we're just four guys with a sad excuse for living."

But Piper's father. . .

Colton pursed his lips. "Now listen here. I appreciate what y'all are trying to do, show me your support 'nd all, but—"

"Support? If I needed support, I'd buy a jock strap." Max snorted. "Dude, you haven't learned a thing have you? A team. Inseparable. Already down one man, we cannot stand without you."

"We won't." Midas shook his head. "Not happening."

Colton eased onto the bench, hung his head as he propped his arms on his legs. "I can't do this." Go after Piper's father, find him—rescue her father while her actions killed his? "She lied to me, deceived me, and I thought I loved her. I hate her."

Max joined him. "Hate is a very intense feeling." His dark eyes looked up at him. "I know. You helped me work through a lot of that—well, you and Marshall's face."

"Leave my face out of this."

"But I'm here," Max continued. "I'm not leaving you. Neither are any of the guys. Whatever's going on, whatever you're feeling, we feel it, too."

"I can't do this. I can't."

"Then it's settled." Griffin assumed a seat across from them. "We don't go. We turned in our keys. The warehouse will be demolished within a week. Nightshade will cease to exist." He shrugged. "It'll be over."

Though his heart seized, Colton tried to bolster his vanishing courage. "I know what you're trying to do."

"I don't think you do," Griffin said. "This isn't fancy talk. This is *real*, Cowboy. Together. All of us. Or none of us."

Colton hung his head. *Not because of me.* He couldn't let the team fall apart because of him. "You don't understand. I'm not quitting because. . ." Why couldn't he get the words out? "Look, I just can't keep going. I can't live knowing. . ." Why couldn't he say it was because of Piper—*Ke-whatever-her-name-is.*

"You got it bad for the girl. I see that. We understand. You love her, let her into your life and your home, and she did this thing to your family—to us. Each of us. Like Frogman said—we all feel it."

Each of the men around him stood strong and resolute in their commitment to the team. Every one. Except him. How had he gotten so offtrack?

"What you're feeling right now, it's all right. We aren't asking you to change that. We are your brothers."

Colton raked both hands through his short crop and pushed off the bench. He walked a circle and gave himself some room. He shifted, pressed his fingers against a metal locker. Four men sat in this room willing to sacrifice their careers as a pledge of camaraderie and solidarity. Despite the war within, he couldn't abandon them.

He ached, wanting his father not to have died for nothing. "What was Lambert's plan?"

"Snatch-and-grab," Midas said.

"Well, if it were that simple, we'd probably be there and back already," the Kid said.

Max strode toward him. "It won't be easy, we'll be disavowed if captured, and chance of success is next to nothing."

Griffin laughed. "Sounds like our kind of mission."

Max's eyes darkened. "We're already down one man, and if you aren't with us, then there is no us."

"I swore I'd never go back to Israel."

"Why?"

"My sister. . ." Bloody images swam at him, plucking at his courage, pulling at his mind. He shook his head. "My sister died there."

* * *

Yeshua. . .forgive me for what I've done to Colton. I never meant to hurt him. The door opened and closed again, but guilt kept her at the window, staring into the dark night. Having her godfather here was such a comfort. He'd seen through her facade to the truth of her feelings for Colton. She drew in a breath, fearing what truth or decision he'd returned to deliver. She smeared the tears away mumbling, "I fear Colton won't forgive me."

"Reckon the chances are slim."

Piper spun at the voice—Colton's voice. He stood, hands fisted as his sides, his shoulders tensed, and eyes dark. She searched. . .hunted . . .for something that would bridge the gap between them, but what could she offer? What could she say? Sorry seemed empty, trite. But it was all she had.

"I'm very sorry, Colton."

"See there?" he said, an edge hardening his words. "That's a problem. You know my name. I don't know yours." His shoulders hunched. "Come to think of it, I'm not even sure I know who you are."

"My name—" She licked her lips. "I'm still the same person."

"Yeah." His left eye twitched. "Seems to me that's part of the problem. The person named Piper kept secrets. Didn't come clean."

Palms out, she took several steps toward him. "I tried. When your—" She stopped cold, remembering his mother's scream that had cut off her confession. Even now, that sound scraped against her soul.

"Go on." His nostrils flared. "Finish what you were saying."

Piper couldn't bring herself to say the words.

"Finish it!"

She jolted at his anger and looked at him, begging he wouldn't make her do this. But he was. And he didn't care how much it hurt her. "I was about to tell you when they killed your father."

He nodded, his lips pulled into a thin, almost invisible line. She understood the emotion written on his face. What it meant—Colton wanted someone held responsible for his father's death. She'd want someone to pay if her father died.

"That's why I tried to leave town. I tried. You stopped me." Her heart felt like it was about to leap out of her chest.

He drew himself straight. "So it's my fault?"

"No!" She shook her head quickly and looked down. "I just want you to believe that I never wanted you or your family to get hurt." She brushed the hair from her face and stalked to the window. "I knew they'd found me, and I was trying to get away before anyone got hurt. It's why my bags were packed when you came that night."

Quiet bathed the room, save the clanking of a flag pole out the window and across the open parking lot. Hands on the rusty window frame, she leaned out a bit and tried to catch a crisp scent of the water. Instead, a wash of stale, dank odors drifted up from the Dumpster parked below the window. She winced and slumped back. Turned around.

Colton ran a hand over the back of his neck. "How'd you know they found you?"

"We had this way to communicate, a code that I could send through a griefer—"

"Come again?"

"A griefer, a person who likes to cause grief for Web sites, normally for gamers. They go in, send flying spaceships through a site just to irritate people." She shrugged. "Annoying, but very effective. My father arranged to have one work as a median between us."

"Go on."

She seized the tenuous thread that said he might not hate her for the rest of her life. "The last time I tried to send a relay to my father, the griefer denied me access. Said I had the wrong site."

"Did you?"

Shaking her head, she gave a caustic laugh. "Trust me—my father's life depended on me going to the right site. I wasn't going to make an idiotic mistake typing in the wrong URL."

Emotion flickered through his face, through his lips, and nearly halted her willingness to tell him any more. But she'd told him once that she would give him the entire truth, and if she was here till midnight, she'd make sure he knew everything.

"I insisted he get a message to my father. That's when the griefer said I'd been found and to get out." Massaging her temples didn't help the throb in her head.

"How'd he know?"

"Either he saw something in the codes—maybe tracing sequences or whatever—or the message was actually from my father, somehow. So I stayed at a hotel that night, then the next day ran home, packed, shut down all my utilities, and was ready to leave town, but..."

"But?" Colton folded his arms. Unfolded them. Folded again. Then planted his hands on his belt. "Lambert sent me in here. Said you have something I need, that the team needs."

Her heart skipped a beat. "They're—you're going to help save my father?"

Ironically, even though she'd spent very little time with the man, she knew him. Knew that right now, he was working very hard to control his emotions—particularly his anger.

"I think," he continued with a long exhale, gripping the back of a chair. "I think he wants us to kiss and make up."

Piper's gaze popped to his.

He straightened, towering over her. "But that's not going to happen. Got it?"

Regret pushed her into a chair at the opposite end of the table.

"Because the woman I dated, the woman I let into my life is Piper Blum." His chest heaved. "And she doesn't exist."

Disbelief squirreled through her. "Is that..." She couldn't say it. Though she tried to put the shock into words, she couldn't. Instead, she planted her hands on the table and pushed to her feet. "If you really think a name is all it takes to wipe me from your life, you're not half the man I thought you were."

"And you're not the woman I thought you were at all."

"I am still Piper. I am still the woman you kissed, the woman who birthed Firefox's foal with you."

"Hershey died in the fire."

His words smacked her back. "No..."

"Try something else."

"What is this? A competition?"

"Just trying to figure it out."

"Figure what out?" She raised her hands. "I've told you everything."

"Have you?" His boots scuffed over the wood as he sidled toward her. "Have you finally told me all your dirty little secrets?"

"Yes!"

His thunderous expression exploded. "Then why in God's name didn't you tell me a week ago so my father didn't have to die?"

Piper lowered her head. "Because I didn't want my father to die."

"Well, therein lies the problem." Colton pivoted and walked to the door. Tried to open it. Banged on it. "Open up!"

Piper flinched each time he banged on the door, tears—the stupid, burning tears—streaking down her cheek. She swatted at them. "Forgive me for fighting for something as trivial as my father's life."

Colton rounded on her, slamming her heart into her throat. "Oh, want to try that on me? Try to make me feel guilty to appease your conscience?"

"That's not. . . I didn't. . . You haven't exactly been the most forthcoming person either. You aren't a saint, Colton."

"Never claimed to be."

"But you never bothered to tell me who you are, or what exactly you do. You deceived me, allowed me to think you were out of the military, knowing you were still entrenched in military actions."

He held out a hand to stop her. "Wait." He patted his chest. "Remember, you love me." Head cocked, he eyed her. "So tell me, Piper—or whatever your name is—who am I?"

"Kelila," she muttered.

Unbelievable. "Avoiding the question." He shook his head. "Well, let me tell you about the man you think you fell in love with. I'm a sniper. I use a long-range scope and place bullets in the gray matter of terrorists all over the globe. I do it with such lethal precision that I haven't missed yet." He arched an eyebrow. "Last night, I put a .308 in the skull of the guy who killed my father."

"And it didn't help, did it?"

The words hit center mass. "We don't have time for this." He turned back to the door.

"I see it in your eyes." Piper rushed around him and caught his arm. "You're still livid; you're still hurting." She took a step closer.

She wouldn't have if she realized how close he was to losing it.

"Killing. . .retribution doesn't solve it, doesn't help."

The rush of his thrumming pulse roared in his ears. "Oh, it helped all right."

Brows knit, she considered him. Then shook her head. "No, you don't believe that for one second," she said quietly. A fierce determination glittered in her caramel eyes. "I may not have known that you were a sniper, I may not have known about this team I've met today, but I do know the heart of the man standing before me."

The storm brewing in his gut shifted. Enough for him to notice, but not enough to wave off the torrent of his anger. He didn't back down. Towered over her, ready to pounce.

"That's what I fell in love with, Colton. Your heart. The tender man who's frantic when his daughter isn't where she's supposed to be. The son courteous enough to endure his mother's nudging to get married and settle down, and the son humble enough to listen to his father even though he's a grown man."

Every beat of his heart thundered. He watched, disbelieving the way she faced his fury, the way she entered the eye of the storm without blinking. Her hand raised, clenched, then flattened as she pressed her fingers over his chest. Over his heart.

She raised her eyes to his. "I pray. . .some day. . .I can earn your forgiveness."

The coolness of her touch seeped through the fibers of his button-down. Each breath felt like a thousand-pound weight beneath her fingers.

He removed her hand. "Forgiveness isn't earned." *It's given.* Something he wouldn't—couldn't do.

But the team would be watching. Lambert was watching. He knew what they wanted him to say, what they expected him to do. If he didn't go into this mission with his head in the game, they'd all back out. Despite harboring this anger against her, he knew the mission was somehow important—a whole country seemed to depend on Nightshade's covert action.

He would play their game. Do the mission. Get it over with. Go on with his life. . .without her.

Only then did he feel her eyes assessing him, and it forced him to step away from her. She'd seen into his soul once already. He didn't need her figuring this one out.

"Colton?"

"We'll go in," he said, bending over the table and harnessing his focus. "Find your father and get him out." He felt her at his side now. "You can trust the team; they're the best. If anyone can get your father out alive, it'll be them."

Since when had he started referring to Nightshade as *them*?

"What just happened?"

He met her gaze, narrowed with suspicion. Who cared if she read past the false exterior and knew what he was doing? "It's time to move on."

CHAPTER 20

Ten rows, more than forty seats. . .roughly twenty-three feet separated them. But even from back here, Colton heard her laughter. He shifted in the seat, angling his booted foot into the aisle in the hopes of stretching his cramped legs. He glanced past the teen with the mullet and the woman cradling the infant and just beyond the flight attendant to where sandy blond hair barely touched the collar of Midas's navy blue button-down. They'd chatted nearly the entire umpteen-hour flight.

"How's your neck?"

Warning his partner to veer off with that stupid smirk, Colton cast a sidelong glance to Max, who sat squished between Colton and the overweight, middle-aged man sawing some serious logs.

"After eighteen hours of straining to see her, you've got to have a crick in that thick neck of yours."

"How would you know? You snored louder than mammoth guy there for two hours."

"Hey, can I help it if you don't know how to relax?"

Colton snorted and slumped back against the seat. Pushed his shoulders into the thick cushion as he readjusted. "These stupid seats were designed with short people like you in mind."

"Cowboy's gettin' cranky."

Another burst of laughter snagged his attention. His gaze shot toward her seat before he realized it. Then started to look at Max and thought better of it. Which made Max laugh again.

"Sounds like they're having a good time." Max yawned. "That'll be interesting. Far as I know, he only does first dates." This time, he stretched across Colton and peered up the aisle. "Yep, they look pretty cozy."

Colton glared at him. Curled a fist.

With a nod, Max shrugged, looking guilty—fake guilt, that was. "I'm sure Midas just wants to maintain cover." When another laugh erupted from Piper, Max grunted. "Hm, never known Midas to be funny. They must be getting along really well."

"Do you want my fist up your nose?"

Max busted up laughing. "You are such a sap. And you say you don't care about her anymore?"

"Partner, you're treadin' some dangerous ground there." Head tilted back, Colton closed his eyes and told himself to get some shut-eye, but with the anger over Max's teasing churning his gut and Piper's voice and laughter plucking at him each time he'd start to drift off, it left him angrier. . .and exhausted.

By the time the plane landed at Tel Aviv International Airport, Colton had more cricks and aches than he'd care to admit. But it wasn't the aches and cricks that antagonized his foul mood. It was the way Piper seemed oblivious to the sacrifices the team had made for her, the fact that his father died. That she'd ripped his heart out.

He couldn't help but eye her when she and Midas crowded the aisle with dozens of passengers. The whole scene reminded him of a herd of cattle trying to wrestle their way out of the line-up pen on auction day.

He and Max waited for more passengers to fill the space, allowing more distance and less cause to be noticed or connected to the supposedly happy honeymooners, before he stepped into the aisle and exited. As he glided through the airport, his gaze roved the crowds, searching for Piper. Just wanted to make sure they were following the mission, that's all.

As he strolled past the fountain, a brightly lit set of arches snagged his attention. His heart chugged to a stop. Emelie.

"Look, Colton! Mickey-D's in Israel. Who'da thunk it?" Her laughter had mingled with the throng of passengers. "Think a Big Mac will taste as bad here in the Holy Land as it does back home?" Her infectious giggle drifted through the planes of grief and death right into his chest as he remembered how she'd been so excited, commenting on everything, comparing. Like Christmas morning when she was a kid. So happy.

So much vitality and vibrancy.

Just like Piper.

"You okay?"

He blinked and darted a glance to his partner. "Yeah, sure." Hitching his pack farther onto his shoulder, he navigated the sea of people.

Already, he felt his decision to come trembling beneath Piper's betrayal and the all-too-fresh memory of Emelie's death. It'd been five years. He should be over it by now. Not her death—he'd never be over that—but hearing her voice so clearly. Remembering things as if they were happening in front of him. Right now.

Had all the makings of a bad flashback. A really bad one. He'd all but kicked them since joining Nightshade. At least the big ones that left him feeling as stupid as Guernsey's hogs.

When he stepped into the arid early morning, he paused at the long line of limos and private drivers loitering nearby.

Emelie had squealed as he pointed her to the sleek black vehicle. *"You got a limo?"*

With a shoulder nudge, Max started toward a blue sedan with a Taxi sign. "Let's grab that one."

As Colton turned toward the car, Piper and Metcalfe stepped from the terminal, dragging their bags...and holding hands. Like the happy couple their passports said they were. She pointed to something out across the road and jabbered on.

Only then did it really hit him that this was her home. Her country.

Midas tapped a stranger, handed him a camera, and asked him to take a photo. Colton gripped the straps of his bag tighter, knowing full well it was all for appearance, but also knowing that Metcalfe was probably doing this to rub it in his face. The idea to pair the two had come from Lambert, said it was for the best considering Colton's feelings.

Colton hadn't argued. Because he agreed. Mostly. Though he hadn't said anything, it bugged him, the thought of her with anyone else. He shouldn't care.

Yet seeing them together—Midas's arm around her—did things to Colton. He ground his teeth as they strode toward a limousine. For a woman who'd declared her undying love to him just days ago, she sure seemed content to be on another man's arm.

Furious, he gripped the padded strap of his pack tighter and strode toward the car. The driver shuttled them to a hotel. After they checked in and dumped their bags in the room, they headed down the back stairwell.

"Hey, let's grab a bite for the road," Max said. "Nearby, I saw a café."

Colton's boot slipped out from under him and nearly landed him on the concrete steps. A café. . .Israel. . . He recovered but descended the stairs a bit slower. "Not hungry." He punched open the door and stepped into the warm, arid day.

"Well, I need to eat."

"No time," Colton said, nodding to the black SUV parked along the curb.

They climbed in and were greeted by a man in a suit. He extended a hand. "Daniel Ben-Haim, deputy foreign minister. Welcome to Israel, gentlemen."

"Thanks," Max said with a quick shake. "Got any food around here?"

Colton grimaced at his partner's request, and introduced himself.

"Sure, I know the perfect place," the minister said as he barreled through the city.

Focused on their surroundings, Colton tensed as they pulled to the curb of an indoor/outdoor café. Patrons sat at tables along the street, laughing and eating. His gut roiled. He searched the crowds on the street for hostiles. The cars appeared normal, but how could one pick out a suicide bomber just by looking at the outside?

"Be right back," Max said as he leapt out and rushed into the place.

Fist over his mouth, Colton remembered how thrilled Emelie had been to be in the same country where Jesus had walked. He brought her here so she could have fun, celebrate the huge accomplishment of earning a full merit scholarship to Harvard. He'd never been prouder of his kid sister. He was young and had money from his career with the Marines. So he treated her to the all-expenses-paid trip. . . .

Straight to the grave.

"Just one more rugelach. Please?"

She'd loved those stupid little pastries with nuts and fruit. And just like that, she'd disappeared into the café once more to buy another. . .

Thud!

Heart jack-hammering, Colton flinched. Snapped out of the memory by the slamming passenger door...*door*...not the bomb that had ended Emelie's life.

A pair of dark eyes considered him. "You okay?" The question held no mirth, no lightheartedness.

Colton could tell Max thought he'd had a flashback. Maybe he had, although to him, it was just a bad memory, a nightmare. "Just want to get there. Get it done." Stretching his neck, Colton roughed a hand over his face. Glanced at the driver, who was watching him, too. "How long to rendezvous?"

"About an hour."

Closing his eyes, Colton leaned back. Anything to get Max off his back and give his mind time to breathe. The jouncing felt familiar and almost comforting, reminding him of riding in the back of a Humvee and barreling through desert.

"Want something?"

"No, I'm stuffed."

She planted a kiss on his cheek, her hands resting on his shoulder, which she squeezed. "You are the best big brother I have."

He chuckled. "I'm the only *big brother you have."*

"Case in point." With another kiss and pat, she said, "I'll be right back."

Behind him, brakes squeaked. He glanced over his shoulder as a hefty woman emerged and walked toward the café. His gaze shifted to the café.

To the car driving away.

Instinct pushed him out of the iron chair. He checked the café as the woman entered. Through the small crowd and dim lights, he saw Emelie smiling at him. She waved.

No. The woman. The woman in the burka. He saw her reach beneath her head covering—a bomb!

He surged forward, but his legs felt like jelly. "Emelie. No!"

Something hit Colton in the gut. He jerked and blinked.

Black eyes stared at him again. "We're here." Max's eyes darkened as the driver—the deputy foreign minister—pulled into a large, gated facility. "Are you?"

Colton didn't answer. They were just memories, bad ones, right? It wasn't a flashback. Not a real one. Right? Swallowing hard against his thundering pulse, he tried to shake off the adrenaline still zinging through his veins.

When the car stopped, he climbed out and grabbed his bag. Trailed the deputy through the open level toward a door and stairwell. His heart hadn't evened out, but at least the effects were fading.

"Hey."

He ignored Max's hissed word. Hopefully he'd leave him alone.

A hand clapped onto his shoulder. "Hey." Max tugged him around, scowling. "What was that back there?"

"Nothing." Colton tried to shrug free, but the hand only tightened on his shoulder.

"Bull!" Max gave him a light shove. "You came to like you were on another planet."

Colton clamped his jaw, stared at the pile of dirt collecting in the corner under the stairs. Just like the memories that had collected at the back of his mind. If only he could sweep them into a bin.

"What happened?"

"A bad dream."

Dawning cleared the fury from Max's face. "You mean a flashback."

Looking away did nothing to ease the guilt and dread pooling in his intestines. He wanted to argue, rationalize, but he couldn't.

"Is this going to be a problem? Because I have a team out there that I'm responsible for—and you're part of it. So tell me, Cowboy. Is this going to be a problem?"

How could he answer? There hadn't been a flashback, not a bad one, in more than two years.

"Answer me!"

"No! I'm here. I'm doing this." Colton shouted, his voice ringing off the high well of concrete they stood in. He grabbed the rail and propelled himself around them and up the stairs. "Get off my back."

"I'll ride your tail from here to kingdom come if you quit!"

Quit? Colton was quitting? Agape, Piper stood at the entrance, watching Colton jog up the stairs.

Metcalfe trotted toward the team leader. "What was that about?"

Piper joined them. "He's quitting? He can't quit out here, can he?"

The little muscle at the corner of Max's jaw twitched as he broke his gaze from Metcalfe and completely avoided Piper. "We have an AHOD meeting upstairs. We're late."

Stumbling back didn't distance her from the roiling hatred she saw in Max's dark eyes. Somehow, she had a feeling she would never gain his approval.

Metcalfe touched her elbow. "Hey, don't worry." Kindness in his tone buffed out the smear of hurt. "Cowboy isn't going anywhere but on the mission."

"How do you know?"

"It's what we do—the mission. Tensions are high. Words are gruff. We do the job and get it done, no matter how much we hate it."

"He hates me?"

Metcalfe smirked. "Sorry, wrong choice of words. I meant, no matter how we feel about it. We're soldiers. Our priority is to the mission. And I know for a fact that's Cowboy's priority, too." He bobbed his head toward the steps. "Come on. Before Frogman starts yelling again."

Upstairs, the team had gathered around a long counter. A man in a navy suit removed a folder and set it atop his briefcase.

"'Bout time y'all showed up," the Kid teased as he straddled his backpack.

Though she would wear a vest and participate as a part of the team, Piper felt anything but a part of the team as she stood here. How odd that even in her homeland she felt like an outsider. She shirked it off as the tension emanating through the room. And from Colton.

He sat against the nearby wall, arms folded. No matter the man's rugged good looks, he didn't look well right now. Dark circles under his eyes made them appear even more blue. The scowl seemed to have taken root in his forehead.

"Okay, listen up," Max said. "This is Deputy Foreign Minister Daniel Ben-Haim. He'll be our Intel and primary contact." He nodded to two men standing next to the Kid. "The grunt with the scar is Harry Weiss, former SEAL."

The man with white-blond hair nodded at them but said nothing.

"Next to him is John Dighton, also a former SEAL."

"Man, a whole herd," the Kid said.

Dighton's gaze barely flickered to the much-younger team member.

"Don't mind the Kid. He's all mouth." Max grinned. "Weiss's call sign is Scar, and Dighton—"

"They call me Squirt."

"Why?" the Kid snickered.

"Those around me tend to squirt blood." The menacing look silenced the Kid.

Laughter dribbled around the room and faded just as quick. Yet tucked in a corner, Colton didn't smile or engage in the banter.

"Deputy," Max said. "Go ahead." Almost as one, the teasing died down, and the mood shifted to a much more somber note as the team focused on the suited man.

"I'll dump the facts and then sort them for you. Here's what we know: A key IRG general is dead; Yitshak Rosenblum is missing, as are a young woman and an assassin."

"Are assassins ever *not* missing?" The Kid chuckled.

Everyone ignored him.

Deputy Ben-Haim picked up a stack of papers. "The first photo was taken three nights ago at a dinner party in honor of Prince Razak, eldest son of one of Saudi Arabia's wealthiest nobles."

Piper glanced over Max's shoulder to the photo. With his hooked nose and thick eyebrows, the prince seemed fattened and content.

"Nearly five hundred guests attended the dinner. We believe, however, this party was a front for General Bashar al-Jafari to meet with some very important brass, businessmen, and money."

Daniel set down the papers. "Understand that al-Jafari is a prime player, and I guess you could call him a recruiter, for the Iranian Republican Guard. We've long suspected him of many things but never been able to pin things on him." Wasn't that always the way with the wicked?

"Al-Jafari has the ear of very powerful men in many countries. Or I should say, he *had* the ear. He was killed the night of that party. Two bullets to the brain, point blank. Assassinated."

"Killer is brave." Max rubbed his jaw. "Five hundred guests and he walks in and kills the general?"

"The killer is a Palestinian assassin." He flung another page onto the table. "A bounty put out by Palestinians for his head."

"He must've gone solo or ticked someone off."

"What about my father? Did the assassin go after my father?"

Deputy Minister Ben-Haim hesitated. "Please, let me work through the information as I have it. You can draw your own conclusions."

That wasn't exactly comforting, but Piper still nodded.

The minister bobbed his head toward the stack of photos and papers. "That second image is al-Jafari's daughter. Nobody knew she existed until this party. Apparently, her father intended to sell her to a prince as part of an arms negotiation."

Midas dropped into a chair and shrugged. "She's a beauty, but why do we care?"

"She's missing, along with the assassin—and I mean, they're together. His identity is unknown, and as you can see, he's elusive."

The photograph showed a partially concealed profile. It could be anyone of Middle Eastern descent.

"He wasn't on the guest register, and nobody knows him. Mossad is working on his identity." Daniel passed a piece of paper around the group. "A source spotted him at a hotel near Ein Gedi approximately two hours ago. A team has been deployed to monitor his movement."

"What significance does this assassin or missing girl have to our mission?" Max folded well-muscled arms over his chest.

"Every significance. We intercepted a cell transmission about two weeks ago that al-Jafari had taken possession of a large package—Yitshak Rosenblum."

Yanked into the meeting by the mention of her father's name, Piper felt the breath snatched from her lungs. She straightened. "My father? He's alive?"

Deputy Ben-Haim gave her a sad smile. "We do not know."

"But he was two weeks ago?"

He nodded.

"Do you know what my father found, why he went into hiding and sent me away?" Did the desperation in her voice ring as loud in the room as it did in her heart?

"My best guess is that he found evidence, perhaps a trail of evidence, of a threat against Israel." He sighed and licked his lips. "Miss Rosenblum, it's my personal theory that he discovered Datan Katz, one of his associates, was connected to the IRG. Mossad arrested him right before your father appeared in the custody of al-Jafari."

Piper's mouth fell open. "Datan went to synagogue—I saw him!"

"The best of men hide evil intentions behind piety."

"So…" Max scratched the back of his head. "This man, the assassin, was at the palace. Where al-Jafari was killed." He looked at Colton. "I'm not getting it. Why would a guy risk hundreds of witnesses to his dirty deed and then take the girl? A lovers' quarrel?"

"That's what we don't know," Daniel said. "Just before we captured the intelligence on the hotel, one of our contacts reported that she returned to her father's palatial estate with the assassin, who killed a guard and apparently held the girl hostage."

"So, we need to be prepared to fight an assassin."

Daniel looked at them both. "The only way to stop an assassin is to kill him."

CHAPTER 21

You're not going."

Her chin tilted up, her beautiful eyes streaked with defiance. "That's not up to you. Don't make this personal."

Personal? She wanted to go there? All right. "Aren't you?" *Easy there, Cowboy. Ratchet down that pulse.* "If it wasn't your father out there, would you be going on a black ops mission?" He arched an eyebrow. "Last I heard, you weren't real fond of the military."

"I spent two years in the Israeli Army, and that was more than enough for me. But this is my father's life, and I'll defend it to the death." She stuffed her hands on her hips. "Do you know how to speak my language? Do you know what my father looks like?"

Colton stalked to the table, snatched up the photo, and held it up. "Yitshak Rosenblum." He pointed to where a helicopter waited outside the building. "Pilots are Jewish, both born here. One raised in Syria and knows Arabic and Hebrew." He bobbed his head, feeling justified and relieved he had enough ammo to keep her out of the game. "Reckon we'll do just fine without you."

Midas appeared beside them and handed Piper a vest and helmet. "Suit up. It's almost time."

Triumph stomped over her face as she took the items.

Colton rounded on Midas. Grabbed the helmet from Piper and glared at Midas.

The man stepped back with one foot, both arms drawn as if ready to fight.

"Hey!" Max shouted over the din of the chopper engines whirring into the bay.

"I said she's not going," Colton growled to Midas.

Palms raised, he back-stepped. "Take it up with the Old Man, dude. He said she goes on every leg."

Colton's heart beat a hard cadence. She couldn't go. She'd get killed, get *them* killed. "This ain't right."

Midas grinned as he hooked an arm around Piper. "Maybe you're just jealous. She traded in a cowboy for a golden boy."

Red lit through Colton's vision. "This is about the safety of the mission." Fire raced through his veins, itching to pummel the surfer.

"Hey, cool. Then I'm glad." Midas turned toward Piper, took her hand, drew her into his arms. "She's pretty and has enough fight in her. Maybe we could go out, see where things lead."

Crimson infused Piper's cheeks. She tried to step back.

Midas held her.

The grunt was trying to provoke him. Why, he didn't know. But he wasn't going to bite. He'd ignore the howling of his pulse in his ears. Had to stay in control. Disregard the throb at the base of his skull.

"Heck, I might even go on more than one date with you, babe."

Restraint gone. He dropped the helmet, grabbed Midas's collar, and jerked him up on his toes. "You want me angry? Is that what this is about?"

"Yeah," Midas grunted.

"Hey, hey, hey!" Feet raced toward them.

A circle formed around them, uncertain what to do, but ready to do something.

Max dove between them, pushing both back several steps. "What in the mad world is wrong with you two?"

"At least now we know Cowboy cares about something other than himself. I was getting sick of him being all morose and closed focused."

Max gave Midas a shove backward. "Get your ruck ready."

"Man." The Kid chuckled. "Even I'm not stupid enough to start something with the Cowboy."

Though he wasn't looking at his friend, Colton could see the rise and fall of Max's chest. The man was angry.

Colton glanced down at the helmet, his own chest feeling like an anchor sat on it.

"She's going, and as of this moment, you're officially tasked with her safety."

Head snapped up, Colton glared. "I'm a sniper. I won't—"

"Am. I. Clear?" Max tugged the helmet from Colton's hands and passed it over to Piper.

Without a word, Colton turned and walked away. It wasn't right, Piper going into combat with them. Nobody knew what they'd encounter or find. What if her father wasn't alive?

Why did he care?

He knelt beside his pack. At the carefully placed items. Meticulously packed. Twice. Didn't have anything better to do with the hours while they waited for nightfall. He rested a hand on it and closed his eyes. He'd never been this far out of the game.

A moment later, movement beside him drew his attention round. Behind and to his right, Piper stood in the flak vest with the helmet in her hands. "Max said I needed to stay near you."

Why was his friend doing this? Max knew how he felt about Piper, yet he saddled him with the responsibility of seeing to her safety. Wasn't he afraid he'd let her die or something?

"Then get that on 'cause we're about to board."

She set the helmet on her head. As the dome wobbled, she fumbled with the catch. The thing nearly fell off her head.

Colton pushed to his feet and stepped closer. "Here." He worked the straps, tightening, tugging, securing. Why a woman who'd been in the Israeli military didn't know how to put on protective gear. . . He patted the top. "Looks solid."

Her eyes rose to his.

Colton stilled. She did know how to put on a helmet. She'd wanted his help.

"Please don't hate me."

"Gather round," Max shouted from the end of the bay. Within seconds, the team crouched around Max's hand-drawn rendering. "Okay, this is the hotel. Our objective is the assassin. He is in room 166, which is on the side of the hotel with a garden patio."

"Beach." Midas grinned. "Sounds like my kind of place."

"There are exits here, here, and here," Max explained. "The interior has a peep hole, but also lots of traffic, which is why we'll be beaching here, hoofing it down to the patio door. If necessary, we can enter through the rear access. But I'd rather it be in and out, snatch and grab."

"Is the patio door glass?" Midas asked.

"Yes, but all images coming back show a curtain covering it. No line of sight, Cowboy."

Not a problem. He had his thermals.

"Midas, Cowboy, you'll insert with me. Scar and Kid, you'll hold position near the extraction point. Legend and Squirt cover the rear entrance to the hotel in case someone does something stupid like try to run."

"I'm all for stupid," Midas said with a grin. "Is the assassin alone?"

"Unknown, but suspected to have the girl, possibly Rosenblum. Okay, that's it. Let's prep and load." Max looked at Colton. "Cowboy's going to pray over the mission."

The words jerked Colton straight. "Hey." He tried to keep his voice low. "I'm not really up to it."

Max shrugged. "Who ever is?"

The team gathered, including the two newbies and Piper. In a huddle, they bowed their heads. Waiting. For him.

Colton yanked off his helmet and rubbed a hand over the top. "God," he began, feeling as if he'd have more luck plucking the Golden Gate Bridge from its pylons. "Keep us all in Your arms. Safe. Grant us wisdom. . . ." What else? What else could he pray? Was God even listening anymore? He'd never felt so blocked.

"Bring us all home safe and with all our pieces in the right place," the Kid added.

"And help us kill some bad guys," Squirt said.

"Oorah!" Griffin clapped his hands as the huddle broke up. "Let's do it!"

"All right, load up!" Max said as the rotors of the Russian helo cranked and screeched.

Colton paused and scowled at Piper. "You don't have the experience for this."

Her chin tilted upward. "In the Israeli Army, I faced bombs and militants every time I stepped out of my home."

"You couldn't even get the helmet on." He didn't ease up. "I'm not kidding, Piper. This is dangerous business. You shouldn't be going. I don't like it."

Clearly, his words agitated her. She straightened. "You don't like me either, so what's the difference?"

When she tried to go around him, Colton stepped into her path. "The difference?" He looked up, swallowed, then glanced at her again. "The difference is in one, you stay alive."

"Really?" She said, her eyes glassing over. "Because it feels like I'm already dead to you."

He wasn't the same man she'd met back in Virginia. Or the one she'd kissed at his house. The new version terrified her. His rock-solid focus and determination seemed blurred with his obsession of hating her. Grief circled her heart as she headed toward the chopper.

"Hey," a voice broke into her thoughts just as a hand gripped her arm. Max tugged her to the side. "Let's talk."

Obediently, Piper followed him back inside, where the drone of the helicopter didn't pound her eardrums. "Is everything okay?"

"Yeah, listen." Max swiped a hand over his mouth. "Keep an eye on Colton."

She blinked. "Me?"

"That thing with Midas—I haven't ever seen Colton that far gone."

A knot squirmed through her stomach. "I've noticed he's. . .not the same. But Midas pushed him."

"And any other day, Colton would've let it roll off his back." Max gripped her shoulder. "He's tore up—about his dad, about you, about his sister, who died here a few years back in a café bombing in Jerusalem."

Piper's stomach swirled. "Here?" Only then did the memory rush back to her of him telling her about his sister dying. "He told me she died, but never told me how or where. No wonder he was so furious about coming on this mission." Did that mean he wasn't really angry with her? No, she'd seen that clear as day.

Despite his terse behavior, Piper had this very quiet but strong voice telling her he was acting out of fear. She regretted her words to him before he got on the chopper.

Max grinned. "Don't let the oaf fool you. He's still got it bad for you." Dark eyes darted to the chopper, then back to her. "Come on."

Piper didn't know whether to be bolstered or weighed down by the information. She couldn't imagine Max revealing so much about his partner, but if he had, that meant he was worried. Which worried her as she climbed up the steel ramp into the back of the helicopter. She squinted into the darkness until she spotted Colton near the front. Trudging past the others, she determined to sit by him no matter what. No matter the glare. No matter the hostility.

Instead, she'd let his heart speak to her. The strength of the man within. She'd fallen in love with him because of that. It would take a lot more than angry words to push her away.

The buzz started at the back of his brain as Piper lowered her lithe frame onto the rack next to him. She darted him a furtive look, which he caught in his periphery. He wasn't sure what made him more frustrated—the pleasure at having her close, or the anger that she was close. How could a man be so messed up?

Airborne, the rickety old Russian bird lifted the team and sped them toward their destination. The hotel in Ein Gedi where the assassin lay holed up. Colton worked to keep his thoughts and arms to himself. But with Piper so close, it proved impossible. More than once, he bumped her when they hit an air pocket.

What felt like mere minutes later, the chopper began its descent through the dark night. Colton flipped down his NVGs and let the wash of green illuminate the interior of the helo. He glanced to the side before he could stop himself. Piper nodded at him.

He scooted onto the edge of the rack as the rest of the team hovered, ready to rush onto the beach. By the time his feet hit the soft terrain, his adrenaline had surged. With a glance back to confirm she was with him, he rushed down the stretch of empty beach. They'd chosen a good hour, and the assassin couldn't have picked a better place to expose himself.

Within fifty yards of the hotel, the team regrouped at a steep embankment that concealed them from the building. Gently, he moved Piper behind him. Eased himself up to the top of the sloped surface. Light trickled toward him from the flood and pool lights. Colton tugged the thermals from his pack.

"What ya got, Cowboy?" Max's voice came through the coms.

"Two bodies. One prostrate. One by the window, watching."

"Our assassin?"

Not with the shape and location of the heat signatures. "Negative. Female."

Was the assassin asleep? That'd be too easy, but that's the way it looked because he certainly wouldn't leave a hostage alone. But sleeping. . . ? Colton lowered the thermals. It didn't make a lick of sense.

"Let's go!"

For cover, the team raced along the sloped surface, giving Colton's thighs a good workout. When he checked on Piper, he was pleased to find her right behind him. The four of them slithered up to the side of the building and crouched low beside the wall that formed a perimeter to the garden patios. Unfortunately, the bleached wall only came to his shoulders, so he felt like one of those shooting ranges at the fair back home with his head as the target. He inched lower as he moved.

Pausing at the point where the wall ended, they peeked toward the room.

Again, Colton eased his thermals out and peered through the walls, steel, glass, and curtain. The woman still stood near the door, apparently looking out. On watch perhaps? Another figure lay prone on a bed, he guessed. He signaled to Max and Midas what he saw.

Max held up a hand with three fingers.

Two.

One.

They launched around the corner, darted for the private patio. Hopped the iron gate that afforded no privacy. As Colton made the bound, he saw the curtain flutter. He yanked up his weapon and swept an arm around to once again nudge Piper into a secure position out of sight and behind him.

Max shoved a booted foot against the door frame.

The glass door popped open.

A scream stabbed the night.

By the time Colton made it inside with Piper, Max had the girl in a stranglehold, a hand over her mouth. "Don't say a word," he hissed in Arabic.

The girl stilled.

Colton and Midas rushed the room. Midas hovered at his elbow and nodded to a door near the main entrance. Together, they scissor-stepped toward what looked like a closet. His partner knelt at the side, gripped the handle, then waited.

Weapon at the ready, Colton gave the signal.

The door flung open. He shuffled forward, sweeping his weapon over the closet—side, side, top. . .bottom. "Clear," he whispered.

Immediately, they whirled toward the bathroom. He slid the chain over the main door and flipped the deadbolt, securing it. At the threshold, he stared down the barrel of his M4 and scanned the semi-darkened bathroom. The sink with soap and a washcloth. White tile stretched floor to ceiling. The toilet and half-empty roll of the paper. Two towels draped over the rod of the shower curtain that had been pushed back against the wall.

"Clear." They pivoted back to the main area, and he eyed the form on the bed. The old man. Rosenblum, he recognized from the picture Ben-Haim had provided.

Max had secured the girl to a chair in the far corner using plastic cuffs. "She had a phone. Talking to our assassin, no doubt." He pointed to the bed, where Piper stood, hand over her mouth as she stared down at the bed. "Midas, check it out."

Seeing her like that pulled Colton forward. He glanced at the still form on the bed. Bruised and bloodied face, a graying bearded also stained with blood. Bandaged hands. But a steady rise and fall of his chest.

Midas darted to the bed and dropped to his knees. He unloaded a pack as he felt for the man's carotid artery.

Slowly, Piper knelt. "Baba?"

"No!" the young girl shouted, looking toward the elderly man. "Don't touch him!" The girl's brow flickered as she saw Piper beside the bed. "Leave him alone. Don't hurt him!"

Next to him, Max asked, "What kind of assassin leaves his objectives in a hotel room?"

"One who knew we were coming?" Colton didn't like the idea, but it was the only one that presented itself.

Glaring, Max joined the scene at the bed. "What've you got, Midas?"

"Severe dehydration, obvious damage to the hands, no broken bones as far as I can tell." He grunted. "I don't know what else."

"He make him sleep," the young girl mumbled in broken English. They considered the old man.

"Now why would a killer have his victim sleep?" Max shook his head. "This is too weird. Prep him for transport, Midas."

On her knees, Piper reached with trembling fingers toward the bruised face. Blood mottled the beard that looked plucked out in several spots. "Baba," she whispered. "Baba, it's me." She pressed her lips to his face. "It's Lily."

Heart in his throat, Colton ached for her. Ached at the sweet name he'd never known. Ached to ease the pain so clearly gouged into her face. He stood at the foot of the bed, watching. And he had to admit that he'd do just about anything to remove this pain from her.

She smoothed a hand over the tussled hair. "Oh, Baba. . ."

"Baba?" The girl balked. "It can't be!"

"Quiet!" Max stuffed something in her mouth.

After swabbing down a swatch of the man's forearm, Midas slid an IV into his arm, which elicited a soft moan. The former Green Beret medic then carefully unwound the soiled bandages from their objective's left hand.

Just then, Yitshak Rosenblum's eyes fluttered open.

Piper hauled in a breath and pushed up on her knees. "Baba, can you hear me? I'm here. Your Lily is here."

A raspy noise issued from the old man. Then he cleared his throat. "How. . . ?" came his strained question. Then his face screwed into sheer panic. His arms flailed. "No, no! You must. . .leave."

Surprise pushed Piper back, but just as quickly, she tried to quiet him. "Shh." She eased onto the bed beside her father.

Only then did Colton realize how thin and frail Mr. Rosenblum truly was—so much that his body didn't take up much of the narrow bed. Matter of fact, it sickened Colton when he thought Mickey would've filled the same amount of space.

Midas slid another needle into the IV and depressed the plunger.

Aged, bruised, and bloodied fingers wrapped around Piper's arm. "Bombs. . .they're moving them. . . ."

The words pulled Colton straighter—and he saw Max do the same. A bomb? Nobody mentioned a bomb. Within seconds, Max stood at his side with a scowl that could create its own nuclear blast.

"No tiimmme. . ." He shook his head. "Get me out of here." His voice sounded stronger. Clearer. He pushed up.

"Hey!" Midas snapped, and when they looked at him, he tapped the IV bag. "Relax or you'll rip this out."

Max keyed his mic. "Legend, Squirt, we need you in here. Two friendlies. Kid and Scar, watch for the assassin. He is unaccounted for."

"Roger that," the Kid's voice came through unaffected.

Seconds later, Colton unlocked the hall door for Legend and Squirt.

"Give us a hand here," Max ordered as they shifted the old man onto a stretcher.

"Movement on the lawn!" Legend's voice snapped through the coms. "It's the assassin. He's scoping the room."

"Take cover!"

The others scrambled as Colton caught Piper's arm and tugged her toward the closet. He directed her inside, scanned the room—Max behind the Saudi girl, Midas tucked in the corner next to the bed, Legend on his belly, his weapon tucked under the blanket hanging off the empty bed, and the Kid slipping into the bathroom. Colton pulled the door to, leaving just enough of a crack to aim his M4 but not give himself away.

Behind him, he heard Piper's uneven breathing. He glanced over his shoulder at her, surprised to find her huddling very close.

Those caramel eyes he loved rose to his, streaked with fear. . . uncertainty. "What if he kills my father?"

Colton peeked into the room again. Satisfied it was clear, he returned his attention to Piper. "He won't."

She inched closer. "How can you be sure?" she whispered.

"Quiet," he hissed. Even though she'd whispered, he didn't want to alert the assassin to their presence. But right then, he saw her near-tangible fear. And his heart hitched into his throat. He caught her hand and set it on the drag strap of the flak vest. Then gave a gentle pat as he shifted back to monitoring the room.

As he stood there, his mind reaching for the assassin huddled out in the darkness beyond the hotel, he felt her catch the other side of his vest, too. Soon, her weight pressed against his right shoulder. When he checked, he found her resting her forehead against him. The sight tangled his mind something fierce, but he quickly reminded himself that she sought comfort, that's all. A normal response to anyone not battle hardened.

But it was Piper. And he liked her being close.

Mentally, he shoved her away, remembering his own father. Hers lay on the bed, here in her homeland—the same homeland where his sister died—and his lay in a coffin awaiting burial.

"I do love you, Colton."

Colton squeezed his eyes shut.

"Please. . .please don't let my father die," she whispered in a voice hoarse. "I know. . . I know you're angry with me because your father died. But please don't let my father die."

He glowered at her. How could she think that of him? Did she really think he valued a human life so little he'd do something like that? Hurt spiraled through him like a heady venom. He jerked back to the door.

The curtain fluttered.

Yeshua, I beg You—save my father!

Loving the man hadn't blinded her. Colton was a skilled, lethal soldier. He knew what he was doing and did it better than anyone, Midas had said on their way to the rendezvous point. Despite that, she didn't think for a minute he'd just let her father die to get revenge on her. Knowing an assassin stood within killing distance had set her on edge and made her panic, saying things she didn't mean.

Though it was dark in the closet, she didn't miss the outrage in Colton's expression. She'd wounded him with her words. She'd just been so desperate. Her father—less than ten feet separated them, yet she could do nothing to help him.

Even now with his broad shoulders completely blocking her view of the room, Colton stood tensed and ready to engage the enemy. She could feel his rigid stance and hoped it didn't go all the way to his heart. There had to be a way to mend the rift between them. She couldn't lose him. . .or her father.

What if she lost both?

Piper let her head drop against his flak vest again, not for the strength and comfort she felt being close to him, but for the ability to detect the way he tensed. Despite the vest smelling of dirt and sweat, she could detect the faint scent of the man she loved. And would always love.

A second later, he straightened, and she felt his arm come up with the weapon. When Colton slid back to line up the weapon, Piper shifted away to give him room. Her heat skipped a beat as almost simultaneously she heard the change in air pressure—the door had opened.

The assassin had finally come.

CHAPTER 22

Get down! Get down!"

Colton rushed from the closet, his M4 trained on the stout young man with death in his eyes. Weapon almost pressed against the man's head, Max forced him down.

The guy sprang up and swung a back-handed fist at Max. Though he stumbled, Max never released his weapon.

Griffin lunged into the fray. Both hands grabbed at the man fighting Max. A kick darted up and caught Griffin in the knee. "Aagh!"

Max rammed a hard right into the guy's face, quickly followed by a swift undercut to the gut. But the assassin seemed unfazed. He rammed Max hard.

Stepping in again, Legend caught a fist—but not the one that nailed his jaw. Flames erupted from the large man's eyes. He sliced both hands against the assassin's shoulders.

With the way those three were going at it, Colton couldn't risk taking a shot. No telling who he'd hit. He glanced back to Piper, relieved to find her hovering in the closet.

Crack! Crash!

"Stop him!"

The noise drew him back around. A tangle of bodies left the door propped open. Squirt and Legend wobbled to their feet. Struggling to extricate himself from a tangle of cords from the overturned TV, Max cursed and jerked free. Unbelievably, the assassin had slipped away and escaped the room. Max scrabbled to his feet and flung open the door.

Sparks flew off the metal frame as Max pushed into the open, but he ducked and kept moving, followed closely by Griffin.

How did that guy take down two of their best?

With a deft move, Azzan landed a punch that dropped the first guy. He'd no sooner taken a step than another brick wall slammed into his back. He hit the beach, face first. Grit puffed in his face. He swiveled around, trying to lock his legs around the guy, but the rock-solid abs seemed to be a mile wide.

The guy flipped him over.

Azzan used the man's over-eagerness and managed to spin out of the man's grasp and leap to his feet. The big guy was just as fast—and enormous. But what frightened Azzan was the fluid moves that belied his size.

And the guy knew how to fight.

Despite his best technique, the gorilla avoided a lethal strike. He wasn't even trying to kill him, but to knock him out and get on with things. They'd set a trap, he'd fallen into it, but he wouldn't get downed again.

Raiyah.

The thought of her spiraled adrenaline through his veins. He had to get back to her and to the old man. Had they already killed him?

The gorilla of a guy shifted and dove in fast.

Azzan came at him from the outside. Slid a hand around his neck. Used the other to swing the guy around in a corkscrew move, then retraced the steps, landing the guy on his back. The gorilla landed with a thud.

Go, now! Azzan launched over the broad chest, but the guy raised a hand, caught Azzan's foot. He flipped forward. His hands dusted the beach. He used the momentum to roll himself through and bounce upright. Kept moving.

"Stop, or I'll shoot!"

He made the fatal mistake of looking back. Saw the muzzle aimed at him. The determined gaze behind the scope.

Dressed in black, head to toe, the guy aimed an M4 at him.

Breathing hard, Azzan slowly rose to his full height, wiped the dribble of warmth sliding down his chin. Muscles twitching, firing neurons told him to run. But the look in the man's face. . .the way he held the weapon with a relaxed yet determined pose made him hesitate.

"You can run," he barked, "but you'll only die tired."

"Go ahead." With an evil grin, gorilla pushed to his feet. "Run." He sneered. "Please make my day."

The wiry guy spoke from behind. "He's never missed yet."

Rhetoric like that had tricked many of his kind.

So had whizzing bullets.

"I just wanted to help the old man and the girl."

The man was slipperier than a brand new foal, and for that reason, Colton wouldn't lower his weapon till Max and Legend had the assassin secured. "Help them, what? Die?" He watched as a very ticked off Max came up behind the guy, grabbed his arm, and yanked it back and up, forcing the man to his knees.

"Help them by running?" Max cinched plastic strips around the guy's arms.

He and Legend hoisted the assassin to his feet. They trudged back to the hotel, and Colton felt the tension knots mount at the half-dozen patrons watching from their patios and windows. He lowered his weapon to the side and held it at an angle that hopefully wouldn't put anyone into a panic. They had witnesses, and that most likely meant authorities.

Speaking of...that wail in the distance was probably their personal escort to the local prison.

"Short on time," he mumbled to Max as they crossed the paved entrance to room 166.

Inside, Max and Legend moved the man toward the bed—but he stumbled. Slumped against the bed—and used the momentum to bounce back up. He thrust a foot into Legend's gut, doubling him. Then he flung around and did the same to the Kid, who flew back into the TV.

Piper screamed.

With a wicked move, the guy hopped through his arms, bringing his hands to the front. He threaded his fingers, then spun and looped his arms around Piper's neck. With a thrust, he pulled her into a stranglehold.

Weapon snapped up, Colton felt everything in him go cold. "Let her go!" Colton roared, sighting the guy. He could take him, but the risks were tremendous, especially with a weapon he wasn't intimately familiar with. He could miss and hit Piper. Or Midas hovering over Piper's father.

"I want out of here," the assassin said. "And I don't want anyone following."

"Not happening," Griffin said with a fierce growl as he came to his feet, holding his stomach. "The only place you're going is six feet under."

"Stop—stop—stop!" Piper held out her hands to both Colton and Griffin, her stomach arched out as she tried to maintain her balance. Her eyes were wide—but not with the terror he'd expected at being the personal shield of an assassin.

"That's right," the assassin said with a sneer. "Listen to the lady."

Something glinted in Piper's expression. "Colton, don't shoot him. Please—I promise, he won't hurt me."

"How do you know that?" Yet even as he asked, he couldn't help but notice the matching eyes.

"He's. . .he's my cousin."

With the issued Glock trained on the assassin, Colton held firm but still.

So did the assassin. He peeked over Piper's shoulder. Then shifted. "Lily?" The disbelief pitched his voice. "I don't. . .understand." He released her.

That was all the team needed.

Griffin pounced on him. Rammed his fist into the guy's face. Immediately, Max was on him, too.

With another scream, Piper shuffled back as the three wrestled. She spun to Colton. "Make them stop. Please!" Tears rimmed her eyes.

"You saw what he just did."

"Azzan, please—tell them you'll listen, you'll cooperate."

They pressed his face against the floor as the Kid worked to secure his hands and feet. It looked as chaotic as trying to wrestle a squid.

"Okay, okay. . ."

Everything went still. Could they believe the guy?

Not on their lives!

Max palmed the guy's face, pressing downward, and leaned close. "One wrong move..."

"How do I know I can trust you people?" the assassin—Azzan—asked.

"You don't." Max eased off him, his weapon held firmly on the guy.

On his back, Azzan looked up at them, his hands held out in surrender.

"Get up, nice and slow. You've already made enemies with my team. I'm sure Legend won't hesitate to split your gray matter."

Griffin hoisted the M16 higher. The way his former MARSOC buddy hugged that weapon made Colton hesitate, that and the venom pouring out of his eyes.

With a wicked look at Piper, Max said, "You've got things to explain." He pointed to Azzan. "He's Palestinian—inherent Jewish enemy. An assassin." Breathing hard from the fight, Max glared at her. "Any other surprises we should know about?"

"It's not her fault." Azzan slowly rose and settled on the edge of the extra bed, gripping his knees as he caught his breath. "She didn't know. Nobody knew."

"Except me."

Colton's gaze slid back to the old man, who pushed himself out of the bed.

"Whoa, wait." Midas shoved to his feet. "You shouldn't be—"

Rosenblum waved him off. "I am fine."

"Like he—"

"Hey." Glaring at the medic, Azzan stood.

Griffin jerked visibly.

Azzan lowered his head. Raised his palms again.

But the guy's eyes showed no submission. He was placating them. Buying time. And another thing registered—Azzan had the exact same eye color as Piper. Even same skin tone. The similarities stopped there. Their differences included the scar above his left eye that bore testament to the guy's hard edge. Crooked nose. Scar behind the left ear—bullet scar, if Colton wasn't mistaken.

"There are bigger threats than Azzan now, *nachon*?" Rosenblum said as he shuffled toward Max. Very close.

Max shifted. Stared down at the man with gray, mussed hair. "Yeah?"

Most people didn't like others invading their personal space. Especially anyone with military training, because it weakened their tactical advantage. It meant death. Even Colton felt tiny balls of tension beading at the base of his neck. There was too much happening here that the team didn't know about. That left them vulnerable.

Again, Rosenblum inched closer. Why was the old man pushing it?

"Back up, man," Max said, an edge hitting his words.

This time, Piper dove into the fray. "It's just—" She hesitated when the Kid moved toward her. "Would you calm down?" Her voice piqued.

Max glowered. "We'll sort this later. Let's move out."

"No, listen," Azzan said. "The reason my uncle went into hiding is because right now six messengers are either entering or are already within the borders of Israel with backpack nukes."

CHAPTER 23

Hold up."

At Max's terse words, Piper turned to her father, noticing the way he wobbled, and wrapped an arm around his shoulders. Were they bonier than before?

"Nukes? Are you serious?" Colton's voice scraped down her spine.

"I thought this was a simple snatch-n-grab," the Kid whined.

Her stomach rumbled, having not eaten since they'd been on the plane, but also from the threat hovering in this hotel room. She glanced at her father. At Azzan. Why had her father entrusted her cousin with the reason why they went into hiding? And how long had Baba known his nephew was an assassin?

Assassin. The world nearly buckled her knees. Killing. . .how could he do that after Bazak's senseless death? She'd definitely need to talk to him at length later.

"The longer we stand here talking, the closer they will be to their targets, nachon?"

"What's with the nachos?" the Kid asked.

"*Nachon.* It's like saying *right,*" Piper answered without thinking.

Midas grinned. And popped the Kid's head. "He's just messing with you."

"I'm going to hit the next person who does that."

Baba moved toward the Kid. Pointed a finger. "You are in Israel, and we will do as my people do. Respect your elders, nachon?" The emphasis on that last word and the sparkle in his eyes couldn't be missed despite the bruises and cuts.

"Dude." The Kid backed up a step. "Step off." He returned to the door and peered through the pulled-to curtain. "I'll scout it out." With that, he rushed into the night.

"Enough," Max said with a growl. "We move out. Rendezvous back with Ben-Haim."

"We must go to Be'er Sheva."

"Ben-Haim." Max held his ground.

So did her father.

"Shh, Baba." Hands on her father's chest, she tried to steady him. These men were on edge, and her father's rambling—innocent but insistent rambling—worsened the mood. Azzan certainly hadn't helped. Even now he looked at the large black man in a silent challenge, which Legend matched. The two would kill each other before this was over.

"Kid gave the all clear," Midas called from the door, where he peeked out into the night.

"Okay, let's go." Max motioned to Colton. "Help them if they need it."

"We're fine," Azzan said.

Her father, though slight after his captivity, was still heavy. She wasn't sure she could make it. Shrugging her shoulder under his arm for better positioning, she glanced at Azzan. "We might need that help you just shoved away."

His piercing eyes snapped to hers. Full of anger. "We're fine. If I have to, I'll carry him before I let them—"

"No." Baba groaned. "No, we must go to Be'er Sheva." He glanced at Max. "Please, if we don't, it will be too late. Al-Jafari has mobilized."

"Not my problem. Back to base." Max gave signals to the team.

Why wouldn't they listen to her father? Didn't they understand this wasn't about just them...about her father only? He'd done all this, endured long hard months of hiding and captivity, to save millions of people. *My people.*

"If my father believes there is danger—"

"Piper," Colton's voice sailed from behind, warming her by its strength. "Leave it. We can't break orders."

She looked back at him, disappointment chugging through her veins, and yet—it hit her. He wasn't glaring at her like he'd been doing just a few hours earlier. Even here in the middle of a mission and dressed in tactical gear, she saw the cowboy she loved. The man with a tender heart. The man with unwavering resolve.

Her father stumbled, almost dragging her down with him. Together with Azzan, they got him back on his feet. But he twisted around to Max, who stood near the door, watching as two of the guys left the room.

"You must listen, nachon?" Baba moved forward. His forward momentum forced her to aid him lest he fall. "There is no time. Be'er Sheva."

"All quiet," Max said.

Piper swallowed hard.

Baba shifted to Azzan. "How can we make them understand?"

Almost instantly, two M4s snapped up—Legend's and Colton's.

"Go on," Legend's words seemed to seep from his very being. His lips hadn't moved. Challenge darkened his eyes. Body angled straight at Azzan, he looked ready to riddle her cousin with bullets.

The expression in Colton's eyes held the same determination.

She couldn't blame them. Learning about her cousin unseated any confidence she'd had in him, especially learning he had worked for the Palestinians. Nervous didn't come close to explaining what she felt. Though he'd been raised in Palestine, they'd visited through the years, and their relationship had always been strong. But this man—the man with balled fists and sneering lips—she didn't know him.

"Quiet," Max said with a snarl. He signaled to Legend, then to Azzan. "You two. Together. Go!"

Hesitation gripped both men, as if their feet were planted several feet underground. They considered each other. Then Legend grabbed Azzan's collar and yanked him out the door. Her stomach swirled, remembering how her cousin had never liked to be handled. Legend would figure that out soon, she imagined.

"Cowboy, we'll cradle the old man." Max hooked an arm under her father's shoulder, his eyes on hers. "Stay with us."

Huddling close, she kept a hand on her father, feeling somehow as if she were helping, even though the tangle of legs as she tried to keep pace with the three men made it almost impossible. Just as they cleared the grassy area, she noticed the steady *thwump* of a helicopter. The noise intensified as they fought the shifting sand to get to the big craft sitting up the stretch of the beach.

Wind ripped at her. Beads of sand pepped her face. Eyes squeezed shut, she pushed onward. The force of the rotors seemed to push her back. She stumbled. Pulled herself up—and fell again. The ground gave way, making it impossible to gain traction against that and the gale-force winds of the helicopter.

An arm came around her and hauled her up, dragged her toward the bird. She tried to blink and clear the sand from her eyes so she could board. Her shin banged against the narrow step. She pitched forward—her hands planted on the interior.

In a humiliating move, someone gave her backside a shove, propelling her inside. Piper scrambled, feeling the heat rush up her neck and into her face as she climbed into the canvas rack seat. Wiping her eyes, she tried to make sense of the interior, but the dark hour made it next to impossible.

A weight dropped next to her.

"Two years Israeli Army, huh?" Colton's near-shout increased her embarrassment. The helicopter lifted, pressing her against the seat— and yet to the side as the nose dipped, then pulled up and leveled out.

Though she wasn't sure, Piper thought she heard a smile in his words. Still she didn't know what to say, and the thought of him pushing her through the door by her rear end renewed the heat infusing her face. Humiliating! She'd never been so clumsy. And it had to be right in front of him that she fell and couldn't gain traction. She couldn't even see! The sand kept shifting.

What was the use? She'd proven his point that she wasn't trained and capable to be here. Yet. . .she'd made it. They'd completed the mission—well, almost. Just a few more minutes, and her father would be safe.

He leaned forward and shouted something to Max, who sat by the open door as they sped through Israeli airspace. Because of the deafening roar of the engines combined with the air rushing through the chopper, she couldn't hear what they said.

When Colton sat back, his broad shoulders overlapped into her space, pressing her against the interior hull of the helicopter. A second later, he seemed to relax, and now she felt pinned. Oddly enough, she found comfort in the position, as if he were protecting her. Piper met Raiyah's gaze and the smirk lingering on the girl's pink lips.

Shaking and shuddering, the bird numbed her entire body. Almost without effort, her eyes started to drift closed.

"RPG, three o'clock, incoming!"

Piper's eyes snapped open.

The chopper veered left. Hard.

She gripped the seat tightly.

A bright flash shattered the night. Pain darted across the back of her head. In a blink, darkness devoured her.

Smoke billowed up in a thick, dark cloud, blotting out the pale moon. Colton jerked himself upright, coughing. He dragged in a long, ragged breath as he extricated himself from a tangle of supplies and people. Rosenblum lay beneath him, holding Colton off his chest. The world had tilted—no, not the world. The helicopter lay partially on one side.

"You okay?" Colton asked, noting his ears felt plugged.

The old man nodded.

On his knees, Colton let his instincts absorb the information in a split-second recon. An RPG attack. Meant shooters. Meant someone would hunt them down. And those someones were probably on their way already. They had to clear out.

"Move out before they find us or this bird blows," Max shouted, as if reading Colton's mind. He dragged himself to the rear of the Mi-17 toward the hatch that now hung open.

Blinking, Colton helped Rosenblum to his feet. "You steady?"

The thick tendrils of smoke trailed through the cabin and encircled the old man. He smoothed his shirt, but then his eyes widened. "Where is Lily?"

The question jerked Colton up. He probed the figures looming in the smoke at the tail of the bird. Not there. He twisted around and searched the disarray. He flung boxes aside. "Maybe she's already—"

There! He lunged to his right, where he saw her legs in the tangle of supplies. "Piper!" Ripping packs off her, Colton worked, his heart thundering. "Piper." He dropped to the metal floor and turned her over. She flopped. His heart rammed up into his throat. He bent closer. *No!*

"Is she breathing?" her father asked, his voice riddled with the same fear Colton fought.

"Cowboy, out. Now!" Max clambered into the bird toward Rosenblum. "Rabbi, come on."

The old man straightened as he looked toward Max. "I am not—"

"Now!" Max shouted.

Colton gathered Piper into his arms and rushed out of the chopper, trailing her father. He'd no sooner cleared the opening, when he probed the huddle of men for the doc. "Medic!"

Midas turned. Even with the smoke and darkness, the moonlight seemed to glow against his widened eyes. He jogged toward them. "What happened?" He pressed two fingers to her neck.

"Dunno," Colton said he laid her on the ground.

"Pulse is fine." With a small blue light, Midas checked her eyes.

Piper groaned and turned away.

"Easy there," Midas said.

A wash of relief dumped into Colton's gut as Piper rolled her head—then winced. Her eyes opened, then pinched closed—apparently because of Midas's light.

"Piper, what hurts?" Colton asked as he knelt beside her.

"Hey," Midas said, "I'm the medic."

"Right." Good thing it was dark and they couldn't see the red heat plowing into his face.

"My head," she mumbled as she tried to sit up, then yelped and grabbed the back of her head.

Midas shifted around. "Whacked it pretty good. There's a bloody spot, but it's not oozing still, so that's good. I'll clean it up in a sec." Crouching before her, he held up the pen light. "Follow my light."

Piper grimaced, but followed the light through pinched eyes.

"How many lights can you see?"

"One—and it's bright."

"I think you've got a mild concussion." Midas chuckled. "Okay, let me clean it up." With his kit, he did his best to clean up the spot and put a bandage over it. "This will probably hurt more when you remove it and pull your hair out with it." He tied up his kit. As he stood, he pivoted to Colton. "Keep an eye on her for the usual—nausea, dizziness, you know the drill."

Colton nodded.

"Okay, people," Max said. "Heard from Ben-Haim."

The tone in Max's voice forced Colton's attention away from Piper.

"We're on our own." His eyes held the fury Colton had seen far too often. "Since we aren't supposed to be here, let's make that true. We have roughly four kilometers to the facility."

"No, we must go to Be'er Sheva."

"Sorry, old man," Max said as he slung his pack over his shoulder. "We're getting our tails back to the base before someone makes Swiss cheese of us."

This was his chance to gain their trust. Not to be pals with them. But to maneuver this situation in his favor. "I know a place we can go." Azzan glanced at Raiyah and tucked aside his roiling emotions.

The leader, they'd called him Frogman, looked at him. Eyes dark and foreboding. Questions lingered but also a desperation that nearly made Azzan smile. They had no choice but to trust him. Out here in the open with Bedouins. Islamic radicals. Israeli police. It really didn't matter who shot them down. If the Americans were caught here, there would be a merciless uproar and slaughter.

Azzan seized the man's hesitation. "We head northeast two klicks. There's a village—people, cars. . ."

Frogman's lips drew into a smirk. His hand coiled around the M4 cradled across his chest, his meaning clear. If this went bad, he'd take it out of Azzan's hide. Still looking at him, Frogman called, "You heard the man. Two kilometers northeast. Fast and quiet."

Azzan rushed to Lily and his dod. He swept past the large man who'd carried her out and tucked an arm under her shoulders. "Come, we will get to a shelter."

Dod bent closer. "You must help me convince them."

"Convince them of what?" The Cowboy hadn't moved away. Hadn't he taken the hint that he wasn't needed here? Besides, Azzan didn't like the way the man doted over Lily. It was too familiar. And he was American.

"This way. Hurry." Ignoring the question, Azzan shifted and met Raiyah's steady gaze. A feeling like butterflies flitted through his stomach as she tentatively stepped forward. When this was over, he would make sure she was taken care of. Perhaps even take care of her himself. Would she have him? If the smile in her full lips was any indication. . . The thought spurred him on.

He led them toward a small hill that would provide barely the cover they needed to make it the two kilometers to the village. There, he could surely find a vehicle to steal—borrow. Finish the mission he'd started. Could he contact Nesher?

No, it was too dangerous. Although the Americans were following his lead, the trust wasn't there. He would wait. There was still a measure of time.

Or he would have to force their hand.

CHAPTER 24

Y ou're sure this is safe?"

Piper eased her father onto the chair in the darkened corner of the small home, her gaze locked on Colton, Max, and Azzan hovering by the door. Midas knelt beside Baba, removed the IV line, then placed a small bandage over it.

"I own it. It's okay." Azzan walked to a cabinet that sat under a curtained window on the opposite wall, opened it, and drew something out. "Give me ten minutes, and I'll be back with a vehicle big enough for all of us."

"And where are you going to get that?" Legend seemed to suck up every extra inch not occupied by the ten people filling the one-room abode.

"I can't tell you." Azzan stopped and shifted to the other men. "Listen, I have more invested in seeing this thing finished than any of you, save my uncle." His eyes, a mirror of her own, seemed to implore the team to trust him.

At least he was smart enough not to ask them for trust.

"I'm going with him," Legend said.

"Agreed."

"No!" Max and Azzan stared at one another after they'd spoken in unison.

Her cousin combed his fingers through his closely shorn hair. "I can move quicker and with less notice than I could if a large, black man were with me. He stands out. I don't. The people know me."

"He's right." Piper blinked, realizing those words were hers. When the others looked over at her, squatting next to her father, she straightened. "Legend will be too noticeable here."

But she had to admit she didn't entirely trust her cousin right now. "And accents," Piper said. "Surely Azzan's will be noticed. Anyone can tell he's not from here."

Her cousin puffed his chest. "The people know me, know I travel for business."

"What kind of business?" Legend asked.

"My own." Azzan's confidence hadn't wavered. He pointed to Max. "I'll take you, but keep your mouth shut."

"Fool—you don't give orders." Legend folded his thick arms over his barrel-sized chest.

Azzan's eyes glittered under the low lights. "Here, I do. You don't know where you are or where you're going."

The Kid stepped up next to Legend but looked a midget beside the oversized man. "We didn't get to be the best by being stupid."

"No, just ignorant and narrow minded."

Piper covered her mouth, disbelieving her cousin. He'd always been forthright, but his boldness bordered on belligerence—and stupidity with the men in this room. Without thinking, she hurried to Azzan and touched his arm.

But it was too late.

Legend tensed. Unfolded his arms. "You want to try that—"

"I'll go." Max nodded. "Legend, one hour."

Features taut, Legend glowered.

When he yielded, Piper felt the kinks in her stomach lessen—but only a little.

Creaking, the open door afforded a somber wash of moonlight into the home for a second before darkness once again descended as it shut.

"Okay, people. Lights low, voices even lower." Legend moved through the house and propped himself against the front door.

Colton stalked out of the shadows, cradling that weapon. "Eyes out. Windows and doors." He walked through the house and out of view, past the curtained-off room that no doubt held a lone bed.

The others situated themselves at the remaining windows and back door. Joining her father at the table, Piper felt the weariness seep into her muscles, the cold night aching her bones. She should be happy to see Baba—and she was—but there were so many secrets, so many things he'd never shared. Yet it all seemed so silly to harbor resentment over that when, according to what he'd said at the hotel, they were fighting for the survival of their nation.

"You are angry."

His wizened voice drew her gaze from the knots of the small table. "Hurt."

"Don't you understand?" he whispered. "I could not tell you, or you would have been in danger."

Piper jerked forward. "I *was* in danger, Baba! It was unfair to send me away, not knowing what I was fighting or running from. They came after me, hunted me down. They killed Colton's father!" she kept her voice tight and controlled.

"Colton?" He shrugged. "Who is this?"

"It doesn't matter." Oh but it did, so very much! She quickly tucked away the deep feelings and hurt to focus on the issue at hand. "The point is you sent me away, did not tell me anything, and they still found me."

"Forgive me," he whispered. "I do not know how they found you. We did everything we could to stay out of their sight and control." His cold hand settled on hers. "Who is this Colton? Why did his father get killed?"

She swallowed, her ears burning as she wondered if Colton had overheard them. Yet no sound came from behind her at the rear of the house. She braved a glance but could not see him through the curtain.

"The tall man, he is Colton?"

Bringing her attention back to her father, she gave a slow bob of her head. "I. . .I think if it were not for him, we would not have come."

"These men. . .they came because of him—and his father was killed?"

Though she did not want to relive that night, she had to tell her father about the great sacrifice. "They came to my apartment, tried to get the transmitter."

"Ah."

"But Colton stopped them. Killed one of the men. Soon, they brought more to his home and attacked." Burning started at the back of her eyes. "I heard his mother scream. We ran through the house. . . and found his dad there, dying." A tear slipped down, remembering Colton's grief and the brokenness she'd seen. The way his heart had hardened toward her, sealing off the hope of any future with him.

"He all but quit, right in front of me, but the other men, they must have convinced him to join the mission to save you." Piper sighed. "His sister died here, years earlier in a café bombing."

Her father's eyes rose behind her, focused so intently on some point that she turned to see if Colton had appeared. When she looked back at her father, his lips parted. Then he slowly shook his head. "He came to help me when our enemies killed his father?" The disbelief hung thick in her father's words. A twinkle shone in his eyes. "This is why you love him, nachon?"

Piper straightened, her pulse racing.

He chuckled. "So, I was not delirious from deprivation." He stroked the unkempt beard. A few minutes later, he pushed from his chair. Started for the curtained room.

Heart stalled, Piper gripped the back of her chair. She hissed, "Baba, no."

Shoulder propped against the wall, Colton peered through the narrow slit into the darkness. He lifted the handheld scope and scanned the distance. Unsettled at being here, knowing they were sitting ducks had kept the adrenaline pumping through his veins.

He'd seen the way Piper had sided with her cousin when Max had called the shots. And that hurt. Made him wonder if she'd ever felt anything for him, or if she was just trying to bide her time while her father sorted out the affairs of a nation.

Nah. He didn't believe that, but his heart and mind needed ammo to keep going, to make sense of this twisted mess. Bouncing the scope in his hand, he peeked down the darkened street. Homes lined the sliver of a dirt road. Most decent people were asleep, unaware of the team of Americans huddled in their midst. And he'd like to keep it that way. Get out of here. Get home to Mickey and his mother.

And bury my father.

Squeezing the thought out of his mind, Colton lifted the scope and once again scanned the surrounding areas. He flipped it to thermal, hoping to give himself some reassurance.

A noise rustled near him. He pulled the scope away from his eyes—and flinched.

The old man stood right in front of him, watching.

A swirl of adrenaline and warmth washed through Colton's gut. "You should be resting." He put the scope to his eye again, glad he didn't have to stare into those eyes any more than necessary.

"The village is quiet, nachon?"

Colton lowered the device but maintained his vigil watching the perimeter. "Reckon so." Come to think of it, there was an unnatural quiet here. . .not just in this village, but this entire country. And it had him on edge.

"My apologies for the loss of your father."

Colton darted the old man a look. "This isn't the time or place for—"

"For as long as the nation of Israel has existed, there have been those who have sought to destroy it." Yitshak Rosenblum bore a vehemence, despite the deep bruises and heavy beard. "Long has the Kingdom of Darkness waged a war to wipe God's people from the face of the earth. Nation after nation killed or attacked Jews, slaughtered the firstborn males time and again. Never against any other race has there been such deep-seated hatred." He drew in a breath, his thick bushy eyebrows knotting together. "Germans died protecting Jews. And British. Even Americans."

What was his point? That they were all going to die here, waiting for the man's nephew to return? Or was the assassin bringing death upon them while they just sat here waiting for it?

"Your father's life was taken to protect our country as well."

No, no don't react. Keep it tight. Controlled.

Colton pushed his head down, battling to strangle the first reaction—to lash out at the man. They had to keep it quiet, not draw attention. Forget it. He couldn't do it. Colton narrowed his eyes at Rosenblum, unwilling to let the justification stand. "My father was on *my* property, heading to bed. He wasn't here; he wasn't fighting a war. And he didn't have a choice."

Yitshak smiled. "You are here to help Israel, nachon?"

Colton clamped his mouth shut. He wasn't going to play into this man's hands.

"Even though your father was killed?"

Each breath came harder, faster.

"I do not think the apple falls far from the tree. You are like your father, yes?"

Colton nodded—didn't mean to, but he did. Wished he hadn't because he didn't want to give this man any ammo to pelt him with.

"Why are you here?"

Swallowing, Colton pushed off the wall. Turned to the window. To the curtain where the others stood guard on the other side. "We don't have time for this."

"What you do not have time for, Colton, is to allow an enemy in your camp."

His heart caught. Enemy? Was he referring to Azzan?

Holding up a hand, Yitshak stayed him. "No, I do not refer to a man. There are already many enemies out there, coming for us, but the one to which I refer, the one you do not need is in here," he said, tapping Colton's vest-protected chest. "Bitterness is a defeat you cannot afford."

"Bitter—" Colton chomped down on the word. His chest hammered. He tried hard to breathe, saw his nostrils flare.

A somber expression stole into Yitshak's face. "I ask your forgiveness for the pain that all this has brought upon you. No doubt you feel my daughter has betrayed you."

Colton looked away. Hating the way this man read his soul like an open manual. Yes. . .yes, Piper had betrayed him. Cut the heart right out of him, not trusting him, hiding secrets, keeping him at arm's length and a lifetime from the truth.

"Deep betrayal can cause us to close our hearts to our own experiences of forgiveness." Yitshak came a step closer.

Colton nudged him back. "Stay out from in front of the window." But really, it was the proximity of the man's soul-probing gaze that upended his frayed nerves.

"I see in you, Colton, the light of Yeshua Himself."

Wiping a hand over his face, Colton tried to fix his attention on the street. The desert. Anything but this old man.

"You are a believer in Yeshua, nachon?"

"Yes," Colton said between ground teeth. Not because he wanted to deny Christ, but because he felt like he'd just handed this guy an RPG to take down the defenses that had barricaded Colton's heart.

"Do we not all have the guilt and blood of *Yeshua* on our hands? There is no greater betrayal, yet we have his unconditional love." Yitshak let out a breathy laugh.

"Quiet," Colton said, knowing full well the man wasn't loud—yet the words screamed through his thick skull.

"There." Yitshak pointed toward the east. "Not far from that turn in the road is Abraham's Well." His eyes glittered. "You know it, nachon?"

The change in subject startled Colton. But at least Rosenblum had left off the lecture. "No."

"When Jacob, son of Isaac, came to the well, he saw his kinswoman, Rachel." He smiled. "You know the story, nachon? He worked for seven years only to be tricked—"

"Look, we should be—"

"Jacob's firstborn son by his beloved Rachel was Joseph. The treasured and favored son."

"His brothers sold him."

"Yes, sold." Yitshak nodded as his gaze rested on something out in the window, his eyes seemingly lost. "To Bedouins. A slave in Egypt. Countless years he spent not as the son of the promised one—Israel—but as a slave to pharaoh."

"Sometimes life sucks."

"Isn't fair." Yitshak all but glowed. "When presented with a moment of reconciliation, what did Joseph say to the very brothers who preferred cold silver to the loving warmth of their own brother?"

Dawg, he'd stepped right into it, hadn't he?

"'And now, do not be distressed and do not be angry with yourselves for selling me here, because it was to save lives that God sent me ahead of you.'" Yitshak tilted his head. "Did not Joseph, of all men who have been wronged, have the greatest reason to hate and become embittered?"

"Look," Colton said, his voice and heart tangled amid Rosenblum's words. . .the *truth* of those words. "I know you—"

"Yeshua seeks to use you for His purposes. Are you a man that you would dictate to God how He would accomplish His purposes?"

How dare this man! "I've prayed night and day for God to lead me, guide me, to make me stronger and prepare me. Yet, I am tormented with memories, suffer debilitating flashbacks, and now—now my father is killed. And you're going to stand there and tell me it's God's will? Why should I pray? It hasn't done me much good."

Yitshak drew back, his brow again knotted. "What? You think

praying is supposed to make life easier? If the great I Am answers your prayers, it is not to make life easier, but to prepare you to handle more!"

The words silenced him.

"My Lily loves you." Rosenblum's chest puffed out. Though Colton wasn't sure, he thought a healthy rosiness filled the old man's cheeks. "You love her as well. I see it, rooted deep, which is why the secrets she kept from you hurt all the more." He clamped a hand on Colton's shoulder and squeezed. "Forgiveness is for our own good."

"Heads up." Legend's voice came from the front of the house. "We got movement."

CHAPTER 25

So far, the man had followed his lead without question. If he could just get him in the building. . . "Almost there." He let them in and guided the man they called Frogman to the lower level. Hustling down stairs, he said, "Frogman—so, you were a Navy SEAL once."

Their feet thudded against the steel steps.

"I wonder at your team. An interesting arrangement of men and experience." Just one more floor. So close. . . Frogman hadn't spoken yet. No doubt this diversion had the man sweating his decision to come with Azzan.

"Your silence tells me everything." They reached the lower level, the basement, and he walked swiftly toward a steel door. He reached for the knob.

"Don't move." Frogman's terse order slammed Azzan's hopes to the ground.

Azzan turned around. Found a gun trained on him. His hopes plummeted. Even with the weapon holstered at his ankle, he wouldn't have time to grab it before Frogman fired. He did not want to have to kill this man, but they could not play these games much longer.

"I'm not seeing a vehicle," Max said, as he held his stance.

"Just beyond the door will explain everything."

"You got me alone." Max tilted his head. Strong shoulder muscles. Arms. Biceps. Pectorals. The finger resting on the trigger. All these told Azzan the man was prepared to cut him down. "They won't stick around if I don't show up."

"Exactly."

A layer of confidence sheared off the man's posture.

Azzan pointed to a small vent in the ceiling. "On my command, that vent will release a deadly toxin." There could be no other way. "All I ask is that you let me enter this room. It will explain everything."

As Colton shoved Baba into the corner, he took a rigid defensive posture, peering out the window into the night.

Piper hurried to her father and huddled with him. Not only for the comfort of her father's touch, but also for the strength she drew from being near Colton. Even when he wasn't speaking to her. She'd overheard little of what Baba had said to him, their voices whispered and low out of necessity because of their situation.

"Two in my sights," Colton hissed to the other men, who also relayed information. In total, they'd tallied close to a dozen.

Colton glanced at her. His gaze sharpened. "Get back!" He thrust a hand back toward the middle of the house. "Go. Now!"

Scrambling to draw her father with her, Piper hurried around the curtain. She'd no sooner rounded the soft corner than the first crack of gunfire rang out.

"Taking fire!" Legend groused.

"Down, down, down!" the Kid rushed them and shoved them to the dirty floor. "Stay down or you'll get hit." On his belly, he crawled to the far corner, where he slid up against the wall and brought his weapon back up.

Crack! Thwat!

Her father wrapped his hands around hers. "We should pray, nachon?"

With a furtive glance back to the curtained area, she nodded. Wet her lips. "Yes." For Colton. For all of them. "How did they find us?"

"Yeshua, we seek Your protection over these men, over our bodies and minds. Guide their bullets to the targets of those who oppose us and seek to wipe out Your people."

Scooting a bit to the right gave her a better view of the. . .curtain. No matter how she repositioned herself, she could not see Colton. Verify he was okay. Unhurt.

One. . .two. . .three holes in the dingy fabric. It swayed under the forced movement.

"Ammo! I need ammo," Midas called as he motioned to a sack

that lay a few feet from them.

Baba patted her hands. "Stay. I'll get it to him."

Oof!

The sound came from Colton. Piper scurried the six feet to the curtain. Squinted through the dust-filled haze. Squatting, Colton made hand signals toward the far wall. "Go," he bit out the word. "No, back. Back!"

Colton dove toward the wall.

What. . .what was he doing? She glanced to the others. The combined efforts of the seven men devoured the room in a deafening cacophony of bullets and shouts. But. . .Colton. It didn't make sense. Who was he talking to?

She scrambled toward him.

Thwat!

A trail of fire lit across her arm. An unseen force swung her around. She spiraled to the ground.

"*Emelie!* Emelie, you okay?" Colton dragged her to the wall and propped her against the plaster. "Where are you hit?" His hands patted her down, but not. . .not aligned with her body, off-center by a fraction. "Emelie, talk to me." Eyes narrowed, lips taut, he had jerky movements.

Emelie? Why was he calling her that?

He looked over her. At the wall above her head. She peered up. Nothing but the peeling plaster that covered the cinder blocks. Yet his gaze seemed to roam as if sighting targets.

"Colton?"

He glanced down. But instead of the clear, focused eyes, they were distant, as if not seeing her. Was this. . .was *this* what Max was talking about? Her courage leapt into her throat when he seemed to dodge something, swaying back and forth. She pulled herself up—until their eyes met. "Colton." Tentatively, she reached out to touch him—

Pain jolted down her arm. She didn't care. She had to reach him, deep down, and pull him out of this. "Colton, are you okay?" Piper cupped his face.

Colton blinked. Again. Several times. He shook his head, and his drawn brows loosened. He looked around. At her. "Piper." The way he said her name, the huskiness, the emotion weighted with disbelief. Then, his expression fell.

"A—are you okay?" She smoothed a hand along his jaw. "You. . ." What could she say? Already she saw the humiliation clouding his face. "You looked lost."

His gaze bounced around her—and finally fastened onto her arm. "You're shot."

Huh? "I am?" She checked her arm, surprised at the blood trailing down it. "I—I don't think so. Just grazed, maybe." She shrugged, forcing a smile as she peered up at him. "Are you okay?"

He scowled. "I'm fine." He crouched in front of her. "Stay down." With that, he returned to his position, aimed out the window, and fired.

The repetitive whack of the weapons drowned her thundering heart. Colton was not fine. He'd been haunted by the past, his mind possessed by atrocities that laid claim to his faculties. She ached for him. Knew that if the others found out, Colton would be humiliated. But what. . .what if he got "lost" again. . .during a pivotal moment?

"With one word, your girlfriend dies."

Azzan stilled. Raiyah. Would the team of men really kill an innocent girl? Did he really care? His thoughts roamed her features, her smile, her eyes large as dates. . . .

"Just let me open the door."

"Why?"

"We cannot stop al-Jafari without what's in there." Azzan shrugged. "And truly, what choice do you have? I won't go back without what I've come for."

Frogman stared him down. Gave a curt nod.

Though he wanted to smile, he feared it would be taken wrong. As a sneer. He accessed the security panel, entered his code, then pressed his thumb against it. The door whooshed back, sliding into the wall and disappearing from view.

Azzan stepped across the twelve-inch threshold, noting the stale swirl of air that met him. He turned just as Frogman entered.

Two men leapt from the sides and tackled Frogman.

"You've done well."

Azzan shifted toward the voice. Smiled. "It was easier than I expected."

Shaking off the last flashback proved. . .difficult. Now, an annoying buzz lingered at the back of his head. His muscles still felt weak and his pride dented more than ever before, especially "coming to" and seeing Piper's frightened expression. Fear. Pity.

Colton blinked. A shadow moved between the houses. He took aim and fired, wishing the loud *crack* of the M4 could sever the greedy claws of the past just as it severed the threat to the team.

"Clear," Legend called.

Scanning the road, the narrow stretch of road that sliced the small village in two, Colton searched for more unfriendlies. Inside the house, he heard the clear signal given by everyone else on the team. Finally satisfied there were no more living enemies out there, he lowered his weapon. Let out a ragged sigh.

Almost instantly, Piper stood at his side, her hand on his arm.

It was her. She was the reason he'd had the flashback. He'd heard her coming, saw her in his periphery as she hurried toward him. But it shouldn't matter what triggered it. And it didn't. He'd never make it through this alive if he couldn't keep his mind in one piece. He had to keep it together. And keeping it together meant keeping her away.

"Cowboy!"

Colton jerked around.

Near the curtained divider, Legend stood a half-dozen feet off. "You clear?"

"Yeah."

Legend thumbed toward the door. "We need to move out." He looked at the others. "Which way did the assassin go with Frogman?"

"East. Not sure where," Squirt said. "I managed to keep them in my sights for the first klick, but then lost them."

"Then we move east. Can't stay here and get pumped full of lead. We'll skirt the village, stay in the shadows."

Could he do it—could he carry out this mission without succumbing again to the demons that had once controlled his life? Why now? Why had this returned with such unrelenting force?

"Bitterness is a defeat you cannot afford."

A soft touch on his arm, however, drew his gaze to Piper. His gaze flicked to Rosenblum, who stood watching him. Colton looked down. How. . .how had he gotten so far off track that he couldn't keep himself together? He'd had enough of this long ago. Living with flashbacks was no kind of life. He didn't want it. Wouldn't live like this again.

I just want to walk out into the night and keep going.

Again, he looked at Piper. He wished things could've been so different. That he could go back and change a few things.

"Hey!" A slap on his chest snapped him around. Legend grabbed his lapels. "You with me?"

Surprise lit through Colton, along with a lump of humiliation. He stumbled back, then gave Legend a shove. "Back off."

"You with us, Cowboy?"

"We weren't sure you'd come."

Azzan clasped the arm of his handler and nodded. "I wasn't sure either." He turned and nodded to the guards pinning Frogman on the floor. "Get him up."

The two hauled their prisoner to his feet, tugging his hands behind the back so that Frogman's chest arched forward.

"You must understand, in my profession, no one can be trusted." Azzan stood eye-to-eye with him.

"Likewise," Frogman bit out through a bloodied lip.

"Release him." Azzan sighed.

When released, Frogman shuffled forward and regained his balance, looking every bit the vicious soldier he was. Ready to fight. Ready to kill. Ready to do whatever it took to get out of here and back to his team.

Nesher stepped closer. "Your team has been attacked."

Frogman's eyes blazed.

Though Azzan glared at the handler—Nesher really must learn to allow Azzan to handle things—he folded his arms over his chest. "This is my handler." Again, he glowered at Nesher.

"What?" Nesher shrugged as he bobbed his head toward Frogman. "He needs to know."

"What he needs to know is that a team of mercenaries helped protect his pinned-down team." He held out his hands, hoping to calm Frogman, whose gaze flitted between fury and uncertainty. "They are fine. En route toward us even as we speak. That is a good thing."

A deep chuckle. "You have grown soft, Azzan."

He flashed a look at Nesher. "We have a larger purpose the eve of this dark day in history."

"What is that?" Frogman wiped his lips.

Tapping the keys on a control panel, he entered a code. "It is true that I am Palestinian. Also that I am an assassin." He glanced at the man. "But what you are not aware of is that I am a Mossad agent."

Frogman stood, waited.

"I double for Israel." With one final keystroke, he accessed the secure room. The wall before them vanished, revealing a bustling control center. "What you see at work here is the best intelligence within the Israeli borders." He started walking, motioning Frogman with him. "You are a soldier—"

"Sailor."

"A subtle difference." Azzan moved to another station and logged in. Within seconds, images filled the screen, but he instead watched as the American's face registered shock. "Ah, as it should be. Realize that nothing happens that we are not able to ascertain the truth about." He shoved his hands into his pockets. "In truth, your name is Max Jacobs. A Navy SEAL with eight years' experience. You have a wife, a s—"

"What do you want?" Max's hands balled into fists.

"Forgive me. It was not my intent to anger you."

"What was your intent?"

Azzan folded his arms. "For you to understand that when I say we have a larger purpose, when I said we must go to Be'er Sheva as my uncle indicated, it is not a light thing I am saying." He spun toward the keyboard and drew up six images. "It is a known fact that seven messengers have been dispatched to attack Israel from within tomorrow."

Nesher joined them. "Israelis have grown soft, believing the separation fence will keep them safe." He pointed to pictures in the lower left. "The first two are Iranian. Part of the Republican Guard. There you will see both of them seated at a dinner with Bashar al-Jafari." He clicked and zoomed. "Last night, these two checked into a hotel in Be'er Sheva." He pointed to the screen again. "Under Israeli names."

Frogman didn't understand. Azzan could see it by the lack of intensity in the man's eyes. Perhaps because Israel was not the man's country, he could not be expected to care.

Nesher leaned against the desk, gripping the edge. "Do you understand the significance of Purim, Mr. Jacobs?"

Max's glare lengthened.

Nesher continued. "Purim is a holiday when children dress in costumes, sort of like your Halloween, except that here in Israel, there are no little witches or wizards or pumpkins. Cowboys, and of course little Queen Esther's." He smiled, but Azzan had seen that smile before. It hid the man's animosity. "Many of us feel that Purim has become a kind of European Carnival."

Azzan wanted to make sure Max understood so the team would understand. "Tomorrow, children—hundreds of children—will gather in the streets with their families to celebrate this holiday." He straightened. "Thousands of Israelis in one place."

"It won't be the only place they hit."

Azzan drew back, surprised by the intelligent comment from the American. "You are correct. The seven messengers are being dispatched throughout Be'er Sheva and the surrounding lands. We have managed with the help of my uncle to identify all but one of the messengers. They are there before you now. The elusive one, we must trust our instincts to help us locate."

"Can't imagine anyone slaughtering children like that." Frogman's gaze tracked over the wall-to-floor images, clearly processing the images and information. "Where else are you expecting trouble?"

Azzan shared a look with his handler.

Frogman shrugged. "That's why you brought me here, right?"

"The one place we are not allowed to place guards," Nesher said.

"And that is?"

Azzan held Max's gaze evenly. "The nuclear plant at Dimona."

CHAPTER 26

Take cover!"

The hissed order came from the front, where Legend knelt beside a small home. Behind him crouched the Kid. With a fluid move, Colton guided Piper, her father, and Raiyah into the shadows of a building.

"What is it?" she asked.

"Not sure." Colton pressed his shoulder against the wall and peered toward his team.

Piper wrapped an arm around her father. "Are you well?"

"Yes, yes. All will be well, nachon?"

Wide, dark eyes considered Piper as they stood under the moonlit night. "Are we safe?"

Raiyah was a very beautiful woman, and for a moment, Piper couldn't help but wonder if there was more than his job as an assassin that kept her cousin from killing the beauty. Even now, the woman's expression seemed saturated in wide-eyed innocence. "What of Azzan?"

Surprise drew Piper back. Didn't this girl understand assassins were ruthless? And if he served Palestine—which his nationality dictated, did it not?—what about his loyalty to Israel? Yet the woman seemed scared to be without him. "He'll come back," Piper whispered. But she could only hope. Assassins were not exactly the kindest of men, and it made her curious what type of man her cousin had become. Confusion cluttered Piper's thoughts. If this girl was the daughter of al-Jafari, why had Azzan kept her alive? Wasn't the girl afraid he'd kill her?

"He promised to bring me to Israel." She gave a soft shrug and winced. "I wasn't sure if he had left me because he'd fulfilled his promise."

"I—"

A loud roar barreled onto the street. Seconds later, a wave of nauseating diesel fumes washed over her. She glanced around Colton. Though she expected to see headlights, the darkness prevailed. Leaning closer, she still couldn't see.

Only as she strained to look around the corner did she notice Colton easing into a position and taking aim down the street. The sight pushed her back.

A strange whistle carried through the night.

"Let's go!" Colton grabbed her hand and pulled her into the open.

She scrambled to catch her father's hand, drawing him behind. As Piper stumbled up the slight incline in the road, she glanced behind them to make sure her father and the girl had followed.

"Move it!"

Max's voice jerked Piper's attention back to the road. There, in the middle of the intersection, sat a rumbling black van. It looked large, and the windows were covered with steel plates. Colton dragged her to the back, where Max stood with Azzan. And a half-dozen men dressed in black. Her breath lodged in her throat. Mossad. Cruel, ruthless men, loyal not to their own morals and ethics. Their loyalty was in one place only—Israel.

"What are you doing with them?" Piper bit out at her cousin.

Azzan's expression darkened. "Get in." The whispered command held more punch than a fist. He'd brook no argument. Then almost as quickly, his scowl vanished as he looked at Raiyah. "Hurry."

"Come on, people. Time's our enemy," Max growled.

Colton nudged Piper inside, then took a seat across from her. As she helped her father, she glanced back to the doors. The rest of the team filed in behind. Only as the doors shut did she see another vehicle. No doubt for the black-attired and black-hearted men Azzan had brought. Did he not realize the dangers?

He's an assassin. Of course he knew the dangers.

The vehicle bounced over the pothole-laden road, jostling them against each other. Her father's shirt rubbed the graze on her arm, making it burn. She tensed and pulled it away from him, shielding the spot.

"Midas," Colton said and pointed to Piper. "Check her arm."

Her father lifted his arm and glanced down at hers. His eyes widened. "Oh, my child, why did you not tell us?" He reached into a pocket and pulled out a handkerchief.

"Got it," a voice said from the side. Midas shifted around the others with his pack. He drew out a bundle and unwound his medical kit. As he swiped a wet, antiseptic cloth over it, she bit down on the hiss that nearly escaped. Midas grinned as he applied a bandage. "You're one tough lady."

"A scrape makes you say this about me?"

Midas stuffed the pack between his feet and kept his spot next to her. He folded his arm over his chest and settled in for the ride. She glanced down at the rest of the men who had already filled the hole he'd left.

Her gaze collided with Colton's. . .and held. The scowl darkened his sky blue eyes, and the scruffiness of a face normally clean-shaven added to the severity in his expression. Slowly, he pulled his attention away.

Her heart hung heavy. Without thinking, Piper slid across the aisle and squeezed into the space between him and Legend. Colton darted a glance, his scowl deep but the uncertainty much deeper.

She placed a hand on his forearm and leaned close so she would not have to shout. "Will you not talk to me?"

At first, he glanced down and to the side. Then his eyes met hers, tormented, yet. . .he seemed to reach for the olive branch she offered. Finally, he turned his head, and his lips parted.

"Listen up!" Max wedged himself between packs and the tangle of legs, kneeling. "We're heading to Be'er Sheva."

Colton cleared his throat and shoved his attention to his leader, deflating Piper's hope that they could heal the rift between them.

Silence dropped on the team.

"Didn't we have a plan to go straight back to the base and head home?" the Kid asked.

Max held up a hand. "If anyone wants to bail, there's the door."

Piper's gaze skidded to Colton, and she held her breath. Would he step out of the mission? Would he walk out on her now? He'd tried to before they left Virginia.

"What's with the ninja guys, Frogman?" The Kid's expression was taut. "Please tell me they're not who I think they are."

Max frowned. "They have their orders, which is to protect and back us up. Our end goals are the same."

"What's that?" Midas leaned forward, his weapon laid over his legs.

After a furtive glance to Piper, Max sighed. "The assassin and Rosenblum were right. There's an attack scheduled for tomorrow during some holiday with a bunch of kids."

Her heart skidded into her ribs, knocking the breath from her. "Purim."

Max nodded. "We neutralize seven messengers and get out of here."

"Seven?" The Kid balked. "That's—"

"The assassin brought reinforcements—"

"I don't trust him," Legend said, his deep timbre voice rattling.

"With good reason." Max gave a curt nod. "Still, we are short on time and resources."

Legend sat forward. "You think we should do this?"

The muscle in Max's jaw flexed and popped. "I do." When Legend started to object, Max patted the air. "We have backup. We have autonomy."

"Backup?"

"The Israeli Army is on alert and made aware of our presence." Max looked at each man—Colton, Midas, the Kid, Legend, Squirt, and Scar. "I have complete confidence in Nightshade. But if anything goes wrong, the onus is on me."

"This ain't about you," Legend said. "We're a team. We get it done. Together. Remember, Frogman, *in all things prepared*."

"What's the plan?" Midas asked.

"We split into teams of two and spread throughout the city." He turned to Colton. "I'm teaming you with Scar. He has experience sniping. I want you two on the roof of a building—I'll show it to you. The entire mission will hinge on you stopping the seventh contact from reaching his target."

"Destination?"

"Still Be'er Sheva. But the assassin's people believe the final messenger has a very specific and different target. Shouldn't be too hard to spot someone with a backpack emitting chemical signatures."

Colton leaned forward, his fingers threaded. "What target?"

"Dimona."

"Dimona?" A heavy weight dropped against Piper's stomach. No, it couldn't be. She blinked. Drew away. Blinked again.

"Why?" The Kid's face went slack as he looked at her, then to Max. "What's she afraid of?"

Max held her gaze as he answered the Kid. "It's a nuclear power plant."

A heavy sense of doom descended, but nobody argued or objected. They were a team on a mission. Everyone was in. No questions asked.

"So, even if we hit our marks," Squirt said and nodded to Colton, "and he misses. . ."

Legend banged the back of his head against the wall of the truck twice. "I knew that assassin was trouble."

"It's not his fault."

Everyone turned toward Piper, and she glared back.

"She's right," Max said. "Azzan's trying to stop this. He didn't start it."

"My cousin may be many things, but he is first and foremost loyal to Israel." He always had been, and if he was with those men—Mossad—then that proved his loyalty.

"Cowboy, you good?" Max slapped his knee.

The question jerked Piper round. She looked at Colton, her concern ratcheting. Even when he gave a short nod to Frogman, she knew there was too much of a storm behind his ocean-borne eyes.

As the team worked out the details, Piper prayed—prayed hard and silently that Yeshua would be with them, would help guide their actions and alert them to danger, and that she could restore her relationship with Colton. She wouldn't give up on him. Not now. Not ever.

About a half hour later, the vehicle came to a slow crawl. When the rear doors opened, Azzan stood there with three men.

Max joined him and glanced around the vehicle. He shifted back to their vehicle. "Legend, Kid, your stop. Let's go."

Azzan handed them radios and papers as they huddled together. He was too far away for her to hear his instructions, but within seconds, Legend and the Kid jogged down the street, the early-morning darkness enshrouding them, even against the white plaster buildings.

A few more stops divested the rest of the teams into the city, leaving Piper, her father, Raiyah, and Azzan with Colton, Scar, Frogman, and Midas.

Max scooted toward Piper. "You're going with Azzan." It seemed he expected a reaction or something from her. "You realize. . .who and what he is." Dark eyes probed her, then her uncle.

"My nephew has made decisions I question—"

"He's Mossad," Max said pointedly.

Her father nodded. "But if he is truly Mossad, there is nothing he will not do for Israel." Though she heard her father's brave words, the inflection in them told her he was concerned, too.

But what worried Piper more was Colton. The flashback he'd had when they were under attack back at the house. The distance in his gaze now.

"Piper?"

She jerked her focus back to Max.

"You okay?"

She nodded. "He's my cousin." She turned to the girl. "I believe she is very important to him, as well. I will be fine."

"Okay," Max said. "You'll be within a klick of Colton. If anything goes south, find him."

"What is this place?"

Azzan powered up the laptop and bank of computers. With a look back, he confirmed they were all inside. He pointed to a side door and looked at the medic, who helped his uncle into the room. "Take him in there. There is a couch—but angle it so he can see the monitors."

Midas nodded and helped his uncle into the room.

Azzan glanced at Lily, then pointed to the entrance they'd just used. "Lock it."

Irritation skidded across her features, no doubt unhappy that he hadn't answered her questions. Again. She'd always been too curious, even as a child. Still she complied. And that was all he cared about right now.

The monitors sprang to life. He slipped the ear mic into place and tested the coms. "Bravo One, this is Eagle. What is your twenty?"

"Bravo One in position."

At the sound of Frogman's voice, Azzan felt a measure of relief. Somehow he knew he could depend on the Americans, though it went against everything in his training. "Teams two, three, and four, report." Once the agents reported their situation, he accessed the grid that Nesher had set up, allowing them to monitor the square.

The blue hues of dawn did little to chase away the specter of night. Even on this fine spring morning, clouds shifted and moved, forming a formidable backdrop. Rain? That would complicate things.

"Azzan, why. . .how?"

He smirked at his cousin. "Lily, sit down before you hurt yourself with all the worrying." But he could not resist stealing a glance at Raiyah, who sat next to him, eyes fixed on him. The adoration was apparent. The trust implicit. He wished it weren't.

"Dod, I need you to monitor the screens." He nodded to the instrumentation in front of him. "Tell me if you see anything that causes you concern."

"Me?" his uncle called from the room.

"Yes, you've researched this the longest, which means you've studied things I couldn't begin to contemplate. It is my hope that something in your large brain will be triggered and put us on the path of our seventh messenger."

"Why did you never tell me, Baba?" Lily's plaintive voice carried hurt buried amid anger and outrage. "You would trust an agent of the Mossad over me?"

Azzan stood and walked to a small cabinet, where he retrieved a bottle of water. "Of course he did." He could not help but taunt her. It'd been their way since they were children. He returned to the command station. "You have always been too sensitive, too moved by feelings."

She whirled on him. "What do you know of my feelings?"

Oh, he couldn't resist. "Your feelings for the one they call Cowboy are quite obvious."

Her cheeks glowed.

Azzan laughed.

"And what of your feelings," she shot back.

"My feelings?" What did she mean?

"Yes, for her." Lily shifted toward Raiyah and glowered at her. "Your father is our enemy. Which means, there is no greater enemy on

Israeli soil than you. Don't you realize, his job—even above family and faith—is to kill Israel's enemies?"

Raiyah flinched and tucked her head.

"Leave her!" Fury rose within Azzan. "She is here because I killed her father."

"But. . .it doesn't make sense. If you killed her father, why is she still here? Why would she trust you?"

Azzan couldn't answer that. He wasn't sure why she'd ever trusted him. Or why he'd felt such a powerful desire to protect her. "She is none of your concern."

A shadow near the door moved. "But she is very much my concern."

Heat jolted through Azzan's gut as the man materialized to the side. No visible weapon. But the threat lingered all the same.

"Hamzah!" Raiyah started for her brother, but Azzan grabbed her hand. Held her back. "What are you—"

"What do you want?"

Raiyah struggled against him. "He's my brother. What are you doing?"

Azzan knew the man standing before him was Hamzah al-Jafari. Which was exactly why Azzan lifted the weapon from his belt holster.

"I am no threat," Hamzah said as his gaze locked with Azzan's.

Lily slipped out of the room as Midas rushed into the open, his M4 trained on the intruder.

The reinforcement bolstered Azzan's confidence. "I'll decide that." He lifted the weapon toward the Iranian. "What are you doing here?"

"Yes," Raiyah said to her brother. "Why are you here? How did you find us?"

Hamzah pointed to her. "The necklace. Our father did not trust you."

"A tracer." Why hadn't he thought of it? Azzan cursed himself. "How many are with you?" What capabilities did it have? How long had they been tracked? Is that how they'd found them in the village and nearly killed Dod? Or in the last village where the team had to fight their way to safety?

"I am alone." Arms out, Hamzah looked too serene.

Uncertainty stole over Raiyah's beautiful face. As her hand curled around the pendant, she hesitated and looked at Azzan. "I—I. . .did not know." She snapped it off and let it fall to the floor.

"Turn around and walk out the door." Azzan stared down the sights at the man's chest. The Iranian wouldn't get across the threshold with breath in his lungs. Azzan would make sure.

Raiyah leapt in front of the gun. "No, please! He's not our enemy." Behind her, Hamzah's face darkened. "Azzan, please. He is not like my father. He's not wicked." She looked up at the hulking man with complete adoration. "Hamzah has always been kind and generous to me. I trust him. You should, too."

The silent challenge in the brooding eyes told Azzan otherwise. He backed toward the control panel, toed the cable leading to the outlet and dragged it under his shoe. The screens zapped off.

Hamzah's eyebrows rose.

"Eagle One, this is Team Three. We have movement." Azzan flinched at the message coming through his ear mic. He couldn't verify what was happening or provide aid with the monitors down. He motioned to Midas.

"Take him into the hall and secure him." Azzan nodded to the American medic. "Keep him covered. If he moves, kill him."

Azzan waited until the men had cleared the room, then hurried back to the computers. It took several long, agonizing minutes for the systems to reboot. When they did, he scanned the positions of the various teams. His heart backed up into his throat.

Team Two. . .the camera showed them down. Dead.

Azzan gulped down the panic seizing him. "All teams. Eyes out. We've been compromised."

CHAPTER 27

What does he mean, compromised?"

Stomach pressed against the roof of the three-story building, Colton propped his arms under the rifle and peered through the scope. It bothered him that a team had been taken out and he hadn't heard a single thing through the coms, nor had he been able to intervene—which he should've considering his situation on top of the roof and being a sniper.

This reminded him of Emelie's death. The vacuous pressure of the explosion had sucked his hearing out. A concussion had slammed him backward. He'd woken up...to a crumbled building. And a dead sister.

"Nightshade report."

His mind hauled itself back to the present at Max's order. With a practiced eye, Colton swept his weapon up the lonely stretch of road that led to the plant.

"Midas here. We have an uninvited guest to our little party."

Tensed, Colton listened—Midas was with Piper at the command center. Who'd shown up? Their team was still in control if Midas wasn't calling for backup or screaming for them to beg off.

"Keep your eyes open, folks. I have a bad feeling."

"That doesn't sound good," Scar said.

Swallowing, Colton aimed the weapon back at the plant. Black of night surrendered to the blues of dawn. Few people moved about the city at this hour, and even fewer a mile out at the plant. Crosshairs on a mother and her child opening a fruit stand, Colton's mind zigzagged through the information. The people were just going about their days ready to celebrate Purim. And some sicko was out there, wanting to wreak devastation on the people.

Piper's people.

The thought pushed his eye away from the scope. The mile-off plant blurred as the scene around him came into sharp focus. Piper had kept the wool over his eyes all this time. Her father. Her cousin. Who knows what else. Staring out over the roof to the white buildings where the first streaks of the sunrise bled against the sky. *Why am I here?*

Because. He believed in missions like this. In protecting the innocent.

But he'd had enough. Was it worth it? Was it worth it to sear images into his brain and live with them night after night so someone half a world away could sleep when he couldn't? Was it right? Sacrificing his peace for theirs?

"Cowboy, report."

Max. Max wanted his progress, wanted his observations. Though Colton felt Scar look at him, he fixed his gaze on the horizon. They wanted him to nail the mysterious seventh messenger. Nobody knew what he looked like. Nobody knew what to expect. It could be a woman. Or a child.

He squeezed his eyes shut.

A child. . .

The ten-year-old they'd rigged with a bomb to ambush him. Hold him captive. Torture him. The stench of his own flesh burning during interrogations. His screams echoing like a warble as if his head had been dunked underwater. He blinked, sweat dribbling down his temple despite the cool morning temperature.

Israel. . .Israel. . . I'm in Israel.

His pulsed increased.

Easy. . .Israel. . .

"Cowboy!"

Colton shook his head. Wiped his face. Scanned the plant. Tried to push his mind into focus, which felt like trying to squeeze Jell-O with his bare hands.

The. . .plant. Watch for. . .backpack.

"Scar here. We're in place."

Ear trained on the guy, Colton monitored his own heart rate. His errant thoughts. He had to hold himself together. A subtle buzzing at the back of his brain warned him to relax, bring his heart rate down.

It went up.

Dawg. He could feel it coming. He fisted his left hand.

"You okay?" The voice snapped against his conscience. Agitated him.

"Eyes on target."

What if the target was in a car, and they couldn't get a bead on him in time? What if the teams were all killed, and they were left to fend for themselves? Why was he here and trying to get himself killed— for Piper? Her father? For a country he'd never lived in? True, God had chosen this land for His people. And Colton could appreciate it. But—

Crack! The sound streaked through his coms, followed by curses and grunts.

"Team Four under fire."

There. That was a sound familiar to him. "Where are they?" Colton asked without thinking.

Scar dragged the map that lay between them closer "Quadrant B2, center."

Colton adjusted his sniper rifle and nudged it to the location just outside the site where the Purim celebration would take place within the hour. Shadows drifted in and out of view. Finally he had the team in his crosshairs. Sorting friend from foe proved difficult. But finally, he assessed the situation. "Target acquired."

"We aren't supposed to engage them," Scar said. "Our orders are to focus on the plant."

Colton eased back the trigger. The tiny sonic boom almost proved a sound of relief and familiarity that he could relax with. "Broke one-third mil right." He immediately chambered another round and located another target as he waited for Scar to report on his accuracy.

"Cowboy! Negative. Stand down. Stand down. Do not engage." Azzan's voice nearly shouted through the coms. "I repeat, do *not* engage."

"They're killing our men," Colton finally barked.

"I don't care if they take everyone out. Do *not* compromise your position."

"A bit late," Scar said.

Anger roiled through Colton. Who was this assassin to tell him how to manage his position and operations?

A wall of fire rushed over him. He ducked, slid to the side and buried his head in his arms. Pebbles rained down on him. Screams tore at the very fiber of his being.

"Cowboy!"

Looking up, he frowned. The overcast sky vanished into a broiling, sun-baked morning. Heat blasted him. Crunching beside him jerked him around. A man, a soldier hollering at him, but the voice was lost. Who was he? He didn't remember bunking with this man or riding out with him on the Black Hawk.

A disguised enemy?

Fear sped through Colton's body as if a direct IV. He scrabbled away from the man. Drew up his weapon.

The man cursed.

"Stand down," Colton shouted at him.

"Cowboy, report!"

Colton blinked. His hearing popped, returned. The gray overcast sky returned. His realization returned. Another flashback.

Scar stared at him, scowling. "What's wrong with you, man?"

"Cowboy, what is your situation?"

"Dude, you going to answer or what?"

Indignation. . .humiliation. . . His stomach was ready to hurl the contents of his dinner—which wasn't much. He wiped a hand over his mouth, swallowing the bitter taste that filled his mouth.

Shaken and limbs trembling, he low-crawled back to his rifle. Worked to steady his breathing. Cursing himself for being so messed up he couldn't keep it together under pressure. They had to do this. For Israel. . .

Piper.

"Cowboy, are you there?"

This time it wasn't Max calling his name. It was Piper. And the sound of her voice spiraling through the coms nearly sickened him. She didn't belong here, not in the middle of a fight like this. He didn't want her in his head. Didn't want anyone in his head.

"Please. . .Col—Cowboy, talk to me."

He yanked out the ear mic. Breathing hard, he tried to shake off the adrenaline that drenched his system. Shook his head. Ran a hand over his face and crown of his head.

"Hey, what're you doing?" Scar stared at him. "It's almost time."

Colton rolled twice toward the far side of the roof, then hustled down the stairs that led to the alley. He stepped onto the dirty road.

Walked away.

"Why isn't he answering?" Piper looked at her cousin, whose face bore the pallor of panic—chalky, a sheen over his brow.

"I don't know. His mic could be out. Or the radios may be jammed." Azzan growled. "His location—I can't get the cameras to work."

"Please, Lily, some water."

Frustration scraped along her worry. "What. . .? Oh. Water?"

"Please." Baba smiled.

Only when he said that did she hear the weariness in his voice. She gathered her frayed nerves and drew in a deep breath. Patted her father's hand. She went to the cabinet and opened it. Empty. "Azzan, where can I get water?"

He glanced back quickly before returning his attention to the boards. "Uh. . .through the room with the couch. There's. . ." He messed with more dials. "There's another door. It leads to the kitchen. You will find more in the cabinets."

Hands on her waist, she stared at the map of the city. Particularly at the location in the southwestern corner where a giant X marked Colton's location. Where was he? Why wasn't he answering the calls for his name?

What if something had happened to him—like getting shot? Or killed!

Someone would've reported that, nachon? Azzan had promised her that Colton and his spotter were in the safest location, situated the farthest from the team.

She pushed herself from the room, anxiety tightening every muscle she possessed. As she wandered past the darkened office, opened the other door that let into a semi-darkened room, she tried to steady her racing heart. Stale air swarmed her. Dust tickled her nose as she walked toward the white cabinets. Despite his reassurances, he had certainly lost his calm composure when Colton had killed one of the attackers that had hit the Mossad agents. A trickling sunbeam streaked through the darkness, glinting against her eyes as she crossed it.

She stopped, Azzan's words ringing in her ears as she eyed the beam of light. *If they so much as see the glint of sun off his scope, they will destroy that building, and with it, our hopes of stopping this attack.*

Piper leaned against the cabinet door. A sob leapt into her throat. She covered her mouth and tried not to imagine Colton. . .dead. Like Bazak.

She pushed herself upright. "No," she ground out. "Yeshua, protect him!"

Heart heavy, she searched the cabinets for more water. She hurried through the dusty storage units, wanting to get back, hoping for news of Colton. Finally, she discovered the stash and reached for several bottles.

Thud!

Bam! Oof!

Piper stilled. Her gaze shot to her left. A door sat ajar. Light flowed from the open area. The front foyer. She glanced back toward the command room. Who was out in the foyer?

She rushed to the door.

A body fell into view, nudging the door opened. *Midas!*

Raiyah's brother must've overpowered him. She drew in a breath and held it. Piper leapt back, plastering herself against the wall.

A stream of Arabic flowed through the hall. Her mind reeled—he'd just given away their position! Suddenly, she was grateful for dear Mrs. Mukhtarian, a neighbor lady born in Israel but of Arabian descent, as she listened to him speaking. . .to someone. Who?

"I will take care of them. But you must not let him take that shot. . . . I don't care how you do it; just do it!"

Piper bolted to the side and rushed back through the small office. Around the sofa. Into the command center. "Azzan! He's loose. He's—"

The door burst in.

Azzan came up out of his chair with a weapon in his hand.

Without hesitating, Hamzah rushed forward and dragged his sister backward by the hair, pulling her into his chokehold.

"Leave her!" Azzan shouted.

Hamzah jammed the gun against Raiyah's head.

Baba hurried toward Piper. He prodded her into the office, but she struggled to stay where she could see the altercation.

"Please," Raiyah said, her form so slight and petite against her brother's tall muscular build. "Please, Hamzah. Why?"

Face pressed against hers, he sneered at Azzan. "Did you think, little sister, that nobody would find out what you did to our father?"

"Let her go," Azzan ordered again as he inched closer. "She did nothing. It was me. I killed your father."

Hamzah chuckled. Gripped his sister's face. "Were you so blinded by her beauty that you could not see the little murderess for what she was?" He took a step back. "Did she not tell you? She poisoned our father." His fingertips turned white as he squeezed her cheeks.

Tears streamed down Raiyah's sweet face. "Please," she whimpered. "You know what he did to me." She clung to her brother's arm, strangling her.

Azzan started forward.

But the man swung the gun toward him. "Stay." He hauled Raiyah toward the door. "It is true he was not a good father, but he was a great general. And now, our people must know that his murder will not go unanswered."

Raiyah cried. "Please, no!" She looked at Azzan. "Help me!"

Piper trembled, her hand cupped over her mouth.

Crack!

The sound of Hamzah's weapon firing rammed through Piper. Slammed her eyes closed. She turned away just seconds after a spray of red hit the wall.

A flurry of noise erupted.

Arms encircled Piper, drawing her into the familiar warmth of her father's arms. "Don't look." Baba held her firmly, rocking, praying.

A guttural cry—Azzan.

Several gunshots. A thud. Another one.

Finally, silence reigned.

Slowly, Piper lifted her face from his soggy shoulder. She glanced into the room. Her cousin walked back from the doorway, where Hamzah's body lay still and crumpled. Azzan crouched next to Raiyah. Blood pooled out and reached toward the walls, as if seeking escape.

A sob escaped Piper. Tears streamed down her face. How. . .how could anyone kill their own sister? Especially such a sweet, gentle girl as Raiyah? Had she really poisoned her father? She'd all but admitted to it, which made Piper wonder what the general had done to his daughter.

Azzan pushed to his feet, staring down at the dead girl. Seconds dropped hard and deafening against the silence of his fury. He fisted a hand. Then he turned toward them. Stalked out of the room.

"Where are you going?" Piper choked out.

"To check on Midas. Then we need to clear out. They know where we are."

"I heard him—" She gulped back a ball of grief. "I heard him say he would take care of us, but. . . Oh, Yeshua!"

Her father caught her shoulders. "What is it, Lily?"

"He told whoever he was talking to that he was to make sure he couldn't take the shot."

Azzan knelt over Midas, who groaned and peeled himself off the floor. "That means they know where the sniper is. It also means that our suspicions were accurate. They're going for the nuke plant."

He jogged back into the command center, and Piper followed. Grabbed a headset. "Bravo One, this is Eagle One."

"Go ahead," crackled over the speaker.

"Have you made contact with Cowboy?"

"Negative. No contact."

"Listen," Azzan said. "They are going after him. You have to get him word."

A curse zipped through the speaker. "How soon?"

"Now!"

Another curse. "The children—they're coming. We can't leave!"

Her cousin banged his hand against the console. Gripped both sides and shook it fiercely.

Feeling hopeless and helpless as Azzan unloaded his frustration, Piper looked away—and her gaze hit the map on the wall. Tears over Raiyah's death stilled on her cheeks; she wiped them as her mind harnessed a thought. A bold, terrifying thought.

"Is. . .is this where we are?" She pointed to a spot less than a mile from the large *X. Colton.*

Azzan nodded as his eyes darted over the monitors, the map, apparently searching for an idea. "We can't be this close and fail."

She was pretty certain she knew what was wrong with Colton. And unless someone went to him, they'd all be burned to a crisp within the hour. "I'll go."

CHAPTER 28

If he could hack out the parts of his brain that contained the memories, he would.

Colton squatted in the alley, head in his hands. "I can't do this anymore, God. . . . I just can't." Back against the plaster wall, he stared up at the wakening sky. Clouds tumbled and rolled over one another. Just like the memories that churned in his mind.

Anger welled up within him, but at the same time, he heard the wizened voice of Yitshak Rosenblum quell the storm. *"Yeshua seeks to use you for His purposes. Are you a man that you would dictate to God how He would accomplish His purposes?"*

He slumped to his knees. Buried his face in his hands. Meredith. . . Emelie. . .his father. What if God needed to use McKenna? Or his mom? Or Piper?

The thought plunked against his heart and knocked him back. He dropped against the hard earth. Piper.

He struggled to his feet, leaned against the wall, and waited to regain his equilibrium. His head—*Merciful God!*—his head hurt. Doubled, he clutched his knees and clenched his eyes shut. He counted. One. . .two. . .three. . .

Drawing in a deep breath, he straightened.

A ghoul wavered at the end of the alley. Dark and ominous.

Colton's heart shifted. He reached for. . .his weapon. He'd left it on the roof. After a quick glance up, he realized his mistake—dropping on the wrong side of the building. No ladder. No way back up.

He shot a glance at the person.

Gone.

Colton spun, searching his surroundings. And only in the humming chaos of his mind did he recognize that when he'd seen that ghoul, the lighting, the very buildings were different. A flashback. Borneo. His mind had flipped back to the battle that had killed his spotter.

He turned around, rammed his fist into the wall. Pain spiked his hand. Darted past his wrist. Up past his elbow and into his shoulder. He crumbled against the wall. Cried out. "Why. . .why can't I stay. In. The. Present?" He kept his voice low, his words ground out.

He flung himself around, threw himself back against the building. Dropped to his knees. He felt beaten. Defeated. Nothing left of him to fight for. He'd lost his ability to function under stress. Lost his father. After this mission, after walking away from the team. . .

The team.

Max.

Griffin.

Canyon.

Marshall.

Slowly, their faces swam before him. Max with his incredible intensity that left Colton exhausted just watching the guy. Griffin with his absolute loyalty and dedication to the team and mission. The impenetrable barriers that kept Canyon focused but quiet—so steadfast. And then the Kid, with the mouth too big for his head, but his indomitable courage and spirit.

Colton couldn't leave them.

They're depending on me.

The entire nation of Israel was depending on him.

But he couldn't. . . . They didn't understand what it took for him to stay in one piece, mentally. He wanted to be there for them. More than anything. But there wasn't enough left of him anymore. He was empty.

"You will keep in perfect peace him whose mind is steadfast, because he trusts in you."

The verse seemed to sail on the cool morning breeze, teasing his face with a soft fragrance Colton could not identify. Yet the words tormented him. "Don't You get it?" he cried out to God. "My mind is not steadfast. I have no peace!" He gripped his temples and growled. "Oh God, please—I want it to be! More than anything. Please, merciful God Almighty!"

A shout whipped him around.

Another shout.

His gaze rose to the roof. Scar!

God. . .oh God, help me.

Another torment seized him—the thought of abandoning his friends, being the cause of their deaths because things got a little too difficult.

He smeared the tears away. Dragged himself to his feet. Stared down into the alley that brightened with each minute as the sun rose. Weary, ragged. Colton closed his eyes. "God. . .give me strength. . .the strength to do this."

He could deal with the terrors, the flashbacks.

He couldn't deal with failing the team, himself, God. And in that split second, he saw the line he'd drawn in the sand between him and God—the one that said if God didn't do things on his terms, Colton was out of the game.

"Forgive me, God."

"The Lord gives strength to his people; the Lord blesses his people with peace."

And for a second, an eerily silent second, he stood there, feeling no different, yet insanely different. He pivoted. Scanned the roofline as he scurried around the side of the building. He scaled the wall, using the windows.

He scrabbled over the gritty rooftop as a beam of sunlight struck him. Ducking his head, he low-crawled up to his rifle.

"Where the—never mind. 'Bout time you came back." Blood oozed from Scar's upper arm, but the guy was in the game, working, watching their site.

"Sitrep?"

"They were shooting, but it stopped."

"Means they're moving in on us." Colton peered through the scope. "Time's short."

"You're a genius."

The scathing comment rolled off Colton's back, knowing the guy was just letting off steam. Colton deserved the sarcasm, and more. "Location is clear." As he nudged the scope around, a blur snagged him. He jerked back. "Wait." He dropped the distance. Scanned the road. His instincts blazed. There. A half-mile down sat a van on the side of the road. A man emerged from the back with something cradled in his arms.

This. . .looks bad.

"RPG! Incoming, eleven o'clock!" Scar shouted.

No sooner had Scar's declaration sounded than Colton noticed a second man walking away from the van, a red pack situated between the man's shoulders. "Target acquired."

"Dude! An RPG!"

"Eyes on the target." They couldn't afford to run. They couldn't leave. This was it. Had to take out the seventh messenger. He sighted the target. *"Peace. . .whose mind is steadfast, because he trusts in you."* Colton harnessed his mind, his heart rate. He could do it.

His mind warred with the actions as the RPG left a frightening trail of smoke, leaving the launcher.

Boom!

Colton's teeth rattled. Vibrations needled his body.

Crack!

Plaster trembled beneath his forearms, numbing his ribs.

A scream behind him.

He jerked—Scar! In the split second that Colton realized his spotter had scrambled away, Colton lunged to catch the man.

The roof pitched. Fell out from under them.

Head first, Colton dropped.

"No, you can't go!"

Piper started for the door, only to be jerked around—right into Azzan's arms. "Release me!"

His hands tightened around her arms. "Listen to me!"

"No, I will not. I am going out there to find Colton. I know what's wrong. I can help him."

"Cousin, there are IRG out there, hunting him down—they know where he is. If you go out there, you're as good as dead."

Piper yanked free of his hold, her heart pounding. "Then let me die out there." She took a step back. "I have to try. He needs help. I can't leave him out there. He doesn't know the city, and. . ." Tears, large and fat, blurred her vision. She slumped, the words she'd let die on her lips had frozen her. What if he'd lost his mind again? What if he was stuck in another time, lost in another battle, and couldn't find his way out?

"It's too dangerous, Lily."

"I'll take her." Midas appeared beside her. "He's part of my team. I'm not going to sit by while he's out there."

Azzan frowned. Grunted. "No, you must stay—"

"Sorry, dude, but I don't report to you."

"Listen to me!" Azzan's eyes flamed. "Stay with my dod. I will go with her. You don't know the city, you can't speak the language. If they come up on you, you are as good as dead."

Piper stared at her cousin, stunned. "You? You'll go with me?"

"I don't know. . . ." Midas said.

Azzan smirked. "You're trying to decide if you can trust me." He rushed to a cabinet and pulled out two jackets and radios. "Don't waste your time. You can't." He tossed a coat to Piper. "My only loyalty is to the Mossad." Turned to Midas and handed him an orange radio. "Channel 5."

"You don't believe that, Azzan," Baba said.

Piper glanced at her father, understanding rippling through her. She turned to her cousin. "He's right. If you cared only for Israel, you'd have left us long ago."

After smashing the necklace Raiyah had worn, Azzan knelt and lifted her hand, kissed it, then removed a ring. He stood and stalked to the door. "Let's go." He tossed a key to Midas. "Lock yourselves in. I'll radio if we need you."

Just before they stepped through the front door, Azzan paused. Looked at her. "You would die for this man?"

She stilled, surprised by the sincerity of his question.

"Because once we leave this building, there's no turning back. You may never see your father again. You may never reach this Cowboy." Azzan glanced toward the glass door, where a filter of light trickled into the foyer. "You hesitate."

"My hesitation is not because of Colton. It's because you question it."

"He's American."

"Yes."

"What are his loyalties? The Americans I've known are loyal only to their own whims and fortunes."

Piper smiled. Reached for the door. "Then you'll need to get to know him. His loyalty is to his family, to his team—which, by the way, is out there trying to save our country."

Azzan grunted. "True enough."

They sprinted across the road, down Sycamore.

Boom!

An invisible force knocked her sideways. She yelped as Azzan steadied her. She pushed wide eyes to his. "What was that?"

"A sign we're too late."

CHAPTER 29

Thunder had nothing on the booming rattling his head. Colton dragged himself to his knees. A grunt. Then onto his feet. Shoulders hunched, he waited for the swooning to subside. Warmth gushed over his face, spilling down his neck and into his shirt. He shrugged, rubbing his shoulder against his chin. He had to get back onto the roof. Take the shot. Kill the seventh messenger.

Pain lanced through him, nearly dropping him. He stumbled forward. Raised a hand to his head—only to pull it away sticky and red... but...blurry...double. Colton shook his head—a thousand daggers stabbed him. Bearing through the sheer agony raking his scalp raw, he tucked his chin and peered through knotted brows at the rubble around him. He took in a long, ragged breath and dust swirled into his mouth. He coughed. But what bothered him was that there was two of everything. Two left feet. Two right hands. Two support walls.

Palm against the wall, he tried to shake off the disparity in his vision. Fire ripped through every nerve ending in his body. Panic wrapped a vise around his throat, making it hard to breathe.

I'm seeing double. "No..." This couldn't happen. "No—no—no—no!" He had to take the shot! Stop the messenger. Where was his rifle? Mind focused, he glanced up. Excruciating pain pushed against his vision. He blinked. A cursory glance gave him no sign of his weapon. Must be on the roof still. Four paces to his right, a hole revealed the first floor in ruins. Where...where had Scar gone? What happened to him?

Didn't matter. Colton had one mission—take the shot. If the rifle was down there, he was out of luck. He'd just have to believe it was still up top. The rubble swirled, his double vision blurring things, making everything seem all over the place. That combined with the blood told him something must've hit him when the roof gave in. No way could he see straight or clear.

His pulse raced. He had to take the shot. Or they'd be wiped out. Millions of people—of *God's* people—wiped from the earth. Careful to avoid the gaping maw in the floor, he shifted around, looked for the stairs—and of course, on the other side of the chasm, swirling from one. . .two. . .one. . .two holes.

Touching his head, he tried to think. Tried to find a coherent thought. Up. Had to go up. Take the shot. *You can't see straight.*

God would help.

He had to believe that. No way would he accept they'd come all this way to lose, to have Israel deep fried. Colton turned around. Light stabbed through the windows—a window.

That gave him an idea. He scanned the room, doing his best to make sense of the confusion his mind created with the multiple images. "If it's not a flashback, it's got to be something tormenting me, eh, Lord?"

Squinting against the incredible throbbing at the back of his eyes as sunlight poked his vision, Colton stepped up on the ledge of the window. Aimed himself to the right, where the roof of the building hung almost completely vertical, having only come to a rest thanks to the floor of the second level. But. . .there was enough of a slant—he could use that. As long as it didn't cut loose and slide off into the lower level, he'd be fine. If it *did*. . .

"Keep your mind stayed on Him," Colton whispered as he eased onto the wall. He reached for a groove—only to miss and slide. Raw burning scraped his calf. Quickly, he grunted and reached for the other groove. Forget the pain. Forget the obstacles. He had a mission to accomplish. His fingers dug into plaster.

He peered up, gauging his next move. Blood dribbled down his face and into his eyes. Though he blinked, it didn't help. Wherever his head had taken the injury, it was bent on reminding him he was injured.

A sniper who can't see. Yeah, that's gonna work real well. The image at the back of his mind of a mushroom cloud filling the Israeli sky propelled him up the ten-foot incline.

Finally, he caught the upper level. Arms trembling, head pounding, he dragged himself up with a loud growl. Heaved onto the unstable roof, he lay on his back, trying to make sense of the multiple versions of objects that his corneas couldn't align into a coalesced image. Like his rifle. . .rifles.

Dawg.

They—*it* dangled precariously on the edge of the collapsed roof. With great care, he rolled onto his belly and low-crawled toward it. The multiple rifles almost seemed comical. The whole "will the real Remington stand up" feeling kept his mind above the agony.

Tense and rigid to keep the shrieking pain at bay, he reached. His fingertips brushed against the stock. With a grunt, he stretched harder, farther. Fingers coiled around the weapon, he dragged it from the drop and over the ledge, careful to keep his head down—and attached. Because no doubt the terrorists were still down there, waiting to see if he'd survived. He righted the weapon and set it up.

It flopped to the right.

He tried again.

It flopped again.

Colton nearly cursed when he finally made sense of what the double vision portrayed. One leg of the bipod was broken. With a grunt, he piled pieces of concrete and compensated for the stand.

On his belly, he put his eye to the scope.

Two blurry images. He adjusted the scope to eliminate the fuzziness. But that's when he realized it wasn't the scope. His eyes. . . they were getting blurry.

And darker.

I'm going blind!

The target. He had to stop the target. Colton took a deep, cleansing breath. This wasn't about him. Maybe that's what he should've figured out long ago. "God. . .be my eyes. Show me where this man is." With great effort, he scanned the roads. The paths.

The strain made him dizzy. He lowered his head and closed his eyes. Everything ached. Throbbed. Blood had saturated his shirt, which now stuck to him.

Do it! Take out the messenger.

He lifted his head and exhaled. Peeked through the scope. He saw the fence along the perimeter of the plant. Dark forms moving along the street. Too many people. How would—there! A blur of red.

But was that the backpack? Or someone else wearing a backpack—or a red jacket?

Colton studied the splotch of color. No. It wasn't a jacket. The spot was too narrow. This was a backpack. And he doubted someone would be walking toward a nuclear power plant this early in the morning with a red backpack.

No, this was his target. The seventh messenger.

His conviction that he'd found the messenger firmed. He worked to figure the variables. To dial the gun. . .the spinning numbers, his mind frantically working to make out the numbers.

"Whose hope is in the LORD *his God. . ."*

"I get it, God," he mumbled as he peered through the scope again. Aligned the sights. Targeted the red spot in the middle. He'd watched them swim and spin—but always around a center point.

Finger on the trigger, he let himself relax. Ignored the blood sliding down his face. Over his nose. Down his neck. Tickling. . .sticky. . .

His vision darkened.

He tensed. Closed his eyes.

No! He had to finish this. He stared through the scope. The scene quickly washed gray.

In that second, he heard that familiar scream again of an RPG.

"Take the shot," he ordered himself.

"Roger," he replied to himself. "Taking the shot."

Another scream.

Colton eased back the trigger. A sonic boom sounded from his rifle.

Boom! Booooom! BOOOM!

He plummeted, darkness devouring him.

CHAPTER 30

W hat was that?" Panting from running through the city, Piper stared wide-eyed at her cousin just as another rumble rattled the ground beneath her feet.

Azzan grabbed her arm and tugged her against the side of the building. "RPGs. Stay close." Together, they darted down the alley. To the right, across another street, and into another alley. He motioned forward. "The building should be just ahead."

Piper rushed the last dozen feet from the dark shadows of the alley toward the bright, sunlit street. "There! I see it." As she raced toward the cobbled street, a strange noise streaked through her awareness. A low, whining, shrieking noise.

As her foot hit the stone, Azzan stopped cold. She plowed into him. He shoved back, his arms down and to the side, holding her back. "Get down!" Without warning, he spiraled around and dove into her.

SCREEECH!

Confusion raked over her as she tried to cushion her fall. Her shoulder impacted hard, jolting the breath from her lungs. Slow motion choked the moment. Azzan rolling to the side. A streak of gray whizzing past the alley. Flames licking the air. Smoke trailing it.

"Wha—"

BOOOM!

Seconds later, an invisible weight slammed her backward. Thunderous and deafening, a roar barreled into them. Dust and pebbles rained down. The ground shook violently.

Piper glanced over her shoulder, past Azzan, who pushed to his feet—

The. . .the building. . .*Colton*. Jaw slack, she stared. As if a sand castle was being washed away, entire walls collapsed in a heap. Plumes of dust and smoke erupted, enshrouding the building.

"No. . ." The word caught in her throat.

As the haze of dirt and smoke cleared, the far side of the structure loomed like a beaten, wounded sentry over the rubble.

Panic jerked her to her feet. Piper tried to breathe. Tried to scream. Only a guttural sound warbled from her. "No!" She darted forward.

"Lily, no!" Azzan's fingers glanced off her arm, but she didn't stop. Hurrying over what had seconds earlier been a threshold, she ignored the thundering panic in her chest. She stopped. Opened her mouth—and choked. Coughed. Eyes burning from the smoke and dust, she peered through the film snaking through the air.

"Colton!" Throat clogged, she covered her mouth and whirled around, searching, probing, panicking. "Colton, where are you?" She pivoted, powder-fine dust grating between her teeth. Rocks crunched as she moved and searched, her gaze stabbing every pile. Every heap. Mound. He had to be here.

Behind her, the clatter of rock and plaster. She turned. Instead of finding the man she loved, she was met with a crumbling wall, pieces still breaking off and dribbling to the piles.

"We can't stay in here," Azzan said as he eased over the debris. "It's going to come down."

"I won't leave without him," Piper said. He'd come to Israel for her, to help find her father. He didn't want to, she knew that much. But he'd come. Sacrificed. . .everything. "Colton?"

Azzan's blue green eyes met hers. She saw defeat, surrender of what had happened.

To Colton.

But she wouldn't accept that. "He was on the roof, so he'd be closer to the top if he got buried, nachon?"

Slowly, Azzan glanced around the building. "We have to—" His sudden silence jerked Piper in the direction of his gaze. Words stopped. A foot stuck out from beneath several feet of rubble.

She rushed forward with a yelp. "Colton!" On her knees, she started digging.

"Lily, no! The wall!"

Plaster scraped her fingers and knuckles. "I don't care." Blood bubbled up, a stark contrast to the fragments and the paleness of her flesh. "I won't leave him here like this. I can't." Tears streamed down her cheeks.

A strange groaning reached out to her from the right. Sunlight peeked down at her, momentarily blinding Piper. Shielding her face, she looked to the sky. Where was the light coming from? She squinted. The wall. . . It looked like it was. . .leaning!

A scream climbed up her throat.

"Li—" Azzan's shout was lost amid a resounding crack. He caught her shoulders and jerked her back.

Piper struggled against him. "No!" She reached for the foot. The stone wall groaned again and tilted inward. Over her. Then dropped. *Smack!*

"Colton!" she screamed.

Hands hooked under her arms, Azzan dragged her back. "We have to get out. The IRG is going to bury us alive"

"I can't leave him."

He yanked her back again. "We must." With that, he managed to stronghold her against his chest.

Tucked into his shoulder, Piper sobbed. The image of the boot seared her memory. The green pants—

She jerked up. Blinked. "It wasn't him!" Grief bottomed out.

"What do you mean?"

A shaky smile flittered across her lips. "The pants—Colton had black tactical pants on. I saw olive green pants on the leg with the boot." Renewed hope swirled through her veins. She pushed to her knees. Onto her feet. "That means he could still be alive somewhere. . . here. We have to find him!"

Hand clamped over her mouth, Azzan looked toward the opening. "Quiet."

Only then did she hear the voices. . .drawing near. . .in the street.

Together, they scooted behind a large mound and ducked. Curled against the rock that poked into her shoulder and side, Piper wiped the tears from her face. She couldn't give up. She wouldn't. Not even if she had to move every rock with her bare hands. Colton had sacrificed everything to help them stop this massacre. Now, she would give up everything to save him.

She peeked up at Azzan. "Do you think he stopped the seventh messenger?"

Her cousin, the assassin, the one who used strategy and analysis every day, considered her for a moment. Stole a glance over the mound. He stared down, then shook his head. "No, he was up against too much."

The sprout of hope withered under his words. Yet she ached to think of Colton failing. He was a sure shot.

Crack! Crack!

The noise reverberated through her chest and ears. She tried to peek at the opening, but rock and dirt spat at her, forcing her back down. She turned and found Azzan kneeling, his weapon aimed out as he fired. *Thwat! Thwat!*

Silence dropped on them. She dared to look back to the street. A man stretched out in a dark pool, a weapon several feet away.

Faint noise drifted on the morning breeze.

Piper lifted her head, tilted it to the side, and frowned. What was it? She shifted, the rocks and dust grating beneath her weight.

"Stay." Azzan pointed to their position, then leapt from behind the mound.

No time to object, Piper watched him scurry toward the street. He reached out and snagged the machine gun. Fire raped the quiet morning. He spun into the safety of the wrecked structure. Dropped to a knee and fired through a large hole in the remaining wall. Piper flinched at the sound, but also at seeing her cousin engage without hesitation. He was no longer the boy she'd played with so long ago in their small village.

Behind her. . .the noise again. She glanced around, wary. Scared. Had the IRG come around the back of the building? If they did, they'd have a clear shot at her. At both of them.

Only piles of rock and plaster, dust and dirt sat in the tease of the early morning sun. The building across the alley stared back, defiant. Silent, eerie.

Nothing moved. Then, something shifted. That's when she saw—

"Colton!" She dove over the rubble, her gaze riveted to his form pinned beneath a large section of the rear, fallen wall. He lay on his side, unmoving. Was he alive? Breathing? The questions propelled her over the ruins. Concrete poked into her palms. Slices of glass and metal scraped and pricked her knees. But she kept going. "Colton, can you hear me?"

"Lily, get down!" Azzan shouted.

She dropped to her belly.

Shards erupted around her. More gunfire swallowed the day.

Arms over her head, she buried her face—yet kept her gaze on Colton. Still not moving. "Oh Yeshua, please. . ."

When quiet ensued, she looked back at Azzan, who relaxed just enough for her to believe there wasn't an immediate threat.

Piper scrabbled the remaining half-dozen feet to Colton, heedless of the pain scoring her flesh. The large slab concealed all but the crown of his head. His black hair looked wet. "Colton? Colton, can you hear me?" When he didn't answer, she tried to ascertain if he was alive. She slipped her hand around the side of his head to his neck and tried to feel for a pulse. But with her own erratic and frantic nerves, she couldn't detect anything.

She had to get him out. Could she do it alone? She crouched low and peered under the slab. His shoulder was wedged, but it didn't look like concrete trapped the rest of his body.

Pressing against the wall, she tried to push it off him. She strained and pushed, the stone digging into her arm and scraping her face. But it didn't budge. Not an inch. Maybe she could unwedge him and draw him out from under the weight. She slumped beside him. Reaching in and under his left shoulder, she grabbed his armored vest. But when she pulled, her fingers slipped free. . .as if. . .wet. What. . . ? She glanced at her hands—and paled. Blood. Her gaze shot to Colton. Her stomach roiled as she realized his wet hair was bloodied hair.

Urgency spiked through her. She had to get him out *now*. Feet propped on the slab, she dug her hands in under Colton's shoulders, dug her fingers around the drag strap, and with a quick move, she twisted and slid him to the side, freeing his torso.

He moaned.

Her stomach seized. "Colton?" When he didn't respond, she tightened her grip, used the leverage of her legs, and hauled him backward. He came out a few inches. Relief spurred her on. She dug in and repeated the move.

Finally, when she'd cleared him from the debris, she collapsed. His head dropped into her lap, facing away from her. She glanced down. He hadn't moved. Blood trickled down his face and marred his handsome features. Her hand trembled as she touched him, longing to see the dimples that had always made her smile. The sky-blue eyes that always held a smile.

Was he—?

She severed the thought. "Colton. . . ?" Piper shifted around, still cradling his head in her lap. Smoothing a hand down the side of his cheek helped her determine the blood wasn't from his face. Gently, she turned his head and found a gash at the back of his head. Blood soaked her khaki pants. "Oh Yeshua. . ."

Biting back the tears, she eased him down, trying to situate him so the wound wouldn't be aggravated. Maybe she should turn him on his side. Piper scooted around and—yelped.

Blue eyes looked up at her.

"Piper?" He blinked, confusion rippling over his bloodied brow. As he rolled toward her, he groaned. He frowned. "Piper, tell me it's really you." His eyes didn't seem focused.

"Y–yes."

His strong hands grabbed her, yanked her down into his arms. "Oh, thank God!" He crushed her against his chest, holding her tight. Squeezing. His breath skated along her neck and rustled her hair. He tightened his hold. "Thank You, God." He kissed her ear. "I love you. Dawg, I love you!"

Though the double vision lingered, he'd never felt more focused or had more clarity than this moment right here. "I never thought I'd see you again. When they hit the building, I thought that was it."

He reveled in the way she held onto him, tight. Slowly, she lifted. "Shh, you should keep still."

"I—I can't see." Then the situation slammed back into his memory. "The IRG! They were hammering us." The world spun. Gray washed over his vision.

"Colton?" Panic edged into Piper's voice.

He tightened his grip on her arms. He felt himself falling. . .deep into a black void.

"Over here!" a garbled voice shouted.

"Will he live?"

M16 in his hands, Azzan stood over the medic, who attended the cowboy. Beside them, his cousin watched, her bloodied hand over her face.

"Pulse is weak—loss of blood." He nodded to the cowboy's head as he probed his body for further injuries. "We've bandaged the injury, so that should slow till I do stitches. I don't detect any broken bones or internal injures—but that's not a guarantee."

The medic pushed back onto his haunches. "We need to get him out of here, have that head wound checked out ASAP."

Shadows shifted near the entrance.

Azzan snapped up his weapon and trained it on the four men ambling into the building. His defenses relaxed as he recognized them.

Frogman jogged over the rubble. "What happened? How is he?"

"Unconscious," Midas said as he stood. "We need to evac him out of here *stat*."

Azzan could not help but marvel that these men were more concerned about their team member than about Israel. He would need to redirect their focus. One man against a million souls. . . "What of the seventh messenger? Did he stop him?"

With a shrug, Frogman watched his friend. "No word. Coms are down."

"Can't you find out?" Legend said as he joined them, his large boots crunching over the debris. "Don't you have endless connections?"

Azzan eyed the man, then lifted his phone. Dialed. Pressed it to his ear and waited.

"Well done, Azzan," Nesher said. "You were wise to trust the Americans."

"It is done, then?"

"It is."

The weight that lifted from him seemed tangible. His first clear breath in weeks traveled through his lungs. Around him, the men patted each other's backs, congratulated one another. A moan came from Cowboy, effectively drawing the attention of the team.

Movement drew Azzan's focus. He glanced to the right—Legend bent over the foot Lily had originally thought to be the cowboy's. Stone by stone, the large man started clearing away the debris. "Looks like we lost a rookie," Legend said.

Frogman turned. "Scar?"

Wiping his hands, Legend nodded and stood. "He's been there a while. Blood's already drying."

Dark and long, a shadow stretched toward the building.

M16 up, Azzan took aim in Legend's direction.

The man froze, widened his eyes, then grabbed for his gun.

Azzan fired—at the shadow behind Legend that had coalesced into the form of an IRG gunman who'd leveled a Glock at the black man's head.

Just before he fell, the enemy darted a look to something behind Azzan. Knowing the Nightshade team had huddled to the left, he pivoted around to the right in the direction the gunman had looked. Another form stepped into the open.

Azzan fired again. The man dropped to his knees, then slumped into the rocks. He scanned the perimeter, noting Max and the others were doing the same. Finally convinced they were not in immediate danger, he lowered his weapon.

A hand clamped onto his shoulder. He looked up into the ebony face of Legend. Dark, serious eyes probed him. Then, the large man shook Azzan's hand. "This doesn't change anything, you saving my life."

"It was a mistake. My aim was off."

"Hey," Midas called as he knelt beside Cowboy. "He's coming around."

Frogman glanced back at Azzan. "Yeah, so is someone else."

Marveling at the way his chest seemed to swell as if absorbing the man's praise, Azzan kept his distance. The strange feeling left a heady aftertaste in his mouth. He needed to get out of here before he was compromised.

Slowly, Frogman and Midas helped Cowboy to his feet. Head bandaged, scratches clawing his face, Cowboy wobbled. "I—I can't see."

The mood visibly shifted. Midas and Frogman steadied him, exchanging concerned looks. Everyone hesitated.

Except Piper. She strode to him, wrapped an arm around his waist, and settled one of his arms over her shoulder. "We'll get you home safely." The man cupped her face, peering down at her, his eyes squinted as Frogman assisted him on the other side.

Watching them made him ache for what he'd lost. Raiyah. He'd never forget watching her brother kill her. In cold blood. With such cruelty. At least Hamzah al-Jafari was dead now. As was his father and the messengers. Israel was safe.

For now.

CHAPTER 31

Grief strangled him. The team had spirited out of Israel almost as soon as the helo landed back at the base. To avoid implication or suspicion, they headed to Cyprus, where a doctor ran tests on the head wound. Although there wasn't internal bleeding, there was a bit of swelling. The doc didn't make promises but felt when the swelling went down, Colton's vision would return.

For now, he was in the dark. Literally. He hadn't seen Piper—or rather, the wobbly gray shape of her form—since they left the base. When he finally wanted to see her, wanted things to be right. . .they were separated.

"How's the noggin?"

"Thick." Colton mumbled as he peered up at Max, cringing at the way the simple act of looking at someone tugged at the ligaments around his retina and felt like someone was using those ligaments as a bowstring. But the comment had made his friend laugh, and that was enough. "The double vision should subside within the week. Hopefully the rest will come back right and proper soon, too. I'll have a full scan when we get back."

"That'll be interesting." With a chuckle, Max eased into the chair next to him in the hotel room. "We head out tomorrow."

Which meant Colton would be farther away from Piper. He pushed aside the thought, unable to bear it. "What happened to Ben-Haim? Nobody has told me anything. Surprised he didn't come thank us. Maybe he's too proud."

"Too dead is more like it."

"Come again?"

"The seventh messenger—nailed by your bullet—was Ben-Haim."

"Dawg." He chewed over the news. The man Lambert trusted betrayed them all. It explained how they'd been found in the small village. "Does the Old Man know?"

"Just got off the phone with him."

"Bet he wasn't happy."

"That's putting it mildly." Max chuckled. "And seems we scared off the assassin."

"Azzan?"

"Vanished about an hour after we got orders to clear out." Max's pushed to his feet. "Which is what we need to do again, now. A security detail is on its way to get Rosenblum and his daughter."

"Rosen—Piper? But how?" Colton's heart rapid fired in his chest. "They stayed in Israel."

Max laughed. Hard. "You're a loser, ya know that?" He chuckled again. "They were flown over separately for security reasons. They're here, in the hotel."

Here? The word knocked his courage sideways. She was here. Why did just her name make his chest feel like he was swimming in the deep sea? She hadn't responded when he professed his love. And now, he was blind. *Likely* to heal up but not guaranteed. How much more broke could a guy get?

"You going to do something about that?"

Colton glanced at Max's gray-like silhouette. "Come again?"

Max shook his head as he looked out the open bay. Sunlight bounced off the gunmetal gray floor and glowed against his dark eyes. "About eight months ago, you slapped the back of my head and said I was pathetic."

With a quiet snort, Colton started to shake his head, but stopped when pain lashed through his skull. "Don't remember calling you that."

"If you didn't have fifteen stitches, I'd repay the favor." Max huffed. "Don't. . .don't let it end this way, Colton."

His friend had used Colton's first name only a few times. And that drew his gaze up—along with a fresh streak of pain. "This is her home, where she lives." *I'm practically blind. I have flashbacks.* Broken-down cowboy. She deserved better.

"She belongs with you, and to quote a thick-headed, equally pathetic friend, 'any sane person—and I do qualify that with *sane*—

could see she loves you as much as you love her.'"

Colton had to smile at the way Max had used his own words on him. They'd been in the Filipino jungles, rescuing missionaries—and Max's then-estranged wife—when Colton had tried to haul Max up straight with truth and direct talk.

"That's just the thing—I can't see."

"Maybe when we get back, the doc can actually put a brain in that noggin of yours." Max grunted. "You are lame, ya know that?"

"Israel's her home." Rising to his full six-two height, Colton sighed. "I doubt she'd go back to Virginia and leave her homeland. Besides, after what I did to her, I don't deserve her."

"Got that right," Max said. "Rosenblum and Piper are treating us to dinner. If you're going to give her the cold shoulder, don't blame me when things get ugly."

"Come in, come in!"

Piper stood back from the door, rubbing her hands down her slacks as her father welcomed the men into the humble—*very* humble—home. The entire flat could fit into Colton's living room, or could have before his home had been destroyed.

The Kid let out a long whistle. "Who owns the place?"

"In a moment, in a moment, nachon." Baba motioned everyone inside as if this were his home.

Piper skated a look to one of her father's dearest and oldest friends, Dr. Admes Golding, who'd welcomed them into his home for as long as necessary while the chaos that erupted over the attack settled and they could safely return to Be'er Sheva. She could not help but wonder if her father had spent some of his time hiding here. Dr. Golding held a twinkle in his eye as he stood at the doors to the open patio. Beyond him, the ocean sparkled and a wave tumbled inward, as if reaching for them.

"What is this?" Max's worry was palpable as he eyed Dr. Golding.

Colton stepped in, his presence sucking every available cell of oxygen from her lungs. A bandage covered the back of his head, and he walked stiffly. *Still he cannot see clearly.*

Heart clenched, she went to him. Slipping her hand into the crook of his arm. "You look well."

His smile came easy, dimples winking at her as he placed a hand over hers. "I don't look at much."

Her heart swirled and jumped into her throat as she led him to a chair and directed him into it. When she straightened, she could not help but notice the way the team tensed and stood awkwardly. Realizing their concern over safety and being identified, Piper scrambled to concoct an excuse for the presence of so many men in their flat. "Dr. Golding, these men are friends from America. Here on. . .on an archeological dig."

Dr. Golding wrinkled his brow. "Friends?" He looked at her father, then back to her. "What does she mean? I see no one here save you, dear Kelila, and your old, graying father."

Piper stilled at the man's assertion. Surely. . .she glanced at Colton, then at Max and Legend, who exchanged slow grins.

"Now," Dr. Golding said. "Where are the falafels and babka you baked for me earlier, Kelila?"

Stunned at the quick change in topic, she blinked. "I—I will get them." She placed a hand on Colton's shoulder, whispered, "I will return," and strode to the small kitchen, where she retrieved two platters of food. After she placed them on the table around which sat the cushions, she returned to Colton's side.

"Come, my friends," her father said as he plopped down at the table. "Let us eat!"

"I'll prepare you a plate," she said to Colton.

"No." The gruff tone stopped her short. Colton's eyes darted back and forth, and his face seemed twisted in anger.

Almost instantly, the conversation died down. Then resumed, but lighter, quieter.

Colton must've noticed. His face grew red; then he relaxed marginally and nodded to her. The next hour was spent in conversation about the food, the weather, and cars. The men of the team never fully relaxed, especially in the presence of Dr. Golding. Although Piper understood their guarded behavior, she wished she could convince them he was a good man.

Next to her, Colton sat with his gaze fixed on the floor. He'd said little in the hour that passed, and only grew more pensive and withdrawn. Hesitantly, she moved away from him to clear the plates and refresh drinks. When she returned, Colton was gone.

She stopped, glanced at the chair he'd just occupied, then around the room. The Kid shifted closer to her, and nodded toward the back doors. She looked out into the dark night and just made out the light color of Colton's shirt. With a small smile to the Kid, she excused herself and stepped out of the house.

A cool breeze rushed over her, coming in off the sea. She plodded across the sandy beach to where Colton stood with his hands tucked in his jeans as he faced the sea.

"Are you okay?"

"No, reckon not." He didn't move a muscle, not even his eyes.

The water sparkled beneath the gentle caress of a full moon. Waves rolled in, then tumbled back out to the great deep. Colton's quiet, unmoving posture made her heart beat a little faster. Was he upset that her father had brought them here? Had she insulted him by offering to help him get a plate? Or maybe it was Dr. Golding.

"I hope Dr. Golding did not alarm you or the others."

"Took us off guard, that's for sure." He shrugged. "But he knew how to ease our minds. He a family friend?"

"He was the godfather of Bazak, my brother—the one who died."

"Ah," he said, a grin pinching the dimple in his cheek. "The brother whose death made you hate the military."

She couldn't help but laugh now. "Which made you afraid I'd hate you."

"Do you?"

His question stopped her. She frowned up at him. "What? How could you ask that?" Though she tried, she couldn't hide her disappointment.

Colton shifted and started walking, head down. He reached up and rubbed his shoulder as she trudged alongside him.

"What's wrong, Colton?"

Finally, he stopped and again faced the ocean with a long sigh. "I thought I'd made my peace with God, with things. . . ."

"But?"

"I can't see straight."

"How did that change your peace with God?"

Jaw muscle popping, he looked down. "It shouldn't. But I just don't get why—"

"Baba said something to you when we were on the mission. Do

you remember?" The soothing *whoosh* of the rolling tide eased her mind as she waited for Colton to respond.

"He said a lot."

"He said that if we're given success, it's not to make our lives easier, but to prepare us for the next battle."

"I should be Hercules by now."

She smiled. "Perhaps. Wouldn't it be better to think of this as another path God is taking you down so you can help someone else, rather than soak up the pity and self-loathing that would drown you?"

He smoothed a hand over the back of his neck. "Dawg, woman. You don't pull any punches, do you?"

She'd spoken too boldly. "Baba has raised me to speak plainly. I should not have—I'm sorry."

"No." He stepped closer. "You're right. I just want. . ." He huffed. Turned to her. Turned back to the water. Back to her.

Piper couldn't stop the smile.

"What I said back in Israel, when you found me. . ." His brow knitted. "I meant it."

Her heart rattled in her chest.

Colton's fingers closed around hers. "I. . .the team's. . .we're leaving tomorrow, first thing."

She nodded, her mouth dry as linen. When he lifted her hand to his lips and kissed it, Piper pulled in a quick breath.

"Israel is your home. Your father is back," he mumbled, his thumb running over knuckles as he stared down at her. "Imagine that makes you happy."

"It does, yes."

"Reckon you'd want to hang around, take care of him."

Her heart careened into her ribs. *That's what this is about.* "Actually. . .no." She licked her lips. "Yes, I love my father, but—" Oh that she felt free to speak her heart.

Colton inched forward. "I don't want to leave you, Piper. I can't. The thought of going back, being without you, eats my insides."

Breathing grew difficult. "Then don't—"

"I have to." He spun away, rolling his head side to side as he walked, the sand softly crunching beneath his feet. "Mickey needs me. My mother—I have to bury my father."

Piper moved to him, placed a hand on his chest, and waited for him to fall quiet. "You interrupted me." She waited for his expression to smooth out. "I was trying to say, don't go back without me."

He blinked. "I can't see your face clearly." In the way his eyes roved her face, his breathing shallow, she saw him trying to process her response, daring to hope she meant what she wasn't saying.

"Don't leave me, Colton" she whispered. "My heart has been yours since you first walked into the store and bought towels for your mother."

His hands slipped up her arms.

"Yeshua brought us together, I believe, for more than to save this country." She stood completely vulnerable before him. "I can't believe He meant for us to do this fantastic thing, knitting our hearts together, only to tear us apart." Braving his heart-stopping eyes, she smiled. "Just as I'm not a perfect person, I know you aren't either. If you were, then once I'm added to your life, perfection is breached." A swell of emotion rubbed against her throat. "I love you. Always have."

"I want to be whole. For you. To give you the best—of me, of everything." His head tipped toward her. "I love you, Piper. So much it's making me crazy." His hand slid around her neck and tugged her closer. His lips dusted hers, gentle and testing at first. Then he captured her mouth with his.

The force drawing her further into his embrace felt warm and exhilarating. His arms around her. . .his strong hand nudging her against his chest and tucked into his embrace.

Then he drew back. Cold air swept her as his large hands cupped her face. He squatted a bit so that they looked eye-to-eye. "And I disagree—God made you perfect. For me." Another kiss, this one deeper, longer.

Piper melted into him, so relieved to have the past behind them. To start anew. To start together. She hooked her arms under his and slid her hands up his back, savoring the moment, afraid the waves would capture this dream-come-true and wash it away.

"Oy! What is this?"

At the sound of her father's stern voice, Piper broke the kiss off and lowered her head, but Colton held her close, his breathing ragged.

"What is the meaning of this?" her father railed.

Colton straightened and shifted to the side, effectively forming a barrier between her and Baba. "Sir, I—"

"Come in here." Baba glanced around the open beach, then back to the house, then them. "Now!"

Even shielded behind Colton, she saw her father's dark scowl. "Baba, what—"

"Quiet, child!" He waved them into the house, then shut the door before turning on Colton. "What is the meaning of this, defiling my daughter in public?"

"Sir, I meant no—"

Piper whirled on her father. "Baba, stop. You know very well those are traditions old and abandoned. I love Colton. We are going to marry. There is no defiling."

"This is true?" Her father's bushy brows rose as he shifted to Colton. "You intend to marry my daughter?"

When Colton hesitated, his gaze wrought again as he surfed the circle of friends who surrounded them, including Dr. Golding, Piper worried she'd jumped to the wrong conclusion. But. . .he said he loved her. He didn't want to leave her. Didn't that mean marriage?

Colton's arm came around her shoulder. "Yes, sir. I love your daughter. If you'll grant me her hand, I'll marry her as soon as we return to the States."

"States?" Baba's voice pitched. "You will do no such thing."

Colton took a step forward. "Sir—"

"I said no, and that is it." Her father stalked to the back room.

Panicked, Piper rushed after him. "Baba, please do not do this. We love each other; you yourself told me you could see that. I want to marry Colton. Allow me to go with him."

He retrieved a bag he'd brought in earlier and started for the main room, his expression resolute.

"Baba, I beg you."

Colton had followed. "Sir, I assure you I will guard her honor."

"Guard her honor," her father said with a chuckle. "Yes, indeed." He pulled a tall cup out of the bag and a small box. He glanced at Dr. Golding. "You are ready, nachon?"

Golding retrieved a folded paper from his pocket. "Indeed."

Only then did Piper see the mischief in her father's eyes. And Dr. Golding's.

Colton drew away, his shoulders squaring. He glanced to the side. "Max, what's going on?"

She glanced at his friend, only to find him sniggering.

Smoothing out the paper, Dr. Golding straightened. He produced a small, thin book.

"Yes," Baba said, poking his finger at Colton. "You will marry my daughter."

Colton warily regarded her father. "I will?"

"And here is a minister to officiate the ceremony according to our mutual faith—you do believe in Yeshua as Savior, nachon?"

"I d—yes." He darted a look to Piper, and she could already feel the flush filling her face probably matched the one in Colton's

"Admes's brother works in the marriage office. He has all that is needed. The marriage certificate has your names, and it is registered with Cyprus. All that is left is the ceremony, nachon?"

CHAPTER 32

The world spun.

Colton blinked, trying to shake off the dizziness. This couldn't be happening. He'd wanted time to think, to. . .to prepare for taking Piper as his. . .*wife*. Warmth splashed his gut. Wife. Dawg. "Look, I appreciate—"

"I'll be best man." Max slapped his shoulder, nearly knocking Colton to the floor from the pain.

"Here," her father said, handing him a small black box. "This is a ring she can wear until he buys her a real one."

Max popped it open. "Sweet."

"Now listen here," Colton said, an edge in his voice but he didn't care. He had to stop them. But. . .who did he stop first? The father? Max?

Though he couldn't quite see it, Colton was certain a challenge sparkled in her father's eyes. "You love my Lily, nachon?"

"There he goes with the nachos again," the Kid mumbled.

"He told me he did," Midas said with a grin.

Max snapped the ring box closed with a wicked grin. "And everyone can tell."

Colton's heart chugged through the unyielding support of the team. "Now look, I don't need help from y'all."

"Actually," Max said, patting his arm. "I think you do. If it were up to you, this wouldn't happen for a looong time. You'd think about it, pray about it, think about it more, do some recon on it—"

"There ain't nothing wrong with praying about this."

"Except when you're hiding behind it."

"Baba." Piper tugged at her father's arm. "It's not right to force this."

Lips pursed, her father stepped toward Colton. "Do you not?"

It felt like he'd taken an RPG to the chest. "Yes. I love her, but—"

"And you asked to take her back to America—and you realize, she is my only child, the only family I have left. Yet you expect to steal her from her homeland, from her own father, without a true and honest commitment?"

Colton scowled at the man. "I didn't say that." He ran a hand through his short crop and hissed as his fingers tracked over the bandage. "Listen, I just. . .I need time. . .to prepare. Think." Why did he feel sick to his stomach?

When his gaze caught Piper's, even with the still-damaged vision, the hurt was obvious and glossed her eyes. He couldn't move. Couldn't talk. She was misunderstanding, thinking he didn't love her, didn't want her as his bride. He did. But this whole situation felt like horses rushing out of the gate at a race.

Stepping forward, Legend murmured, "Gut it up, Cowboy."

"You think too much," the Kid said.

"This is obscene," Max said. "You've lined up the shot, now *take* the shot."

Marry her? Now? Colton looked at her again. The panic was unfounded. The most wonderful thing that ever happened to him stood before him right this instant. Why should he wait? Slowly, he held out his hand.

She sniffled, and he squinted. Was she crying?

Colton left the huddle of friends prodding him. Took both her hands. "I'm sorry—I didn't mean to hurt you. I do want to marry you." He glanced back at the others, who grinned like banshees. "Just don't like being ambushed." Sliding a hand along her jaw, he felt the tears. He smoothed a thumb over her cheek. "Your father has a point." Wow, was he really going to do this thing? "Will you marry me?"

A sob shook her willowy form. She squeezed her eyes tight, crying harder and shaking her head.

Colton pulled her into his arms. Kissed the top of her head. "I love you, Piper. I'm ready to marry you, even though rushing it scares me."

Her arms snaked around his waist. "I love you, too." She drew back. "But I don't want to marry you, not like this, not if it scares you."

The grin was sheepish and small; he felt it. "The Kid's right—I think too much."

"D'ya hear that? He said I'm right!"

"Shut up," Max said as he popped the Kid upside the head.

Colton rolled his eyes, and Piper laughed. He bobbed his head toward her father. "Ready?"

She nodded through her tears, and together they stood before Dr. Golding, who officiated the short, simple ceremony. Colton marveled at the way God had dragged his reluctant carcass out of self-pity and loathing to bring him to this beautiful place of surrender.

As he slid the gold ring inscribed with Hebrew lettering on her finger, he couldn't help but think of his father smiling down on him now. Mickey would be thrilled; she'd long said Piper would be her mom. The picture she'd drawn flashed in front of his memory of them—him, Piper, Mickey, and two other children.

Just not soon, Lord. He wanted time with her, time to get to know each other, live without having to fight for their lives. Regular husband and wife.

"I thought it would help."

With a nod, Colton acknowledged Piper's words but could not tear his attention from the building where she'd stopped the taxi. Pieces of that terrible day flickered through his internal movie screen. His muscles buzzed. Fear of another flashback plucked at him. And yet his mind no longer felt stranded in the past. They'd married nearly five days ago, and with the peace and happiness that flooded his life, his vision slowly returned. Almost perfect save a few fuzzy edges. But not enough distortion to ruin this moment.

"It is my hope," Piper said, her voice soft, alluring—though she probably didn't intend it that way, "that my homeland will hold good memories for you. That it won't be painful anymore to think of Israel."

Another nod. "My sister loved this country." He drew off the sunglasses and squinted against the blinding sun. "She wanted to walk where Jesus walked."

Piper smiled at him. "I am biased, of course, but Israel holds many miracles."

Colton grabbed the handle and opened the door. He climbed out and stepped onto the sidewalk. Hands on his belt, he wished for a Cattle Baron or Stetson to block the sun that tugged at the back of his corneas, a leftover from the concussion. Mingled with the noise of traffic and the city, the thud of the car door reached his ears. Soon, Piper stood beside him. Hands stuffed in his pockets, he ambled around the gutted building.

"I don't get it," he mumbled as he kicked a stone out of the way.

"What?"

"Every time I've thought of Emelie—the memories alone are enough to toss me into the past." He shrugged. "But I'm standing here. . .staring at it, and though I remember, I don't feel like I'm back there." He turned to her. "I should be panicked or freaking out right now."

Piper smiled. "Should you?"

He glanced around, disbelieving his clear mind. "You don't understand. . . ."

"Perhaps it is you who does not understand. Have you not prayed for healing?"

"Of course, but I've prayed for years. Never been healed." He shifted and pointed indiscriminately to the side. "I flipped out the morning of the mission. Couldn't tell friend from foe. It's why. . .it's why Scar died instead of me. I left the roof."

"And you went back. Then, despite unimaginable odds, you took out the messenger. You saved Israel, my home." She offered another sweet smile. "Colton, I don't know why God hasn't granted you complete healing of your mind, but I think now that you've faced this place, maybe it will help."

"Reckon so," he said. His father had told him not to squander the days, not to let things come between him and his love for Piper.

He shifted toward her. "I messed up."

She frowned, confused.

"I was angry at God, angry at life, but too bullheaded to see the truth." He scratched his head and winced at the stitches. He huffed. "Nah, that ain't entirely true. I could see, but I rejected it. Rejected you."

She looked down.

He might as well get it all out. Time for him to start clean. "I wanted someone to blame for the things going wrong in my life, and I blamed you. That was the only control I had, and I exercised it." He inhaled and let it out. "I'm sorry. You didn't deserve the way I treated you."

She tucked a strand of her long, tawny hair behind her ear. "I understood. I can't say it didn't hurt, but I understood." Her gaze drifted away, sadness lingering there. "It's in the past; let's leave it there."

He nodded, then lifted her hand and kissed the wedding ring. "I have the rest of our lives to make up for it." Once more, he took a glance around the place that had taken Emelie's life. A sign hung from two hooks over the door and read COMING SOON: EVA'S CAFÉ. He touched the edge of it. "Looks like someone's going to rebuild."

"Life goes on."

So it does. Despite his every effort, his heart continued beating, and life came at him full speed. He turned and smiled down at Piper, his *wife*. "I'm ready to rebuild."

EPILOGUE

What if she hates me?"

Colton tucked the pillow under his side and reclined next to his wife. *Dawg*, he liked that word. "Why would you think she'd hate you?"

On her back, she stared up at the ceiling of their temporary home, a three-level brownstone he'd leased until the ranch house was rebuilt. "Look at what happened, what my being in your home caused—your father is gone." When Piper glanced at him, a tear spilled over her cheek.

He swept the drop aside. "My mom is a very reasonable woman."

"I am a reasonable woman, but. . ." Her chin trembled, and she smoothed a hand over his face. "I would find it very difficult to forgive someone who caused your death."

Kissing her palm, he closed his eyes and prayed for the right words to say. He wanted to ease her fears, but he had his own misgivings about his mother's reaction to the news of their marriage—not to the marriage itself, but to the quickness. "You weren't the cause. A sniper was the cause. No more talk like that, agreed?"

Hesitating for a few seconds, she searched his face. "Then you've truly forgiven me?"

"I think God smacked some sense into me the day I nearly died. I said and did a lot of things that I'm right ashamed of. I'm sorry. I was lost in anger, in fear that my life had finally collapsed despite me trying to hold it together."

"I've seen the change in your actions, but what changed in here?" She pointed to his chest, directly over his heart.

"I realized it wasn't mine to hold together. My mother told me not to let what happened be a reason to lose you. She was right." He kissed her. "If you hadn't been so steadfast, so ardent in your love for me, I don't know that I could've realized how much I love you."

She nodded. "You should have phoned her, told her we married. What if she gets angry?"

"That's not something I wanted to tell her with thousands of miles between us." He scooted closer. "Besides, whether she's happy or not, it's done. I have no regrets."

Something sparked in her eyes.

At that second, he saw where her concern lay. "Darlin', nothing or no one but death could separate us. I'm yours. You're mine." Colton brushed silky strands away from her face. "I married you because I love you. Whatever may come, we face it together."

She wrapped her arm around his neck and hugged him. Colton gathered her close and buried his face against her shoulder. He planted a kiss there, then one next to her ear. His passion rose, and he swept his lips over hers. Her fingers traced a teasing line down his back, causing him to deepen the kiss.

A sharp gasp came from behind. "Colton Benjamin!"

He jerked up and looked toward the door near the foot of the bed. "Mom!"

She caught McKenna's shoulder and spun his daughter away. "What is the meaning of this?" Her silvery brows knitted together as she scowled at the two of them. "I raised you better than to. . .to. . ."

"Mom," he said, pushing to his feet. "It's not what you think— well, yes. . .yes, it is. But—" His mind clicked into gear. "Wait, how did you get in the house? You weren't even due till lunch."

She bristled. "We took an earlier flight because we were anxious to see you." With a key in her hand, she glared. "The real estate agent overnighted the key to me. I knocked, but no one answered. And never mind changing the subject."

Colton turned to Piper and held out his hand. She was dressed modestly, even in bedclothes, but he could see her trepidation. Piper slid her hand into his and stood beside him.

"It took longer than expected to get back stateside because I took a blow to the head. I almost couldn't see at all—"

She motioned to the bed. "What does this have to do with your . . .your—"

"Easy, Mom. It's not inappropriate when you're married."

"Marri—" She gasped.

With a sheepish grin, he nodded. "We got married in Cyprus."

"We could not be married in Israel because Colton is not of Jewish lineage," Piper said, her words tumbling over one another. "But in Cyprus, you can marry on a day's notice if arrangements are made." Her hand tightened in his, and instinctively, he pulled her closer.

His mother's mouth opened slightly, then closed. Tears enlarged her blue eyes.

"You got married?" Mickey spun around, her blond hair whipping into her face. She rushed forward and threw herself at Piper, who lifted her up. "You're my mommy now!"

But Colton noticed his mom hadn't moved. Closing the three feet between them, he hoped to head off any bad feelings. She wasn't supposed to come in and find them like that. He'd wanted to tell her over dinner or on the way home from the airport. "Mom?"

She shook her head, crying. "He told me you'd marry her." She drew up straight and swallowed the tears. "I just. . .didn't think it'd be so soon."

"Maybe you and I are too much alike." Colton chuckled. "The guys helped me see I would've thought this thing between me and Piper to death. I love her. She loves me. I know God wanted me to marry her, so what was there to think about or wait for?"

She glanced across the room, and he followed her gaze. Piper sat on the edge of the bed with Mickey in her lap. She'd given her the necklace and ring they'd bought for Mickey in Cyprus.

"She's afraid you hate her," he whispered.

His mom sucked in a breath. "Hate her?"

"I'm not sure she has forgiven herself for her role in that night."

Head tilted, she considered him. "And have you?"

"Reckon it's only natural you ask." He ran a hand over the back of his neck, regret thick and churning in his gut. "I was just so angry about Dad, scared. . . . What she did for her father was no less than I would do for those I love or am sworn to protect. She didn't mean for it to happen. I can see it now."

She touched his arm, eyes wide and glossed. "I am so relieved. I wasn't sure you could ever let go of it after your father's death."

"Honestly, I didn't intend to. But God knocked me upside my head—literally."

"Sounds like I have some stories to hear later." With a small smile, she tiptoed up and planted a kiss on his cheek. She composed herself, then strode across the room and stood before Piper.

Nervously, Piper's gaze drifted upward. She swallowed hard and came to her feet, but Mickey climbed into Piper's arms again, hugging her. Colton wanted to extricate his daughter, but feared interrupting the moment. He fisted his hands and forced himself to stay put. They needed to do this.

"Ben always knew you'd be a part of our family. He's gone now."

Oh dawg. Maybe this wouldn't end well. His muscles contracted, and he started forward—

Stay.

"But you've loved Colton from the start, and though he couldn't see it at the time, I know he loved you. Now you've left everything you know and love—including your own father."

Piper darted an anxious look to him, and he gave her a nod. "Baba must remain behind and in hiding, for a while."

"You two will have to tell me what transpired later, but for now, I just want you to know that while I would've preferred a right and proper wedding, I am so very glad you're my daughter-in-law."

Surprise leapt into his wife's beautiful face. She half smiled, half cried. "You are?"

"Of course. You belonged here from the start." His mother pulled Piper into a hug, tears streaming down her face. "I only wish Ben could've seen this." She eased back and smiled at Colton. "He was always so proud of you—but this, this would've been a dream he wanted to see."

After a couple of minutes, Piper mumbled, "I'm so sorry. Thank you. Thank you."

"No more of that talk. Agreed?"

Piper laughed. "Colton said the same thing."

Hands on either side of Piper's face, his mom smiled. "Welcome to the family, Piper."

"Daddy," McKenna said as she bounced off the bed and into his arms. "When do I get my baby brother?"

As soon as he'd turned loose of the reins, life had taken a swift turn for the better. Two months had passed, but Colton still couldn't quite wrap his mind around it all. God had blessed him in ways he'd never imagined possible—the home rebuilding went faster than expected. Just another month or so, and they could move in.

But there were situations that caused a man to think long and hard about the way he conducted himself.

Like Nightshade. With a beautiful wife, a daughter, and a mother he provided for, it got a man's mind racing. Wondering at the risks of being part of an elite group. Made a new ache twist his intestines.

As he strode into the warehouse, light dimmed through the grimy windows that lined the upper rim of the perimeter. He had to put it all in God's hands when he got called out on missions. He'd come clean with Piper, explained about the team, about the need to keep their conversations short and vague when referencing Nightshade. And that he could never reveal anything about the missions. He could see her fear, felt it almost as if it were his own. Come to think of it, maybe the fear was his own.

Griffin, Midas, and the Kid sat in the lounge, a loose term for space furnished with two faded wingback chairs and the torn leather sofa that leaned to one side because of a missing foot.

"Cowboy," Griffin said. "How's the wife?"

"Doin' all right." He shook hands with the man, then moved to Midas, who patted his shoulder.

The throaty twang of a motorcycle ripped through the hanger, reverberating off the exposed steel rafters. Max drove right up to the edge and killed the engine. Seconds later, the Old Man's 300 slid into the bay.

"Gentlemen," Lambert said as he climbed up the four steps with Max right behind him. "Thank you for coming. I know you all have plans for this fine Saturday morning, but I felt you would want to hear this news."

Colton slumped against the sofa as Max joined them, setting his helmet on the cheap, badly scarred coffee table. He ripped the zipper open and stood braced. Something about his posture put Colton on edge, though he wasn't sure what.

"You will be pleased to know that we are adding two men to the team. They've both been through extensive checks—background, psychological, criminal, you name it. I've had them tested over the last few months to verify their appropriateness for Nightshade."

Griffin scooted to the edge of the wingback chair. "We don't have a say?"

"Already have." Max held his stance, arms folded over his chest. "Squirt survived the mission, performed beyond my expectation. I gave him my full recommendation."

"I can buy that," Griffin said.

He might have agreed, but Colton saw the hesitation in Griffin's expression and heard it in his words. Colton understood. Every person on the team took the lives of the others into their hands. A precarious situation. Even more so when dealing with someone you didn't know.

"What about the other?" the Kid asked.

"This changes nothing," a voice spoke from the shadows.

Colton pivoted, stunned to find the assassin emerge from the shadows.

"Oh snap! Where did he come from?" the Kid balked.

Griffin punched to his feet. "This?" He pointed to Azzan. "This is who you're putting on the team?"

"Yes. Mr. Yasir served undercover in the Israeli Special Forces; then, as you know, he joined the Mossad."

"He's an assassin," Griffin hissed. "They work alone. He doesn't know the first thing about teamwork. He's not even an American."

"And that makes me deficient how?" Azzan held Griffin's gaze, a defiant challenge gleaming in his eyes. "Besides your arrogance, what do you have that I do not?"

"Man, this is awesome." The Kid laughed.

Griffin flashed a fiery glare at the youngest member of the team, who snapped his mouth closed.

Hands in his pockets, Lambert tilted his head to the side. "When Max suggested you might object to his recommendation, I told him you were above things like that." There would be no doubt who ultimately controlled this team—and it wasn't that he was power hungry. Colton could see in Lambert's eyes the man had spent long hours considering this decision. "I reassured him this team would make the integration of these two men seamless."

Colton eyed the assassin—Piper's cousin. Piper would love to know her cousin was here. But he had to admit Griffin had a point. Assassins were trained to work on their own, trust no one, look to themselves and no one else for help. Conflicted, he dropped his gaze.

"You do not have to like my choices, Mr. Riddell, but I do expect you to work together."

Griffin stabbed a finger at Azzan. "Start right there with Teamwork 101." Without another word, he strode out of the warehouse.

Max, Canyon, and Marshall huddled around Azzan, shaking his hand. Squirt joined them, receiving the same congratulations.

Colton offered his hand to Azzan.

"You hesitate."

A slow nod.

"Good. I could tell you were a thinker." He didn't lessen his grip. "I wouldn't have accepted the offer if I wasn't committed to this, to the team."

In the eyes that mirrored his wife's, Colton saw the uncertainty, the hesitation, even if Azzan never uttered a word. So maybe this man wasn't all "guns blazing" the way Griffin had suggested. Azzan had a solid head on his shoulders. And he had experience.

"Griffin will come around."

Azzan cocked his head and quirked an eyebrow. "Not easily, I expect."

"Nothing's easy when it comes to him." Colton squeezed his hand. "Welcome to Nightshade."

ABOUT THE AUTHOR

An Army brat, Ronie Kendig married an Army veteran. They have four children and two dogs. She has a BS in Psychology, speaks to various groups, is active with the American Christian Fiction Writers (ACFW), and mentors new writers. Ronie can be found at www.roniekendig.com or www.discardedheroes.com.